THE
COURSE
OF ALL
TREASONS

THE
COURSE
OF ALL
TREASONS

AN ELIZABETHAN
SPY MYSTERY

Suzanne M. Wolfe

CROOKED
LANE

NEW YORK

Copyright © 2019 by Suzanne M. Wolfe

Published in the United States by Crooked Lane Books, an imprint of The Quick Brown Fox & Company LLC.

Crooked Lane Books and its logo are trademarks of The Quick Brown Fox & Company LLC.

Library of Congress Catalog-in-Publication data available upon request.

ISBN (hardcover): 978-1-64385-178-5
ISBN (ebook): 978-1-64385-179-2

Cover design by Mimi Bark
Book design by Jennifer Canzone

Printed in the United States.

www.crookedlanebooks.com

Crooked Lane Books
34 West 27th St., 10th Floor
New York, NY 10001

First Edition: December 2019

10 9 8 7 6 5 4 3 2 1

In Memory of John McEntee,
my beloved grandfather

And as in the common course
of all treasons, we still see them reveal
themselves, till they attain to their abhorred ends,
so he that in this action contrives against his own
nobility, in his proper stream o'erflows himself.
—All's Well That Ends Well

DRAMATIS PERSONAE

Simon Winchelsea: Agent working for Sir Francis Walsingham.

The Honorable Nicholas Holt: Spy, adventurer, owner of The Black Sheep Tavern, Bankside.

Robert, Earl of Blackwell: Nick's older brother.

Francesco del Toro: Spanish diplomat.

Edmund Lovett: Acquaintance of Nick's from undergraduate days at the University of Oxford; currently an agent in the employ of the Earl of Essex.

Sir Robert Cecil, aka the Spider: Nick's immediate boss under Sir Francis Walsingham.

Elizabeth I: Queen of England, Ireland, and Wales, Defender of the Faith, etc.

Robert Devereaux, Earl of Essex: The Queen's favorite, step-son to the Earl of Leicester and former ward of Baron Burghley.

Codpiece the Fool: The Queen's personal spy at court.

Hector: Nick's Irish Wolfhound.

John Stockton: Nick's childhood friend; runs The Black Sheep.

Maggie Stockton: John's wife.

Bess: A parrot formerly owned by the playwright Christopher Marlowe.

Henry and Jane Stockton: Maggie and John's children.

Matty: A former cinders from Whitehall Palace who now lives at The Black Sheep.

Will Shakespeare: A young, aspiring playwright.

Kat: Madam of a Bankside brothel; Nick's friend and occasional lover.

Joseph: Kat's business partner; formerly The Terror of Lambeth, a retired wrestler.

Harold: An unsuccessful rat-catcher.

Sir Francis Walsingham, Secretary of State: Head of the Queen's spy network in England.

Lady Annie O'Neill: Daughter of the exiled Hugh O'Neill, Ireland's future Earl of Tyrone.

Henry Gavell and Richard Stace: Agents working for Essex.

Sir Thomas Brighton: Agent working for Walsingham.

Eli: Jewish doctor who lives in Bankside.

Rivkah: Twin sister of Eli, doctor in all but name.

Sir John Staffington: Gentleman who lives in the same lodging house as Sir Thomas Brighton.

Mistress Shrewsbury: Landlady of Sir John Staffington and Sir Thomas Brighton.

Sundry other minor players.

PROLOGUE

Wood Wharf, London

"Satan's pizzle!"

Simon Winchelsea cursed as he sank ankle-deep in the revolting effluent running like a river down the center of the street. A cold rain had been steadily falling since late afternoon; he was wet as a witch on a ducking stool, and now he was literally wading through shit. And all because Sir Francis Walsingham had tasked him to shadow a mark to a nighttime meet.

Not for the first time, Simon thought with nostalgia of his poaching days on the great estates near his childhood home in Windsor. How he longed for the great spreading canopies of leaves that sheltered him from the worst of the rain instead of the filthy torrents that cascaded onto his head from overflowing gutters. What he wouldn't give for the musky tang of fox and badger in his nostrils instead of the reek of raw sewage; for the merry trilling of a stream in his ears instead of obscene curses.

The two-legged animals he now hunted were not only far more stupid than the four-legged variety but infinitely more dangerous. He hated London for its noise and filth and rapacious venality. Query the dubious contents of a pie, and the beefy matron who sold it to you would likely knee you in the bollocks; challenge a tavern owner over the outrageous price of the piss he called ale, and you could find yourself flat on your back while a crowd of inebriates did a Morris dance on your head. The only good thing about London, in Simon's opinion, was the abundance of whores who lounged in doorways, hung out of windows, flashed a leg at street corners, and generally advertised their wares with a lewdness that Simon—still a country lad at heart—found thrilling. And unlike the solitary drab in his home village, a long-in-the-tooth widow with six children to feed, the London whores were willing, nay eager, to do anything for a shilling.

Simon knew he shouldn't complain. Walsingham had intervened when Simon would have been hanged for taking a brace of pheasants from a royal park despite being a mere ten yards inside the boundary when he loosed his arrows. Since when was Mother Nature the exclusive right of kings and queens? he had asked the magistrate. Since when was it a crime for the landless poor to eat? The magistrate, whose ponderous belly proclaimed him to be a man of substance, both literally and figuratively, had given a mighty yawn before sentencing him to death.

Simon had been crouched on the floor of a dark and airless cellar underneath the magistrate's manor, miserably contemplating his fate, when there was a rattle of keys, the door creaked open, and he was unceremoniously hauled into the presence of a dour man dressed in black. The man, Simon later learned, was Sir Francis Walsingham, Secretary of State and head of Queen Elizabeth's spy network.

Thinking his time on earth was up, Simon had not been able to take in what the man was telling him. But when the man courteously bade him take a seat and offered him a cup of ale, Simon realized that a proposition was being put to him: work for Walsingham's spy network in London or swing from the gallows. It was the easiest choice Simon had ever made. Ever since, he had been Walsingham's best tracker, the difference being that now he hunted in the city and not in the verdant woods of his youth.

The man Simon Winchelsea had been tasked to follow on this night was a fast walker, and Simon had to concentrate. His difficulty did not lie in his comparatively shorter legs but rather in the foul weather. Not only did the pelting rain reduce visibility, but it had turned the roads into a noisome torrent, ankle-deep in some parts, and Simon was hard-pressed to keep his quarry in sight while watching where he put his feet.

One advantage to the miserable weather was that the mark took no precautions to elude a possible shadow and did not once glance back over his shoulder to see if he was being followed. Admittedly, it was late and the streets were deserted, all decent folk safely tucked up in their beds. Aside from the taverns, still rowdy with late drinkers, the buildings Simon passed were shuttered and silent, dark shapes looming at the edge of his vision. The night watchmen had forsaken the streets and were no doubt keeping dry in the same taverns they habitually patrolled. A mercy on a night such as this, Simon knew his unsuspecting quarry must be thinking. And one that allowed him to pass seemingly unseen through the streets of a foreign city.

But the man Simon was following was mistaken if he thought he was alone, that his nefarious purpose remained undetected.

Simon grinned to himself as he flitted silently and invisibly through the streets. What matter a bit of mud? He could always clean his boots. Despite the weather, this was turning out to be an easy night's work, and Simon was looking forward to getting paid handsomely when he reported in.

Only once did Simon think he was going to lose his mark. Just as the man turned onto Fleet Street, a whore appeared out of a dark doorway and beckoned to him. The man stopped, and Simon saw the whore draw him into the dark overhang of the doorway. Simon prayed fervently that his quarry would not disappear into the whore's rooms and leave him standing for hours outside in the cold and rain. Much to his relief, the man stepped back out of the doorway and continued on his way. Simon waited a moment to give the whore time to leave, then followed. When Simon glanced into the doorway as he passed, it was empty.

The man turned west on Fleet Street and now turned south toward the river and Wood Wharf. He stopped at the wharf and leaned against a piling, clearly waiting, his shoulders hunched miserably in his cloak. The lantern fixed to the piling to guide wherrymen in the dark swung crazily in the wind as if someone were signaling the alarm. Simon crouched down behind an abandoned shed and waited, praying it would not be for long. He had promised Joan, one of the whores who plied her trade in Smithfield, where Simon lived, that he would see her tonight. If he didn't get back by midnight, she would ditch him for another punter.

Simon pictured Joan naked in his bed, the youthful perfection of her body more than making up for the sourness of her breath and the front teeth lost in a fight with a rival who had trespassed on her patch. If he closed his eyes and breathed through his mouth, he could almost imagine he was fucking Venus herself.

Then he tensed. Someone was approaching.

"It's me," the newcomer called out.

"About time. Your wretched English weather will be the death of me."

Simon could hear not only impatience in the man's voice but contempt. Although valuable and assiduously recruited by foreign powers, traitors were despised the world over. And the newcomer was certainly a traitor. Not only was he an Englishman, but Simon had recognized his voice, had seen him drinking in The Angel earlier that night with a man who was built like the side of a privy. He was straining to hear their conversation over the sound of the rain when a sudden gust of wind sweeping off the river made the shed door swing back on its hinges with a bang.

"What's that?" Simon heard the foreigner say.

"Probably nothing. I made sure I wasn't followed."

"What do you have for me?" the foreigner asked.

"What about payment?"

"Later."

"I need the money *now*."

Simon could hear the note of desperation in the traitor's voice.

"You think I carry such a sum at night in this God-forsaken hole? You think I want to have my throat cut? Besides, you have yet to give me anything of value."

The door banged again.

Chancing a quick glance along the side of the shed, he saw the dark outlines of the two men standing stock-still on the jetty, the traitor with his head raised like a dog snuffing the air. Silently,

Simon shrank back against the wall, looking down so the pale oval of his face would not give him away. Then he heard footsteps approaching the hut, and for the first time that night, fear clutched at his chest.

"Who's there?"

The door of the shed creaked and Simon heard someone step inside, threads of light from the lantern showing feebly through the rotted planks. Now was Simon's chance to escape. But no sooner had his mind registered that fact than he felt a searing pain in his thigh. For a moment, he thought he had pierced his flesh on a nail; then he realized he had been run through with a sword. Gasping, he tried to rise, but his left leg gave way and he stumbled and fell. Clawing at the mud, he began to pull himself into the chest-high weeds behind the shed, his injured leg trailing uselessly behind like a leveret with a broken back.

This is what it felt like to be hunted, he thought, and felt a sudden stab of pity for all the creatures he had slain. Then he heard the sound of wood splintering, and hands gripped his legs and began pulling him into the shed. Simon twisted onto his back and clawed at his attacker, trying to reach his throat, his fingers snagging on something but not enough to do any damage. Kicking with his uninjured leg, he again tried to claw at the shape above him. Then everything went black.

★ ★ ★

When he came to, Simon thought he was back in the woods at home. What he'd first thought were branches slowly came into focus and revealed themselves to be the wooden planks of a roof. He was lying on his back in the shed, his arms bound to his sides by something cinched so tightly around his chest he had difficulty breathing. A belt, he thought.

A dark mass loomed over him.

"I know you," a voice said. "You are Walsingham's bloodhound."

Simon tried to control the fear coursing through his body, turning his bowels to water. Whatever happened, he vowed, he would not disgrace himself but die like a man. And die he would, he realized. For his attacker could not afford to let him live now he knew he had been discovered. For a brief moment, Simon had a vision of Joan waiting for him in his rooms, wondering why he did not come. Then he smiled mirthlessly to himself. No, she would not be missing him; she would be missing the money he gave her. When he did not return, she would curse him and go back to the streets. In less time than it took for a couple of pennies to change hands, he would be forgotten. Suddenly he wished with all his heart that he had married the girl in the village his parents had picked for him, that he had sired children. And he was overcome with a terrible sadness that no one would grieve for him, no one would remember him in their prayers when he was gone.

"Tell me what you know. Whom have you told?"

"Go to hell."

Simon saw the tip of a blade hover over his left eye, then heard an animal screaming. It sounded like the high-pitched cry of a vixen or perhaps a stoat caught in a trap.

"*Sweet Jesus!*"

Simon heard himself calling for his mother, something he had not done since he was five years old.

Then the world, and all he loved in it, shrank to a point and winked out.

CHAPTER 1

The Spotted Cow, Oxford

Nicholas Holt, younger brother of Robert, Earl of Blackwell, was sprawled on a bench, booted feet up on a table, in a hole-in-the-wall tavern tucked behind New College, Oxford. Although Oxford was his hometown, he was there that day on business. Spy business.

His immediate master, Sir Robert Cecil, aka the Spider, had ordered Nick to see if he recognized an agent. Cecil's source at the port of Dover had informed him that a man looking suspiciously like a Spaniard but speaking flawless English had stayed one night in a Dover inn and then set out the following day for London. This would not have provoked much interest if not for the fact that England and Spain were on an unofficial war footing and Mendoza, the Spanish ambassador, had been expelled for complicity in an assassination plot on the Queen. Sir Francis Walsingham, the head of Queen Elizabeth's spy network and Cecil's superior, had ordered that any Spaniard entering England was to be closely watched.

It didn't take a genius to figure out that the man's name was an alias. Under half-closed lids, Nick thought that if the black-haired, brown-eyed man was John Smith, then he, Nick Holt, spy, adventurer, and owner of The Black Sheep Tavern in Bankside, London, was the Man in the Moon. He had recognized the man immediately as Francesco del Toro, a member of the Spanish ambassador's retinue in Paris. Nick had picked up his trail in London, then followed him to Oxford. What should have taken a day of hard galloping on a fast horse had instead taken a wearisome four days to cover the fifty-one miles. Del Toro's sorry nag had thrown a shoe outside Henley-on-Thames, and it had taken him a day to find a blacksmith. On the third day, a rainstorm that turned to blinding sleet at dusk forced del Toro to seek shelter in an inn at Abingdon. Wet, cold, and miserable, Nick had slipped a boy a farthing so that he could bed down in the stables.

Now, sitting in The Spotted Cow, his arse sore from days in the saddle, his head aching with what he suspected was a fatal dose of influenza (his friend Sir Thomas Brighton had come down with it just before Nick left London) and filthy despite his icy ablutions in the horse trough of the inn the previous night, Nick heartily wished del Toro's soul to the devil.

In reality, del Toro was probably feeling closer to heaven at that very moment. His hands were full—literally—of a surprisingly delectable trollop with flowing blond hair who straddled his lap while he nuzzled the large white breasts barely contained by her low-cut, flame-colored bodice. A group of undergraduates who should have been discussing the finer points of Cicero with their tutors were boisterously cheering him on. Just another reason, Nick concluded morosely, why he had grown to hate the man, enemy agent or not.

And he was undeniably an agent, of that Nick had no doubt. Unfortunately, he had not seen him meet with anyone suspicious either on the journey or during his two-day stay in the city. In fact, the man had behaved like a tourist, wandering aimlessly around the city gawping at the colleges and interiors of the chapels. He looked more like a man who was killing time than a man on a mission. But whoever the man was supposed to meet had not shown up, and now del Toro was getting ready to leave, if the packed saddlebags by his feet were any indication.

"Nick."

Nick's heart sank at the familiar voice, but he quickly plastered a delighted smile on his face as his older brother, Robert, shouldered his way through the throng of inebriated students. "What are you doing here?" Robert said, sitting down on the bench beside Nick. "Why didn't you tell us you were in town?"

By *us*, Robert meant Elise, his wife, and Agnes, their widowed mother, who lived with them at Binsey House. Robert did not know Nick was a spy, that Nick had, in fact, been coerced into working for Cecil because of Robert's own actions. A letter Robert had written to an old Oxford friend, a Jesuit, had been intercepted by Cecil. He had threatened to investigate Robert for communicating with a Catholic order that had vowed to unseat Elizabeth from the throne and return England to the one true faith.

As Nick and Robert were from a prominent recusant Catholic family, this threat had been very real and hung like the sword of Damocles perpetually over their heads. Essentially, Nick was at Cecil's mercy, especially since he knew Robert had deep sympathies with those who would like to see England return to the old faith.

"How long have you been here?" Robert asked. Then, before Nick could reply, he bawled, "Ho, there, Alan. Ale, if you please."

"Righto, Your Honor." The tapster behind the counter, Alan, was a wizened, gnomelike man, with a bald head as wrinkled as a winter apple left too long in the barrel. Old enough to have known Robert and Nick since they were students at the university, he seemed not to have aged a day. Grinning toothlessly, he toddled over with a jug of ale and another cup.

"Thanks, Alan," Robert said. "How's the missus?"

"Tolerable, I thank thee," Alan said. "And her ladyship and the young'uns?"

"Well, thank you, Alan."

"And you, young master?" the tapster asked, his rheumy eyes surveying Nick affectionately.

Nick hid a grin. However old he got, he suspected Alan would always address him as he used to when Nick was fifteen and had first come up to Oxford. "Not so bad," he returned. "Still serving the same old rot-gut, I see." He lifted his tankard in a salute.

"Better than the piss you serve," Alan replied equably. He and Nick had a harmless rivalry about the respective quality of their ales.

Over Alan's shoulder, Nick saw the whore climb off del Toro's lap and, taking him by the hand, lead him toward the back door of the tavern.

"Speaking of piss," Nick said, getting up. "Nature calls."

Quickly, he pushed through the knot of undergraduates crowding the doorway, but when he got to the alley, the prostitute and del Toro had vanished.

"Hell and damnation!" Nick ran to the end of the alley and looked up and down St. Helen's Passage, then ran to New College Lane. Aside from a few students shying stones at the gargoyles jutting out from the sides of the college chapel—something Nick himself had done in his undergraduate years—the street was empty.

"Seen a man and a whore come this way?" Nick called.

At the word *whore*, they sniggered and nudged one another, falling over their barge-sized feet like overgrown puppies.

"I wish," one of the lads said. "She might have given us one for free."

"Not you," said a runt of a lad with shocking pimples. "You're too ugly."

With their sticking-out ears and chins as smooth as a baby's bottom, Nick thought it more likely they would have run a mile if any woman approached them, let alone a woman of ill repute.

"I'm sure she would have found you all irresistible," he said kindly.

They grinned, oblivious to Nick's irony.

Nick stood for a moment considering his options. He could, of course, follow New College Lane to the High and hope to find del Toro there. But he suspected they had disappeared into a room where the woman plied her trade, and there were hundreds of such rooms in a college town catering to randy youth on the razzle. It would have been like finding a needle in the proverbial haystack. In addition, Robert's unexpected arrival meant Nick was not free to pursue his quarry without giving away his real purpose for being in Oxford. Cursing himself for a fool, Nick returned to the tavern.

Walking in, Nick saw Robert in conversation with a man who was fair-haired and approximately his own height. Nick found himself looking into a face he recognized but couldn't place.

Then the penny dropped. "Edmund?" he said. "Edmund Lovett?"

The man gave a sheepish smile and stuck out his hand. They shook. "It's been a long time," Edmund said. "I'm amazed you remember me. I thought I recognized your brother, the earl."

When Nick looked surprised—Robert had long since gone down from Oxford by the time Edmund was there—Edmund added, "He's well-known in the county."

That was true: next to Robert Dudley, Earl of Leicester, Robert was one of the biggest landowners in Oxfordshire and was held in high regard for his honest dealings, like the old earl before him.

Edmund Lovett had been a year below Nick at Oxford. The son of a gentleman farmer near Binsey House, Nick's ancestral home, he had spent his first year trailing after Nick and his best friend, John Stockton, the son of his family's steward. Both Nick and John had found Edmund's company tedious and embarrassing. Nick seemed to remember something about a scandal involving Edmund's father illegally enclosing common land, thus depriving the locals of their ancient grazing and wood-gathering rights, but he couldn't be sure. At fifteen, Nick had been more concerned with chasing dairy maids and had paid little attention.

Now Edmund seemed to want to chat about old times. In truth, Nick had barely any memory of the man at Oxford, as he had been much too busy living it up with John to spare Edmund much attention. What he did recall was a gangly youth with a shock of blond hair falling over his eyes and a habit of swiping it off his forehead with fingers whose nails were bitten to the quick. In Edmund's second year he had finally gotten the message and left Nick alone.

The bones of Edmund's face had thickened, giving his face a square look; his hair had darkened to a pale brown, but he still favored an untidy fringe as if determined to preserve the last vestige of his youth. Though hatched with lines at the corners, his blue eyes retained a wide-eyed innocence, and his nails were still bitten. In short, the boy was still recognizable in the man.

Robert got up. "Must be off," he said to Nick. "Got to meet with the lawyer."

Nick raised an eyebrow.

"Don't worry," Robert said. "I'm not disinheriting you, however disreputable you've become."

"That's a relief."

"Just some land leases that need sorting."

Edmund was following their conversation with avid interest, and Nick felt a small stab of irritation. One thing had not changed. Edmund was ever the hanger-on.

"Will you be staying over?" Robert asked Nick. "The snowdrops are coming up in the orchard."

For a moment, Nick felt a pang of homesickness, remembering the joy he had always felt as a boy when the first white froth of spring had appeared miraculously beneath the winter-bare trees.

"Besides," Robert added. "Mother wants to talk with you."

"She can always write to me," Nick said.

"She prefers face-to-face."

Agnes, the Dowager Countess of Blackwell, was a formidable woman, and although she and her husband, the old earl, had dutifully attended Anglican services once a month, Nick suspected she still practiced her Catholic faith in secret. Robert, too, for that matter. The prospect of the authorities finding a priest hiding in Binsey House kept Nick awake at nights. It would only take one servant to betray them and all would be lost.

Nick's heart sank, as this suggested that what his mother had to tell him was too dangerous to be committed to paper.

"Tell her it will have to wait," Nick said. If he was following a Spanish spy, Nick could not afford to tangle his family up in his business. It was imperative that no one else in his family have any contact with Catholics from abroad. He did not elaborate but saw understanding flare in Robert's eyes. People habitually took his brother's blocky, stolid appearance for bovine slowness, but Robert was far from stupid.

Even though Robert did not know Nick was a spy, he did know Nick sometimes worked directly for the Queen. Just last winter, the Queen had commissioned Nick to track down the murderer of two of her ladies-in-waiting. Robert correctly interpreted Nick's laconic reply to mean he was again on the Queen's business and must return posthaste to London.

"Give my love to Elise and the brood," Nick said. "And to Mother."

"Next time you are in Oxford, come and stay at the house," Robert said. "We miss you." It was Robert's way of telling Nick that what their mother wanted to communicate was important.

Nick nodded. He felt guilty about not seeing his family more often, but he dreaded finding out that his mother was still practicing the old religion, even harboring priests at Binsey House. One day soon he would have to broach the subject with his mother, and his brother.

Robert shook hands with Edmund and left.

"Fancy another?" Edmund said, lifting up the flagon.

"I really must be going," Nick said, "before I lose the light." He would have to look for del Toro in all the inns along the London Road. If he didn't find him, he would have to report his failure to Cecil. Not something he was looking forward to. This knowledge increased his impatience with Edmund, although he knew he was not being fair to the man.

"One more can't hurt."

"All right." Inwardly cursing himself for being weak, Nick picked up the tankard Edmund had filled. Maybe it was a guilty conscience. He remembered Edmund standing forlornly in the middle of the quad at Balliol as Nick told him he and John had things to do elsewhere. And Edmund was not invited.

"So, Edmund," Nick said. "What have you been up to since going down from Oxford?"

"This and that," he said vaguely. "I'm returning to London today."

Nick's heart sank. It looked as if he would be stuck with Edmund's company all the way back to the city.

"I fell in with the Earl of Essex's set," Edmund explained. "Did some work for him and then got hired on as one of his agents." He brushed the hair off his forehead and casually picked up his drink. Even in the half gloom of the tavern, Nick could see he was watching Nick for his reaction. Nick was careful to give none, although he cursed inwardly.

★   ★   ★

The twenty-one-year-old Robert Devereux, second Earl of Essex, was a thorn in the side of Sir Robert Cecil. Passing to the wardship of William Cecil, Baron Burghley, after the death of his father in 1576, Devereux had grown up with Robert Cecil. They had spent their boyhood engaged in a jealous rivalry for Burghley's affection, a mutual antagonism that had only grown worse as they attained manhood. That alone should have made him a favorite of Nick's. But the man was a spoiled brat, puffed up from being the pampered scion of an ancient aristocratic line and first cousin twice removed of the Queen.

Essex was a man who modeled himself on *The Book of the Courtier*, a handbook on courtly manners written by Castiglione in Henry VIII's reign, the favorite read of useless toffs. The fact that Henry had also taken Castiglione's book as his personal bible did nothing to recommend it, given that the syphilitic king's definition of courtly love was to lop off the heads of two wives, divorce two, lose one in childbirth, and be outlived by another. Not a stellar track record, in Nick's humble opinion. And, indeed, Essex had a reputation with the ladies to rival Henry's, although no one at court was brave enough to tell the Queen.

Nick considered Essex to be a dandified lightweight who would have been laughable had it not been for Elizabeth's outrageous favoritism. The spectacle of the aging queen flirting with a man young enough to be her son was both embarrassing and sad. Even Nick's friend, Richard, the Queen's dwarf, known to the court as Codpiece, went quiet when Essex was around. It was rumored that Essex was the replacement for longtime favorite Robert Dudley, Earl of Leicester, who was currently in Holland aiding the Dutch in their revolt against Philip II of Spain. Only Baron Burghley had had the balls to warn her about Essex.

"Don't be ridiculous," she had retorted. "Robin makes me laugh. Which is more than I can say for you, Old Woman," she said, vindictively using the nickname Burghley's enemies used behind his back.

Burghley had wisely taken the hint and never raised the subject of Essex again.

Much more serious than the Queen making a fool of herself, in Nick's opinion, was the fact that Essex had set up a rival spy network to Walsingham's. It meant that, in practice, spies were often working at cross purposes to each other, as neither side knew the identity or allegiance of the other, and in addition, inside each separate network, agents were often ignorant of each other's identities. This only added to the chaos. In short, Essex was a rash, idealistic troublemaker with enough money and royal favor to make him dangerous. Somehow Nick wasn't surprised that the gullible Edmund had taken up with him.

"I hear we're in the same business," laughed Edmund, toasting him with his tankard. "Who would have thought?"

Who indeed? Nick mused. He had never known anyone to be so prone to hero worship as Edmund. Nick raised his own tankard in polite acknowledgment but kept silent. It was not his habit to blab about his employment in strange places and to people he had just met. Painfully, Edmund's willingness to do so seemed an attempt to prove that he was just like Nick.

Nick was just wondering if one tankard of ale was enough for old time's sake or if he was duty-bound to gag down another when the tavern door opened and a man stuck his head in, caught Edmund's eye, and closed the door again.

"It's for me," Edmund said, leaping to his feet. "A message I've been expecting," he explained over his shoulder as he went to the door.

Edmund left the tavern, shutting the door behind him. Nick was surprised he didn't bring the man in to get warm by the fire, which was crackling merrily in the grate and putting out a fair bit of heat. But shortly after Edmund went out to confer with the man, he returned alone.

"Sorry about that," he said. "An urgent message that needed a reply." Edmund said this as if he wished Nick to know he was even now on Essex's business, but once again, Nick did not react.

Instead, he stood. "I've got to be going," he said. "As long as the weather holds, I hope to make it to Wallingford by tonight."

"I'm going that way," Edmund said. "We can keep each other company."

This wasn't what Nick had planned, and he was not best pleased. After the day's debacle, he had no stomach for company, least of all Edmund's, now that he had seen how little the boy he had known had changed. But he tried to put a good face on it, telling himself that, once they reached London, they could go their separate ways.

CHAPTER 2

The London Road

Once they had cleared Headington Hill and Cheney Lane, Nick set a punishing pace on the London Road, justifying this to himself by observing that the sky was looking leaden, as if it might snow. In truth, it meant he and Edmund had no chance to talk. He had been surprised that Edmund did not seem curious about Nick's life since going down from Oxford and was more interested in talking about himself and his achievements. But if Nick was being honest, this was a small price to pay for the way he had ignored Edmund when he was a lonely adolescent in a strange new town.

They had been riding for some time and were approaching Didcot when Nick spotted a lone horseman ahead. He was sitting on his horse in the middle of the road. Immediately wary, Nick slowed down, then reined up within hailing distance of the man.

"What is it?" Edmund said, pulling up beside him.

"Not sure," Nick replied, studying the stranger carefully. He was wearing a soft cap pulled low on his forehead and a muffler around his neck so that most of his face was hidden. He was turned sideways on the road, effectively blocking it, one hand holding the reins of his horse, the other concealed by the angle of his body. Instinctively, Nick moved his cloak back over his left hip and, transferring his reins into his left hand, placed his right hand on the hilt of his sword.

"I'll go see what the fellow wants," Edmund said, and before Nick could prevent him, he was spurring his horse into a canter toward the stranger.

"God's teeth!" Nick muttered, and dug his heels into his horse's flanks. "Hold up, Edmund," he shouted.

But by now Edmund had reached the stranger and seemed to be conversing with him. Just as Nick drew up, the man brought his right hand from behind his body and pointed a small crossbow at Nick. For a moment, Nick stared in freezing disbelief at the deadly iron tip of the bolt pointed straight at his heart, before he flung himself sideways from his saddle. Simultaneously, he heard the wicked snap of the bolt being fired, then the ground rushing up to meet him with bone-jarring impact. He rolled desperately away from the lethal surge of hooves stamping and rearing around him and managed to make it to a ditch at the side of the road. Crouching for cover in case the assailant had managed to reload, he drew his sword and peered over the top of the bank before scrambling up and running to Edmund's aid.

But it was all over.

Their assailant was slumped over his pommel, and as Nick approached, he slid slowly down the side of his horse, smearing the terrified horse with his blood, and fell to the road, where he lay still. The horses were prancing and rearing in panic at the smell of blood, and Nick could see Edmund struggling to master them.

Nick dragged the man clear of the horse's hooves, then placed the tip of his weapon against the supine man's chest. But there was no need. The man was dead, pierced through the throat, his eyes regarding Nick with grotesque surprise, his mouth open as if in midshout, the front of his jerkin drenched in gore. Nick did not recognize him. Swiftly, he glanced around, looking for another rider, but the fields on the other side of the hedges were empty.

"Is he dead?" Edmund asked, at last managing to dismount. He was clutching his shoulder.

"You're hurt."

"It's nothing. Just a scratch."

Nick noticed that the dead man was holding a dagger; his crossbow lay on the road. He must have discarded it as soon as he realized he had missed and dropped it in favor of the knife. Crossbows were notoriously slow to load in a skirmish.

Nick tore off a piece of linen from the dead man's shirt and bound up Edmund's arm. The three horses had calmed and were now cropping the grass on the verge of the road as if nothing had happened.

"Do you know this man?" Nick asked, squatting down and going through the dead man's pockets. When Edmund didn't reply, he glanced up. Edmund had turned pale, as if he had just realized he had killed a man. He shook his head.

The only thing Nick found on the body was a small purse of gold.

"A cutpurse?"

"Perhaps," Nick replied. But the manner of attack seemed too deliberate for a spontaneous robbery. It was almost as if the man had been waiting for Nick. He saw again the iron bolt aimed directly at his heart. There was no happenstance here. The man had been sent to kill Nick. He wondered if Francesco del Toro had spotted Nick tailing him and arranged to have him taken off the board.

"We have to report the death to the local magistrate," Nick said, getting to his feet. "Can you ride?"

Edmund nodded.

"Then let's get out of here."

Nick caught up the reins of the dead man's horse, soothing it in a low voice to keep it calm. Edmund held it steady while Nick heaved the corpse across the saddle and tied it on. Next, he looped the reins over his pommel and mounted his own horse. Edmund did the same, although Nick could see he was in pain.

"What were you saying to him?" Nick asked.

"I asked him if he needed help," Edmund said.

"What did he say?"

"He said he had a message for you."

Nick frowned. "For me specifically?"

"Yes. The Honorable Nicholas Holt."

Then not a robbery but an assassination. Del Toro.

"Then you arrived, and, well . . ." Edmund trailed off. Glancing at him, Nick saw he was swaying slightly in the saddle. His wound must have been more serious than he had first thought. Edmund's sleeve was red to the wrist, and blood was dripping down his hand and onto the neck of his horse.

Nick held his questions and concentrated on getting them both to Didcot, where Edmund's shoulder could be properly treated. He tried to remember what Eli and Rivkah, twin brother and sister doctors in Bankside and his closest friends after John, had told him about infection. Something to do with cleaning the wound with wine and then smearing it with honey before binding it in clean linen. It had sounded more like a recipe for a ham to Nick, but he would do his damnedest to follow the instructions to the letter if such things as wine, honey, and clean linen could be had. Such was his faith in his friends' medical skills.

Their friendship had begun when Eli found Nick bleeding in the streets of Bankside and stitched up the deep gash in Nick's face that had been meant for his throat. Now a neat white line ran down from his right temple to just under his right jaw. Nick thought the scar gave him a dashing, piratical look; Rivkah said it made him look like a Bankside cutthroat.

Nick smiled to himself as he remembered what Rivkah had said. Sitting on a stool in their tiny kitchen the night he was wounded, he had not known whether he was in shock due to blood loss or from the sight of Rivkah in a flowing nightgown inadequately covered by a cloak. At first he had thought her Eli's wife, but when he realized they were twin siblings, his heart had given a great lurch, and he wasn't sure it had ever recovered. Perhaps that was why every time his friend Sir Thomas Brighton eyed Rivkah with more than gentlemanly interest, he wanted to throw him through the nearest window.

★ ★ ★

The death of the unknown assassin, albeit killed in self-defense, took two days to sort out. The local magistrate—a gentleman farmer—was not the sharpest tool in the shed, and it took repeated explanations to satisfy him that the killing was lawful. Neither Nick nor Edmund said anything about assassination but let the magistrate believe it was a robbery gone bad.

"Here's your gold, then," he said, handing Edmund the small bag. He had assumed Edmund had been the target, as he was the one wounded.

"Er . . ." Edmund said, looking embarrassed.

"Thanks for your help, sir," Nick said before Edmund could blurt out the truth, steering him firmly to the door of the magistrate's home. They had accepted the offer to stay for a couple of nights at the manor; Nick was concerned for Edmund, but he also needed to find out the identity of the man who had tried to kill him. Leaving Edmund recovering at the manor, he galloped back along the way they had come to make inquiries, but no one seemed to know the man or have any information about an accomplice. On the second day of fruitless searching, he gave up, aware of how late his report to Cecil was going to be. He just hoped Cecil didn't learn of del Toro's escape before he, Nick, could break the news to him.

Edmund's arm was in a sling, but he said he could ride. The wound had been small but deep, and he had lost a fair amount of blood. The magistrate's wife had patched him up proficiently, even putting in a couple of stitches.

"We have five boys," she told them, breaking off the thread and surveying her handiwork with complacence. "You have no idea how many cuts and scrapes I've patched up in my time." Nick had been pleased to see her clean the wound with wine, but when he mentioned honey, the woman had looked at him as if he were mad, although she grudgingly complied. "Never heard of that," she said. "Must try it next time one of my lads lops something off." She said this quite cheerfully. Nick admired her spirit and thought she would make a good battlefield nurse. She was far more intelligent than her husband, for one thing. And much younger. Her firm round body filled out her bodice quite charmingly, he thought.

"God go with you," the magistrate said, waving them off. He seemed pleased that his first dead body had been sorted so quickly and he hadn't had to go fagging the length and breadth of the county in search of a murderer. Judging from his girth and easygoing nature, Nick thought the magistrate was the type to settle for the obvious solution of an attempted robbery. If it had been him, Nick would have left the case open and continued the search for the family of the dead man in order to identify him. Nick left a letter to be sent back to Robert by the magistrate, asking his brother to make further inquiries into the identity of the man.

Nick gave the magistrate a few coins to bury the body decently.

"That was good of you," Edmund said, "seeing as he tried to kill you."

They were, once again, riding east on the London Road. This time Nick was careful to set a gentle pace so as not to jar Edmund's shoulder. Unfortunately, this meant there was ample opportunity to talk.

"He wasn't a suicide," Nick replied, conscious of the men he himself had dispatched into eternity. "He had the right to a decent burial." Even suicides deserved to be buried in a churchyard, Nick thought. In his opinion, most people's lives were so brutish and short, it was no wonder some poor unfortunates gave way to despair and decided to off themselves. If everyone who felt despair was going to hell, then heaven was going to be a very sparsely populated place. Perhaps that was what the clerics wanted: paradise as an exclusive gentlemen's club.

"I really don't feel comfortable keeping this," Edmund said, trying to give the gold back. "It feels wrong somehow. Like blood money."

"You saved my life," Nick said. "If anyone deserves it, you do."

Nick realized that not only was he was in Edmund's debt, but he had misjudged him. Edmund's reaction to being given the purse of the dead man indicated he was a decent man with a conscience.

CHAPTER 3

The Palace of Whitehall

"What do you mean, you lost del Toro and then he tried to have you killed?" Sir Robert Cecil said.

Nick had walked into his office, ignoring the cries of Cecil's flunkies that their master was not to be disturbed. Even though Cecil was only in his early twenties and a relative newcomer to court, he had already established a reputation for ruthlessness. His remarkable memory and his penchant for compiling lists of names in his own personal code of those foolish enough to make disparaging remarks about Queen and country kept his underlings in a state of silent, feverish employment. The son of Baron Burghley, he was rumored to be being groomed as the successor to Sir Francis Walsingham as head of the Queen's spy network. Until that happy day, he effectively ran the day-to-day business of the spy network, answering only to his father, Walsingham, and the Queen.

Nick made his report, offering no excuses for his failure.

"I don't know for a fact it was del Toro who hired the assassin," Nick said. "But the coincidence seems too great."

Cecil steepled his fingers and, resting his chin on them, regarded Nick across his desk. His thinking pose. Nick wondered if he practiced in a mirror. From this angle, Nick could hardly see the hunch on his back. It was his bent-over creeping gait that had given him the sobriquet of the Spider. That and the fact that he was seldom seen outdoors, preferring instead to lurk silently in dark corners.

His deformity was also the reason he chose to receive visitors sitting behind a desk littered with piles of parchment, which were covered in Cecil's precise, minute script. The desk was a symbol of his power and it made him seem almost normal, like a clerk or a librarian.

But Nick wasn't deceived. Cecil, he was convinced, was more encyclopedia than man. Open up his skull and there would be more lists with more names on them. Names of traitors and informers and double agents and recusants. Nick's name. His brother, Robert's, name. Hell, his whole family, living and dead. In 1559, the former earl, Nick's father, and Nick's mother, Agnes, had been forced to comply with the Act of Uniformity of Common Prayer and Administration of the Sacrament, which made it compulsory to attend Anglican services and established the Book of Common Prayer as the liturgy of the land; nonattendance at services was punishable by the massive fine of twenty-five pounds a month, imprisonment, or, as was increasingly the case as Elizabeth's paranoia grew, death.

When the Act of Uniformity had first gone into effect, Nick had been in long skirts and Robert twelve. Nick had grown up in the Anglican Church but was well aware of what this change of spiritual allegiance had cost his brother and parents. On his deathbed, the old earl had repeatedly called for a Catholic priest to come and shrive him, to take away the sin of his apostasy to the old faith. However, in return for their compliance, Nick's family had been able to keep their title, their hereditary lands, and most importantly, the Queen's trust.

Despite the risk of losing everything, including their lives, Nick suspected that his brother and mother still practiced their faith. As a boy, Nick had accidentally discovered a secret panel in the library that led to a tiny priest hole deep within the walls. He had never told anyone of his find and was afraid to discover that it was still in use. However cunningly priest holes were hidden, Walsingham's men were adept at discovering them, and Nick sometimes woke up from a nightmare of torches flickering on the stone walls of the

Tower torture chambers while the screams of his brother, sister-in-law, and mother being racked echoed in his ears.

★   ★   ★

"Tell me again exactly what happened," Cecil said.

When Nick got to the part where he had checked the pockets of the dead man, Cecil interrupted for the first time.

"Are you sure there was nothing else on him?"

"I'm sure."

"And you have no idea who he was?"

"Not a clue."

"What did he look like?"

"Very dead."

Cecil scowled. "I meant, was he an Englishman?"

"Not a Spaniard, at any rate." The dead man had been fair-skinned and blue-eyed.

"What about your friend Lovett?"

"He's an Englishman too."

Again, Cecil gave him the evil eye.

Nick sighed. He was getting tired of this. "He didn't know him either."

"But definitely not an attempted robbery?"

"No," Nick said. "It didn't play like that. The man was waiting. He told Edmund he had a message for me."

"And Lovett told you he himself was working for Essex?"

Nick shifted impatiently. "Yes. Before. At the tavern. I already told you that."

Cecil tapped his fingers against his lips, his expression introspective. He looked as if he were praying, only Nick couldn't imagine what kind of prayer Cecil would be capable of offering. Or to whom, for that matter.

"What?" Nick demanded as the silence stretched out.

Cecil looked up, as if surprised to see Nick still sitting there. "Instead of del Toro, perhaps our Boy Wonder is trying to eliminate his rivals?"

"Essex, you mean? Surely not. Even he is not rash enough to start murdering Englishmen."

"You don't know him the way I do," Cecil said. "He cannot tolerate being bested by anyone, especially if it has to do with what he laughingly calls his *honor*. He doesn't give a fig for the law. Thinks his exalted birth and the Queen's favor make him exempt."

Nick suspected Cecil was thinking of the times Essex had pinched his toys when they were boys. In addition, Cecil's own mother had been of comparatively low birth, and this was, Nick thought, the root of the bitter rivalry between the two men: Essex had the birth; Cecil had the brains. For the first time in their acquaintance, Nick suspected he was witnessing Cecil's emotions getting the better of his judgment. He was fascinated but also deeply worried. The last thing Nick wanted was to end up in the middle of a feud between Cecil and Essex.

"I thought Essex was in the Netherlands," Nick said.

The previous October, Robert Dudley, the Earl of Leicester and Essex's stepfather, had been sent to the Netherlands to aid the Protestant Dutch in their uprising against Catholic Philip II of Spain. Dudley had promptly appointed Essex his General of the Horse, an act of blatant nepotism. It was rumored that the twenty-year-old Essex had spent the staggering sum of a thousand pounds kitting out his entourage and had occupied his time in Holland by feasting, performing pointless military exercises, and generally quarreling with anyone who crossed his path. Essex, and his close friend Sir Philip Sidney, viewed war as a type of chivalric sporting event where the man with the most trophies won. A veteran of several bloody battlefields, Nick was not only amazed at such naïvety but also deeply disgusted at the callous disregard for those killed and maimed, usually the pikemen, archers, and foot soldiers of the lowest social rank.

"He's back," Cecil said sourly. "Apparently the Dutch told Leicester that if he didn't curb his stepson's excesses—he and his friends had been raiding the local villages for food and women and whatever else they could snaffle up—they would assassinate him themselves. So Leicester sent him back to the court carrying dispatches for the Queen and told him not to hurry back."

"That old chestnut. I'm surprised Essex didn't twig to it," Nick said. Much employed on the battlefield since the time of Julius Caesar, the "urgent dispatches" ruse was a way for generals to get rid of useless officers without political blowback.

"I'm not. Essex was delighted, apparently. Came galloping up to Whitehall in a lather as if the Visigoths were at the gates." Cecil snorted in derision. "All Leicester had written to the Queen was, 'I beg you to keep my stepson in England for as long as possible.'"

Given Essex's reputation for mayhem, Nick could imagine the heartfelt tone. "How long has he been in London?"

"Since January."

So, plenty of time to stir things up, then, Nick thought. It was now April.

The previous summer, it had been the talk of the court when Essex had announced he was establishing his own spy network to work "hand in hand" with Walsingham's. While the court toadies had lined up to congratulate him for his patriotism, behind his back they sniggered at his vainglory and correctly interpreted it as yet another instance of his rivalry with Robert Cecil, who had just arrived at court to work for Walsingham.

The chief spymaster himself had been furious. Dressed in his customary black and looking like a disgruntled crow, he had stalked in to see the Queen, intending to ask Elizabeth to order Essex to cease and desist. Instead, Elizabeth had waspishly reminded him of his failure to prevent the assassination attempt on her life when William Parry had hidden in the grounds of Richmond Palace and then leapt out of the bushes with a knife. Surrounded only by her shrieking ladies, Elizabeth had faced down her would-be killer with breathtaking hauteur, commanding him to stop trampling the lavender and put down his weapon forthwith.

"Where were you when Parry popped out of the shrubbery?" Elizabeth had raged.

To this Walsingham had wisely given no reply, seeing as William Parry was, in fact, one of his own spies who had been recruited by the Spanish. Not his network's finest hour.

Parry had refrained from carrying out the assassination only because he was overcome, he later confessed, by the Queen's uncanny likeness to her father, Henry VIII, whom he revered. Despite her being ten stone lighter, not to mention the wrong sex, it must have been Elizabeth's bowel-loosening tone of command that did the trick. In Nick's opinion, Parry's fondness for Fat Harry more than confirmed the fact that he was a complete loon. This did not, however, save him from a traitor's death.

Nick got to his feet. "I'm off to see Her Maj. I'll give her your best, shall I?"

He had received the royal summons as soon as he entered the palace but had chosen to make his report to Cecil first in order to get the confession of his botch-up with del Toro over with and alert the network so that the man could be found. He hoped the Queen would not be aware that he had made a detour. She took a narrow view of being kept waiting.

At the mention of the Queen, Nick saw a tremor of discomfit pass fleetingly over Cecil's face before he schooled it into its habitual mask of impassivity. Only a few months before, the Queen had sent one of Cecil's spies to the Tower, thinking him—erroneously, as it turned out—a suspect in the murders of two of her ladies-in-waiting.

In reality, Sir Thomas Brighton was working for Cecil, who had tasked him to uncover a tax fraud at the Custom House. When Elizabeth had learned of Sir Thomas's true identity, she had flown into a monumental snit. Ever since, she had treated Cecil with glacial politeness. So glacial, in fact, that Nick was sure Cecil had a severe case of frostbite in his extremities. Something that cheered Nick immensely.

Let the Spider sort out his own problems, Nick thought as he left Cecil's rooms. Nick had enough on his plate. To wit: someone, as yet undisclosed, was out to kill him.

★ ★ ★

Next stop, the Queen. Nick had arrived back in London only a few hours before and had not even dumped his saddlebags back at The Black Sheep in Bankside but had ridden straight to the palace. Edmund had veered off toward Leicester House near the Middle Temple while Nick had continued along the Strand and then south on King Street to Whitehall. Nick was once again saddlesore and hadn't bathed in days. Still, perhaps the fact that he reeked would encourage the Queen to cut the audience short. He had no idea why she wanted to see him but fervently hoped she didn't have a job in mind. The previous winter he had identified the "Court Killer"—the nickname given to the murderer by the people of London—and this had convinced Elizabeth that Nick was now her personal fixer, much like a trusted plumber when the sewers started backing up and she found herself knee-deep in shit.

Once again, Nick found himself outside the royal apartments trying to gain admittance from the granite-faced guards.

"I assure you, she'll want to see me," Nick said. When that got no response, he pulled out his ace, a bit of gossip he had overheard in The Black Sheep. "Hey, Bill," he said to the bigger of the two. "Heard you got into a bit of fisticuffs last month. Tried to choke the royal cook with his apron."

"A misunderstanding," Bill managed to say without moving his mouth. Royal guards were not supposed to speak while on duty.

"Not what I heard. Something about broken fingers and how he can't hold a ladle anymore, let alone whip up those fairy cakes the Queen is so fond of." Nick grinned nastily. "Wonder if the Queen knows you're the reason her food tastes like crap nowadays."

"You bastard," hissed Bill. Then, to his younger companion, "Let him in, Lenny. Maybe Her Majesty will send him to the Tower."

"Live in hope," Nick said. "I'll tell the cook you'll send flowers." This as an aside as he ducked under their crossed pikes. He was still smiling to himself when he found himself face-to-face with Elizabeth, who was standing on the other side of the door. He hastily made a leg. "Your Majesty."

"Look what the cat dragged in," was his august monarch's response. "We were just talking about you."

It took Nick a moment to figure out that Elizabeth's use of *we* was not the royal prerogative but grammatically precise. Reclining on a cushioned settle in front of the fire was a young fop resplendent in a peapod doublet of white-and-black silk scintillating with silver thread. The effect was calculatingly blinding, as were the long legs, also clad in white hose, indolently stretched out in front of him. He wore no breeches that Nick could see, just the doublet and hose. It was the latest French fashion and designed to highlight the manly parts. In Nick's opinion, it made him look like a rent boy, albeit an improbably handsome one. The head above the elaborately starched ruff was blessed with abundant brown curls, the dark eyes surprisingly penetrating for a young man with such a profligate reputation. One arm was flung carelessly over the back of the settle; in his other hand he held a glass filled with wine that was perilously close to dripping onto the Queen's priceless Turkey carpet.

Talk of the devil, Nick thought, making the smallest bow he could get away with. *It's that toffee-nosed git, Essex.*

"Heard you and my agent were attacked on the London road." This spoken in an upper-crust drawl that made Nick feel ashamed for his own class. "Bad luck, old chap." As if he had lost a game of tennis. Essex must have come tearing over to Whitehall after hearing the news from Lovett. He would have relished telling his monarch that one of her agents had been saved by one of his own. Nick watched Essex's face to see if there was any sign of complicity in the attack but could discern nothing except idle curiosity.

"That's why I wanted to see you," Elizabeth said, seating herself in an upright chair, the stiff brocade of her skirts spreading worryingly close to the fire. "Tell us what happened. I will not have my agents attacked in my own realm."

Nick caught the use of the plural. Essex had also used it. The last he'd heard, he had been the only one who had been deliberately attacked. Admittedly, Edmund had been wounded in the ensuing scuffle, but he was definitely not the target. Trust Essex to exaggerate in order to make his own network look important in the Queen's eyes.

Nevertheless, a request from Elizabeth was tantamount to a command, so Nick went through it all again, stressing that the assassin was unknown to him and unknown, apparently, to the people in Didcot and all the villages and hamlets along the London Road near where the attack had occurred. He omitted any mention of del Toro, as he didn't want Essex sniffing around an operation run by Cecil. This was not so much out of loyalty to Cecil as it was a desire to keep well shot of the virulent rivalry between them. Thank God Edmund had not seen del Toro in The Spotted Cow; otherwise Essex would know that too.

"It's a puzzle, to be sure," the Queen said gravely. Then, with a certain pointedness, "Perhaps he was an outraged husband?"

Essex chuckled, and Nick shot him an irritated look. *Pot calling the kettle black* was the phrase that crossed his mind. The trouble with his cover as the dissolute lad about town was that people assumed he was a promiscuous rake. Like Essex.

"I did not recognize him, Your Majesty," he repeated.

"Well, you wouldn't," she replied, "necessarily."

"He was hired, of that I'm certain," Nick said. "The plain way he was dressed did not tally with the bag of gold on his person. It was obviously payment for services rendered. And the weapon itself, a crossbow, is a professional's weapon. People acting on their own for personal reasons favor what's to hand. Knives, usually."

Elizabeth sniffed at the mention of the sordid lives of her citizens and their crude manner of settling disputes. It occurred to Nick that ordering people's heads lopped off was pretty crude as well, but naturally, he kept that to himself.

Essex stirred on the settle. "If I may, Your Majesty?"

Elizabeth looked at him fondly. "Of course, Robin. You know how much I value your counsel."

"It's obvious what this is all about," Essex said. "The man was hired by the Spanish to eliminate one of Her Majesty's agents. To wit, Lovett. It was he, after all, who was wounded."

Nick opened his mouth to say that a crossbow pointed at his heart was definitely something he wouldn't mistake, but Essex lifted a schoolmasterly finger to forestall him.

"In order," the earl went on, "to throw *my* spy network into disarray."

"Do you think so, Robin?" exclaimed the Queen. For the first time, she looked worried, as if Nick's personal health, namely his ability to stay alive, was of piddling importance compared to her favorite's reputation. As it probably was, concluded Nick glumly. No wonder Codpiece was not in the room. Five minutes with this pair of lovebirds and he probably wanted to hang himself. Nick certainly did. It was profoundly depressing to see a woman of Elizabeth's intellect, not to mention mature years, reduced to a simpering, brainless ninny.

"Absolutely," Essex said. "Lovett is a valued agent. The Spanish would love nothing better than to destroy my network."

Nick tried to keep his face straight at this staggering display of vanity and self-delusion, not to mention the ludicrous exaggeration of Edmund's importance.

"Then what you need is someone like Nick here," the Queen said. "I used him last winter to find the killer of two of my ladies-in-waiting." She smiled at Nick, and he was forced to smile back, although he felt like screaming. He knew what was coming. He was being loaned out to Essex like some prized hunting dog.

"I'll have a word with Walsingham," Elizabeth said.

In court parlance, that meant she would be issuing an order. Nick's fate was sealed.

"Thank you, Your Majesty," Essex said. "I accept."

As well you might, thought Nick. *You've just successfully maneuvered the Queen into stealing a rival agent.* No one had thought to ask if Nick agreed with this arrangement. On the contrary, he could do nothing other than bow at the Queen's apparent graciousness. In truth, he felt like jumping out of the mullioned window.

"I'll send a man over to fetch you at your tavern across the river," Essex said to Nick.

"I cannot wait."

"Splendid." Essex got to his feet and stretched. "Sure you don't want to come riding with me, Your Majesty?" he said. "I fancy a bit of hawking."

"I'm afraid not, Robin. I have to see a deputation from the Dutch."

"Those fat butter-boxes," sneered Essex. "Can you believe they told lies about me to my stepfather?" His face had flushed with anger, his mouth twisting petulantly. Suddenly Nick saw him as a spoiled little boy who had been denied something he wanted. This was the face Cecil had known in their boyhood. For the first time, Nick felt that Cecil was not entirely crazy to suspect Essex of being behind a plot to get rid of Walsingham's agents.

"Holland is an important ally," the Queen admonished with a tiny glimmer of irritation.

"Oh, well then. Needs must, I suppose," he replied sulkily.

The Queen rose to her feet. "You can escort me to the audience chamber, Robin." She said this like a mother trying to coax a spoiled child into good humor by offering it a sweetmeat.

Immediately Essex brightened. "I would be honored to, Your Majesty."

She linked her arm in his, and together they left the room. Before the door closed, she looked back over her shoulder at Nick. "Sort this out," she said. "You're no use to me dead."

Nick bowed, and they were gone.

Immediately a diminutive figure stuck his head round a door leading into an inner chamber in the suite of rooms.

"Has Fancy-Pants buggered off, then?"

It was Codpiece, the Queen's Fool, a dwarf who might have been cursed with a small body but had been blessed with a large wit.

"Hello, Richard," Nick said. "Hiding under the bed again, I see."

"Too right." Codpiece jumped up on the settle where Essex had just been sitting. "And it's as dusty as the Arabian Desert under there, I can tell you. Those lazy good-for-nothing slatterns never do a proper job of sweeping."

Bemused, Nick watched as Codpiece picked bits of fluff and cobweb off his doublet, then rubbed the rim of Essex's abandoned wine glass with his sleeve and took a deep quaff.

"Ahhh, that's better."

Nick flopped down in the Queen's chair and helped himself to a drink. "I gather you heard that I've been loaned out to Essex."

"Bad luck, old chap," Codpiece said in a perfect imitation of Essex's upper-class voice.

Nick couldn't help but laugh. Then, as the enormity of what the Queen had done to him sank in, he lapsed into silence, miserably contemplating the hours, days, weeks, and, God forbid, months he would be forced to spend in Essex's company. He fervently hoped the Spanish would attack the Dutch and send Essex storming back to Holland to save the day.

"You could always abjure the realm," Codpiece said.

Nick glanced up and saw that the Fool was watching him with a look of amused pity on his face.

"Tell me, Richard," he said. "How does the Queen tolerate Essex? He's far more trouble than he's worth."

"Maybe," Codpiece said. "But then again, you know how Her Maj likes to play one side against the other."

"Burghley and Cecil versus Essex, you mean?"

Codpiece nodded. "And Walsingham. While they're busy getting up each other's noses, they forget to nag her about policy. I suspect that is one of the reasons she's lent you to Essex. On the one hand, it will infuriate Walsingham; on the other, it will provide him with access to Essex's network. Quite clever, if you think about it."

Nick considered this and still thought it wasn't worth it. Especially for him.

"Too clever by half, if you ask me," he said. "And, of course, no one did. Ask me, that is." He drained his wine and poured more. "Problem is, Richard, I'm caught between a rock and a hard place. Cecil thinks Essex tried to have me killed; Essex probably thinks Cecil is trying to kill off his own agents. Either way, I'm fucked."

"Cheer up," Codpiece said. "This is your chance to undermine Essex's network."

Unspoken between them was the Queen's infamous vanity. It was almost as if she set out to play the hoyden in order to dispel any notion that she was an old maid. But Codpiece, Nick knew, would never say as much.

Fiercely loyal to the Queen, Codpiece was Elizabeth's personal spy at court. As a Fool, he could go anywhere the Queen went, and nobody took him seriously. His madcap antics and witty, obscene banter were the perfect disguise, even more perfect than Nick's dissolute-nobleman act. Beneath Codpiece's foolery lay a capacious intelligence. His given name was Richard, and that's how Nick thought of him. They had become friends the previous winter when there had been a murderer on the loose butchering the Queen's ladies-in-waiting. Richard had trusted Nick with his real identity in order to be his eyes and ears at court. With Elizabeth's blessing, of course.

"Carrying on with Essex has taken her mind off the problem of that Scottish minx, however," Codpiece said. "So I suppose we have to thank the little turd for that."

The Scottish minx was Mary, Queen of Scots, kept under house arrest by Elizabeth since 1568 and long the figurehead in numerous plots to assassinate the Queen and set Mary on the throne in her stead. Now rumor was rife that there was another plot afoot. Nick had picked up hints that Walsingham was running some sort of covert operation that would lead Mary into a trap that would finally be her undoing. Nick was just thankful Walsingham had not involved Nick in his devious game. In truth, Nick felt sorry for Mary and thought she had led a tragic life, but as a Catholic recusant, he knew it was more than his life was worth to say this out loud, even to Codpiece.

"I can't believe Essex thinks someone is out to discredit *him*," Nick said, getting to his feet.

"Well, he would, wouldn't he?" Codpiece said. "His self-regard makes Narcissus look like St. Francis of Assisi."

Nick grinned.

"Seriously, though, what are you going to do?" Codpiece asked. "Aside from watch your back."

"Not sure yet," Nick replied.

"Take care, my friend. These are naughty times we live in."

CHAPTER 4

The Black Sheep Tavern, Bankside

Nick was sitting in front of the fire at The Black Sheep, his sword belt and cloak laid aside on a bench. The enormous head of his Irish Wolfhound, Hector, lay in his lap, and Nick was sleepily fondling his ears. Hector's rapturous baying at Nick's approach several hours before had no doubt roused the entire neighborhood. It had certainly alerted John and Maggie Stockton, the married couple who ran the daily business of the tavern for him, and a cup of ale and platter of food were waiting for him when he opened the door. Nick was so weary that even the greeting of "Who's a poxy whoreson, then?" from Bess the parrot—won in a game of dice from Kit Marlowe and renowned in Bankside for her execrable vocabulary—failed to put a blight on his happiness at being home.

John was the younger son of Nick's father's steward and a childhood friend who had followed him to Oxford, ostensibly as his bodyservant but more accurately as his partner in drinking, wenching, and, later, soldiering on the Continent. In short, John was his bagman.

John came over now and sat down on the bench. He had his seventeen-month-old daughter, Jane, in his arms. Her head was lolling against his shoulder, her limbs completely loose in sleep as only a child's could be. Nick envied her.

"What happened?" John asked in a low voice. Maggie was wiping down the board on which the tavern served ale in preparation for the night's customers, and Matty was stacking cups.

Matty was a relatively new addition to The Black Sheep family. Nick had interviewed her as a witness the previous winter when she had been a lowly cinders at Whitehall only a crust of bread away from starvation. Then she had been a sticklike waif with a ghostly pallor, as her job of cleaning out the fireplaces in the palace was conducted mostly at night. When the Queen had asked Nick what he wanted for a reward after he apprehended the murderer of two of her ladies-in-waiting, he had asked if Matty could come live at The Black Sheep to help with Jane, the baby. Now she had filled out amazingly, her skin blooming milk and roses.

When Nick had first encountered her, he had thought Matty about ten years old, so stunted by malnutrition and neglect she had been; now she looked more like her actual thirteen years, still much too young for what Henry, Maggie's fourteen-year-old son, obviously had in mind, but not too young to be developing the first tentative hints of a womanly figure. Nick had seen the way Henry had been ogling her since Christmas and was relieved Maggie had noticed it too and was careful not to leave the youngsters alone.

Nick saw John glance at his family and knew this was John's way of telling him that whatever was bothering him, they were to keep it between themselves, especially from Maggie. Not that she wasn't as brave as a lion, as evidenced by the firm way she dealt with unruly customers in the tavern who couldn't keep their hands to themselves, but she was a mother and wife and worried for the safety of her children, John, and now Matty. She did not mind the occasional tavern fight among some of the lowlifes who frequented The Black Sheep—she had been running a tavern since she had married her first husband at the age of seventeen—but she feared the world Nick inhabited, a world of suspicion and shadowy figures, a world where someone could smile and smile and be a villain. Sometimes Nick fell afoul of her when it was his fault John had been drawn into danger. But telling John to stay home where it was safe was not an option. And on this night, John had known the moment he laid eyes on his friend that something was amiss. So Nick told the story one more time, adding an account of his visit to Whitehall and the fact that Essex had managed to convince the Queen to lend him Nick.

"To find out who tried to murder Lovett," Nick concluded.

"But it was you the man was trying to kill!" John exclaimed.

"Tell Essex that," Nick said morosely. "He takes everything as a personal slur on himself. Probably even the weather if it has the temerity to piss on him." Nick crashed his tankard down on the bench, making Jane stir on John's shoulder. She began to whimper.

"Sorry," Nick said, feeling even more miserable. Now he was taking out his problems on nurslings.

John got to his feet and carried Jane into the back of the tavern, where he and Maggie had rooms. On his way back, after having put the child to bed, he swiped another cup off the counter and picked up a jug of wine.

"I reckon we need something stronger than ale," he said. He poured for both of them and sat down again.

A few customers wandered in, and Maggie and Matty were busy serving them. The low hum of voices at that end of the room gave them the cover they needed.

"It's more likely del Toro is behind the attempt on your life. We have to find him," John said, leaning forward and pitching his voice low.

Nick pulled a face. "I agree. But it looks like I'm stuck in London dancing attendance on Essex. I have no idea where del Toro might be. Probably back in Spain by now."

"I can go to Oxford and try to track his movements," John said.

"Wait until after I see Walsingham. It's possible del Toro is back in London." He had received no summons yet but was expecting one at any moment. Nick wasn't looking forward to it. By now, Walsingham would know he was expected to turn over one of his best agents to a man he detested.

"I think you were targeted because you are Walsingham's agent, not just *an* agent," John said. "He left the tavern before you in order to set up the ambush. His man was waiting for you."

It made sense. Nick remembered the whore. Perhaps she had been in on it too?

"I suppose the proof that it is somehow political will be if there is an attempt on another agent," Nick replied. And if this happened, then Spain must be trying to provoke an international incident that would lead to an open declaration of war. They were already building ships for an invasion as fast as they could. Nick himself had reported this to Walsingham. When they were ready, they would attack.

"Or another attempt on your life," John said.

Their conversation was halted by the arrival of Will Shakespeare, who immediately came over to them. For once, he was not drunk, although there was plenty of time for that, Nick thought, shaking his friend's hand.

A relative newcomer to London, Will had been born in Stratford-upon-Avon, the son of a glove-maker, but had burned to become an actor. Even more than acting, he longed to write plays of his own and was always trying out bits of dialogue and plots on his friends. As far as Nick knew, he kept body and soul together by stabling the horses of theatergoers. Lately, he had joined Essex's acting troupe. Will was always hard-up, so Nick was willing to run a generous tab at The Black Sheep for his friend because he sensed Will had enormous talent and would go far. Besides, he liked Will and found him one of the most intelligent men he had ever met. Even in his cups, Will was witty and charming. Unlike Nick's other playwright friend, Kit Marlowe, who grew bitter and morose when inebriated.

Will leaned forward. "I heard about what happened on the London Road."

Nick threw his hands up. "It seems like the whole world knows." Another proof, if Nick needed it, that London was really a glorified village with a preternaturally efficient gossip mill.

"Edmund told me."

Then Nick remembered that Will too was familiar with Essex's set because Essex had taken over the day-to-day patronage of his stepfather's acting troupe, the Earl of Leicester's Men, established by royal patent in 1574. It seemed that Essex was always taking over that which others had established—the spy network, an acting troupe—as if he lacked the essential imagination to found some-thing unique. In this way, he was like a flea, a parasite that feasted on a host, Nick thought. "How do you tolerate Essex, Will?" he said. "I was in his company for ten minutes this afternoon and I wanted to do him a mischief."

Will shrugged. "His stepfather is a patron of the theater. Besides," he added. "He's not so bad once he's away from court."

Will drew up a stool and sat down, his dark eyes flashing with intelligence. "It's actually quite fascinating to watch, the change that comes over him when he's at court and in the public eye. It's as if he becomes another person entirely. When he's at home, he's relatively normal."

"Ha!" Nick said. "Define normal."

"Well, not *normal*, exactly. What nobleman is?" Then he became aware of what he had said. "Not you, of course, Nick. You're *immensely* normal. Superlatively normal." He cocked his head, reminding Nick of a giant robin eyeing a worm. "That was a contradiction, wasn't it? Or was it an oxymoron? I get them mixed up. How about *normally* normal?"

Nick laid a hand on his arm. He knew his friend's love of words, and Will could go on like this all night. "Go get yourself a drink."

"Bugger off, you mean?" he said with a grin. "I can take a hint." But he got to his feet, nodded to John, and sauntered over to the bar, where they heard him address Maggie: "Shall I compare thee to a summer's day?"

"The usual then, Will?"

★   ★   ★

Kat's Brothel, Bankside

Nick was up to his neck in hot water.

Submerged in a tub in the back of Kat's brothel, he was soak-ing off the accumulated grime and sweat from his abortive trip to Oxford. He was having less luck washing away the memory of the crossbow pointed at his heart.

There was a small shriek and the sound of water slopping onto the tiles.

"What are you doing with your foot?" Kat demanded. She was sitting facing him in the bath. It was a tight fit, but Nick thought that just made it all the more interesting.

"Just exploring," he murmured, his eyes closed.

"Well, you can stop exploring right now. I have to get dressed. I've a business to run, in case you hadn't noticed." Kat was the madam of a Bankside knocking shop. She and Nick had been friends and occasional lovers for five years.

"Call me Sir Francis Drake of the bath," Nick said. "I don't need an ocean to discover new lands. My ambition is far more modest."

"There's nothing modest about what you're doing."

Nick opened one eye and grinned. Then he grabbed a shapely ankle. More water slopped onto the tiles.

★ ★ ★

"Harder," Kat gasped.

"I'm trying," Nick grunted.

There was a knock on the door, and before either of them could move, the door opened and Joseph, Kat's business partner and a former wrestler, stuck his head round.

"There's a messenger arrived for Nick," he said, and closed the door.

"You didn't pull it tight enough," Kat said, "but it will have to do."

Nick obediently tied the strings of her corset. "Can I help roll up your stockings?"

In reply, Kat threw his doublet at him. "I would have thought you'd seen enough. Now hurry up and get dressed. It seems you're wanted outside."

When Nick emerged fully clothed, he spotted a disreputable-looking character slouched on a stool. The man's eyes were glued to the young ladies in various stages of undress who were sitting at a long table in the main room. It was morning, so the brothel was empty of customers and the girls were having breakfast. Some were feeding small children on their laps and one was nursing a baby. None of them was paying the newcomer the least attention.

"How goes it, Harold?" Nick said. He recognized him as one of Walsingham's runners, a wizened runt of a man with lank hair and a face like a ferret. He looked like a rat-catcher, which, oddly enough, was exactly what he was.

"His Nibs wants to see you," Harold said, jerking his thumb at the door, as if Walsingham were sitting in a coach and four outside. "It's urgent," he added when Nick grabbed a hunk of bread and a cup of ale off the table.

"Not urgent enough to miss breakfast," Nick said between mouthfuls. Then, seeing Harold's doglike slavering, he tossed him a small loaf and handed him a cup of small beer.

"Ta, Nick," Harold said, devouring the bread. He drained his cup, wiped his mouth on a rancid sleeve, and stood up. "I'll tell His Nibs you're on your way, shall I?"

"Don't nag, Harold," Nick said. "I'll be there as soon as I can. I have to pick up something first." He tossed the man a small coin. "Make sure you spend that at my tavern," he said. Then, seeing Harold looking wistfully at the whores, "Forget about it. You can't afford the prices here. Especially for all the unnatural things you want to do." This provoked a fierce blush in Harold and a gale of raucous laughter from the girls as Harold fled.

CHAPTER 5

Seething Lane

The something Nick wanted to pick up was Hector. He had missed his dog on his trip north and wasn't about to leave him pining at the tavern all day. But this wasn't the only reason he had delayed: not only would Walsingham have been fully apprised of his cock-up with del Toro, but he would also have been told that the Queen had ordered him to lend Essex one of his best agents.

Nick was glad when John insisted on accompanying him.

"You can bribe the turnkey for a swank room when Walsingham has me thrown in the Tower," Nick joked.

Judging from his expression, John did not seem to find this amusing.

"Don't forget to drop in at the Guild," Maggie called after them.

In answer to Nick's questioning look, John said, "Maggie is thinking of brewing her own beer so we can join the Brewers' Guild. What do you think?"

"Fine with me if she has the time."

"Now that Matty helps with Jane, she has more time. Besides, she wants Henry to learn a trade. She's worried about him. He's been hanging around the bear-baiting ring with the actors." Henry was Maggie's fourteen-year-old son by her first marriage and John's stepson. As the euphemism went, he was going through an "awkward phase," mooning over anything in a skirt and writing idealistic verses about the fairer sex. Considering that the "fairer sex" were the toothless hags who made up the tavern regulars and supplemented their meager income by quickies in the alley, his poetry was startlingly Platonic in nature. Nick had once had a quick peek when he found Henry's notebook left on the bar. There were lots of references to beautiful shepherdesses and lovesick swains, a tremendous feat of imagination considering that Bankside was populated mostly by whores and criminals.

"Will's all right," Nick said. "So is Kit Marlowe beneath all the bravado." They crossed onto London Bridge and headed north over the Thames.

"Henry wants to be a poet," John said glumly. "A poet, God help us!"

"He'll grow out of it," Nick said, clapping his friend on the shoulder.

"What if he doesn't?"

"We'll cross that bridge when we come to it."

"I see you've been taking lessons from Codpiece," John said sourly, but Nick had seen his mouth quirk up in a slight smile.

They continued across the bridge; turned right on Thames Street heading toward Billingsgate Fish Market, Hector's nose twitching at the pungent smell; took a left at All Hallows church by the Tower; and arrived at 35 Seething Lane hard by the Crutched Friars. The house resided in Tower Ward within the walls of the ancient city of London. Nick had often wondered if Walsingham had chosen the location so he could gaze at the Tower from his garden, knowing that at any given time a traitor he himself had caught likely languished there, awaiting death.

A gangly youth was just leaving as Nick arrived, a hat pulled low over his forehead. Mumbling an apology for momentarily blocking the doorway, the lad hurried off, face averted. He looked too young to be an agent. Probably a runner like Harold the unemployed rat-catcher, Nick thought, stepping over the threshold.

On the few occasions Nick had been inside the house on Seething Lane, it had looked as if a bomb had gone off in a paper factory. This visit was no exception. There were sheets of parchment everywhere, covering the wooden floors, piled on chairs and tables, emerging from open chests like stuffing out of feather bolsters. The scene gave the impression of utter chaos, and yet, Nick knew, Walsingham and his secretaries had the uncanny ability of laying their hands almost immediately on whatever document they needed and extracting a single name from the hundreds, even thousands, contained within the house's four walls.

It must make cleaning a nightmare, Nick thought, as he tried to tread only on the infrequent glimpses of floorboard. It made him feel as if he were traversing a river on stepping stones. A river of paper. He traversed alone, as John and Hector were told firmly by Walsingham's chief secretary, Laurence Tomson, that they must remain outside. John said he would pop along to the Brewers' Guild with Hector and meet Nick back at the house in an hour. The Guild was located not far away in Cheapside.

"His Honor's feeling a bit poorly today," Tomson whispered as he led Nick upstairs to his master's study.

That was an understatement. Walsingham had been in ill health the whole time Nick had known him. Long suspected of being a hypochondriac famous for his kidney ailments, he had recently been diagnosed with testicular cancer. It was now rumored that the Queen's Secretary of State did not have long to live.

When Nick saw him, he believed it. The man's face was the color of parchment and deeply lined, his body emaciated. He held himself carefully, as if he were in acute pain, but it was typical of the man to be at work. Nick had heard that when he was forced to keep to his bed, he ordered his servants to prop him up on his pillows and put a large tray on his lap, on which papers were placed by Tomson, who sat beside him on a chair. Nick didn't know whether to admire the man for his Calvinist work ethic or pity him for an obsession with traitors that bordered on mania. But one thing Nick knew for certain: Walsingham was fanatically loyal to the Queen and to Protestantism. Unlike Essex, who was fanatically loyal to only one man: himself.

Walsingham was sitting hunched over his desk writing when Nick was shown in.

"Just a moment," he said without looking up.

Tomson waved Nick to a chair and left. The only sound was the scratching of Walsingham's pen, and Nick had the strange feeling that the room he had entered was the inside of the spymaster's mind—a cluttered space filled with secrets and dark corners. Against the wall he saw a chest labeled A BOX OF RELIGION & MATTERS ECCLESIASTICAL and knew that it contained, among other things, the names of Catholic recusants, his family's names included. At any time, Walsingham could decide to fish them out and institute an inquiry. It was the reason Nick was sitting here now. When His Nibs asked for a meeting, it was prudent to show up. Especially if you had ballsed up an assignment and were now working for the competition.

At last Walsingham stopped writing, meticulously sanded the wet ink, shook the sand off, then picked up a small bell on his desk and rang it.

A man of slight build with a blond beard came in so quickly that Nick got the impression he had been waiting outside. He did not so much as glance at Nick but went straight to his master. Nick recognized him as Thomas Phelippes, fluent in many languages and a genius at deciphering and creating codes.

"Code this in Petty Wales Standard, will you, Tom?" Walsingham said, handing over the sheet of paper. "And then seal it with the usual. It must be delivered into the hands of Captain Shawe of the merchant ship *Arachne* by the evening tide."

"Very good, Sir Francis," Phelippes replied. He bowed and left the room.

At last Walsingham sat back and surveyed Nick with surprisingly placid brown eyes, considering he must have been enraged by the Queen's request.

"Thank you for coming," he said in a low and mellifluous voice.

Walsingham was famed for the politeness of his speech. As a staunch Protestant, he abjured all coarse language and despised metaphor and flights of rhetoric, preferring cold, hard facts. More than once, Nick had wondered how Walsingham would react if he ever came into contact with Bess, his parrot. The parrot's previous owner, Kit Marlowe, had taught the bird a few choice words concerning the dour spymaster. But that meeting, of course, would never happen. Walsingham considered Bankside to be nothing less than a worldly precursor to hell itself. He had been heard to remark that, detestable papist though he was, Dante had gotten it right when he created the Inferno, and if it were up to him, he would condemn all actors, whores, Jews, Catholics, and thieves of Bankside and Southwark to the flames there. As that neatly categorized almost all the people Nick called friends, he was pretty sure where Walsingham thought he was headed in the afterlife. Now he gave Nick a particularly disarming smile.

Here it comes, Nick thought, bracing himself. He had a sudden conviction that his family's names had indeed been plucked from that ominous chest in the corner. With mounting panic, he thought of the ruin of his family's fortunes, their imprisonment, perhaps even death. Even though the room was chilly, he had begun to sweat. This was what those poor unfortunate sods Walsingham personally interrogated must have felt like, he thought. Either that or Walsingham was very, very pissed off about Nick losing del Toro.

"The body of Simon Winchelsea was found floating in the river the day you left London for Oxford," Walsingham said.

Nick blinked. Having braced himself to be given a bollocking for losing del Toro, to be forced to listen to a rant about Essex and the Queen, this was the last thing he'd expected. His conversation with John came back to him: if another agent were killed, in addition to the attempt on Nick's life, they would know the Spanish were behind it. Walsingham wouldn't have bothered to mention it if Winchelsea's death had been accidental.

Nick hadn't known Winchelsea well but vaguely recalled a slight, wiry man with the weathered face of someone who had spent most of his life outdoors in all weather.

"His death was . . . unexpected."

This was as close as Walsingham would ever get to expressing dismay, Nick realized. The spymaster was gazing at Nick, but his eyes were sightless, turned inward on his own thoughts, as if he were pondering his next move after an opponent had unexpectedly checked him.

The spymaster grimaced. "Throat cut. After his eyes were put out."

If Walsingham could imagine Winchelsea's state of mind as he was being blinded, then murdered, he gave no sign. His voice was low and uninflected. As always.

The defining experience of Walsingham's life, one that explained his fanatical hatred of Catholics and had hardened his resolve to establish an English Protestant state, had been when, as English ambassador in France, he was in Paris during the Massacre of St. Bartholomew's Eve fourteen years earlier. There he had witnessed the wholescale slaughter of French Huguenots—men, women, children clinging to the skirts of their mothers, babes in arms, and the infirm elderly. Bravely, he had given sanctuary to as many of the terrified populace as the embassy could hold and barred the doors. Then he and his staff had stood guard with drawn swords all night, refusing to give up the Huguenots under his protection to the baying mob while the streets of Paris ran ankle-deep in blood and the screams of the dying had continued unabated throughout the night like a hellish chorus.

Like Dante emerging from the Inferno, without the consolation of the Paradiso, Walsingham had returned to England a changed man, his soul seared by the sights and sounds of unimaginable horror, by the dark knowledge of what man was capable of doing to his fellow man in the name of God. Perhaps that was the reason he dressed all in black, Nick thought. Not because he was a Puritan, but because he was in perpetual mourning.

"Judging from the lack of bloating," Walsingham continued, "we think he went into the river the night before. Your physician friend confirmed this at the scene."

Walsingham was referring to Eli, the Jewish doctor who had performed the examination of the body of Lady Cecily, the first lady-in-waiting to be murdered at court. Rivkah had examined the body of the second lady-in-waiting. The Queen had sanctioned their involvement, knowing that Nick thought highly of their medical skills. Cannily, she also knew that a Jewish physician would keep silent about what he discovered because Jews were tolerated in England on sufferance. As long as the Jews proved useful, she would turn a blind eye to their faith and leave them unmolested.

As for Walsingham, he was not above recruiting people he would ordinarily abhor if it served his purposes, especially if they were protected by the Queen's favor. So long as they remained useful to him, they were relatively safe.

Still, the fact that Walsingham had taken it upon himself to enlist the help of Eli made Nick profoundly uneasy, as if the tentacles of the spy business were reaching across the river and encircling the sanctuary Nick had built for himself in Bankside. He knew he had only himself to blame. It was he who had suggested Eli examine the body of Cecily in the first place.

"He found three sets of footprints at the scene of Winchelsea's death," Walsingham continued. "The actual murder took place in a shed near the wharf. I am proceeding on the assumption that this third unknown person murdered Winchelsea."

"But surely a third set of footprints cannot tell us who murdered whom?" Nick said. "Just that there were three people. They could easily have been left by a witness or left there days before?" Nick was astonished that Walsingham should be so sure the murderer was the third man and not the mark whom Winchelsea had been tracking. The obvious series of events, in Nick's mind, was that the man had discovered he was being followed and had deliberately led Winchelsea to a deserted place so he could kill him.

"I am certain the third man killed Winchelsea." Walsingham's eyes were shuttered. Nick could read nothing in them. But this fact alone told him there was something more at stake here than just the murder of one of Walsingham's spies.

Nick waited for Walsingham to elaborate, but he did not. Instead the spymaster picked up a quill, then thought better of it and put it down, clasping his hands on the desk so tightly his knuckles whitened. Another sign that His Nibs was profoundly disturbed. As with Cecil and his obsession with Essex, Nick wondered if the normally unflappable Walsingham was coming unraveled. Witnessing this made him feel as if he had stepped into quicksand and was sinking fast.

"It is imperative that you find this third man," Walsingham said. "Do you understand?"

Nick didn't understand a damned thing except that something had gone terribly wrong with the spymaster's grand design, whatever that might be, and he knew it was useless to ask. An actor had stepped from the shadows onto the center of the stage, one who had not been written into Walsingham's script, and had irrevocably altered the plot.

"How am I going to find this man?" It was not an unreasonable question, Nick thought.

"I will come to that," Walsingham replied testily.

Time to change the subject.

"How was the body discovered?" Nick asked.

"He was bound with a belt, and it snagged on a nail under the jetty. Otherwise we might never have found him."

The Thames was tidal, and bodies had been known to travel miles downstream toward the Wash.

If Nick had been tempted to regard the attempt on his own life as a one-off, he could now forget it. There was clearly something going on—another operation afoot—and it was serious.

He felt a brief surge of relief that his loan to Essex had nothing to do with Catholicism and his family before his anxiety returned. Was he to blame because he had lost a Spanish assassin and set him loose to kill with impunity? He had trudged all over London inquiring at inns before he had finally located del Toro in The Red Bull only a few hours before dawn. At the time, he had chided himself for not starting his search there first, considering the proximity of the inn to the road to Oxford as well as the curious aptness of the tavern's name. Did Nick have Simon Winchelsea's blood on his hands?

Despite St. Bartholomew's Eve, or perhaps because of it, Walsingham was not a squeamish man, nor had he ever balked at sacrificing one of his agents if the larger game he was playing required it. Like Machiavelli's prince, Walsingham believed the end justified the means. No individual life was more important than the holy cause he labored for, the cause of Elizabeth Regina, the great

Protestant Queen. Even his own life was expendable. In this, Nick thought Walsingham had much in common with the religious fanatics who had butchered the Huguenots in Paris, but he was equally certain Walsingham was blind to this terrible irony. Doubtless Walsingham's last thought on earth would not be for his wife or daughters nor even for his own soul poised on the brink of eternity, but for the safety of the realm he had spent his life protecting. In some ways, this made Walsingham admirable; in others, diabolical.

As if reading Nick's mind, Walsingham gave a weary smile.

"Essex's interference has played into our hands," the spymaster said. "I had intended to fire you and let it be known it was because your carelessness led to Simon Winchelsea's death."

When Nick opened his mouth to protest, Walsingham held up his hand.

"Let me finish: that was the only plausible reason for letting you go. However, now that the Queen has commanded you to work for Essex, there is no need."

Nick was glad someone was happy.

"Who was Winchelsea tracking the night he was killed?" Nick asked. "Was he a Spaniard?"

Walsingham frowned. "That does not concern you."

"I need to know if I am to catch Winchelsea's killer," Nick said, allowing his frustration to show. "The fact that he was blinded means that whoever killed him was trying to extract information." This was so obvious to Nick, he was astonished Walsingham had not mentioned it. His disquiet was growing with every word that came out of Walsingham's mouth.

And every word that did not.

"Cecil suspects Essex is behind both the attempt on your life and the death of Winchelsea," Walsingham said, as if Nick had not spoken. "And that there may be more attempts on my agents. Cecil may be right. Essex is certainly rash enough. Now I am informed by the Queen that Essex believes it is *his* agents who are being targeted." Walsingham gave a little wince, whether from pain or disgust, Nick couldn't tell. "Whatever the case, this can be turned to our advantage."

Like the Queen's use of the possessive plural, Nick took this to indicate that Walsingham still considered Nick very much on his team. He was surprised at how relieved he felt.

"Now the Queen has ordered that you be loaned out," Walsingham was saying, oblivious to the way it made Nick sound like a bull passed on to a neighboring farmer to impregnate his cows, "Essex will, no doubt, make overtures to you to come work for him permanently."

"That will never happen," Nick said. "Just to be clear."

"Yes, yes," Walsingham said wearily. "Your loyalty to me is highly commendable. But to return to the matter at hand, if I may: I know Essex well and he would not miss the opportunity of suborning one of my own men. And there is the advantage that you are a man from his own class. He is such an insufferable snob that that will count the most in your favor. Her Majesty's . . . *generous* suggestion that you aid Essex may well work to our advantage."

Generous, my arse, thought Nick savagely. *She's besotted. Her wits are gone.*

"Surely del Toro is a more likely suspect," Nick insisted. "He certainly had time to kill Winchelsea the night before he left for Oxford. I didn't locate him until after Winchelsea was killed."

Walsingham nodded. "Locating him is part of your brief. We believe he has returned to London. But you are also to look within Essex's network."

"You know that I will not be able to act independently," Nick said. "Essex will likely task Edmund to keep me under surveillance."

"Ideally, I would have used Sir Thomas Brighton for this assignment. But as he is ill, and now that the Queen has intervened, that is not now possible. Besides, your past acquaintance with Lovett will go a long way in allaying Essex's suspicions that you are a plant in his network. That and your aristocratic birth. I am not concerned about Lovett."

Easy for you to say, thought Nick. It wasn't Walsingham who had to operate with one hand tied behind his back. Aside from John and Hector, whom he trusted with his life, Nick preferred to work alone. Given the foolishly naïve way Edmund had blithely approached the assassin on the London Road, Nick knew he would be considerably hindered in his investigations by Edmund's rank inexperience. In effect, Nick would be his nursemaid.

"I want you to flush out the rat in Essex's employ," Walsingham said.

That rat would be me, thought Nick, glumly. Out loud he said, "I don't really have a choice now the Queen has taken an interest."

Walsingham didn't even bother to nod. "You are in a perfect position to find out who is murdering my agents and why. This talk of Lovett being the target is complete rubbish. Of course, ultimately the goal is to discredit the earl so that the Queen revokes her favor."

In other words, Walsingham wanted Nick to prove that Essex was complicit in the murder of Winchelsea and the attempted murder of Nick. This case reeked not only of agents double-crossing each other but also of court politics, the nastiest smell of all. And if the Spanish really were behind the killing of Winchelsea, then that threw international politics into the mix as well. Compared to this assignment, Nick's catching of the Court Killer last autumn had been child's play.

Perhaps scarpering off to the Continent, as Codpiece had jokingly suggested, was the wisest thing to do. Then Nick thought of John and Maggie, Rivkah and Eli, not to mention his own family and the perilous future they would face as recusant Catholics without him to keep the likes of Cecil off their backs, and he discarded the idea. That didn't mean he would cease to try to talk sense.

"But why would Essex employ me as an agent if he tried to have me killed?" Nick asked.

"Having you close to him will provide plenty of opportunity to try again," Walsingham said.

That was comforting, Nick thought.

Edmund had not recognized the assassin, but that did not mean the man had not been hired by Essex. There were plenty of men who would kill for a purse of gold, no questions asked. And it would have been an easy matter for Essex to find out that Nick was traveling to Oxford, although Nick had not felt he was being followed, and his instincts had never let him down before.

"He will think that the fact that his man saved your life will count in his favor, but it will not," Walsingham continued. "It will count in ours. He will assume that you now owe his man a debt. He will, therefore, be less inclined to suspect your loyalties." Then Walsingham frowned as if struck by an unwelcome thought. "The meeting between you and Lovett was by chance, was it not?"

"Yes," Nick replied firmly. He saw again Lovett's surprise at seeing him walk through the door of the tavern and his obvious pleasure. Walsingham was devious enough to entertain the possibility that Lovett had been part of the plan to kill him. "Lovett was wounded trying to protect me," Nick said. "He saved my life." And however cynical Walsingham made it sound, Nick was, in fact, in Lovett's debt.

"Essex would be mad to pass up an opportunity of trying to turn an agent like yourself who could supply so much information about my network."

"I would never . . ."

"Yes, yes," Sir Francis said. "That goes without saying. Laurence will supply you with interesting, though ultimately useless, facts that you can pass on. In short, you will be acting as a double agent."

Nick noted that Walsingham had never actually asked him if he was willing to take on the assignment. He flirted with turning him down, then just as quickly discarded the idea. He wanted to know who had tried to kill him and who had murdered Winchelsea. Besides, even if he himself was the son of an earl, there was no way he could refuse a request from His Nibs. He was far too powerful.

"By now word will have got out that you were summoned here. And after you leave, news will leak out that you are in disgrace." Walsingham rang the bell again on his desk, and instead of Phelippes, Laurence Tomson appeared.

"Laurence will brief you on what you are to pass on to Essex," Walsingham said. "And it goes without saying," he added, "it is vital that Her Majesty does not hear about our suspicions of Essex. You are to discuss this with no one outside these four walls."

"Perish the thought," Nick replied.

★ ★ ★

"So that's what's afoot," Nick said. "The usual clandestine horse-shit." He had just finished telling John what Walsingham wanted him to do, confidentiality be hanged. There was nothing Nick and John did not share. They were in a dark corner of The Saucy Salmon opposite Billingsgate Fish Market, and the stench of Thames slime—a particularly noxious variety, considering that all of London's waste was dumped into the river—was overpowering.

"I don't like it," was John's response.

Hector seconded that with a low whine. He was staring mournfully into Nick's face, his ears twitching as if he understood every word. Nick scratched him reassuringly under the chin, but he was not mollified and flopped down with a huge sigh, his chin on Nick's foot. Neither was John happy when Nick told him that Walsingham had specifically ordered him not to take John with him when he was summoned to Leicester House.

"I don't buy the fact that Essex is bumping off agents. Why would he risk a full-scale war with Walsingham?" John said.

"Because it destabilizes Walsingham's network. Essex will simply step in and save the day. He sees himself as a knight-errant riding to the rescue of the Queen."

"Bloody silly, if you ask me. My money's on del Toro. He has far more reason to want you out of the way. You were following him, for God's sake."

Nick stretched. "Oh, I'm not ruling him out, John. I am going to be keeping my eyes peeled, believe me."

"Sheer lunacy," John said, banging his fist down on the table and making the tankards jump.

Nick surveyed his friend affectionately. "No, John, it's not. It's better you stay in the background. I may need you to shadow me." When his friend started to protest, Nick laid a hand on his arm.

"Besides, I have a task for you. Walsingham said that del Toro was back in London. I want you to try to locate him."

John looked slightly mollified.

Nick tossed back the last of his ale. Even to his own ears, this sounded thin. If he was in trouble, it would be difficult to get a message to The Black Sheep. Nevertheless, he smiled reassuringly. "You and Sir Thomas Brighton can be my cavalry."

"His illness means Thomas can hardly sit on a horse right now, let alone ride one." John frowned into his ale. "Walsingham's sending you into the lion's den. Naked."

"That's so that when I get eaten, he'll know who the lion is that's chomping on my liver," Nick replied.

"It'll be a bit late by then."

"I expect Walsingham won't lose any sleep over that." Nick had meant to say this lightly, but it came out laced with bitterness. "He's desperate to pin something on Essex. If he ordered a murder— two murders, if you count me—then the Queen will be unable to ignore that. She might even send him to the Tower."

"What are you going to do now?" John asked as they made their way to the door.

"Pretend to be sulking after being given the boot," Nick said. "And wait for my summons from God Almighty."

"Don't say that."

"Relax," Nick replied. "I wasn't being metaphysical. I was referring to a summons from that prick Essex."

CHAPTER 6

Leicester House

Nick did not have long to wait. The next day Edmund Lovett showed up at The Black Sheep with an invitation from the "Great Man," as he put it.

"Who would that be?" Nick asked, noting bleakly that Edmund seemed to have lost none of his propensity for hero worship as he grew older. "The Archbishop of Canterbury? The Lord High Treasurer? God?"

Edmund looked shocked. "Why, His Lordship, the Earl of Essex, of course."

Nick had been seated on a bench, sharpening his sword. Now he carefully wiped it with oil and sheathed it. Maggie, Matty, and the baby were out shopping on London Bridge, so he had taken the opportunity to refurbish his weapons, safe from curious little fingers reaching for razor-sharp blades. It was also something he did before going on a dangerous mission to the Continent, and this assignment, though in London, felt similarly dangerous. As if he were going into battle. He continued honing his dagger with his whetting stone, aware that Edmund was still hovering near the door. John and his stepson Henry were in the cellar, getting in a shipment of beer. The thunder of the barrels being rolled into place below their feet sounded like the Last Judgment.

"Um, Nick?" Edmund said. "I may have, er . . . *exaggerated* the events on the London Road to His Lordship somewhat."

Nick glanced up. Edmund was shifting from one foot to the other like a schoolboy expecting a whipping. As well he might. But for the fact that Edmund had saved his life, Nick would have been tempted to beat him senseless, so great was his exasperation at Edmund's foolish boasting to Essex.

"*Toad!*" Bess the parrot shrieked from her stand in the corner of the tavern. She had fixed Edmund with a yellow eye and was bobbing her head up and down as if taking a bow. Edmund blinked.

"Don't take it personally," Nick said, buckling on his sword and slipping his dagger through his belt. "Bess hates everyone." He opened the door.

Edmund looked at the way Nick was dressed. "You're not going like that, are you?"

Nick looked down at his stained leather jerkin and baggy breeches. "What's wrong with this?"

Edmund colored slightly. "It's a bit . . . er . . ." He was plainly grasping at an inoffensive way of saying Nick looked like a Bankside cutthroat.

"Workaday?" Nick offered.

"Exactly," Edmund said with relief.

"My party togs are at the laundry," Nick said, snatching up his cloak and whistling for Hector.

★   ★   ★

Essex had sent his private barge, a painted, gilded monstrosity that could have accommodated a large orgy and probably had. His oarsmen sat in frigid misery while the boat rocked violently on the swell. A cold pelting rain was hammering the deck, but Nick and Edmund were at least dry, if not warm, under a gilded roof at the stern of the boat. A servant even brought mulled wine for them to sip while the barge pulled across the Thames, going upriver from Bankside to the northwestern corner where the river veered due south.

"How's your shoulder?" Nick asked.

"On the mend," Edmund replied. He rotated it. "Like new." But Nick had seen the involuntary wince he gave at the movement and felt guilty. He had kept thanking Edmund all the way to

Henley-on-Thames until Edmund had told him that enough was enough and asked that he kindly shut up. But Nick knew he had an obligation to the man and intended to repay him, even if it was only through friendship. Although this was proving harder than he had thought, considering the mess Edmund had landed him in.

Nick could see that any reference to Edmund's wound embarrassed him, so he changed the subject. "To what do I owe the honor?" he said, nodding at the straining oarsmen. "A humble wherry would have been fine." He knew, of course, that Essex was showing off, trying to impress him with how wealthy he was.

"His Lordship wanted to show the proper deference."

At least Edmund had the grace to blush at how preposterous this sounded and how self-aggrandizing. He was obviously repeating Essex's words. "And he feels remiss that he did not show a proper sympathy for your ordeal."

Nick spent the rest of the boat ride contemplating how much could go tits up with Walsingham's plan for him to snoop around Essex's network looking for a killer. What if His Nibs was wrong and the murderer did not come from Essex but from the Spanish? Given del Toro's mysterious disappearance, this seemed much more likely. Despite Nick's deep mistrust of Essex's notorious rashness, he did not believe the earl was capable of ordering the torture and murder of a fellow Englishman in cold blood.

In the meantime, Nick had been forced to switch masters from one he did not like but respected to one he neither liked nor respected. He could not help but feel that he was on a fool's errand; or worse, that he was on a suicide mission.

★ ★ ★

Leicester House was situated on Milford Lane facing the Strand where the site of the Outer Temple had been, part of the headquarters of the Knights Templar in former times. Nearby stood the Inner and Middle Temples, where London's Inns of Court were now housed. Essex didn't have to go far if he wanted to sue someone, Nick reflected sourly as the barge drew up at the house's private river steps next to Wood Wharf.

Originally built almost twenty years before for Robert Dudley, the Queen's longtime favorite and first Earl of Leicester, the house was now occupied by his stepson and heir, the Earl of Essex. Nick thought it indecent that Essex should have already taken over the sumptuous house prior to Leicester's death. In private, Essex was already calling the place Essex House, although he was barred from legally changing the name until after his stepfather was decently in the ground. Since he stood to inherit a vast fortune from Leicester, his stepfather's funeral was no doubt already inked into his calendar.

After disembarking, Edmund led Nick through a tall iron gate, which gave onto a huge garden, if miles of weed-infested gravel paths in elaborate designs bordered by dripping privet hedges could be described as a garden. Personally, Nick preferred a bit more pro-fusion and less military precision. Not to mention a bit more hor-ticultural variety. The effect under a lowering sky was depressing, downright funereal. The only relief was afforded by the occasional ghostly glimpse of a marble breast or shapely buttock peeking coyly around the hedges, but even the statues looked as if they might appreciate a few clothes on this dank, miserable day.

Nick could see the house in the distance, and as they approached, the impression of vastness grew. It was said to have forty-two bed-rooms, a picture gallery, acres of kitchens, a banqueting suite (to justify the kitchens, no doubt), and its own chapel. Not counting the stables and outhouses. By comparison, it made Binsey House, Nick's own ancestral home near Oxford, look like a sheepshearer's cottage. Yet Nick preferred his own more modest home with its hodgepodge of buildings tacked on by successive generations of Holts, causing the present-day dwelling to resemble a cluster of sep-arate houses in different styles mysteriously fused together. Undis-ciplined it might be—an architectural folly it certainly was—but it gave an altogether friendlier aspect than the one he approached now, the new brick making the house look like a stage set, all exte-rior similitude with emptiness behind.

As they neared the house, a confused baying greeted them. Hector gave a warning growl as a pack of beagles raced toward them in full bell.

"Oh, dear," Edmund said. "I was afraid of this."

"Not to worry," Nick replied.

Hector had stationed himself in front of his master, a low and continuous growl thrumming deep within his chest, lips peeled back. The lead beagle stopped ten feet away and the rest of the pack came to a halt behind him, yipping and snarling. Both sides regarded each other for some seconds; then, growing bored with the standoff and possibly irritated with the din the beagles were making, Hector gave a deep baying roar and the beagles scattered, howling, running pell-mell back toward the house with their tails between their legs.

"Well done!" a voice shouted. "Well done, indeed!"

Nick saw Essex striding to meet them. He was bareheaded and dressed in a simple shirt and doublet, seemingly oblivious to the wet and cold but somehow looking more attractive, certainly more human, than he had appeared in the Queen's suite. At twenty-one, he was in peak physical condition and moved with easy grace. It wasn't hard to see why women swooned over him.

"What a magnificent beast," Essex said with unfeigned admiration. "May I?" he asked. Then, when Nick nodded, he held his hand out for Hector to sniff.

He likes dogs, Nick thought approvingly, and was surprised at his favorable reaction.

Essex patted Hector and then turned to Nick, his eyes gleaming with pleasure. "Thank you so much for coming," he said, shaking his hand. "And such a miserable day, too. I hope the row across the river was not too wet." And with other solicitous pleasantries, he led Nick indoors, Edmund following at a respectful distance.

If Nick thought Essex would show off the house, he was mistaken. Instead, he led them to a small room on the ground floor that, judging by an untidy stack of paper piled on a desk and a roaring fire in the grate, looked very like the steward's accounting room. Which, Nick learned later, it was. And judging from the quill propped in a flask of ink on the desk, Essex had been doing his own accounts.

"Welcome to my den," he said.

Nick was puzzled. This was not the earl he had expected to meet. Instead it was as if he had met Essex's more human twin brother, and it made him feel off balance, oddly unsure of himself.

"Sit, sit," Essex said, waving to a chair in front of the fire.

On a small side table rested a tray with a silver ewer and goblets on it.

"Do you mind?" he said to Edmund, waving at the tray. He seated himself opposite Nick.

"Not at all, my Lord," Edmund murmured. He filled the goblets and passed them round, serving himself last.

"I'm afraid I was a bit of an ass to you the other day," he said. Gone was the annoying aristocratic drawl. "I apologize."

Nick covered his confusion by raising his goblet in a toast. It had the advantage of concealing his mouth, which had fallen open, so great was his astonishment at such an about-face.

"The court does something to me," Essex murmured, looking at the fire. "It's like an elaborate play with all the parts scripted: the Dread Sovereign, the Wise and Loyal Counselor (that's Burghley), the Hunchback (Cecil), the Obnoxious Fool. That's me, by the way," he added, smiling. "Don't ask me why it happens. It's very peculiar. And I always regret my behavior afterwards." He looked rueful. "But by then it's too late and I find I have made another enemy. Especially Walsingham."

It was neatly done, and but for the fact that Edmund was still standing awkwardly behind Essex's chair like a valet, Nick would have been impressed.

"I'm afraid I'm on the outs with him too," Nick said. He paused to let Essex reply, but Essex just raised his eyebrows as if mildly interested but too polite to probe.

"He seems to think I am indirectly responsible for the death of one of his agents."

"But you and Edmund were also attacked," exclaimed Essex.

Nick glanced at Edmund and saw that he had the grace to look sheepish. Nick decided to let it drop. He could hardly blame Edmund for wanting to raise himself in his master's esteem, to make himself seem more important than he obviously was. It made

Nick sad to see that, even in adulthood, Edmund had learned nothing from his days at Oxford.

Essex sipped his wine reflectively, then put the goblet down on a table as if he had reached a decision. He leaned toward Nick.

"The Queen wants you to come and work *for* me," he said. "I want you to work *with* me."

While he waited for Nick's reply, Essex casually held up his empty goblet. After Edmund had filled it, he held up the ewer, offering Nick a refill.

"No, thank you, Edmund," Nick said.

"Walsingham was furious when the Queen told him you were coming to work for me," Essex said, clearly relishing the chief spymaster's discomfort and feeling that he had put one over on him.

Nick doubted that. It appeared that the canny old spymaster had gotten exactly what he wanted. A spy—namely, Nick—embedded in Essex's network.

"But what could the old misery do?" Essex gloated. "Young men should stick together, don't you think, Nick? Edmund here has vouched for you, isn't that so, Edmund?"

Essex was animated, even boyish. His hair had dried in the warmth of the room and now curled to his shoulders, spots of color showing on his cheeks. He seemed genuinely excited. Nick was sure he was unaware of how patronizing he sounded.

Edmund nodded. "Yes, my Lord," he said. "Nick and I were friends at Oxford."

Nick thought that was overstating it a bit, but he said nothing. Instead he looked at the fire as if he were mulling over the offer.

"Surely you want to get to the bottom of who tried to kill you and Edmund?" Essex pressed. "And killed this other agent too, of course."

"I can do that on my own time," Nick said, glancing at him.

"I'm sure you can," Essex said. "You certainly caught the monster who murdered those poor girls at court last autumn. No doubt that is why Her Majesty trusts you. But don't you see, Nick," he said, his eyes flashing. "That's exactly what's perfect about you coming to work for me. I only have the Queen's best interests at heart. I don't serve her for preferment or titles." He laughed and waved his hand to indicate the house. "I already have those." His mouth twisted. "Unlike others we know."

This was a not-so-veiled reference to Walsingham. It was common knowledge at court that Essex and Walsingham were engaged in a nasty feud after the Queen had—rashly, in Nick's opinion—awarded Essex's stepfather, the Earl of Leicester, the tax on all sweet wine imported into England. A staggering sum. With Leicester in the Netherlands, Essex had taken it upon himself to openly gloat about this lavish gift, one that Walsingham had thought had been his for the asking, making public remarks about Walsingham's relatively low birth compared to that of his stepfather. This had earned him Walsingham's undying hatred. Since then, Walsingham had been lobbying hard for an equivalent sign of the Queen's favor. So far, Elizabeth had rebuffed the entreaties of her "Moor," as she called Walsingham, a reference to the black he always wore. Playing on this nickname, Essex had taken to calling Walsingham "More," a nasty jibe at Walsingham's perennial need for gold. Considering that the spymaster freely spent his own fortune in the service of the Crown, Nick thought it quite reasonable for him to be compensated by the Queen.

Essex's boast about his own wealth was true but complicated. Like most nobles, he was rumored to be deeply in debt due to his penchant for gambling and high living and was mortgaged to the hilt. It was said that his recent excesses in the Netherlands had depleted his coffers disastrously. However, his credit in London was nigh limitless thanks to the vast inheritance he would receive after Leicester's death. And the Queen's favor opened even more coffers to Essex, as it was a reliable conduit to titles, land, royal gifts, and military plunder.

Even so, Nick knew Essex was not averse to having his hand out for even more largess when it came to his monarch. He too had his eye on the sweet-wine tax once Leicester died, and it was rumored that he sometimes even borrowed money from her to pay her back when he lost at cards to her. That Essex should pay the Queen her due in her own coin was typical, Nick thought. Somehow he always managed to avoid taking responsibility for his own losses by getting others to pay.

That the Queen, usually as sharp as a steel bodkin, should allow herself to be so gulled was a mystery to the entire court. Personally, Nick thought it had less to do with the flirtations of her younger days and more to do with her childlessness. The fact that Essex's mother had married Leicester so soon after his father's death made their relationship more than a bit dodgy, if you asked Nick. Essex was a bit of an Alexander the Great who was supposed to have had a relationship with his mother that was very peculiar indeed. Perhaps Essex's unstable and confusing family life had produced an unstable and confused man. Perhaps Essex was deluded enough to think Elizabeth might make him her heir to the throne.

Nick returned his attention to what Essex had just said and was relieved that Essex's spurt of malice aimed at Walsingham was a return to the man Nick recognized, a man much given to glee over his enemies' misfortunes. What dismayed Nick was when the new Essex—the frank, relaxed, cordial Essex—returned. Nick much preferred the old one; at least he knew where he stood with that one.

"Come, man. What do you say?"

Walsingham had stressed that Nick should play hard to get, but in view of the Queen's order, he could see no sense in this. For all his cunning, Walsingham was not a very good judge of character; Essex was too impatient to wait for Nick to take his time considering his offer. He wanted an answer and he wanted it now.

"I'm honored," Nick said.

Essex jumped to his feet and, grasping Nick's hand, pumped it up and down. He looked like a boy who had received his first sword.

"Splendid!" he exclaimed. "Absolutely splendid."

Edmund also shook Nick's hand, but solemnly, as if this moment were too auspicious for levity. But Nick detected a hint of triumph in his face, as if he were taking the credit for Nick's recruitment, which, in a way, he deserved.

"Come," Essex said, virtually pulling Nick to his feet. "Let's go meet the lads. And the lass," he added with a wink.

CHAPTER 7

Leicester House

The lass in question was a tall redhead perched on a table, nonchalantly swinging her daintily shod feet. The room they had entered, Nick surmised, was the banqueting suite that had been converted into the nerve center of Essex's spy network. The long dining table was strewn with papers, the dining chairs occupied by busily scribbling clerks. Several men stood around the room in low conversation, which instantly stopped as the three men entered. Essex made a beeline for the lady and gave a low courtly bow.

"Lady O'Neill, may I introduce the Honorable Nicholas Holt."

"Call me Nick," said Nick.

"I'm Annie," the woman said, jumping down from the table and, instead of curtsying, giving Nick a firm, manly handshake. He looked into the wide-set green eyes and realized here was a woman as slender and honed as a rapier and just as dangerous. And her name proclaimed her a member of the powerful Ulster O'Neill clan, the head of which was Hugh O'Neill, Elizabeth's favorite Irish vassal. The Queen had backed him in his bid to take over the territory of the rival Lord of Tyrone clan, an offshoot of the O'Neill family, long an enemy of English rule. This bloody internecine war was still raging, drawing the interest of Spain, which—correctly, as it happened—thought they could use it to distract the English from a possible Spanish invasion. So far Walsingham had not sent Nick to

Ireland, but he thought it would only be a matter of time, especially if he became chums with an O'Neill.

Thus, Nick resolved to keep as much distance between himself and Annie as possible. He had no intention of getting embroiled in the "Irish balls-up," as it was called by fellow agents unlucky enough to have been sent to that tumultuous and soggy island. To a man, everyone Nick had talked to about it had been of the opinion that the English, like the ancient Romans, should pack up and bugger off home.

"Annie is my best spy," Essex said. Nick noted the use of the possessive pronoun and caught the brief look that passed between Annie and Essex. Immediately, Nick knew they were lovers. And from Edmund's besotted expression, he was hopelessly smitten.

Then Essex turned to the room in general: "This is Nick Holt, an old friend of Edmund's. I'll leave you to make yourselves known to him. He joins us from Walsingham's crew." There was a mutinous rumble at this.

"No, no," Essex said with mock severity, although his smile belied his words. "We're all friends here." And with that he slapped Nick on the back and strode out of the room calling for his secretary, Henry Savile.

Annie linked her arms through Nick's and Edmund's. "I'll introduce you to the boys," she said.

Despite what Essex had said about being among friends, the reaction of the room was standoffish, if not decidedly hostile. Francis Bacon was familiar to Nick, at least by sight. They shook hands.

Bacon, sandy-haired and plump, looked positively benign, although he was reputed to have the best legal mind in England and was said to be a veritable pit bull in the courts.

"How's Walsingham treating you?" Bacon asked.

Remembering his brief to act the disgruntled agent, Nick said, "Same miserable bastard."

That elicited a grin. "My brother says he is as stingy as ever." Bacon's brother, Anthony, was always grumbling about Walsingham's notorious penny-pinching. As an agent of Walsingham's stationed at the English embassy in France, he was forever moaning about how expensive it was to live in Paris and was always writing home for more money. This caused family problems, as both Bacon brothers were nephews of Baron Burghley, staunch ally of Walsingham, and cousins to Sir Robert Cecil.

Nick took Bacon's comment to be an invitation to give him the scuttlebutt on his firing. He figured that, of all the men in the room, Francis Bacon would be the most sympathetic to Nick's switching of loyalties from Walsingham to Essex, as his brother Anthony was always threatening to do. So Nick filled him in. While he was speaking, the others drifted over to listen.

"Who do you think is killing off Walsingham's agents, then?" a short, wiry man with icy blue eyes asked Nick. "Us?" He grinned evilly. The others laughed.

"This is Henry Gavell," Annie chimed in.

"Did you?" Nick asked. "Kill Winchelsea?"

The group of men laughed even louder.

All except Edmund, who said, "Of course not. We're all on the same side, after all."

"Edmund," Annie said, reaching over and patting his cheek. "You really are too sweet."

"Pah!" Gavell said, giving Edmund a withering look. "Same side, my arse!" His eyes slid back to Nick. "Maybe you're still acting for Walsingham?" he said. "Maybe you're spying on us? What do you think, Richie?"

A man who looked like a Wood Wharf stevedore nodded.

"Could be," the man said, measuring Nick with his eyes as if sizing him for a coffin.

"This is Richard Stace," Annie said.

. Whereas Henry Gavell had the whippet build of concealed strength, Stace looked like a block of granite. He was the same height as his friend but wide, his head seeming to rest squarely on his shoulders without the benefit of a neck, his biceps and chest swelling like ship's cables beneath a cambric shirt. Like Nick, he wore a leather vest; unlike Nick, his gut, which looked as solid and capacious as a brick oven, strained against his belt. Anyone foolish enough to punch it would end up with a broken hand. But Nick knew from experience that strong men were often slow, and that made them vulnerable; an elbow to the throat would probably put him down, one of several illegal wrestling moves Joseph had taught him. Nick looked forward to trying it out, but for now, his brief was to play nice, so he returned Stace's stare and did not react to the implicit challenge in the man's flat, opaque eyes. The last time Nick had been looked at like that was at the Billingsgate Fish Market when he had been buying his dinner. When he got no response, Stace looked about as impressed with Nick as the dead mackerel had been. These were the eyes of a killer, and Nick knew instantly that Stace was Essex's resident assassin. Gavell, he thought, was the brains of the pair.

"And maybe you murdered Winchelsea?" Nick replied mildly.

Stace glanced at his friend, Gavell. "Did we, Henry? I can't remember."

"Probably." Gavell stifled a yawn. "There've been so many. It's hard to keep track."

"Simon Winchelsea was tortured," Nick said. It was all he could do to keep his voice even. "His eyes were put out."

Annie put her hand to her mouth. Francis Bacon looked at the floor.

"Better watch out for yourself, Lordship," Gavell said. "You might be next."

"Is that a threat?"

Gavell shrugged. "Just friendly advice."

"For your information, someone already tried," Nick said. "And failed, thanks to Edmund here."

Edmund mumbled something about it being nothing.

"Why, Edmund," Gavell said, giving him a slap on the shoulder that made him stagger. "I didn't know you had it in you. Hey, boys," he said, "we've got a proper Achilles here."

Everyone laughed.

Nick could see that Edmund played the part of the court jester in their midst. His naïvety and comparative innocence could not compete with their hard-edged cynicism. And like all schoolboy bullies everywhere, it hadn't taken long for Henry Gavell and his mates to figure out Edmund's weakness and exploit it for their merriment.

Annie came to his rescue. "Pack it in, you lot," she said. Then, to Edmund, "Ignore them. They're only jealous."

During this exchange, Bacon had been regarding Nick with clever, assessing eyes. Besides Annie, Nick recognized him as by far the most intelligent person in Essex's household. A lawyer as well as a Member of Parliament, Bacon was known to be a philosopher and a scientist, even though he was only twenty-five. Like his older brother, Anthony, he too had worked for Walsingham as an envoy carrying official state documents between France and England. His ties to Essex were not yet formalized, but the rumor was that he was growing more and more disenchanted with Walsingham's painstaking way of conducting statecraft and craved more immediate results. He was said to be in favor of the execution of Mary, Queen of Scots, even if it meant outright war with Spain.

"Shall we sit?" Bacon said. Indicating a group of chairs placed in front of the fire. He was polite and urbane, as befitted a diplomat and barrister. The men sat down while Annie again chose to perch, this time on the arm of Nick's chair as if she had appointed herself his guardian angel.

Or bird of paradise, Nick thought, with her red hair, sea-colored eyes, and scarlet-and-blue dress. He could smell her perfume—sandalwood—and even, he fancied, hear the soft creak of her corset when she moved. So much for keeping his distance. Apparently enraptured by Hector, she was rubbing the dog behind his ears, a thing Hector adored, judging by the big silly grin and eyes half closed in ecstasy. Annie was murmuring Irish endearments in his ear, calling him "macushla," which meant, as Nick had learned from a sailor describing his doxy, *my darling*. And "a stór." *My treasure.*

"I grew up with Irish Wolfhounds," she said when she caught Nick looking. "They are the dogs of the world."

With difficulty, Nick focused his attention back on Bacon. He knew he must tread carefully; Bacon was an expert at cross-examining witnesses at trial and was known to be tricky. His calm, soft voice asking seemingly innocuous questions had led more than one perjurer to the Clink or the Tower.

And Nick felt as if he were in the dock with Bacon's calm gaze upon him.

Bacon began by asking Nick what had happened on the London Road. Edmund shifted uncomfortably when Nick came to the part where the assassin had asked specifically for him by name.

Bacon turned to Edmund. "I thought you said he attacked both of you?"

Edmund indicated his shoulder. "I was the one who was wounded," he said.

"Quite," Bacon said.

Nick could tell Bacon had already dismissed Edmund as an unreliable witness. He turned his attention back to Nick.

"And you have no idea who this man was?" Bacon asked him.

"None."

"English?"

Good question. Only Cecil and Bacon had thought to ask this. "Yes."

Nick looked thoughtfully at Stace and Gavell, who had settled into a game of dice at one end of the table with the others gathered round. The cheers and groans as well as loud advice provided a strange accompaniment to the calm reasonableness of Bacon's questioning. The clerks were ignoring the hubbub, continuing to write furiously. It was an oddly disjointed scene, with the gentrified Bacon rubbing shoulders with riffraff like Gavell and Stace.

Not for the first time, Nick was struck by how contradictory Essex appeared—the loud, obnoxious Essex given to worldly pleasure, and the calm, ordinary man he had met earlier in his study. Having witnessed the way Essex had treated Edmund, Nick had been surprised at the contented look on Essex's face when he had introduced Nick to his spy network, as if he were revealing a prized piece of machinery like a printing press. Nick wondered if low-lifes such as Gavell and Stace suspected that Essex regarded them as nothing but tools to be used to his own advantage.

"I assume, however, that Essex has sanctioned an investigation into the killer of Winchelsea and the attempted murder of yourself?"

"He has."

Bacon smiled as if he had scored a point against opposing counsel. "Then I think that answers your question. It couldn't have been one of us. Or the earl himself."

Nick nodded as if he agreed. But he was fully aware, as undoubtedly Bacon was too, that there were wheels within wheels and that in a world of double and even triple agents, nothing was ever logical or straightforward.

"When you find your man," Bacon said, getting up. "I will prosecute him to the fullest extent of the law." He looked at Nick thoughtfully. "Whoever he is."

CHAPTER 8

The Angel

"Right," Nick said. "Who wants to go to the boozer?"
Edmund looked at him askance. "It's a bit early, isn't it?
I thought you'd like a tour of the house?"

"I'm game," Annie said, leaping up. "Just give me a minute. I'll meet you at the front." She hurried from the room.

Nick looked after her. "She looks fine to me." Then, shrugging, he turned to Edmund. "What was the name of the tavern Winchelsea was last seen in?" he asked.

"The Angel."

As Nick suspected, this was the closest tavern to Leicester House and Wood Wharf, where, Nick was certain, Winchelsea's body was dumped in the river. "Let's go there."

On the way out, Edmund couldn't resist showing Nick various rooms on the ground floor. Most of them turned out to be offices with more clerks beavering away in them. Nick was impressed by how many people Essex employed. No wonder he was a thorn in Walsingham's side. His base of operations was ten times the size of the one in Seething Lane and must have been an enormous drain on his purse.

When they reached the main entrance and stepped out under the portico, Nick saw a woman leaning on one of the pillars. She was dressed in the scanty and gaudy dress of a whore, brown hair falling in rat tails on her shoulders rather than decently covered by a hood or cap, her bodice so loosely laced Nick was amazed her breasts didn't fall out.

"Wotcha, handsome," she greeted Nick in a Bankside accent so thick he could have curried his horse with it.

"Mistress," Nick said, bowing. "To what do I owe the pleasure?"

"A shilling if you want the full treatment."

Her screeching cackle made Nick's molars ache, but Hector didn't seem to mind. Surprisingly, he was wagging his tail.

Nick studied her face carefully. Now he thought about it, there was something familiar about her. Perhaps she had worked at Kat's?

Then the woman scratched Hector behind the ears and murmured to him.

"Annie?" Nick exclaimed.

"Took you long enough," Annie said in her own voice. She did a pirouette. "Like the getup?"

"You look . . . ravishing," Nick said gallantly. In truth, she looked like a proper drab—more ravaged than ravishing—but, then again, that was the point. He was filled with admiration. "You should be on the stage."

"That's what Will says," Annie replied, slinging a shawl over her head against the rain, which was still bucketing down. "But women aren't allowed. Only pretty boys." She bared her teeth at the injustice of it. Nick saw she had blackened one or two of them. It changed her expression, not to mention her age, amazingly.

"Where did you learn to shapeshift like that?" he asked in wonder. "You are a veritable chameleon."

Annie shrugged. "Came naturally. And then, in the troubles, it helped me stay alive." The light in her eyes dimmed. "My mother and sisters were butchered," she said in a low voice. "I escaped the castle by posing as a beggar at the gate. Tyrone's men didn't even notice me when they sacked the place. Raped my mother and sisters." She shot Nick a fierce look, behind which lay an ocean of pain. "There was nothing I could do."

"I'm sorry," he said, aware of how inadequate his words were. She shrugged, then gave a bright smile. Too bright. It glittered like steel.

"I'm an O'Neill," Annie said, as if the name alone was sufficient. And it was. The O'Neills were a formidable clan where even the women, it was rumored, rode to war. "What's past is past," she said. "Let's go to The Angel."

"How did you know we were going there?" Edmund asked.

She gave him a scornful look. "That was the last place Winchelsea was seen alive."

★ ★ ★

The Angel was situated opposite Leicester House but two streets over. They crossed the Strand, the smartest road in London, made especially wide to allow royal carriages with their numerous retinues to pass in style, then cut through St. Clement's churchyard and crossed Wiche Street. The inn was down a short alley on Wiche, the joke being that any woman patronizing the tavern was transformed from a witch to an angel by a few short steps. As few respectable women frequented taverns, Nick thought this witticism back to front, as it was commonly believed that a woman entering a public house changed from an angel to a witch. Nonsense, of course. His friendship with Kat had taught him that a person's occupation did not necessarily tally with their character. Many people he knew in Bankside, especially women, had been forced into a life of prostitution or crime due to crushing poverty. And he knew plenty of aristocrats who would sell their own mothers for a court appointment. In his opinion, poverty was a better excuse for wrongdoing than naked ambition.

Glancing with fascination at Annie, he saw that with every step she took she transformed herself into a Bankside trollop. No longer striding purposefully beside them, she began to swing her hips and toss her head. She laughed raucously and linked her arms through Nick's and Edmund's. A merchant's wife looked askance at her, but her husband lustfully followed Annie with his eyes until his disapproving wife brought him back to his marital duty by thrusting her overladen basket at him and dragging him down the street.

"I'm known here as Meg," Annie whispered in Nick's ear as they entered the tavern.

The place was heaving with the noonday crowd, and they had to push their way to the bar accompanied by lewd but friendly shouts to Meg and Edmund, who were clearly regulars.

"Fishing for trout in a peculiar river, are you, Nick?" This from a voice Nick recognized.

"Will," he exclaimed, slapping his friend on the back. "I thought The Black Sheep was your regular? I'm hurt."

"It is. I had to run a script by the earl," Will replied. Then he winked at Annie. "Meg!" he cried, puckering up his lips and squeezing his eyes shut. "Give us a kiss, darling."

"A pox on you, Will Shakespeare," Annie replied in her Meg voice, pushing him away with a grin.

"That's what you gave me last time," Will replied, feigning dismay. "The pox."

This was greeted by ribald whistles and mock groans from the patrons propping up the bar and watching this little scene with relish.

"Get stuffed," Annie told him with great good humor.

"That's the general idea," Will retorted. The patrons cheered.

Nick could see that both Annie and Will were enjoying their little drama. He often forgot that Will was an actor too, and he sometimes thought his friend pretended to be drunker than he was in order to better observe his fellow imbibers. Nick had long been aware that Will was a watcher. Not a spy, exactly, more a student of human nature. Perhaps that was why he burned to write plays that dealt with all the vicissitudes of human life, from comedy to tragedy, king to commoner, and everything and everyone in between.

And looking around, Nick could see that the inn was indeed filled with people from all walks of life, from courtiers and bureaucrats fagging up and down the Strand to and from Whitehall, to wherrymen who had tied up their boats at Wood Wharf, to lawyers from the Middle Temple and a host of prosperous merchants and weedy, undernourished apprentices from the more upscale shops on the Strand, to the more homely ones catering to the middle classes on Wiche Street.

"All the world's a stage," Will was wont to say. "And we are players on it."

Nick bought the first round, deliberately overpaying by a shilling. The innkeeper, a florid-faced fellow who looked as if he drank his own stock on the sly, raised his eyebrows.

"A word," Nick said.

The innkeeper jerked his head to the back of the room. "Take over, Molly," he instructed the serving wench, and slid out from behind the bar. "I need to get up another barrel."

"I'll give you a hand," Nick said, following him to a flight of dank cellar stairs, but before the innkeeper could go down them, Nick put a hand on his arm. "Did you know Simon Winchelsea?"

The man nodded, glancing over Nick's shoulder to make sure none of his patrons were within earshot. He needn't have worried. There was such a racket in the main room of the tavern that, unless someone had the ability to lip-read, it would have been impossible to understand what they were saying.

"Was he in the night he was murdered?" Nick asked.

Again the man nodded. "Earlier in the evening."

"Who with?"

The man shrugged, but Nick could see he knew and was afraid. "I give you my word no one will know the information came from you," Nick told him.

The innkeeper swallowed and glanced down the pitch-black well of the cellar steps as if he were contemplating throwing himself down. Instead, he leaned closer to Nick. "He didn't talk to them, but I saw him watching Gavell and his mate Richie."

"Watching?"

"That's what it looked like."

"Did he talk to anyone?"

"He wouldn't, would he?" the man said. "He weren't a regular. Came in from time to time if he were in the area. That's how I got to know him a bit. He told me his name, said how he hated the city. But that night I thought he just stopped in because of the rain, to shelter like. It were a shocking night."

"How long did he stay?"

The man shrugged. "I were busy serving. One moment he were there, and when I looked up again, he were gone. That were just after St. Clement's tolled seven." Situated just across the street from the tavern, St. Clement's was the chief timekeeper for the neighborhood.

An honest answer but not very helpful. Nick knew from experience that time could pass quickly when serving in a busy tavern. What seemed like a brief time could have been much longer and vice versa.

"Thank you." As Nick turned to go back into the taproom, he almost bumped into Edmund. Nick hadn't heard him approach, and as he had left Hector sitting outside the inn by the front door, he hadn't been alerted. Nick didn't know if he had overheard the names of Gavell or Stace and wasn't sure it mattered, as Edmund knew he was investigating Winchelsea's murder. Used as he was to acting independently, this constant shadowing was beginning to irk him. He didn't know if Edmund was acting on instructions from Essex or if he was simply doing what Nick had found so exasperating when they were at Oxford. But one thing he did know: he would have to put up with Edmund's presence if he was to keep Essex sweet. Not for the first time, he cursed the Queen and Walsingham for sending him on this mission.

"Were you here the night Winchelsea was killed?" Nick asked.

"I stopped by briefly," Edmund admitted. "I might have seen Winchelsea, but I wouldn't have known who he was. I bumped into Gavell and Richie on the way in. They were just leaving."

"What time was that?"

"St. Clement's had just tolled seven."

That tallied with what the innkeeper had said.

Returning to the bar, he picked up his tankard of ale and gulped it down. "Right," Nick said, wiping his mouth with his sleeve. "I'm off."

"Where are we going?" Edmund asked. Nick sighed. In the last few days he had heard far too many people use the word *we*, and he was beginning to feel like a twin in a bad play, as if he had a constant shadow at his back: Edmund, Essex, Walsingham, the unknown killer. He would have given anything to have John with him instead of Edmund.

"*I'm* going for a walk," Nick said. "*You're* going to stay here." Something in Nick's tone made Edmund step back.

Nick pushed through the crowd to the door. Annie was sitting on the lap of a man who was clearly drunk, trying to fend off his big roving paws. Despite her laughter, Nick could see the hard set of her jaw, the dangerous glitter in her eyes, and knew she was filled with disgust. He was suddenly overcome by a great weariness. Everyone was pretending to be someone they weren't: Annie, Essex, Will, Winchelsea's murderer—who, even now, could be one of the inn's patrons laughing and joking with people who had no idea he had blood on his hands. Nick himself was playing the part of a disaffected agent. He was sick of the whole business. Without caring if Edmund was following or not, Nick collected Hector and made for the river.

If Simon Winchelsea had last been seen alive at The Angel and Gavell and Stace had left the inn soon after he did, then that insalubrious duo had just risen to the top of Nick's list of suspects. It wasn't unheard of for agents and assassins to go rogue, especially if they thought they could help their paymasters without risking a veto on their actions beforehand. If all went well, they could claim credit; if it went belly-up, then they could disavow all knowledge. But Nick couldn't rule out Essex, drunk on his own ambition, ordering a hit on one of Walsingham's best agents.

CHAPTER 9

Wood Wharf

Wood Wharf was just west of the private river stairs of Leicester House. In former times, it had been a busy wharf used for unloading wood used in the construction of sumptuous houses along the Strand. Now that the area was built up, it had become obsolete and a larger wharf had been built further east where the river was deeper and larger ships could anchor safely. The wharf was still occasionally operational as an unloading dock for exotic woods brought back from the voyages of Sir Francis Drake and in high demand by the rich, but nowadays it was mainly used as a landing for wherries and all manner of river craft disembarking people with business on the Strand.

When Nick arrived, the wharf was deserted aside from a couple of disconsolate seagulls blown inland from the Wash. So miserable were they that they didn't budge even when Hector gave them an obligatory woof. A few wherries were tied up, bobbing forlornly on the choppy swell, but there was no sign of their wherrymen. Probably wisely in The Angel trying to keep dry, Nick thought. Very few craft were on the Thames in this weather. Most of the shipping was further east, riding their anchors with the hatches snugly battened down. A derelict hut completed the picture of abandonment.

Even though he knew he would likely find no signs of blood or a struggle, let alone the three sets of footprints spotted by Eli— the murder had occurred two weeks ago and it had been raining steadily ever since—Nick always found that the scene of a crime spoke to him in some way, if only by allowing him to see the last thing the victim had seen before he or she died. Then Nick remembered that Winchelsea's eyes had been put out, and he shuddered. He would not have seen anything.

Nick did not think Winchelsea's torture was primarily to extract information. The act of putting out a man's eyes told Nick that Winchelsea had recognized someone he knew. The blinding had been a sadistic reference to that, a hellish twist on the concept of the punishment fitting the crime. Much like a cruel nursemaid washing a child's mouth out with lye for swearing. It took a special kind of monster to take joy in another's pain, let alone endow it with irony.

Nick looked about him: the wharf was too far away from the great mansions of Leicester House on the east and Arundel House on the west for anyone to have seen anything through an upstairs window. Besides, at night it would have been as black as Hades. His only hope was that a wherryman or a night watchman patrolling the Strand to the north had seen or heard something untoward, although how he would be able to find a possible witness, Nick did not know.

Squatting down on the edge of the jetty, he ran his fingers over the edge. The sodden wood showed no signs of fresh splinters. The river sloshed over the edge and then was sucked back. Winchelsea must have been dead when he went into the water and had not clawed at the jetty. Nick checked for bloodstains, but the surface was so rotted and waterlogged and the time that had elapsed so long that he was not surprised to find none. He stood and looked around. Hector was pawing at the door of the shed. This was where Eli reckoned the murder had taken place.

Leaning drunkenly against a siding at the far end of the wharf, the structure was so rotted it looked as if it had been built in old King Harry's time. The door sagged on broken hinges. Nick entered. Hector immediately began pawing at the ground, whining. As his eyes adjusted, Nick saw a large brown stain. Hunkering down, he scraped up some of the hard-packed dirt and rubbed it between his fingers. A smear of what looked like rust mingled with dirt stained his fingertips. Blood. Then he put his fingers to his nose and recoiled. The smell of decay was unmistakable. Eli was right. Winchelsea had been tortured here, and judging from the size of the stain, his throat had been cut while he lay blinded and helpless on the floor.

Nick noticed a huge hole in the planks of the back wall, as if someone had kicked it in. He went out of the shed and round to the back. Close to the wall, waist-high weeds in a patch of rampant vegetation had been flattened, and in the muddy ground Nick could make out two deep grooves, as if someone had been dragged backward while their hands clawed desperately at the dirt. There was no sign of blood in the weeds, but Nick hadn't expected any. The mutilation and killing had been done in the hut.

Nick returned to the hut and began to search the floor, sifting through the debris left by vagrants looking for shelter—a broken pipe, a torn playing card—methodically scraping the floor of rat droppings and wood splinters with the blade of his knife. A stone bottle lay in the corner, its base shattered. Nick picked it up and saw dark stains and hairs along its jagged edge. Most likely, Winchelsea had been stunned by a blow to the head. That explained how he could have been tightly trussed with a belt around his chest.

Hector was digging in a spot near the corner, and when Nick went to investigate, he saw a gleam of metal embedded in the dirt. Levering it out with his knife, he saw it was a tarnished silver medal.

"Good boy," he said to Hector.

Buffing it up on his jerkin, he examined it in the poor light of the shed but could only make out a crude design on the front. The back was completely plain. It could have belonged to Winchelsea and fallen to the ground unnoticed, but Nick had the feeling it belonged to his killer. If the killer had torn it from Winchelsea's neck in order to rob him, he would have pocketed it immediately.

Suddenly Hector gave a warning growl, and Nick stuck his head outside. At the end of the lane leading from the Strand to Wood Wharf, he saw Henry Gavell and Richard Stace crowding a third figure, shoving him back and forth between them as if they were playing catch. Nick realized it was Edmund. Then Nick saw Stace hit him in the stomach and Edmund collapse to his knees. A mighty kick sent him sprawling onto his side.

Nick ran toward the men, Hector at his heels. Gavell and Stace were kicking Edmund in the ribs and legs. He was curled into a ball with his hands over his head.

"Mewling little suck-up," Gavell was saying. "Licking Essex's arse by bringing him that git Holt. Useless. Fucking. Prick." These last three words punctuated by vicious kicks.

Nick grabbed Gavell from behind, lifted him off his feet, and threw him bodily into Stace. Gavell bounced off his friend's chest and crumpled to the ground as if he had hit a stone wall. Stace blinked like an ox sighting a red flag, then lumbered toward Nick, a dagger suddenly materializing in his hand.

"Guard," Nick commanded Hector, pointing at Gavell. Immediately the dog placed himself within inches of the prone man's neck, lips peeled back, his teeth showing. Gavell, who had been in the process of getting to his feet, wisely froze.

Chancing a quick glance behind him, Nick saw he had his back to the river. Not good. Stace took another step, a mindless grin stretching his lips, his knife hand held wide, away from his body. Nick's assessment of the man at their first meeting at Leicester House had been correct. Stace relied on strength rather than agility, and it seemed to take an age for him to close the gap between himself and Nick. Just as Stace was within striking distance, Nick sidestepped his knife hand and punched him in the throat. Stace's eyes goggled, and dropping the knife in shock, he sank to his knees, gurgling. Nick finished him off with a kick in the groin. The man toppled sideways and lay there, gasping, like a beached trout.

Calmly, Nick picked up Stace's knife and stuck it though his belt. He relieved Gavell of the dagger on his belt and did the same with it. Later he would show them to Eli and see if he thought either could have been the knife used to kill Winchelsea. He didn't hold out much hope; most men carried knives with which to eat. They were as common as cloaks or boots.

Nick motioned to Hector to stand down as Edmund staggered over.

"Are you hurt?" Nick asked. It was becoming a familiar question.

Edmund shook his head, but he was holding his wounded shoulder as if the stitches had burst, and his face was deathly pale. A trickle of blood ran from the corner of his mouth.

"Nice move," Gavell said, nodding at Stace, who was still gasping, his face a nasty shade of puce. If he was concerned for his friend, there was no sign of it. He got to his feet and casually dusted off his hose.

Nick shrugged.

"Me and Richie don't like you." Gavell spat, the gobbet landing next to the toe of Nick's boot.

"I'm heartbroken."

Gavell jerked his thumb at Edmund. "And we don't like him, neither."

"So far that only tells me you don't have many friends," Nick said. "Must be lonely with only that ape for company. It also tells me that you and your sidekick are cowards. Two against one is not very sporting."

Despite the deadly insult impugning his courage—one that would have instantly provoked a duel if Nick were dealing with a gentleman—Gavell, he could see, was reevaluating the situation. If he had been alone, Nick had no doubt the men would have jumped him and beaten him to a pulp as they'd been about to do to Edmund. Perhaps even killed him. They already knew Edmund was rubbish in a fight, but Hector was another matter. His jaws were large enough to rip off an arm. It would be interesting to see if they were brave or stupid enough to take on not only Nick but also, potentially, his dog.

Gavell stuck his thumbs in his belt. "We were following him." He jerked his head at Edmund. "But seeing as you're here, we might as well give you a warning." He grinned. "A *verbal* warning."

Not stupid, then.

"Stop sticking your nose where it doesn't belong."

"Thanks for the advice," Nick said. "I'll take it to heart."

Gavell gave a sneer. "You toffs are all the same," he said. "Think your birth gives you the right to do anything you want. Treat the likes of us like dirt."

Nick moved forward a pace, but Gavell took a step back. At that moment, Nick knew it was over. He also knew he had made mortal enemies of these men and that they would try to find a way to injure or kill him. Not face-to-face in the open but on a dark night in some deserted alley when his guard was down.

★ ★ ★

"Do me a favor," Nick said to Edmund after Gavell and Stace had left. "Stop following me around."

"Sorry," Edmund said. "I thought I could help."

They walked in silence. Nick's initial impression that the Edmund he had known at Oxford had grown into a man had been wishful thinking. This bumbling ingenue Edmund was the same as the adolescent Edmund. Doglike in devotion, impossible to hate, but always underfoot.

When they reached the front of Leicester House, Nick did not stop.

"Aren't you coming in?" Edmund asked.

"I'm off to see a friend," Nick said. "And before you ask: no, you can't come."

"Oh," Edmund said, obviously crestfallen. Then he brightened. "But I'll see you later?"

"Possibly," Nick replied, suppressing a sigh.

CHAPTER 10

Rooms of Sir Thomas Brighton, Aldersgate

When he walked into Sir Thomas's rooms in Aldersgate, he was confronted by the sight of Rivkah putting on her cloak. His heart did a somersault.

"Oh, Nick," she said, smiling at him. "I was just leaving."

Although Nick knew that Rivkah looked in on Thomas when Eli couldn't get away from the hospital in Bankside, where he held a clinic every morning, he felt an unreasoning surge of jealousy. He glanced across to the bed and saw that Thomas was grinning smugly. At that moment, Nick heartily prayed his illness would keep him in bed for a month.

"Make sure you take the buttercup syrup," Rivkah said to Thomas as she moved to the door. "And, most important of all, make sure you take a small portion of cheese every four hours."

Thomas pulled a face.

Rivkah looked stern. "I'm serious. It might look revolting, but it is the best cure for a fever that I know of."

Nick saw a block of cheese blue with mold sitting on a platter on the bedside table and was about to echo Thomas's revulsion when he caught Rivkah's look and promptly schooled his expression into one of complete agreement. And, indeed, Nick knew that Thomas would do well to heed Rivkah's advice.

As skilled in the art of healing as her brother, she had been denied formal medical training at the University of Salamanca, where her brother had studied, because of her sex. She always joked that she had studied at the "University of Eli." For those who knew Rivkah well—as Nick did—the lightness of her remark could not hide the underlying bitterness. But this exclusion from a profession she loved was not her only sorrow.

Forced to flee their native Spain after a rioting mob burned the Jewish ghetto and their home to the ground, killing Eli and Rivkah's parents and siblings, they had found refuge in Bankside, so called because it was the part of Southwark that stretched along the southern bank of the Thames across the river from London proper. A criminal underworld avoided by the bailiffs and watchmen who patrolled the more respectable northern side of the river, Bankside was a perfect place in which to disappear, teeming with a constantly shifting population of riffraff, cutthroats, prostitutes, actors, sailors, and punters at the bear- and bull-baiting rings. Exiled from her homeland because of her faith, Rivkah was also an outcast from the only calling she loved. Nick couldn't begin to think of the courage it took for her to face each day without complaint or self-pity, focusing only on the needs of her patients.

Like Eli, Rivkah practiced medicine among Bankside's poorest, seldom being paid. But the denizens of Bankside's underworld had taken Eli and Rivkah to their collective bosom and saw to it in myriad ways that they did not starve. Only a few months ago, the roof of their house had been burned by sailors whipped into an anti-Semitic frenzy by rumors that the Queen's ladies-in-waiting were being killed by the Jews. The community had come together, not only to put out the fire in time to save the rest of the structure but also in the aftermath: Kat had taken in Eli and Rivkah until their house was repaired; Tom the Thatcher had put on a new roof in record time, gratis; Black Jack Sims, the most powerful crime boss in Southwark, had let it be known that anyone helping the two physicians would be looked on with favor and anyone trying to hurt them would be dead. In vain did Eli try to explain to Black Jack that Eli's Hippocratic Oath forbade him to cause harm to his patients, even indirectly. Black Jack just grinned.

"Think of death as a permanent cure for their ills," he said.

★   ★   ★

"And you must drink plenty of fluids. Preferably water," Rivkah was saying, eyeing the wineskin Nick was trying to conceal under his cloak. He had stopped by The Angel on his way over to purchase it as a gift for his friend. "I'll be back tomorrow at the same time."

"Yes, Doctor," Thomas said meekly.

Nick would have laughed out loud at the change from tough soldier to cowed patient if Thomas hadn't looked so ill. Nick handed Rivkah her basket, and she gave an almost imperceptible nod at the door, indicating she wanted a private word. He followed her to the landing outside Thomas's second-floor door.

"How is he?" Nick asked, nodding back at the room. "He looks terrible."

"Very ill," Rivkah replied. "But with plenty of rest and good food, he should recover. That's all I can tell you."

Rivkah and Eli were notoriously closemouthed about their patients. Another reason Black Jack Sims had taken a shine to them. He knew they would not blab about his ailments and therefore would not inform his enemies of his poor health.

"I heard a rumor you were attacked."

Nick silently cursed. John would not have told her. His money was on Will Shakespeare, who reveled in gossip as much as in witty word play. Most of Eli and Rivkah's patients frequented The Black Sheep, and Will was almost always to be found there propping up the bar.

"A spot of bother on the London Road," Nick said.

Rivkah raised her eyebrows. "You call an assassination attempt a 'spot of bother'? Either you are trying to impress me with your bravery or you think my sex too feeble to be told the truth? In both instances, you are gravely mistaken."

"Sorry," he said, hoping he sounded as meek as Thomas had done a few moments before. He told her what had happened, careful to leave out all mention of her countryman del Toro.

Guiltily, he allowed her to believe he had been in Oxford to visit family.

"But why would anyone want to kill you?" she said. "Besides me, of course."

"Probably a robbery," Nick said, hating himself for deceiving her. "Lucky that Edmund was with me."

Rivkah held his gaze as if waiting for him to say more. When he didn't, she nodded curtly, gave Hector a kiss on the nose, and was gone, clomping rapidly down the stairs in her stout boots—Rivkah was much too level-headed to wear fashionable shoes with high cork soles in wet weather yet another thing he admired her for. Nick crossed to the window on the landing and looked down. Rivkah had covered her head with a deep hood and was walking purposefully along the street, a small anonymous figure but one he would know anywhere, even in pitch-blackness. At the corner, she turned south toward the river and was lost to view. Nick had the sinking feeling that he had somehow hurt her deeply.

When he returned to the room, Thomas was sitting up in bed. Dressed in a nightshirt, his face looked pale, with dark hollows under his cheekbones. "Thanks for the wine," he croaked. "You're a pal."

Thomas really did look at death's door, Nick decided.

"Sorry, old chap," he said, deliberately lightening his tone so as to disguise his concern. "Your doctor gave specific instructions that you were to drink only water." He reached for a beaker, unstopped the wineskin, and squirted in a generous amount. "But don't worry," Nick said, grinning. "I'll keep you company. Cheers."

"You bastard."

In the end, Nick relented and poured a small amount of wine in the bottom of Thomas's beaker, topping it up with water.

"Tastes like vinegar," Thomas grumbled.

"Just promise you won't tell Rivkah."

"Are you insane?"

Nick surveyed the man who was rapidly becoming his friend despite their underlying rivalry. Sent to the Tower by the Queen a few months before, Sir Thomas had eventually been revealed as a fellow agent working for Cecil. Refusing to clear himself in order to protect the secrecy of his mission, Sir Thomas had impressed Nick by his courage. The only thing Nick had against him was Sir Thomas's obvious attraction to Rivkah. Now Nick was concerned that his friend, like him, was a target for whoever was trying to clear the board of Walsingham's spy network.

"So you think someone is going to come after me?" Thomas asked when Nick had finished telling him what was going on.

"You're a sitting duck here," Nick said. He watched as his friend was overcome by a fit of coughing. At last, Thomas lay back on the pillows exhausted and gave Nick a weak smile.

"More like a crow."

"I'm serious, Thomas. Why don't you go home?"

Thomas was married to the former Lady Wakefield, a distant cousin of the Queen's, and owned a fine house and land on the southern coast somewhere. The trouble was, he and his wife didn't get on and lived their lives more or less apart.

"If I did that, I'd be pushing up daisies in no time," Thomas said. "She's probably down on her knees right now beseeching God to make her a widow." He gave Nick a weak grin. "I'm touched by your concern, but I'll be all right." He drew a dagger from beneath his pillow. "I'm not entirely without resources."

Nick let it drop. Thomas was a proud man, and it would do no good to mollycoddle him. He hoped it was true that Thomas was recovering. The influenza was deadly, and far more people were carried off by it than recovered from it. And the season for it had only just begun. It was an odd phenomenon, but Nick had often noticed that when the weather was at its coldest in late December and January, sicknesses of all kinds seemed to take a holiday. It was only when the season began to turn from winter to spring in late February, when snow and ice turned to rain, that people began to sicken. Eli and Rivkah speculated it had something to do with water in the air. They had long suspected that contagions thrived on fluids, especially in the way they were spread from one person to another through coughing and sneezing. But when Nick had asked them why the plague was more virulent in the drier, warmer months of summer, they owned that they did not know.

"The plague must be spread by some other means we do not yet know of," Eli said, frowning. "But I have often noticed that those who live in clean homes and who keep a cat to keep away the rats are less likely to contract the disease."

★ ★ ★

"Maybe del Toro was sent to Oxford to lure you out. He gives you the slip and hires a thug to kill you," Thomas said.

"Perhaps." But Nick was certain del Toro had been operating alone. When would he have had the time to organize an assassination? Unless there had been another agent already in place, the man Edmund had killed.

Nick had first picked up del Toro's trail at an inn called The Red Bull on the northern edge of the city. Given that *toro* was Spanish for bull, Nick had wondered if del Toro had a sick sense of humor. That certainly tallied with the cruel way in which Winchelsea had been tortured. Or maybe the name of the inn was merely coincidence, seeing as it lay closest to the main road to Oxford. Either way, it seemed like a foolish risk to take for a secret agent. Even as del Toro was setting off for Oxford with Nick shadowing him, Simon Winchelsea's body was being pulled out of the Thames at Wood Wharf. It would have been entirely feasible for del Toro to murder Winchelsea the night before; it was not a huge distance from The Red Bull to the wharf, certainly walking distance for a fit man.

But why would the Spanish send an assassin to pick off English agents on their home turf? Considering the fragile relationship between the two countries since England had sent forces to aid the Spanish Netherlands in their rebellion against Philip II, their hated overlord, it was the equivalent of striking a tinderbox in a room full of gunpowder.

And now Nick had to include Henry Gavell and Richard Stace as suspects. He told Thomas what had happened at Wood Wharf.

"They're certainly vicious enough to torture a man to death," Nick said. "But what I don't understand is motive. Could Winchelsea have discovered something about them that night in The Angel? Seen them talking to someone?"

Thomas shrugged. "Del Toro's a much more likely suspect than those two, I would have thought. Gavell and Stace are Essex's creatures and don't take a shit without his permission. Essex has too much to lose at court if it came out he was eliminating the competition. If you ask me, Walsingham's illness is making him senile. And Cecil has always hated Essex and would like nothing better than to bring him down. I still like del Toro for it. What do you know of him?" A little color had come back into his cheeks, as if talk of their common profession had put new life into him.

"He's a bit of a mystery. Just recently joined the staff of the Spanish ambassador in Paris," Nick said. "He could very well be a trained assassin. We need to find him."

Nick frowned. Although that did not explain how the attempt on Nick's life had been bungled. Trained assassins did not contract out killings but operated alone.

"And you say he didn't make contact with anyone?"

"Not unless you count the whore," Nick replied.

Thomas gave a lewd grin, then fell into another bout of coughing. Nick waited until he had recovered, then got to his feet. "I'll check in with you in a couple of days. Anything you need?"

"More wine would be nice."

"I'll see what I can do," Nick said. "Don't forget to eat your cheese." He grinned. "It looks delicious."

"Most disgusting thing I've ever heard of," Thomas said, eyeing it askance. "Rivkah says there's something in the mold that brings down a fever. Sounds like a load of cobblers to me."

"She's usually right."

"Don't I know it." Thomas stretched luxuriously in the bed and grinned. "She is the most amazing woman I have ever met."

"You're married," Nick said.

"Your point?"

★ ★ ★

Once back on the street, Nick wondered what he should do next. Mercifully, the rain had stopped, so he decided to return to Leicester House.

Instead of entering by the main gate on the Strand, Nick went through a small archway that opened into a side court on the eastern side of the house and followed a path into the gardens at the back. If he was to be acting as a double agent for Walsingham inside Essex's spy network, then he needed to know every mode of exit in case he needed to leave in a hurry. This type of reconnaissance had saved his life on numerous occasions in the past. Few of his friends and family noticed that Nick always positioned himself in a room with a clear sightline to all the entrances and exits; few noticed that he always had a dagger or sword within easy reach, or that, however relaxed he appeared, his body was always tensed for action. In addition, such was the bond between Nick and his dog that the merest twitch of Hector's fur, the slightest growl from deep within his throat, served as an infallible warning of danger.

As Nick rounded the corner of the house, he heard voices coming from a ground-floor room. Judging from its location, Nick guessed it was Essex's study. Signaling Hector to keep quiet, he flattened himself against the wall beside the window and listened in.

"It's good to have you back, Annie."

Nick chanced a peek through the window and saw Essex with his arms around Annie, his face buried in her hair.

"I've missed you. Where did you go? You've been gone for two weeks."

Annie stepped back from the embrace, and Nick ducked out of sight.

"I had to go back to Ireland," she said. "Family business."

"You didn't tell me that." Essex's voice was peevish. "You just disappeared."

"I didn't think I needed your permission." Annie's voice was haughty, and it reminded Nick, and should have reminded Essex, that she was no low-born mistress but a proud scion of an ancient Irish family.

"I worry about you," Essex said, his voice more conciliatory. "One day someone is going to see through those disguises of yours."

Nick heard Annie laugh, a high, derisive sound. "I doubt it."
Then, her voice softer, "No need, my love. I'm well able to take
care of myself."

"I hope so."

Nick heard Essex pacing.

"What do you think of Holt?"

"I think he's very clever," Annie said. "I think he needs
watching."

"That's your job, then. I can't rely on Edmund. Although he
did do us a favor by saving Holt's life. I confess I didn't think he
had it in him. I was trying to come up with a way to get close to
Walsingham's network, and Edmund delivered Holt for us. Walsingham's planning some kind of coup, I feel it in my bones, and I'll
be damned if I'm going to let him make me look like an amateur if
he pulls it off. I intend to use Holt to find out."

"He won't give up anything," Annie said. "He plays his cards
too close to his chest."

"Use your charm, Annie. God knows it worked with me."

Nick chanced another look through the window and saw Annie
put her arms around Essex's neck. Then she kissed him. Essex gave
a deep groan, pushed her against a wall, and started fumbling with
her skirts. Over his shoulder, Annie looked straight at Nick through
the window and winked.

Startled, Nick ducked out of sight. She had been aware of his
presence all along. He felt like a fool.

The most valuable thing he had learned was that Annie had
been away from London for two weeks, exactly corresponding to
the time Nick himself had been following del Toro to Oxford and
back. Essex's comment about Annie's disguises made him wonder
if the whore he had seen in The Spotted Cow had in fact been
Annie. If this was so, who was she working for, seeing as Essex had
not known where she was? Was she a double agent for the Spanish?

Nick suspected that Annie would do anything to reinstate the
former glory of her family, and if the Queen was dragging her feet
in providing money and support, then perhaps the Spanish were
a better bet. Catholic Ireland had long been an ally of Spain, one

of the reasons the English wanted to get a foothold there to prevent Spain from launching an invasion from both east and west.
Was Annie capable of changing political allegiances as easily as she
assumed disguises? One moment a whore, the next a fine lady and
the lover of an earl? No one, Nick suspected, least of all Essex, knew
who the real Annie was. That made her supremely dangerous.

★   ★   ★

Bankside

"Stuff what Walsingham said about you working alone," John said.
"From now on, I'm going to stick to you like glue."

Nick had just finished telling John about the conversation he
had overheard at Leicester House and how Essex was using him
to find out what Walsingham was up to, not just who had killed
Winchelsea. He also told him of his suspicions about Annie.

As the son of the old Earl of Blackwell's steward, John was not
only loyal to Nick as a friend but fanatically loyal to the entire Holt
family. Nick knew it was useless to beg John to reconsider, and
when he thought about it, he concluded that he did indeed need a
guardian angel at his back if he was going to negotiate the treacherous waters he now found himself in.

More and more, Nick was beginning to feel as if he were being
used as a pawn in a very complicated game. He could not put his
finger on who was the prime mover, whether Walsingham or Essex
or Annie, but he was convinced that one of them was orchestrat-
ing these events. Walsingham had stonewalled him when Nick had
asked who Winchelsea had been following that night to Wood
Wharf. He knew he had to find this out another way. Another
reason he needed John.

As for the assassination attempt on him, Nick was becoming
more and more convinced it had something to do with his surveillance of del Toro. But whether it was the missing Spaniard who
had arranged the ambush on the London Road or someone else
and for some other reason, Nick did not know. Perhaps if Nick used

himself as bait while John watched from the shadows, they would be able to lure the assassin into the open. If Walsingham and Essex could play a double game, then so could Nick.

They were walking along the bank of the Thames at dusk in order to keep their conversation from the ears of Maggie and any patrons of The Black Sheep who were beginning to straggle in after work. Maggie had looked at them oddly as they left, obviously thinking it was a strange time to go for a stroll in one of the most dangerous places in London. Nick knew she would pump John for information when they returned but also knew his friend would lie through his teeth, even to his beloved wife, to protect Nick's cover as a secret agent.

"It'll be like old times," John said, punching Nick on the shoulder. He was referring to their Oxford days. "Except that we'll have to let Edmund tag along this time." John pulled a face. He had never liked Edmund.

"He's all right," Nick said. "He did save my life."

"Then you saved him from being beaten up. So, you're even. Let the little milksop look after himself from now on."

"I don't want anyone to know you are helping me," Nick said. "Not even Edmund."

"Do you suspect him?"

"No. But I don't trust his judgment. He'll blab anything we find out to Essex in order to curry favor. You have to be completely invisible."

"Got it," John said.

"You'll have to watch out for Annie. She's very hard to spot when she wants to be." Nick had told John of how she could change her appearance like Proteus.

They had been following the riverbank west, water on their right, a straggle of shops and tenements on their left that began to peter out as they neared Paris Garden, an enormous swath of open land where the river curved south. Across the black expanse of the river, they could make out the occasional flicker of lights in the windows of individual houses, like fireflies in the darkness. But it was the great palaces of Whitehall, the Savoy, and Somerset and

Leicester Houses that were lit up like signal beacons as the river turned south in a wide curve. Only the very wealthy could afford to transform night into day by burning a fortune in candles and pitch; the rest of London went to bed with the sun and rose with it, seeking relief from the dank April nights in their beds. If Nick was honest, that's exactly what he would have liked to do. He longed to hibernate like a bear and only come out when Winchelsea's killer had been caught and Essex had buggered off back to the Netherlands where he would become Leicester's problem and not Nick's.

He and John stood for a moment on the bank looking across the river. Nick remembered how he had felt at the beginning of his murder investigation in the autumn when it seemed as if he were looking into a black void with only occasional lights showing in the darkness. Now he experienced the same feeling of helplessness—as if, like Winchelsea, he had been blinded.

With a sigh, Nick turned back toward The Black Sheep, John and Hector keeping pace beside him.

"At least you don't have to go to Oxford," Nick said. He had told John that del Toro had been spotted in London. "Start with The Red Bull. You never know. He may be stupid enough to return there."

CHAPTER 11

Bankside

Early next morning, Nick and John dropped by the house of Eli and Rivkah. Brother and sister were sitting in their tiny kitchen having breakfast. Eli made room for them at the table, and Rivkah cut more bread and pushed a pot of honey towards them. Eli sloshed small beer into their cups.

"Thanks," Nick said.

John saluted them with his beaker, his mouth already full.

"To what do we owe the honor?" Eli said.

Looking at brother and sister sitting opposite him at the table, Nick was amazed anew at how identical in feature they were. Both had black hair, brown eyes, small, straight noses and wide mouths. Both had the same sardonic and slightly wary gleam in their eyes; both would do anything for a patient.

Eli wore his hair to his shoulders, tied back with a leather thong. Rivkah's hair was pulled back into a thick braid that she had wound at the back of her neck. Mercifully she was not a slave to the court fashion that called for frizzy topknots and kiss curls, making the court ladies appear as if they each had a poodle on their head. As it was the Queen who had set the prevailing fashion with her wigs, Nick had kept his aesthetic opinion to himself. Nick happened to know that Rivkah's hair was so long she could sit on it; he had first seen her in her nightdress with her hair loose. Every time he'd seen her since, he'd longed to stroke the gleaming smoothness, fancying it would feel like silk.

Nick saw Eli's medical satchel sitting by the door. He knew Eli started each day by holding a morning infirmary at St. Mary Ovarie in Bankside for the poor of the parish. The parish priest, Father Anselm, had set aside the church crypt for the hospital, where the sickest of Eli and Rivkah's patients could stay until they either recovered or died. But the siblings also ministered to walk-ins: laborers with broken bones or sprains; children with measles, chicken pox, or the croup; infections from cuts that could develop into gangrene or lockjaw in less than a day; many cases of the flux due to bad water and spoiled food. And when the summer came with the pestilence, the infirmary would be crowded, the graveyard of St. Mary Ovarie even more so.

Anyone with an ailment, whether Bankside resident or traveler coming into London on the Southwark Road, was welcome. Eli would even dispense herbal remedies to those inebriates who had woken in the rushes of the bull-baiting ring or the downstairs parlor of Kat's brothel with a pounding hangover. As their house was situated between the Bear Garden, the bear-and bull-baiting ring, and London Bridge, it was not unheard of for people to knock on their door to pick up some palliative before staggering back across the bridge to face their employer or an irate wife.

Neither Eli nor Rivkah discriminated among their patients, something Nick had always found remarkable, considering that they were Jews and had been burned out of their home in Salamanca and forced into exile. In Nick's opinion, his two friends showed more Christian charity than most Christians he knew. If their patients could not pay them, then they either went without or accepted payment in kind. The house they lived in was owned by Black Jack Sims, the local crime lord, and Nick happened to know that he demanded no rent from them in return for an endless supply of gout medicine that Rivkah prepared in her kitchen.

Rivkah's basket sat beside Eli's satchel. Usually she went first to Kat's brothel to check on the girls who worked there—she was also Kat's personal physician—before joining her brother at the infirmary. This morning, Nick knew, she would be going across the river to see how Thomas was progressing. Nick was hoping they could share a wherry. Anything for a little more time in her company, even if John's amused gaze would be on him the whole time.

John also knew Nick was terrified of Rivkah finding out he was a spy who spent most of his time spying on her countrymen. If she ever found out, Nick was convinced she would believe their friendship was nothing more than a way of extracting information about their homeland. He couldn't bear the thought that she would believe he had been using her and her brother, that he was just another Christian who had betrayed her as she and Eli had been betrayed before.

When they finished eating and Eli had cleared the table, Nick took out the two knives he had taken from Gavell and Stace the day before at Wood Wharf.

"Could these have been used to cut Winchelsea's throat?" he asked Eli, who had examined the corpse.

John looked askance at Nick and tipped his head at Rivkah. He was more traditional than Nick and thought women should be protected from the harsh realities of life, especially violent murder.

Rivkah caught the look and, picking up one of the blades, went to stand behind John. She held the knife to his throat and John went very still. Nick grinned.

"Could this have done the job, do you think, Eli?" she said.

"Point taken," John croaked. "Literally." He fingered the spot where Rivkah had laid the tip of the knife.

Eli tested the sharpness of the knives by paring some cloth. "They could," he said. "The trouble is that they are of standard design with ordinary wood handles. Aside from the wealthy, almost every man carries a knife like this."

"That's what I thought," Nick said.

Rivkah was examining one of the knives closely. "There's some blood in the join between the haft and the blade and on the handle itself, but it could be anything: rabbit, mutton, human. Impossible to tell."

Unless the handles were made of an impermeable material like metal or horn, the untreated wood tended to stain quickly. Most people carried cheap knives with which to eat, and wooden handles absorbed blood, grease, ale, and wine until they were stained almost black. Gavell's and Stace's daggers were no different.

Next Nick placed the silver medallion on the table. "What do you make of this? Some kind of coin or charm?"

Rivkah picked it up and turned it in her fingers, rubbing at the discoloration. Then, going to a shelf in the corner of the kitchen, she picked up a pot and a rag. She sat down again. "Chalk," she informed them. She proceeded to clean the silver with the rag she had dipped first in water and then in the chalk. Soon the medal was as gleaming as the day it was first made.

"Look here," Rivkah said, handing it to Nick. "It's a tree of some kind with writing around it."

Nick squinted at it, then took it over to the window at the back of the kitchen to get better light. "It's an evergreen tree," he said. He looked closer, turning the tiny disk around in his hands. "*Ego permanere.*"

"I will remain steadfast," Eli translated.

"How old do you think it is?" Nick said, handing it to John.

As the son of the steward at Binsey House, John's father had begun to train his eldest son to take over his duties before he realized that John was not cut out for looking after a stately home. John's younger brother had shown much more aptitude for facts and figures and was now steward. But John had absorbed more of his father's teaching than he cared to let on. Silver was one of the things he knew something about, as Nick well knew.

"I would say it was pretty old," John said. "See how scratched it is, and the beveling around the edges is worn down." He turned it over to look for a hallmark, but there wasn't one. Not legal tender, at any rate. A medal of some kind.

"Perhaps a shilling melted down and then stamped with a design. It's a cheap way to make a medallion."

"Isn't that illegal?" Rivkah asked. "To melt down currency?"

John nodded. "But it happens all the time. A local blacksmith could do it and no one would be the wiser." He laid the medal down on the table.

Eli picked it up and studied it. "A family coat of arms, do you think?"

"No escutcheon," Nick said. Then, seeing the incomprehension on Rivkah and Eli's faces, "No shield. It's not a martial symbol. The evergreen means fidelity. The killer must have lost it when he was dragging Winchelsea into the shed. He would not have realized he lost it until after the fact."

"That's the only opportunity for Winchelsea to have fought back," Eli agreed. "After that he was trussed by a belt. He was still bound when I examined him on the dock."

Nick told the others where he had found it—well, where Hector had found it, to be strictly truthful.

"Where is he, by the way?" Rivkah asked. Hector was a great favorite of hers.

"Back at The Black Sheep, sulking," Nick said. "I had to leave him as a substitute for John." He paused a beat. "A more intelligent substitute, or at least that's what Maggie said."

CHAPTER 12

The trip across the river was quick but wet. Nick's opportunity to feast his eyes on Rivkah during the crossing was thwarted by the fact that she was huddled deep inside the voluminous folds of her cloak's hood with only her nose peeking out.

"Bloody awful weather for April," the wherryman said cheerfully as he pulled with easy grace at his oars. Young and with the massive shoulders and arms of a man born to a life on the river, he seemed oblivious to the rain drizzling down. Nick grunted a response and thought longingly of the cover on Essex's barge.

"Do you put in at Wood Wharf often?" Nick asked when they landed and he was handing Rivkah out of the wherry onto the dock.

"Not much call nowadays," the wherryman said. "Now, in my grandfather's day it were another matter. Lots of business doings hereabouts, merchants and such. The toffs at the big houses on the Strand mostly use Temple Stairs. And their own stairs, of course."

All the great houses had their own private landing docks with stairs going right down to the river—York, Leicester, Somerset, and Savoy Palace. Wood Wharf, with its splintering dock, warped stairs, and derelict watchman's shed, was a decaying remnant of a bygone era.

"What about a fortnight ago, late?" Nick didn't have much hope, but it was worth a try. Most wherrymen would not row across the breadth of the river at night, but some would be willing to row along the northern bank, especially where the great river curved to the south because the great houses between the Middle Temple and Whitehall were often lit up with entertainments and there were fares to be made. It was safer to hire a wherry, even in the dark, than to risk the pitch-black London streets at night. Only the aristocracy who could afford to hire an armed guard to discourage the cutpurses and bully-boys who lurked in dark alleys would dare to cross the city at night.

"Funny you should mention that," the wherryman said. "Me and the lads were just talking about it the other night in The Water Beetle. Sam said there were a lantern on the wharf and he thought it were a fare wanting to be picked up, so he made for it. He were down at Whitefriars. Not a hard pull with the tide coming in. Then, as he got nearer, he shipped his oars and glided in silent. Heard two men on the dock arguing. One had a funny accent. Foreign-like."

"Dutch? Spanish?"

The man shrugged. "Dunno, just foreign. The other gent spoke normal. You know, proper English."

Nick saw Rivkah hide a smile at the man's unselfconscious bigotry.

"You say *gent*," Nick said. "You mean he was a gentleman?"

The wherryman shrugged. "Sam didn't say."

Nick had the feeling this was the most valuable information the man could provide. The foreigner was probably del Toro; the Englishman, a traitor, if he were meeting a Spaniard in a deserted place at night. Either of them could have killed Winchelsea.

"Is there any way the second person Sam heard was a woman?" Nick asked. He was thinking of Annie.

The wherryman frowned. "He said the voice was soft, if that's what you mean. Could have been a young gent, I suppose.

"Anyway," he went on. "Sam were about to shout out his rates when one of them left. The other took the lantern and went off over there." He pointed to the shed.

"What time would this have been?" Nick asked.

"Bells had just spoke twelve, Sam said."

That was accurate enough. The noise from all the churches tolling the hours was cacophonous, even at night. A born Londoner could count the hours without stirring in his sleep, so used was he to the din. If all the bells were suddenly to go silent, the townsfolk would wake in a panic.

"Did Sam tie up at the wharf?" If so, then he could be a witness to Winchelsea's murder. But the wherryman shook his head.

"Nah. He decided to call it a night. Shoved off and rowed home."

Nick hid his disappointment.

"Good day to you," the man said, tugging his cap.

Nick paid him above the going rate in gratitude for his information, although he did not think it would lead to anything.

"Is that where the agent was murdered?" Rivkah asked, pointing to the shed. "And his body found in the water along this dock?"

Nick nodded. He took her arm and tried to hurry her on, away from this place of violence and betrayal, but she shook him off. She stood looking at the abandoned wharf and shed. A lone white swan resolved itself eerily out of the tendrils of river mist and silently glided up to the dock. It seemed completely unafraid of them. As swans were normally seen in pairs because they mated for life, it was unusual to see one alone.

Rivkah crouched down and, taking a piece of bread out of her basket, offered it to the swan. It took it from her fingers delicately. Nick shivered. For a moment, he fancied the swan was the spirit of Winchelsea haunting the place of his murder.

"A lonely place to die," Rivkah said.

It was as if she had uttered Winchelsea's epitaph, and it made Nick feel ashamed that he had been too concerned with his irritation at Essex and Walsingham's spy games to have given much thought to the man who had died so terribly and, as Rivkah had reminded him, so alone. As they walked up to the Strand and made their way through the streets to Thomas Brighton's lodgings in Cheapside, Nick vowed that he would bring Winchelsea's killer to justice.

★ ★ ★

Rooms of Sir Thomas Brighton, Aldersgate

Nick, John, and Rivkah climbed the stairs to Thomas's room. The door was ajar.

"Thomas, you old malingerer," Nick called, knocking lightly on the door. "Up for visitors?"

They entered when there was no reply. Thomas was lying across the middle of the bed on his back, his arms flung out, as if he had been sitting on the side of the bed and had toppled back. He was gasping for air, his limbs shaking. A wineskin lay on the floor at his feet, its sticky contents already drying in a brownish stain on the wood boards. Rivkah rushed over to him and put her fingers against the side of his neck.

"His pulse is racing," she said.

Nick bent to pick up the wineskin.

"Don't touch that," Rivkah said. "Thomas has been poisoned."

Now Nick could see flecks of some darkish substance at the corner of Thomas's mouth, his face pouring sweat as if from a high fever, his hands plucking convulsively at the coverlet.

"He must be moved to the infirmary at St. Mary Ovarie," Rivkah said. "But a ride in an uncovered wherry in this weather will kill him."

"John," Nick said, turning to his friend, who was staring aghast at the twitching figure on the bed. "Run to Leicester House. Beg Essex for the loan of his barge. Have it pull up at Blackfriars Stairs, closest to Aldersgate as the crow flies, and wait for us there. Make sure you tell him there's been another attempt on an agent's life. Then return here with Edmund so we can move Thomas to the barge."

"Christ's Hospital is nearest," John said.

Nick shook his head. "Not safe. Whoever did this can find Thomas there and finish the job. We need to get him over the river to Bankside. Besides, it's closer to Rivkah and Eli."

John nodded and left the room.

Nick regretted involving Essex, especially as he did not know who was trying to kill off Walsingham's agents, but felt he had no choice. They had to get Thomas to the infirmary as quickly as possible.

"What can I do?" Nick asked. He had absolute faith in Rivkah's skill; if anyone could save his friend, it was she.

"Help me prop him up on the pillows. He cannot breathe on his back."

Nick lifted Thomas and laid him lengthwise on the bed. Then he stacked pillows behind him so that he was almost sitting up. Immediately, Thomas's breathing became less labored.

"I need water and salt," Rivkah said. "A lot of both." She lifted each of Thomas's eyelids and saw that the pupils of both eyes were unnaturally enlarged, giving him a staring look. "Hurry, Nick."

Nick ran down the stairs and out into the street. Three doors down he found a tavern and burst through the door.

"I need a bucket of water and as much salt as you have," Nick demanded of the tavern-keeper. He placed a silver crown on the bar. "As quick as you can. It's a matter of life and death." Briefly he explained what he needed it for, and the tavernkeeper ordered his boy to draw two buckets from the well and to help carry them to Thomas's lodgings. His wife silently handed Nick a large cake of salt wrapped in burlap.

Back at Thomas's rooms, Nick watched Rivkah shave the salt into a goblet of water and stir vigorously. Then she picked up a bowl of fruit from a table, dumped out the contents onto the floor, and placed it on Thomas's lap.

"Tip his head back and pinch his nose," she instructed.

Seated on one side of the unconscious man, Nick held him up and cradled his neck in the crook of his arm so that his head lolled back, although his body was upright. Then he pinched Thomas's nose while Rivkah poured as much of the salt water down his throat as she could. Thomas gagged and thrashed, trying to resist. It was the first sign of awareness of what was happening to him that Nick had seen. He looked for reassurance to Rivkah that this was an improvement, but her eyes were fixed on her patient, a small frown on her face, watching for any sign that Thomas was not too far gone for his body to reject the poison he had unwittingly imbibed.

Suddenly Thomas arched back, then threw himself forward and violently vomited the contents of his stomach into the bowl Rivkah was holding. His convulsions seemed to go on and on, but at last he went limp and they laid him back on the pillows. Rivkah climbed off the bed with the bowl and examined the contents, swirling the bowl and sniffing it.

"Belladonna," she said. "He was lucky he only ingested a small amount and we found him so soon. Otherwise he would be dead."

Nick thought guiltily of the wine he himself had brought Thomas on his last visit and had encouraged him to drink, despite Rivkah forbidding it. Belladonna, or deadly nightshade, was one of the most common poisons; it grew wild as a weed, and almost anyone could gather it and use the berries or roots. In small doses, it was used as a remedy for palpitations of the heart. In large doses, it sent the heart into fatal arrest. Its name—*belladonna*, or *beautiful lady*—derived from the fact that women used it to enlarge the pupils of their eyes so that their eyes looked bigger.

Rivkah cleaned out the goblet of salt water and refilled it with fresh water from the bucket. Then she held it to Thomas's lips.

"Drink," she ordered.

Thomas's eyes flickered open briefly. "Yes, Doctor," he managed to croak. She hushed him and dribbled some water into his mouth. Exhausted with the effort, Thomas's eyes closed again, and he seemed to slip away into a deep slumber.

"Will he recover?" Nick asked, mopping his friend's brow with a rag he had dipped in the clean water from the bucket.

"Time will tell. He's already weak from the influenza, but he is a strong man and has recovered well from wounds before." Rivkah was referring to the sword and musket scars on Thomas's torso. "But we must get him to Eli."

At that moment, there was a clattering on the stairs, and John, Edmund, and Essex burst into the room.

"How is he?" Essex asked Nick. Then he caught sight of Rivkah.

"I am Sir Thomas's physician," she said to his unspoken question. "We need to move him to your barge with all speed."

If Essex was surprised at Rivkah's gender or her quiet authority, he didn't show it.

"My carriage is waiting downstairs. I thought it easier than carrying him through the streets to the barge."

"Thank you," Nick said. And meant it. In his state, Thomas might not survive being carried in the rain across town to the river. Even with foot traffic impeding the carriage's progress through the streets, at least he would be dry and warm.

Together the men wrapped Thomas in a coverlet and carried him down the stairs. He was still unconscious, but his eyelids flickered occasionally as if he were at least in part aware of movement.

"Will he die?" Edmund asked.

Nick glanced at Edmund's face and saw it was as pale as when he had killed the assassin on the London Road. Another thing that made him unsuitable as an agent: Edmund was squeamish about violence and sudden death.

"We don't know," Nick said.

Carefully, they laid Thomas along one of the seats of the carriage, covering him with furs that Essex had been thoughtful enough to bring. Rivkah climbed in beside him and placed Thomas's head in her lap so she could monitor his breathing.

"You go too, John," Nick said. "Tell the bargemen to row for St. Mary's Queen Dock. They can help you carry him into the infirmary from there."

John nodded. St. Mary's Queen Dock was located at the southern tip of London Bridge, directly opposite St. Mary Ovarie Church.

"Eli will still be there," Rivkah said. "He will know what more can be done for Thomas." What she did not say, but what everyone understood, was that she did not know whether it would be sufficient to save his life. That all depended on how much poison had been purged by the vomiting and how much remained in his body. Only time would tell.

"I will return to The Black Sheep later," Nick said to John. A look passed between them. Their plan for John to watch Nick's back had just gone up in smoke with the attempt on Thomas's life.

And that attempt now made it certain that Walsingham's agents were being systematically targeted.

Nick leaned into the carriage, his voice so low only John and Rivkah could hear. "Watch over Thomas until you can get one of Black Jack Sims' boys to do it. There may be another attempt on his life. And, John," Nick said. "When Thomas is able to talk, find out who brought him the wineskin."

"The wine was fresh," said Rivkah. "So it would have been siphoned from a barrel relatively recently."

"Good to know," Nick said. That meant tavernkeepers' memories would also be fresh and they might remember someone purchasing a wineskin in the last couple of days.

"What's the killer's motive?" Rivkah asked. "Don't tell me robbery."

Nick knew she had worked out that the attempt on Thomas's life was connected to the attempt on his own and was not, as he had allowed her to believe before, a botched robbery.

To avoid the accusation in her eyes, Nick slapped the rump of the leading horse, and the carriage pulled away down Aldersgate, turned right at Newgate, and was gone.

Rivkah's look of sorrow burned in his chest. His refusal to answer her proved that he had been lying to her through omission. Given that she knew Sir Thomas was one of Walsingham's agents, it was no stretch of the imagination to assume Nick was also in the same business. Somehow he would have to put things right between them. How, he did not know, unless he came clean about his secret life. He shuddered at the thought.

When Nick got back to Thomas's room, he found Edmund holding the wineskin. "I thought I would throw it on the midden behind the building," Edmund said. "That way, no one will be tempted to use it again."

"It's evidence," Nick said. "We need to show it to every tavernkeeper in the area and find out who bought it."

"Good," Essex said. "Edmund can do that." He looked at Edmund standing there. "Well, you heard Nick."

"At once, my Lord," Edmund said, leaving the room, face averted.

Nick turned his back on Essex and started searching the room; he was mortified that his friend had been treated so peremptorily in front of him. Once again, Essex seemed oblivious of his rudeness. It was as if he regarded all men beneath his own exalted class as mere servants, tools to be used. No wonder his presence in the Netherlands had been so disruptive; he had the uncanny knack of putting people's backs up without being aware of it. Nick himself was only just holding on to his temper despite his gratitude to Essex for loaning his barge and carriage to transport Thomas.

Essex was a strange, mercurial mix of generosity and callousness, thoughtfulness—witness the fur rugs he had included in the carriage—and utter obliviousness to others' feelings. It was as if there were two men inhabiting one skin—one whom Nick despised; the other whom he couldn't help but like.

And if Nick was honest with himself, he also despised Edmund's servility. Perhaps that was why he had avoided him when they were at Oxford. There was something about Edmund's very desire to please that set Nick's teeth on edge. Nick hated himself for it and suspected it made him more like Essex than he would have believed possible.

To distract himself from these depressing thoughts, and the knowledge that his friendship with Rivkah might be irretrievably damaged, Nick concentrated on searching Thomas's room. He stripped the bed, but found nothing except Thomas's dagger under the pillow, and examined the cracks in the flooring to see if anything had fallen between them. He was looking for some clue to the identity of the person who had brought the poisoned wineskin to Thomas, but he knew it was hopeless. Whoever it was could have placed it in Thomas's room while he was sleeping; it would have been easy enough, as Thomas had not kept his door locked. One thing Nick did know: whoever had tried to poison Thomas knew he was sick in bed and knew he had visitors who brought wineskins. Nick had not only been seen the last time he visited, but he had unknowingly provided the killer with the perfect means to murder Thomas.

"Seems like you have everything in hand," Essex said. "I'll be off. I must report to the Queen what has happened."

Get in before Walsingham has a chance, thought Nick uncharitably. But the Queen would have to be told, and Nick would rather Essex break the news to her than do it himself. He was also relieved not to have Essex hanging over his shoulder while he investigated.

★ ★ ★

Once Essex had gone, Nick went onto the landing on Thomas's floor and knocked on the door opposite.

"Who knocks?" a voice boomed. "Speak, gentle, or forever hold thy peace."

Nick blinked and wondered briefly if he had stumbled into a farce, perhaps as the hapless messenger to a king. "Open up in the Queen's name," he shouted. Mention of the Queen usually did the trick, Nick found, and this was no exception.

The door flew open to reveal a man so enormous that he entirely filled the doorway, blocking all view of inside. Even though it was still morning, he was holding the leg of a capon in one fist and a tankard in the other. His chin was shiny with grease, and as he chewed, he regarded Nick through tiny, intelligent eyes sunk deep into the folds of his face like currants in a suet pudding. His jerkin was fouled with not only his present repast but many earlier meals, judging from its malodorous condition. Nick wrinkled his nose at the sour smell coming off the man, at his unwashed, unshaven appearance. But despite the overwhelming impression of a pig in a trough, the man's expression was cheerful, as if he was delighted to be interrupted in the middle of his breakfast by a stranger.

"Greetings," the man said, waving the capon leg as if it were a royal scepter. "Prithee, enter." He backed away so that Nick had room to squeeze through the doorway. A table groaning with food sat under a window with a chair pulled up to a platter with the rest of the dismembered capon on it. The rest of the room was littered with past meals, shriveled apple cores, bones picked clean, the sour smell of spilled wine and ale. It was truly a sybarite's palace.

"Sack?" the fat man offered, holding up a jug.

"No, thanks," Nick said. "But don't let me stop you. I just have a few questions."

"Please," the man said grandly. He sat down heavily in the chair and carried on eating. "Don't mind me," he added. "I have to keep my strength up."

"Did you see anyone deliver a wineskin to the room opposite either today or yesterday?" Knowing Thomas, he would have poured himself a drink almost as soon as he got the wine.

"So that's where it went," the man said.

"I don't follow," said Nick.

"My daily wineskin. I have one delivered every morning from The Rising Sun tavern, only yesterday it didn't come." He regarded Nick dolefully. "It just goes to show, does it not, that you cannot trust your neighbors. And Sir Thomas seemed like an honorable sort, not one to filch another fellow's tipple." He sighed as if the perfidy of the world weighed heavily upon his soul. "What's this about?"

"I'm afraid Sir Thomas has been poisoned."

The man's face turned pale, and he looked balefully at the tankard in his huge fist.

Before Nick could point out that the man would certainly have known about it by now if his sack had been tampered with, there was the sound of footsteps on the stairs and Will Shakespeare burst into the room.

"Sir John, you old devil," he cried. "How goes it?"

"Will?" Nick said.

"Hello, Nick. Sorry about Thomas."

"How did you hear?"

"We were rehearsing at Leicester House when John came rushing in with the news. Thought I would come over and see if I could help."

Nick sighed. As a spy agency, Leicester House was a joke. It leaked like a sieve. "You obviously know this gentleman." Nick pointed to the fat man.

Will laughed. "Sir John Staffington is a generous patron of our acting troupe."

Clearly overcoming his qualms about his sack being poisoned, Sir John raised his tankard in a toast. "Here's to you, immortal thespians."

So that explained Sir John's initial greeting, Nick thought. He was a theater buff. Which meant that half of what came out of his mouth was pure fiction and the other half pure intoxication. It hadn't taken Nick long to figure out that Sir John was already three sheets to the wind despite it being only midmorning.

"Can we get back to business?" Nick asked.

"Sorry, Nick," Will said. "I'll keep mum." He sat opposite Sir John and, after sniffing at the flagon, helped himself to a cup of sack. The fat man and the would-be playwright chinked tankards. Nick sighed. But for the absence of scantily clad nymphs, Nick felt like a Puritan who had inadvertently stumbled into a bacchanalian orgy.

He pressed on manfully. "You were saying that you did not receive your usual wineskin yesterday from The Rising Sun, Sir John."

"That's right. Most peculiar. I flatter myself I am their best customer."

I bet, Nick thought, eyeing Sir John's enormous girth.

"I heard footsteps and I thought, 'Aha, my wineskin has arrived. Oh, joy!' But when I opened the door a little while later, there was nothing there. Most disappointing."

"Did you see anyone?"

"Not a soul." Sir John looked downcast; then he brightened. "Lucky for me, eh? Otherwise it would be me that was poisoned." Then, as an afterthought. "Poor Sir Thomas."

"Indeed," intoned Will.

"You might ask the landlady downstairs," Sir John said. "A Mistress Shrewsbury." He laughed, a huge sound that boomed off the walls. Will looked at him fondly, Nick not so fondly, as he was sure he was now partially deaf. "Shrew, more like." Sir John slapped his knee with delight at his own wit. "Mistress Shrew." He jerked his head at the floor. "Lives below in the nether regions."

Nick felt sorry for the poor woman. He would not like to have a neighbor the weight of Sir John galumphing around just above his head at all hours of the day and night.

"Thank you, Sir John." Nick could now inquire at The Rising Sun and find out who delivered the wineskin and precisely when. Perhaps Edmund had already done so.

"Not at all, young sir. My infinite pleasure. And please convey my deepest commiserations to Sir Thomas. I trust he will recover?"

"We hope so."

★ ★ ★

The woman who opened the door to Nick on the ground floor was so tiny and wore so many layers of clothing that she did indeed look like a shrew peeking out of its nest. To add to this impression, her long nose twitched at the sight of him, as if Nick had brought the rank odor of Sir John with him; tiny, black eyes darted over his face and clothes, assessing him as a possible threat. Nick had to suppress a smile at the aptness of Sir John's name for her. In addition to a cap, she had a shawl over her head and a blanket around her shoulders.

"Mistress Shrewsbury," Nick said, bowing. "I hear that nothing goes on in this building without your knowledge." A bit of flattery never went amiss, Nick reckoned. "May I come in and ask you a few questions? I am on the Queen's business."

"Is this about poor Sir Thomas?" the landlady said in a surprisingly strident voice that belied her diminutive appearance.

"It is."

"Then you'd better come in," she said. "Make sure you wipe your feet on the mat."

After dutifully wiping his feet on a threadbare rug just inside the door, Nick was free to look around the room. It was cold and dark, with an empty fireplace despite the large basket of logs standing on the hearth. In other circumstances, this lack of a fire would have suggested poverty, but Nick could see that the furnishings of the room were of good quality—a solid oak sideboard with silver candlesticks (candles unlit) against one wall; a threadbare Turkey carpet; a glimpse of a four-poster bed hung with painted cloth through the doorway into the bedchamber beyond. The room was literally stuffed with belongings, and Nick surmised that Mistress

Shrewsbury was a widow who had rented out the rest of her house to make ends meet and had somehow managed to cram all her furniture and knickknacks from the entire house into these two rooms. The lack of a fire and light was probably her mistaken notion of economizing, although he couldn't see that she needed to with the high rent Sir Thomas and Sir John undoubtedly paid in such a respectable neighborhood as Aldersgate.

Nick had often observed that people who lived alone tended to develop peculiar habits. Witness Sir John upstairs. Nick had him pegged as a widower who had decided to eat, drink, and be merry before he died, which would probably be of apoplexy fairly soon, the way he was going. Better than the pinched life of a Mistress Shrewsbury, who was doubtless tormented by the conviction that her renters were engaged in riotous living at the expense of her diminished circumstances. To complete the picture of the batty widow, Nick counted at least six cats in the room.

"They're to keep the rats down," the landlady said, seeing the direction of Nick's gaze. "Sir John's room is a veritable Lord Mayor's Banquet for rats with all that rotting food lying around. If I've told him once, I've told him a thousand times. Throw it on the rubbish heap out back. But does he listen? No, he does not."

Nick had the strange impression he was listening to a conversation that went on inside her head most of her waking hours. He could see that she had focused all her unhappiness, loneliness, and blighted hopes on the gargantuan figure of Sir John. In an odd way, her ongoing war with him probably gave her life purpose. Nick had observed this in feuding neighbors back in Oxfordshire, sometimes over something as trivial as an errant cow grazing on the wrong side of a fence. When one old fellow died, his septuagenarian nemesis often followed within weeks, his reason for living gone.

"Please be seated," Mistress Shrewsbury said, with an oddly touching sort of faded gentility.

Nick looked in vain for a chair that was not piled with clothes or pots or, indeed, a cat. "I'll stand, thank you."

"Suit yourself." She removed a ginger tom from a chair and sat down, arranging the cat on her lap like a fur muff, where it began a stentorian purring. Two sets of eyes, one pair dark, one green, stared up at him disconcertingly. What with Sir John upstairs, Mistress Shrewsbury downstairs, and a poisoner on the loose, Nick was beginning to feel as if he had stumbled into an insane asylum.

"Was a wineskin delivered yesterday for Sir John?" Nick began.

"Must have been," she replied. "Same every day like clock-work. How that man can drink so much and still be standing is anyone's guess."

Nick resigned himself to a flood of irrelevant commentary on Sir John, clearly the landlady's pet peeve.

"But you didn't see who delivered it?"

"I was otherwise occupied." She glanced back at the bedcham-ber and then reddened, as if she had given herself away about doing something shameful like dressing. "But it is usually the boy from The Rising Sun."

"At what time?"

"St. Martin's had just struck the half after nine. I was getting ready to go to market."

"I see." Nick was disappointed. He had hoped that, like all landladies in his experience, she would have been nosy enough to look out her door whenever someone arrived at her premises.

"I went up to Sir Thomas to ask him if he needed anything, poor man."

Nick perked up.

"I tapped on the door and opened it."

"Was there a wineskin outside his door?" Nick asked.

"If you will let me finish, young man," she said, severely. "I didn't go in, of course. It wouldn't have been proper."

Not to mention fear of catching the influenza, Nick thought.

"Sir Thomas was sitting on the side of the bed pouring a drink from a wineskin. He asked me if I had seen who delivered it. I said no. Perhaps it was Sir John? I said. Sir Thomas said that it was prob-ably his friend Nick."

Nick's heart sank. He felt more responsible than ever. "Did he say where it had been left?"

"Just inside his door. He never locked it when he was at home. Only when he went out."

So the boy from The Rising Sun had delivered the wineskin as usual for Sir John; then someone else had spiked it with deadly nightshade and put it inside Sir Thomas's room for him to find when he woke up. Sir Thomas would have thought Nick had dropped by, found him asleep, and, not wanting to wake him, left it for him.

"Did you see or hear anyone else on the stairs after you returned from market?"

Mistress Shrewsbury shook her head.

"Is there a back entrance?" Nick asked.

"Of course."

"Show me, please."

She led Nick down a passageway on the ground floor to a door at the far end. Just to the right of the door was a small staircase. When Nick asked her where this led, she told him to the upper floor and on to the attic.

She opened the back door, and Nick noticed that it was unlocked. He remarked upon it.

"No point," she said. "Sir John uses it to avoid his creditors. Which are legion, I can tell you. He kept losing his latchkey and breaking it open. Cost me a fortune to repair it each time." She sniffed. "So now I just leave it unlocked. Sir Thomas uses it too. I prefer they leave the front door for me. More private."

Nick surmised that her dislike of Sir John was probably stronger than her fear of being murdered in her bed.

The door opened onto the usual tiny garden surrounded by an old-fashioned withy fence, rotting and sagging in parts. A gate at the end of the garden led to a lane. In better times there had been a vegetable garden, but now weeds, overgrown blackberry bushes, and broken household detritus had taken over so that the garden was little more than a junkyard with a beaten path down the center. At the end of the garden to the left of the gate was an enormous rubbish dump. Those householders who were lucky enough to back onto the river merely dumped their rubbish and the contents of their chamber pots directly into the water. Households in the center of the city, like Mistress Shrewsbury's, used their back-yard. A city ordinance decreed that these refuse dumps should be removed every month at the householder's expense, but few people obeyed this rule. Some used the compost heaps on their vegetable gardens—Rivkah and Eli did—but most simply left them to grow huge and noisome, fouling the air of the entire neighborhood and bringing hordes of rats from the river to feast on them at night.

Nick had seen enough. He now knew how the poisoner had gained access to the house without being seen by the inhabitants or people in the street at the front. He would have known the time the wineskin was delivered each day and simply slipped inside and up the back stairs, poured in the poison, and placed it inside Sir Thomas's rooms. The callousness of it bit into Nick's soul. Even as he followed the landlady back into the house and climbed the back stairs to the upper floor, Sir Thomas, his friend, could be breathing his last.

★ ★ ★

Nick searched Sir Thomas's rooms again but found nothing. Once back out on the street, he discovered that the tavern where he had obtained the water and salt was, indeed, The Rising Sun. Seeing as it was only a few doors down from Mistress Shrewsbury's lodging house, it made sense. Now that he had been given a definite lead, and not trusting Edmund's thoroughness, Nick ducked in and quickly ascertained that the same boy who had helped him carry the buckets up to Sir Thomas's rooms was the boy who delivered the daily wineskin to Sir John. The lad had not seen anyone on the stairs when he had dropped it off outside Sir John's door.

"I hope Sir John is not in trouble, sir," the tavern owner said. "He's our best customer."

Nick assured him Sir John was not a poisoner. Unless he was guilty of poisoning himself with gluttony, Nick thought to himself.

★ ★ ★

Although Nick was eager to return to Leicester House to ascertain where Gavell and Stace had been that morning, he knew he must report in to Walsingham. He was now certain that del Toro was a Spanish assassin sent to destabilize the English network prior to some act of war, an act of great audacity, since Mendoza, the erstwhile Spanish ambassador, had been expelled from England two years prior for being implicated in a plot to kill the Queen. It was common for foreign agents to be assigned as low-level diplomats to embassies, Nick knew. It allowed them more freedom of movement and more protection. What better way to cut off the flow of intelligence than to kill an enemy's agents? Not only would it break the line of communication between the continent and London, it would also throw Walsingham's network into utter confusion as they labored to find the murderer. As a ploy, it was crude but effective.

Accordingly, he made his way to St. Paul's and then turned east on Fenchurch Street. But when he arrived at Seething Lane, he found Walsingham being helped into a carriage by his secretary, who solicitously tucked fur rugs around his master's knees.

"Climb in," Walsingham ordered. "We've been summoned to Whitehall."

Only a royal summons could have enticed Walsingham out of his warm study. The man was clearly at death's door, judging by his ghostlike pallor and hands that trembled uncontrollably until he tucked them out of sight under the rugs. Nick marveled at the iron will of the man that could keep his body, and more importantly, his mind, functioning. Even so, the spymaster had been seldom seen at court of late, preferring to use Sir Robert Cecil as his liaison with the Queen. *This must be serious*, Nick thought, placing himself opposite Walsingham in the carriage.

"Before you ask, I know about the attempted poisoning of Sir Thomas," Walsingham said. "So does the Queen."

So Essex had informed her as soon as he left Sir Thomas's lodgings, as Nick had known he would. Although on the periphery of real intelligence work, Essex was eager to appear at its center.

Nick told Walsingham of the conversation he had overheard between Essex and Annie. "I don't think she can be trusted," Nick said. "She seems to be playing some kind of devious game of her own, and she has a habit of disappearing and then reappearing. I think she's up to something."

Walsingham kept his eyes on the window, as if the passing scenes of London were of great fascination.

"My Lord," Nick said, his irritation growing at Walsingham's continued silence, "if there is something going on, I think now is the time to tell me."

Walsingham turned toward him. "Patience, Nick," he said. "Patience."

CHAPTER 13

The Palace of Whitehall

When Walsingham presented himself outside the royal apartments, dressed in funereal black like the Grim Reaper, his gold chain of office glittering around his neck, the guards stood smartly to attention, the stocks of their halberds rapping in unison on the polished floor as they uncrossed the blades to give him admittance. Nick grinned as he followed Walsingham through the door.

"Thanks, lads," he couldn't resist saying. "Keep up the good work."

His grin faltered when he saw that the Queen was pacing up and down the long room. Always a bad omen. Another bad sign, as far as Nick was concerned, was that the Spider was also present. Essex, however, was conspicuously absent.

Walsingham gave a low bow, then tottered on his feet and had to put a hand on Nick's shoulder to steady himself.

"Sit down, Moor," Elizabeth said, "before you fall down." She said it brusquely, but there was a flicker of compassion in her eyes.

"Most kind, Your Majesty," Walsingham murmured, availing himself of a hard-backed chair. Both Cecil and Nick were standing, and Elizabeth did not offer them the same courtesy. Codpiece was leaning against the window behind the Queen, and he raised his eyebrows at Nick. Squalls ahead, his look said.

"Let me see if I understand this," the Queen said, still pacing, her arms crossed, chin down. "There is an assassin out there murdering my agents. One is dead, one is like to die of poisoning, and one"—here she glanced at Nick—"was shot at with a crossbow on the London Road."

"That is correct, Your Majesty," Walsingham said.

"And you have no idea who the assassin is?"

Both Cecil and Nick opened their mouths to speak, but Walsingham forestalled them. "None, Your Majesty."

Nick tried to hide his amazement at the bald-faced lie. From the look on Cecil's face, he too was having a hard time concealing his dismay. Nick saw Richard, aka Codpiece, looking at him intently, a frown on his face.

Oh, bollocks, Nick thought. *Walsingham is running some kind of operation behind the Queen's back.*

To Nick's mind, the need for subterfuge and the monumental riskiness of lying to the Queen could only mean one thing: Mary, Queen of Scots.

Elizabeth had made it abundantly plain that she had no interest in executing her cousin, even though Mary had been used as a figurehead in countless treason plots since her imprisonment nineteen years before. For almost twenty years she had been a thorn in the side of Elizabeth, a thorn that the Queen chose to live with rather than pluck, as Walsingham and Baron Burghley had repeatedly advised. In fact, whenever the subject of her cousin was raised, Elizabeth flew into a fury.

Nick understood why. Her own mother, Anne Boleyn, had been beheaded by her father, Henry VIII. As an anointed queen, Anne's execution was a clear case of regicide. Elizabeth was determined not to follow in her father's footsteps. If an anointed monarch could be executed, then Elizabeth herself could be similarly deposed. The current situation regarding Mary, Queen of Scots, and her chief ministers' desire to get rid of her against Elizabeth's express wishes was one of uneasy stalemate.

Nick breathed a sigh of relief that he had not mentioned del Toro to the Queen when he had first returned to London after being sent to Oxford. Essex had been present, and Nick hadn't wanted him sniffing around someone Cecil had thought bore watching. Nick had thought merely to keep well clear of any rivalry between Essex and Cecil. Now he realized that the presence of a Spanish agent—possibly an assassin—had far more serious implications and that Walsingham was up to his neck in something devious and dangerous.

Cecil was clearly having similar thoughts. His face was pale with anger, although his expression remained impassive as always. He had now realized that Walsingham had kept him in the dark about del Toro. All Cecil had known at the time was that del Toro was a mysterious Spaniard who had landed at Dover and should be investigated. By merely doing his job, Cecil might have compromised an important spy mission. The fact that Walsingham had not seen fit to inform him would not lessen the appearance of incompetence if the mission should fail because of his tampering, however innocent his intention might have been.

"I find that hard to believe, Moor," the Queen said, coming to a halt in front of his chair.

Walsingham rose, one hand on the back of the chair. "We are doing everything in our power to see that the culprit is caught, Your Majesty."

Elizabeth looked at him narrowly, trying to gauge the veracity of his words, but all Walsingham's face betrayed was that he was a deeply ill man near the end of his resources after the jolting carriage ride to the palace. She sighed in defeat.

"You may go," she said. "And you," she said pointing a jeweled finger at Cecil. "You stay," she said to Nick.

For the first time, Nick saw a look of unease flicker over Walsingham's face, and his eyes sought Nick's. But Nick ignored the urgent message in them to keep quiet about del Toro. Like Cecil, Nick was furiously angry with Walsingham. He felt he was being played. And more than his own hurt pride, he was enraged that Winchelsea had been murdered so hideously and Thomas poisoned. He could still see his friend twitching and shaking on the bed, his face deathly white, his hands clutching convulsively at the covers of his bed. Even now, Thomas could be dead. Nick did not care what game Walsingham was playing; he was going to go after del Toro if it was the last thing he did.

"So Nick," the Queen said when the door had closed behind Walsingham and Cecil. "What is really going on?"

This was the moment Nick had been dreading, the moment when he was forced to choose between loyalty to Walsingham and loyalty to the Queen. In truth, it was really no choice at all: Elizabeth was his sovereign, with the power to take away not only his livelihood but also his life.

He had just opened his mouth to speak when there was a loud commotion outside the door to the royal apartments.

"Let me in, God damn you," a familiar voice said. "I'll have your heads for this, you varlets."

A look of extreme irritation passed over Elizabeth's face; whether from the noise that had interrupted her or the unwelcome appearance of Essex, Nick could not tell, but she strode over to the door, wrenched it open, and barked, "Let him in."

Nick had never been so glad to see Essex. And Essex in a snit was a sight to see.

"What is the meaning of this, Your Majesty?" he raged, barely taking time to give a cursory bow to his Queen, a serious breach of court etiquette that would have resulted in a week in the Tower in the days of her father, Fat Harry. "I was told you were in a private meeting with Walsingham and that gutless wonder Cecil. Am I not also your spymaster?"

"Yes, yes, Robin," the Queen said. "An oversight, no more."

"Ha!" Essex replied.

Both Nick and Codpiece exchanged shocked glances. This was tantamount to accusing the Queen of being a liar. Even though there was no such thing as an oversight in Elizabeth's Machiavellian brain, it was simply not permissible to accuse the Queen point-blank of dissembling. But Essex seemed oblivious of the unmistakable signs of the Queen's displeasure: the pallor of her face, apparent even beneath the white face paint; the small tic along her jawline; the way her eyes shrank to pinpoints like twin bodkins.

"I will not be treated like this," Essex said, and actually stomped his foot.

Nick retreated to where Codpiece was standing by the window. It was like watching a reenactment of Chaucer's "The Wife of Bath," a cautionary tale of the miseries and hilarities that ensued when an older woman married a much younger man. At the very least, the Queen was not going to come out of the encounter with her dignity intact, and neither Nick nor Codpiece wanted to witness this.

As if of one accord, they backed discreetly out of the room. The fact that Elizabeth had not given them permission to leave was of little account. The prospect of witnessing the Queen's humiliation at the hands of one of her inferiors, however favored, was a far more serious offense and one that Elizabeth would never forgive.

Once out in the corridor, both Nick and Codpiece drew a ragged breath. Even the guards refused to make eye contact but stood stoically at their stations as if they were carved out of oak while the sounds of Essex's tantrum and the Queen's placatory response came clearly through the door.

Codpiece led Nick to his private rooms father down the corridor. Once inside, he poured them both large goblets of wine, and they sat facing one another in front of the fire.

"What's going on, Nick?" Codpiece eventually said.

"I have to have your word you will not repeat this to the Queen," Nick said. When Codpiece opened his mouth to protest—the Fool was loyal to a fault to his Queen—Nick held up his hand. "There is nothing treasonous. Just politically . . . delicate."

"Oh, shit," the Fool said. "I smell a Spaniard."

"Do I have your word, Richard?" Nick repeated.

Richard nodded glumly.

Nick told him about his suspicions that del Toro was a Spanish assassin sent to destabilize the Queen's spy networks. He said nothing about his suspicion that Walsingham was running a plot somehow involving Mary, Queen of Scots.

"Why did Walsingham conceal this information?" Codpiece asked.

"So as not to worry the Queen," Nick replied, feeling guilty that he was lying by omission to his friend, something he had been doing a lot of recently, he realized sadly, thinking of Rivkah. "Things are politically delicate in the Netherlands, and Walsingham doesn't want to spark reprisals by Leicester against the Spanish before he can bring all his forces to bear to defeat them."

It sounded a lame excuse to Nick's ears, but Codpiece nodded.

"Makes sense," he said. "The Spanish are trying to provoke a response that will give them a reason to invade."

Nick wasn't a bit surprised at the Fool's political grasp of world events. Codpiece was the Queen's spy on her own court. Nothing that went on between the palace walls was unknown to him. Although Walsingham did not know Codpiece was Elizabeth's personal spy, the fact that he kept his center of operations at his house in Seething Lane meant that this part of the spy network was a mystery to the Fool. Nick was hoping to thread the needle of truth between what Codpiece knew and did not know. He prayed that his friend would forgive him when it all came out into the open, as it was bound to do eventually.

"I am trying to track del Toro down," Nick said.

Nick also told Codpiece of his suspicions concerning Henry Gavell and Richard Stace. "I can't rule them out," he concluded.

"You think Essex is eliminating the competition?" Codpiece asked.

Nick thought back to the recklessness with which Essex had accused the Queen of being a liar barely an hour ago. "He acts before he thinks," Nick replied. "That makes him dangerous."

Codpiece nodded. "There have been times when I actually thought he would draw his sword in the Queen's presence, so great was his choler."

They both contemplated the enormity of that. It was automatic treason for a subject to pull a weapon in anger in his monarch's presence.

"One day his temper is going to be his undoing," Codpiece added. "I just wish . . ." He trailed off.

"What?"

"Never mind."

Nick knew Codpiece had been on the verge of saying that he wished the Queen were not so weak when it came to dashing young courtiers of Essex's ilk, that her vanity was not such that she required the illusion that she was a young, beautiful, and above all, eligible woman. But Codpiece was too loyal.

Nick looked at his downcast face with affection. "You're a good man, Richard," he said.

"Well, for God's sake, don't tell anyone."

Nick refilled their goblets. "Tell me what you know about Annie O'Neill."

Codpiece stretched out his stubby legs. "Ah, the beauteous Annie," he said. "That tale is a bloody one, I fear. A veritable Greek tragedy."

"I'm listening," Nick said.

"Annie O'Neill is the great-granddaughter of Conn Bacach O'Neill, granddaughter of Matthew O'Neill, the illegitimate son of Conn. Conn O'Neill was granted the earldom of Tyrone in 1542 by Henry VIII in return for submission to the Crown of England. This provoked a civil war within the extensive branches of the family that is still raging today because of Matthew's illegitimacy. Annie's ancestral home was burned to the ground, many of her family killed, but Annie and her father, Hugh Rua O'Neill, escaped. She fled to England to try to persuade the Queen to restore to her father the ancient title of The O'Neill—sovereign of the dominant O'Neill family of Tir Eoghain—essentially, High King of Ireland— against the claim of his cousin, Turlough Luineach O'Neill, who assumed the High Kingship through force."

Nick blew out his breath. "And I thought English politics were complicated."

"You have no idea. Whatever you do, don't accept an assignment in Ireland. The Irish will never give up their right to rule alone. The fighting will go on until doomsday unless England leaves well alone."

"Then why is Annie siding with the English?" Nick asked.

"It is the only way for her branch of the family to come back to power. Once they do, they will turn on their English overlords. It is the way it has always been. That is why the Queen keeps stringing her along."

"What's the connection with Essex?"

"Annie hopes he will be sent to Ireland with a military force to put her father on the throne of Ireland. It is not an unreasonable hope. The Queen has a habit of sending favorites to Ireland. Especially ones she is beginning to find tiresome."

They both thought back to the ugly scene they had witnessed in the royal apartments.

"What's your take on Annie?" Nick asked. "Personally, I mean."

"She is utterly ruthless." Codpiece smiled. "I like her."

"Do you think she is capable of acting as a double agent for the Spanish and killing off agents?"

"If the Spanish had promised to restore her father to the High Kingship of Ireland instead of making him a mere Earl of Tyrone as the Queen has promised, then anything is possible," Codpiece said. "Annie is getting tired of waiting for the Queen to act on her promises. And remember," he added. "Annie is a Catholic."

CHAPTER 14

Bankside

His head still spinning from what Codpiece had told him of the Irish situation and the internecine warfare between the clans, Nick summoned a wherry at Whitehall Stairs and instructed the boatman to row him to St. Mary's Queen Dock on the southern side of the river hard by the infirmary of St. Mary Ovarie, where Thomas had been taken.

On the long row downstream, Nick wondered how far Annie would go to restore her family fortunes. If he was honest, he could not fault her for joining cause with Protestant England, the enemy of her faith. After all, that was what Nick had done when he agreed to spy for Walsingham, knowing full well that his Protestant spymasters considered England's greatest enemy to be not merely Spain but the Catholic faith itself. In many ways, he was betraying his family while at the same time trying to save it. Caught up in never-ending conflict, Ireland was not the only Greek tragedy; England was a veritable land of woes. In many ways, English Catholics under a Protestant Queen were in much the same position as the Irish under English rule, and there were many who would be happy to see Elizabeth assassinated and her Catholic cousin, Mary, put on the throne.

But to actively participate in plots of regicide was a line that Nick would not cross, however much he longed for his family to be able to practice the faith of their ancestors openly and without fear.

He would never join cause with the enemy of his country, even for the sake of his faith. If Annie was working for the Spanish as a double agent and had tortured and murdered Simon Winchelsea and attempted to kill Thomas and him, then Nick would hunt her down without mercy.

Wearily, Nick paid off the boatman and climbed the stairs of St. Mary's Queen Dock in the descending dusk. Above his head the massive span of London Bridge was still rumbling with life, its wooden road groaning with the weight of the houses built along its length and the heavy passage of carts and foot traffic. It was almost like a separate town from London itself, one that floated in air. Nick knew people who lived on the bridge who seldom went into London or Bankside but lived practically their whole lives suspended over the river. Fleetingly, Nick wondered if there would ever be a time when he could inhabit a spiritual London Bridge between loyalty to his family's faith on the one hand and loyalty to his Queen on the other.

Not in this life, he thought.

Nick knew his thoughts had turned morbid and tried to shrug them off as he entered the church of St. Mary Ovarie and descended into the crypt where Eli and Rivkah had been given space for their infirmary. In truth, he was dreading finding that his friend Thomas had died. He walked quietly between the pallets laid against the wall on either side of the stone chamber. Some of the beds were empty, neatly made up with pillows and wool coverlets that Kat's whores had made; some of the beds were occupied, their occupants coughing with the influenza or merely sleeping fitfully, chests audibly wheezing as if they breathed in water. A baby was whimpering in its mother's arms, a low mewling like a kitten's as if the child was too weak even to cry. The smell in the crypt was a mixture of chest liniment, unemptied chamber pots, and the dank smell of river slime absorbed by the foundations over centuries.

He passed a bed containing an ancient woman with long white hair straggling over her shoulders. One side of her face drooped like melted candlewax. Her eyes were open, but she lay flat on her back with her clawlike hands crossed over her breast as if she had already composed herself for death. Her eyes moved repeatedly to a beaker of water on the floor beside her pallet.

"Mistress," Nick said. "Can I do you a service?"

Again her eyes moved sideways. Suddenly understanding, Nick knelt, picked up the cup, and slipping an arm about her blade-like shoulders, lifted her so she could drink. Most of the water slid down her chin. He mopped it with the edge of her coverlet. She blinked twice at him but did not speak as he laid her down.

As he was getting to his feet, Nick saw Eli watching him.

"An apoplexy has robbed her of speech and movement," Eli said in a low voice. "She blinks to give you thanks. She is so quiet that I sometimes forget she is there, and she gets very thirsty." For a moment, Eli's eyes shadowed with pain. "And the little child over there is dying. There is so little I can do to ease her suffering." Then he summoned up a smile. "But come," he said. "At least there is occasionally good news."

He led Nick to the far end of the crypt. Lying on a pallet, propped up with pillows, was Thomas. His face was deathly pale, but he was alive. When he saw Nick, he gave a weak grin.

"My savior," he croaked.

"Actually, it was Rivkah who saved you," Nick said. "I just did as I was told."

"Wise man."

Beneath their banter, Nick was aware of an enormous burden lifted off his heart. The murderer had failed to kill his friend, just as he had failed to kill Nick. Though monstrous, the killer was fallible, possibly even inept. If so, he could be caught.

In the shadows next to a stone pillar, Nick saw an enormous dark shape.

"Hello, Ralph," he said.

The figure did not return his greeting, nor did he move. Ralph was the bodyguard of Black Jack Sims's ten-year-old grandson, Johnnie, the only living heir to Black Jack's crime syndicate. Ralph was enormous, dumb in speech and wits, and utterly loyal to his young charge. Where Ralph was, Johnnie was sure to be close by, and indeed, as Nick's eyes adjusted to the gloom in the crypt, he saw Johnnie lying on a pallet on the other side of where Ralph kept guard. The boy was sleeping, his breath ragged.

"Influenza," Eli said. "We thought Ralph could keep an eye on both Johnnie and Thomas at the same time."

Nick nodded. Ralph would certainly scare off any would-be assassin. His placid, bovine face was unnerving when coupled with his fearsome skill with a dagger. It was like being attacked by a murderous child. Hardened bully-boys had been known to turn on their heels and flee when they saw Ralph lumbering toward them, a beatific smile on his innocent face.

"How's Johnnie doing?" Nick asked Eli in a low voice. He knew that if the lad died, Black Jack Sims would hold Eli and Rivkah responsible and his revenge would be terrible. This despite the fact that he was fond of them both and relied on their medical skill for his own myriad ailments.

"He's a strong lad and will recover," Eli said in a voice pitched loudly for Ralph's ears. Then, in a whisper to Nick, "It was touch and go at first. Mouse and I thought we would have to flee into exile again." Eli gave Nick a weak grin as if he had made a joke.

But Nick did not return the smile, even at Eli's use of his pet name for Rivkah. She had once explained that her nickname came from her ability to go quietly about her business in public without drawing attention to herself, a skill she had learned in Salamanca.

"We need to move you," Nick said to Thomas.

"Absolutely not," Eli said. "He is too weak."

"He's not safe here," Nick insisted. "I don't want Essex knowing where he is. His own boatmen delivered him here."

"I can walk," Thomas said gamely, although he looked as feeble as a newborn.

"No, you cannot," Eli said sternly.

"I want to move him to Kat's," Nick said.

Thomas grinned. "I can definitely walk."

Nick ignored him. "Ralph," he said. "Would you do me a huge favor? It won't take long. Eli here promises to look after Johnnie while you are gone, and I'll let you have free ale for a week in The Black Sheep."

Ralph frowned and looked down at the sleeping boy. It was clear his feeble mind was laboring painfully with the choice he had to make. Aside from Johnnie, there was nothing he loved more in the world than ale.

"I promise you no harm will come to him," Nick said. "Eli will sit by him and watch over him until you return. Won't you, Eli?"

Eli scowled. "Yes," he said. Then privately to Nick, "If Thomas has a relapse, I will hold you personally responsible."

Taking this for permission, Nick instructed Ralph to pick Thomas up in his arms as if he were a bridegroom carrying his bride across a threshold. Nick then tucked a coverlet around Thomas and over his head.

Once out on the street, people gave them a wide berth, some of them crossing themselves, thinking that Ralph was carrying the corpse of one of Eli's patients who had succumbed to the influenza. As they walked, Nick mused on the aptness of Kat's brothel being situated in Dead Man's Place.

By the time they reached Kat's and Ralph had carried Thomas up the stairs to the third floor where Kat and Joseph had their private chambers, Thomas looked the color of old cheese. For all his good humor, he was clearly still very ill.

"Put him in here," Kat said, pointing to Joseph's room, which was connected to her own room by a door. "You don't mind, do you, Joseph?"

"'Course not," Joseph said. "I can kip down on a bench downstairs." Formerly the Terror of Lambeth, Joseph was a retired wrestler who had fallen on hard times. He had met Kat when she was a street prostitute twenty years before and had agreed to become her protector. Since then, they had built up a lucrative business, and Joseph was devoted to her in much the same way Ralph was devoted to Johnnie, except with far more intelligence and far less homicidal impulses, although he could be fearsome in a fight if any of the patrons in the brothel got out of hand.

Task accomplished, Ralph was eager to get back to Johnnie.

"Thank you, Ralph," Nick said. "Come to the tavern anytime for free ale."

★   ★   ★

Once Thomas was installed in Joseph's bed, Nick breathed easier. Quickly, he told Kat and Joseph what had happened. Eli or Rivkah, he said, would be coming in regularly to make sure he recovered.

"It's best if none of the girls know who he is," Nick cautioned. "We don't want them talking to their johns."

"Leave it to me," Kat said. "I'll tend him myself."

At her words, Nick felt a flare of jealousy.

When Kat glanced at him, Nick avoided her gaze. He knew he had no claim on her, no right whatsoever to play the possessive fool. Why then did he burn with jealousy? Why did he smolder when he saw Thomas looking at Rivkah? Did he believe he had a right to possess the body of one woman and the heart of another?

What kind of green-eyed monster am I? Nick wondered.

Sick with self-loathing, Nick declined an invitation to eat with Kat, Joseph, and the girls before the brothel's nightly business commenced and walked back to The Black Sheep. The streets were now dark and filled with the footfalls, rustlings, scuffles, and mutterings of illicit enterprise. But Nick was well known in Bankside, and no one molested him. He passed Rivkah and Eli's house and saw a light burning through the window. Rivkah was probably alone making dinner, which she would carry to Eli at the infirmary, for he always stayed the night when there was an epidemic of illness, not trusting the elderly priest or his deacons to take adequate care of his patients. When the infirmary was full, Rivkah and Eli took turns nursing the sick through the night.

Nick knew he should knock on her door and beg her pardon for lying to her about the attempt on his life on the London Road; even more importantly, he should explain why he was a secret agent working against the country of her birth. But he allowed himself to keep on walking.

When he stepped through the door of The Black Sheep, Bess the parrot's greeting of "Who's a lily-livered varlet then?" sounded depressingly like the voice of his conscience, but at least Hector's rapturous greeting lifted his mood.

"How's Thomas?" John asked. He had just opened a new barrel behind the counter in readiness for the night. A few early drinkers were slouched at the bar. Nick could hear Maggie, Matty, and the children in the back rooms of the taverns having dinner. John came around the bar with a couple of tankards and put one on a table for Nick, who had his hands full of Irish Wolfhound.

"He'll live, thank God," Nick said, fending off Hector, who had placed both paws on his shoulders and was attempting to rasp the skin off his face with his tongue.

"Down," he commanded. "I'm glad to see you too."

Nick wiped his face on his sleeve, then unbuckled his sword and laid it on a table. He told John that Thomas had been moved from the infirmary to Kat's brothel. He didn't have to tell him not to bruit the news about.

"You think someone from Essex's crew is the murderer?" John asked, frowning.

Nick picked up the tankard John had brought him. "We can't take any chances. But, in spite of whatever game Walsingham is playing, I intend to go after del Toro." Nick then told John what had transpired in the Queen's apartments, describing how Walsingham was keeping the existence of del Toro from the Queen and how he himself had narrowly escaped giving the Queen del Toro's name by the arrival of an irate Essex.

"Tomorrow," Nick said, putting his booted feet up on a stool, "we go hunting."

CHAPTER 15

City of London

Over breakfast the next day, Nick and John discussed how to best go about finding del Toro in a town as large as London.

"It will take at least a week to inquire at every inn in the city," Nick said. "And, for all we know, he is being sheltered by someone in their home. Then we'll never find him. What we need to do is have someone lead us to him."

"One of Essex's people?"

"Possibly," Nick replied. "If it doesn't work, then at least we'll know they are in the clear. The important thing is for you to keep in the shadows. I don't want them to know there are two sets of eyes on them."

"Sounds more like fishing than hunting," John grumbled.

They both put on dark cloaks, the better to remain undetected from recessed doorways. Luckily, it was raining again, so they would not appear suspicious with their hoods up. Both men were dressed in dark clothing, and both were armed with sword and dagger.

"Sorry, old man," Nick told Hector. "You have to stay here today."

The last thing he wanted was to advertise his identity by the presence of his distinctive dog.

Hector gave a sad whine but obediently lay down on the floor, his nose toward the door, to await his master's return.

★   ★   ★

Leicester House

While Nick and John leaned against a yew tree in St. Clement's churchyard across the Strand from Leicester House, they paid a lad loitering outside The Angel—in the hope that someone would buy him ale—to give a message to Essex. He was to tell Essex and anyone else within hearing that Nick was on the track of the assassin who was killing off agents. The lad was to act stupid—not a difficult thing for him to do, Nick concluded, judging from his sleepy-eyed look—when asked exactly where Nick had gone. Only someone who already knew where del Toro was hiding would know where to go. From what Nick had observed, Essex himself did not seem to know about del Toro's existence.

At the mention of agents, the lad's eyes grew round. He swiped at his runny nose with a dirty sleeve. "Are you one of them, then?" he asked. "A secret agent?"

"If I told you, I'd have to kill you," Nick said with a straight face.

The boy took a step back.

"If you do it right, you'll make enough money to buy all the ale you can drink," Nick said, relenting. "So be off with you."

When he had gone, John looked at him. "Threats followed by an appeal to his baser instincts?"

"Did I leave anything out?" Nick asked.

"Nope. You pretty much covered the totality of human venality."

"That's what I thought."

The lad was gone for some time. When he returned and reported that he had told the "posh gent" (Essex), the "hot wench" (Annie), and a man who looked like "a right hard bastard" (Henry Gavell, no doubt), Nick tossed him a shilling, well satisfied that he had put the cat among the pigeons.

They didn't have long to wait. Annie, in her guise as Meg the prostitute with a shawl over her head, slipped out of a side door of Leicester House and walked quickly north on the Strand. A few moments later, Gavell and Stace left by the front entrance and went south.

"Damnation," Nick said. "We'll have to split up. I'll take Annie. You follow the other two. Meet up later at The Black Sheep."

★ ★ ★

Nick followed Annie up Fleet Street, over Ludgate Hill and the Fleet, and past St. Paul's. He almost lost her in the crowd, who were listening to a preacher harangue them about the evils of the Seven Deadly Sins from the steps of St. Paul's Cross.

"You, sir, with the ponderous belly," the preacher shouted, pointing at a prosperous-looking merchant. "How will you account for your gluttony in the next life?"

"I will feast mightily at the heavenly banquet. And so should you, you scarecrow," the merchant bellowed. "You look like you need a good meal."

This provoked gales of laughter. The preacher was, indeed, tall and thin and dressed in a faded black robe, as if he had only one suit of clothes and the color had run with repeated washings. His dour appearance made him look suspiciously like a Puritan, even though public preaching by that sect had been banned. He had opened his mouth to reply when he caught sight of Annie trying to dodge her way through the crowd.

"*Lust!*" he screeched, spittle spraying out of his mouth onto the unlucky people in the front row. "There goes one of the devil's paramours."

Everyone craned to see where his shaking finger was pointing. If Annie was chagrined at being singled out, she didn't show it. Giving a gap-toothed grin, she blew him a kiss.

"He's one of me best customers," she gaily informed the crowd. "Likes to dress up in women's clothes and have his arse whipped for his sins."

Again the crowd roared. The preacher turned crimson. He shook his fist and shouted something, but it was lost in the raucous merriment of the onlookers. Someone threw an apple, and then a whole barrage of missiles made up of rotten fruit and lumps of mud began to rain down on the hapless preacher. He scuttled off the steps of the cross and made off down an alley, his long robes hoicked up around his skinny white calves.

Nick followed as Annie pushed her way to the edge of the riot she had created and turned left toward Cripplegate. He had to admire her practice of spy craft. She constantly doubled back on herself, leading him in circles, apparently wandering the streets aimlessly, sometimes fending off men who thought she was trolling for customers. Once she entered a house, and it was only by chance that Nick, by running down an alley at the side of the building, saw her emerge out of the back entrance now dressed as a young man in hose and a doublet with a slouchy hat pulled low on her forehead.

Something looked familiar about her appearance, but he couldn't place it. He shrugged it off; Annie now looked like any young man with modest means on the streets of London. Nick could not help but be in awe of her ability to change character and gender. He remembered what the boatman had told him about his friend Sam hearing a third voice at Wood Wharf the night Winchelsea was murdered. A soft voice. Could it be that Annie was the murderer? He was now sure it had been Annie in her disguise as a whore whom he had seen at The Spotted Cow in Oxford. Somehow she had recognized Nick and led del Toro out of harm's way. Nick burned with shame when he remembered how easily she had outwitted him.

Nick was now convinced he was following a traitor. It was obvious that Annie had decided to back two horses at once in order to regain her family heritage. By playing the Queen against the Spanish, she was insuring herself against the possible success of a Spanish invasion when it would be Mary, Queen of Scots, in alliance with Spain, who would be handing out favors of land and titles. And given that Ireland was still a Catholic country, in defiance of its Protestant overlords in the north, what better advocate than His Most Catholic Majesty, Philip, King of Spain and Holy Roman Emperor, to plead for the restoration of Annie's ancestral lands? Codpiece had made it plain to Nick that the Irish owed loyalty first to their clans, second to their faith, and only a distant third to their nation.

In Scotland, Robert the Bruce's greatest achievement and the key to his military success had been to convince the clans to put their country first in order to resist Edward Longshanks's invasion of Scotland. No leader in Ireland had yet arisen to do the same.

The bells of London had struck the hour twice before Annie eventually stopped in front of a small tavern tucked away down an alley in Bishopsgate—ironically, not far from the Tower and Seething Lane, as if hiding in plain sight of the authorities. She looked up and down the alley before she ducked inside. Nick went round the back to see if she emerged, but there was no sign of her, so he entered, pulling his hood down over his face.

She was not in the crowded taproom, but he noticed stairs leading to an upper floor. Trying to look as if he had legitimate business there, Nick went up. No one prevented him. Hearing a door close on the tiny landing, he put his ear to it and heard voices— the higher voice of a woman and a man's deeper voice in reply. Drawing his sword, Nick kicked in the door and entered.

The scene that met his eyes was like a frozen tableau in a tapestry—Annie pouring wine into a goblet from a heavy pewter flagon; del Toro seated in a chair in front of a fire about to drink from his goblet. Both of them had turned their heads toward the door when Nick suddenly burst through. The only noise in the room after the crash of the door hitting the wall was the sound of the logs crackling in the fireplace and the ticking of rain against the casement window.

Then time resumed, and Annie picked up the goblet she had just filled and held it out to him.

"Join us?" she said.

Nick had to admire her coolness. "No, thanks."

She shrugged and took a long drink. "I should have figured you set this up to follow me," she said. "I warned Essex you were clever."

"Sit," Nick commanded. "And you, Señor del Toro. Drop your dagger on the floor and slide it towards me with your foot."

Del Toro glanced briefly at his sword lying out of reach on the bed, then looked at Annie.

"Better do as he says, Francesco," Annie said. "I think our friend the Honorable Nicholas Holt means business."

Shaking his head as if in regret, del Toro took his dagger off his belt and dropped it on the floor, sliding it toward Nick. "You are the Earl of Blackwell's brother?" del Toro said, something clicking behind his dark eyes.

Nick picked up the dagger and stuck it into his belt, trying to conceal his shock that del Toro knew who Robert was.

"Why do you think I went to Oxford?" del Toro said.

"Shut up, Francesco," Annie said, sharply. "Let me do the talking."

Nick closed the door and leaned against it, his sword pointed at del Toro. He tried to keep his sword hand from shaking, but cold tendrils of fear were coiling around his heart, making him feel as if he had the ague. He remembered Cecil showing him a letter that Robert had written to an English Jesuit in exile. It was the reason Nick had been coerced into spying for Walsingham. At the time, he'd thought the letter entirely innocent and that Robert was too wise to be in treasonous correspondence with Jesuit agents, but del Toro's words had shaken him badly.

"Are you saying you were in Oxford to meet with my brother?" he said.

"I am interested in talking to all the prominent recusant families," del Toro replied. "Alas, we missed each other, and I did not end up seeing him."

"Keep your mouth shut," Annie said, rounding on him. "Nick knows nothing."

"I know you are a traitor," Nick said, turning his eyes on her.

It was unnerving to see her dressed as a man. She had even stippled charcoal on her chin to make it appear like stubble. If he hadn't seen her enter the tavern as a whore and leave as a man, Nick would have been utterly fooled. She had even walked like a man, striding along, swinging her shoulders instead of her hips.

Annie picked up the heavy flagon. "Sure you won't have some?"

When Nick did not reply, she laughed. "Afraid it's poisoned?"

"Is it?"

In answer, she poured more wine into her goblet and drank.

"Did you kill Winchelsea?" Nick said. "He recognized you from The Angel, didn't he? Couldn't have him reporting that you were working for the enemy?"

"What's he talking about?" del Toro asked.

Annie ignored him and kept her eyes on Nick. "You think you've got everything worked out, don't you?" she said.

"I can't prove it yet, but I will. Once I take you both in."

"How are you going to accomplish that?" Annie asked. Again she refilled her goblet from the heavy flagon.

Nick just had time to wonder why she was drinking so much when she suddenly flung the flagon at him. Instinctively he ducked, and it glanced painfully off his shoulder, clanging heavily off the door behind him. But Annie had distracted him long enough for del Toro to launch himself at Nick and grab him in a bear hug. He was a big man with huge shoulders and long, simian arms. He pinioned Nick's arms to his sides so that his sword was pointing uselessly at the floor. Nick tried to twist free, but del Toro just squeezed harder, crushing Nick's chest so that he had difficulty drawing breath. Spots of light began to dance in front of his eyes, and he knew he was close to passing out. Nick head-butted del Toro in the face and felt the Spaniard's nose break, blood spraying into Nick's face and blinding him. But the Spaniard did not loosen his grip. Through a haze of red, Nick saw Annie coming toward him, an arm raised.

"Hold him," she commanded.

Then he felt a tremendous blow to the back of his head as if a giant elm had fallen on him, and his limbs went slack like a puppet with its strings cut. The next thing he knew he was falling, the side of his face cracking against wooden floorboards gritty with dirt. He lay absolutely still and held his breath. Then he sensed someone crouching beside him.

"He's dead," he heard Annie say.

Nick waited for the sound of the door opening and closing and footsteps moving away before taking a huge, ragged, breath.

Then he did the sensible thing and passed out.

CHAPTER 16

Rivkah and Eli's House, Bankside

Once again, Nick found himself being stitched up in Eli and Rivkah's house.

He had yet to summon the courage to tell Rivkah that one of his recent attackers was a woman.

"Ow!" he said.

"Don't be a baby."

"Easy for you to say. You don't have a hole in your head."

"It's a cut, not a hole," Rivkah said, snipping off the thread on the last stitch. "Made by a fire poker, if I'm not mistaken, judging by the soot in the wound." She put a linen pad smeared with some ointment on the stitches and secured it with a bandage that she wrapped around the top of his head. She frowned. "It's not the cut but the dizziness from the blow that I'm worried about."

When Nick had come to on the floor of the tavern room and tried to move his head, he'd felt like an axman with poor aim was chopping at it in a botched execution. Very slowly he sat up, the room spinning. His stomach heaved. Once he had thrown up, he felt a little better. He found his sword and began the long process of trying to stand.

Once upright, he held on to the walls and staggered onto the landing and down the stairs. His legs didn't seem to want to cooperate, so he had to sit down again in the taproom. No one remarked on his state. He probably looked drunk, he thought, although a tentative exploration with his fingers had told him the back of his head was caked in blood and it had run down the side of his face while he was unconscious, giving him the appearance of a ghoul. Vomit stained the front of his jerkin. One or two of the customers glanced at him but made no comment. Perhaps they thought he had been in a drunken fight. Judging from its dark, smoky interior, the tavern was probably the type of lowlife establishment that was used to brawling and knife fights.

How he made his way out into the streets, over London Bridge, and back to Bankside, he wasn't sure. Vague images came back to him like snatches of a dream: the openmouthed shock of a matron and the way she dragged her child to the other side of the road; the disapproving glance of a cleric plainly disgusted that Nick was drunk in the middle of the afternoon; the grin of a carter as he passed in a jingle of harness. No one offered to help him. Nick felt a bit like the poor sod in the gospel parable who had been attacked and robbed and lay there bleeding while everyone passed him by on the other side of the road. He vaguely wondered when his Good Samaritan would appear.

Somehow he ended up sitting on Rivkah's doorstep, his head cupped in his hands. He hadn't even had the strength to knock, but a local, correctly identifying him as a would-be patient of the Jewish doctors, knocked for him.

"Thankee," Nick croaked. Then, when the door opened, "Hello, Rivkah. Thought I'd drop by."

Silently, she had helped him stand and brought him indoors. Sitting him down on a stool, she had set about cleaning the blood off his face and head so she could get an accurate look at the damage.

Now handing him a beaker of water, Rivkah held up her hand in front of Nick's face.

"How many fingers am I holding up?" she asked.

Nick squinted. "Four?"

"Two," she said. "You're seeing double."

"Two of you can't be all bad," Nick replied, trying to grin but wincing instead as his head throbbed.

Rivkah ignored his feeble attempts at flattery. "You may feel sleepy, but you mustn't go to sleep yet," she said. "We don't know why, but head injuries can lead to coma if you sleep, and then sometimes death. Perhaps due to bleeding inside the skull."

Nick looked at her. She was being wonderful. That was the problem. Her kindness and professionalism meant he was merely her patient. But he didn't want to be her patient; he wanted to be her friend, and perhaps more, and he was terribly afraid that he had irretrievably damaged their relationship with his lies and secret life as a spy.

"Rivkah," he said. "I need to explain a few things."

"Not when you are like this," she said. She began to get up from her chair.

"Sit down. Please," he added when he saw her frown at his tone.

She sighed. "You really shouldn't be talking, you know."

"Will you damn well stop being my doctor for a moment?" Nick said. Then immediately regretted it. "Sorry," he muttered. "But I need you to hear me out."

Rivkah folded her hands in her lap. "I'm listening."

"I'm sorry I lied to you about the attack on the London Road," Nick said. "It was an assassination attempt, not a robbery."

Rivkah did not say anything but bowed her head as if accepting his apology. At least he hoped that's what she was doing. He couldn't bear to think that she was hanging her head in sorrow.

He plowed on. "I am, as you now suspect, an agent for Walsingham." He went on to explain how Sir Robert Cecil had coerced him into becoming a spy. "My family's status as a recusant Catholic family puts us all in great jeopardy," he said. "It means, in effect, that we have to constantly prove our loyalty to the Crown. Or at least I do. That means I cannot afford to turn down any assignment I am given, especially if it has to do with Spain. If I spy on Catholic Spain, then it means that I am loyal to the Protestant Crown of England. Do you understand?"

"Why didn't you tell Eli and me this when we first became friends?" she said. "Did you think we would betray you to our fellow countrymen?"

"No! I . . ." Nick swallowed. "I did not want to lose your friendship." It sounded weak and self-serving. He had not meant it to come out like that. What he'd meant to say was that he could not bear never seeing her again, that the mere sight of her cloaked figure hurrying down a street filled him with gladness.

"And we have been useful to you," Rivkah said, thoughtfully. She was referring to the way she and Eli had examined the bodies of the murdered ladies-in-waiting the previous winter and had been able to help Nick find the killer from the clues left on the bodies.

"No!" Nick said. "I mean, yes, you and Eli were invaluable to me. But that's not why I did not tell you I was an agent." He took a drink from the beaker of water she had given him. The words he had in his head were not the ones that came out of his mouth—at least, not the way he wanted to say them. The conversation was slipping out of his grasp.

Rivkah got to her feet and began to put away the bandages and needle and thread she had used on Nick.

"There is something I must tell you," she said, "so that you understand who Eli and I are, where our loyalties lie. It is a long story, but you need to hear it all."

Nick leaned his elbows on the table. "Go on."

"Our great-great-great-grandfather settled in Salamanca in the last century. He was a physician of great repute, and his colleagues were Jews, Christians, and Mohammedans. These religions were all called the People of the Book, and we lived in harmony with one another."

Nick wished Rivkah would sit down, but she continued to move about the tiny room, placing scissors in a jar, rolled bandages in a basket. It was as if she could not keep still. His head ached, but he concentrated on what Rivkah was telling him as best he could.

"Then Isabella of Castile and Ferdinand of Aragon were married, and they united the north of Spain. They took a holy vow before the Pope that they would cleanse the south of Mohammedans and heretics. This they did with great bloodshed and suffering, calling upon the Inquisition to root out heresy by torture and public burnings. Then their attention turned to the Jews. In

1492, a proclamation of expulsion was signed by Isabella and Ferdinand. Only those Jews who were baptized and became *conversos* were allowed to remain. My great-great-grandfather decreed that the family should become *conversos*. This happened long before my birth, so I was born a *converso*. And so," Rivkah said, smiling at Nick, "you and I are the same. You are a recusant Catholic and I am a *converso* Jew. And this state of things was decided for us, by our families."

Nick stared at her. He had not known this, although he had wondered why Eli and Rivkah did not have contact with other Jews living in London and, although the practice of their faith was banned, did not gather in Jewish homes that were secret synagogues.

"We are despised by those Jews who refused to be baptized," she explained, seeing his expression. "That is why we keep ourselves apart. We are doubly exiled, you see."

"But I have eaten with you on your Shabbat," Nick said.

She smiled at him. "See how we trust you?" she said. "We have delivered ourselves into your hands."

"I would never . . ."

"Do you think we do not know this?" Rivkah said. "We are not foolish, and neither are we suicidal."

She paused and gazed for a long time at the kitchen table, tracing the scarred wood with her fingertip.

"For a while, we *conversos* were safe. In order to wage this religious war, Isabella and Ferdinand had borrowed vast amounts of money from Jewish moneylenders. They needed us. And they needed the skills of the physicians of Salamanca to heal their soldiers and combat the plagues that swept through their armies." She looked at him. "But there came a day when Torquemada, the Grand Master of the Inquisition, turned his gaze on us."

Now she did sit down on the chair in front of him, as if suddenly weary with the telling of such an ancient and oft-repeated tale of woe.

"At first they ordered that we live in ghettos. 'For our protection,' the decree said." She smiled bitterly. "But we knew better.

Always the first step leading to annihilation is separation. No longer were we neighbors to the Christians with children just like them, hunger just like them, illness just like them. Now we were set apart like lepers. Soon we were no longer even human."

She poured herself a beaker of water and drank. "One summer the plague was very bad. Many, many died. The Inquisition began to whisper that it was the *conversos* who had caused it by our hypocrisy in 'converting' and the continued practice of our ancient faith. For proof, they pointed to the fact that far fewer of our people had died in the plague. In vain did our rabbis and physicians tell them that it was because we had never had the custom to have rushes on our floors, that we cleaned our houses each week, that somehow the ritual cleansing of our persons and our household goods kept the sickness away. And then there was the fact that we were separated from the Christian populace in the ghetto, so we were protected, to some degree, from contagion."

Rivkah smiled and looked at Nick directly for the first time. "It was common sense, no? You yourself have seen how spotless we keep the infirmary." She held her arms out. "And this house?"

Nick nodded. It was true. Compared to most every other house in Bankside, Eli and Rivkah's house always looked as if an army of invisible servants cleaned the floors and tabletops every day. And he had noticed that Eli and Rivkah seldom got sick.

"But it did no good," Rivkah went on. "The Inquisition said that only fire could purge the evil spells we had put upon the people, that fire alone would destroy the plague. So they incited the people to set fire to the ghetto so these 'holy' churchmen would not have murder on their conscience."

Nick looked down, ashamed. He was a Christian and a Catholic, tainted by the same hypocrisy that had caused his kind to make the Jews scapegoats for their own evil.

"That is how my family died," she said. "That is how Eli and I came to be here as exiles."

Nick opened his mouth to tell her that she had found a home in Bankside, that there were many, many people who loved and revered them, not least he himself. But she held up her hand to forestall him.

"Let me finish," she said. "You may think that when I refer to 'my people,' I mean my family. That is what you mean, is it not? Your family?"

Nick nodded.

"But for Jews it is different. When we think of our people, we mean the Jewish race and not merely our family or our country of birth. I am a Spaniard, but I am a Jewess first. We are in perpetual exile until we can return to the land that Moses led us to out of the wilderness, to our holy city Jerusalem. Until then, we belong nowhere and everywhere, scattered to the four winds."

There were shadows around Rivkah's eyes, as if the telling of her people's history had cost her all her strength.

"This is why I do not consider that you have betrayed us by working against Spain. And neither will Eli."

"What will I not do, Mouse?"

They looked up and saw Eli step into the room. Neither of them had heard him open the door.

"It seems that Nick is a secret agent working for the Crown," Rivkah said, taking her brother's cloak from him.

Eli sat down at the table opposite Nick and poured himself some water. He drained it and wiped his mouth on his sleeve. "Tell me something I don't know," he said.

"You knew?" Nick said.

Eli smiled. "Hard not to with the Queen putting so much confidence in you to solve last winter's murders and the Spider constantly watching your every move. Not to mention your frequent trips to the Continent."

Nick was flabbergasted. "And you knew, too?" he said to Rivkah.

She shrugged. "It was not hard to guess."

"So why did you pretend you did not know when I told you?" Nick said. He felt humiliated and embarrassed. But, most of all, he felt an overwhelming sense of relief. They had both known all along and still had not withdrawn their trust of him.

"Because you needed to tell us yourself," Rivkah said. "It is clear to us both that you have been troubled and this guilt has been inside you a long time. It is good to let the poison out of an infected wound."

"Ever the doctor," Nick said, a little wistfully.

"Of course," she replied. "What did you expect?" But when she took his hand, it was not to take his pulse but to clasp it tightly in both of hers.

CHAPTER 17

City of London

Still reeling from what Rivkah and Eli had revealed to him and also from his head wound, Nick went with John straight to Seething Lane the next morning. But Nick was told that Sir Francis Walsingham had collapsed and had been ordered by his physician to retire to his country estate to recuperate. Typically, he had taken his most trusted men with him: Thomas Phelippes, his code cracker, and Laurence Tomson, his chief secretary. Nick could not imagine that Walsingham planned on getting much rest. Nick left a sealed message revealing Annie's treachery; he demanded that it be sent straight to Walsingham by courier.

Ordinarily, Nick would have thoroughly searched the room in which he had found Annie and del Toro the previous day, but given the state he was in at the time, he was lucky to have made it back to Bankside in one piece. Now he was going to rectify that omission. He led John through the streets to the hole-in-the-wall tavern, thanking God that the blow to the head had not impaired his memory. The tavern was empty except for two sad cases who had collapsed head-down on the rickety tables and were sleeping it off, and the tavernkeeper who was wiping a desultory rag along the bar. When they went up the stairs, the tapster did not even look up, let alone challenge them, which told Nick he was used to people coming and going to the upstairs rooms.

Nick expected to find the room cleaned up in readiness for another occupant, but he was surprised to find it exactly the way he remembered it from the day before. A pool of his blood had dried on the floor where his head had lain, and a couple of the year's first bluebottles were lazily zooming around the blood.

"Del Toro was sitting there," Nick said, pointing to the chair closest to the window. "Annie was there." This was the chair beside the fire with easy access to what he now realized was the poker. The table with her goblet on it was on the other side of the chair, the flagon still lying on the floor where she had thrown it, the poker discarded near the door as soon as it had done its job.

Together they searched the room, stripping the bed down to the straw mattress and then flipping it over to see if anything was hidden underneath, feeling for loose floorboards, slicing pillows open. Nick even ran the tip of his dagger along the sides of the bricks in the hearth to see if there was one that was loose and could be used as a hiding place. Nothing.

"The room doesn't feel as if del Toro was staying here," John said, looking around. "It feels as if it was only used for meetings."

"I think you're right," Nick said. "We need to talk to the tavern owner."

On the way downstairs, Nick knocked on the other door on the landing. When there was no reply, he lifted the latch and went in. It was empty, the bed stripped, the fireplace swept clean. Except for the fire that had been burning in the other room the day before, this room had the same unlived-in feel as the other one. He wondered how a tavern as poor as this could afford to turn away prospective tenants.

Noting that there were no stairs leading to an attic, Nick and John descended to the taproom.

The previous day when he had arrived, Nick had been too intent on following Annie to take notice of the tavern owner. And when he left, he had been far too groggy. Now he made a beeline for him.

"What can I get you gentlemen?" the tapster asked. He showed no sign of having seen Nick the previous day, nor did he comment on what they had been doing upstairs nor even on the dried blood that Nick had yet to wash out of his hair, making it stand up in spikes like the spines of a hedgehog.

Behind the counter, the man's huge belly overhung his belt and swayed like a sack of oats stuffed down his shirt as he moved. Forced to stand a pace or two behind the bar to give his enormous girth room, he was round-shouldered from reaching across the gap to set tankards down on the table in front of him. He gave them his new-customer smile, which was not as welcoming as he thought, as it only served to reveal the blackened stumps of his teeth; if his belly proclaimed him to be a prodigious ale drinker, his decayed teeth told Nick that the tapster was also fond of sack, a wine heavily sweetened with sugar and lime.

Nick could almost hear Rivkah's voice telling him that sugar was iniquitous to teeth. He could imagine her lecturing the Queen on this point, as it was well known that Elizabeth was fond of sweetmeats, and it had been ruinous to her teeth.

"I haven't got all day," he said, abandoning his friendly demeanor. With his bald head, unshaved jowls, and lowering brows above small, hostile eyes, he had the surly appearance of a bulldog about to be loosed into the bear-baiting pit. "What'll it be?"

Nick stepped back from the charnel-house reek of his breath. "Just a few questions."

The man belatedly registered that they were somehow connected with the authorities and had no business going upstairs. Nick saw a shutter slide down behind the man's eyes like a shopkeeper putting his board up for the night. "As I said, I'm busy."

John pointedly surveyed the two sleeping patrons and the otherwise empty tavern. "He's run off his feet," he observed to Nick. "This place is heaving. We must ask him what his secret is." As a tavernkeeper himself, he knew that mornings were the slackest time of the day.

"When did the Spaniard and the young man first approach you to rent the upstairs room?" Nick asked.

"Don't know what you're talking about," the tavernkeeper replied.

But Nick had seen his eyes shift sideways and knew he was lying. He leaned his elbows on the table, even though it brought him in contact with the man's odious breath. "I warn you that if you do not cooperate, you will find yourself on a treason charge."

The man reared back as if Nick had spat in his face. "*Treason!*" he blustered. "I am a loyal citizen of Her Majesty. I know of no treason. I only wanted to make a few shillings."

This last utterance had been tantamount to an admittance, and the man knew it. He looked at the snoring forms of the men at his tables. "Let me see them off first," he muttered. Lumbering around the bar, he grasped each by the back of his collar and heaved them unceremoniously out the door into the street, where they lay in the mud, blinking blearily in the sunlight. The barman slammed the door and bolted it.

"It weren't no Spaniard paid me for the rooms, nor no young man neither," he said, coming back and standing behind the bar as if glad to have a barrier between him and his interrogators. "It were an Englishman. A gent."

"What did he look like?" Nick asked.

The man rubbed his nose. "Dunno," he said. "A gent."

That was how the boatman had said his friend Sam had described the voice of the man talking to the foreigner at Wood Wharf. The foreigner was del Toro, of that Nick was now certain. But the description of the "gent" from both Sam and the tavern-keeper was too vague to be of use. Nick believed him. People from different classes tended only to notice the general characteristic of a class not their own—velvet instead of fustian; an educated voice instead of the cant of local dialect. To most aristocrats, servants were anonymous beings who did the daily chores they themselves were too privileged to soil their hands with. To a working man, a gent was someone who did not work as hard as he did for a living. Both attitudes lay rooted in contempt.

"Could the gent have been a woman disguised as a man?" Nick asked.

The tapster looked at him incredulously. "Are you having me on?"

"I assure you, I have never been so serious in my life."

"It were definitely a man," the tapster said sullenly.

"Weren't you even a tiny bit curious why he wanted to rent out the rooms?" Nick pressed, not bothering to hide the exasperation in his voice.

The man looked at Nick as if he were daft. "It were money, weren't it? Doesn't pay to ask too many questions in my line of business."

Looking around at the miserable tavern, Nick could well believe it. He suspected that the tavernkeeper turned a blind eye to all kinds of shady business dealings going on under his nose, like the fencing of stolen goods and prostitution. In fact, Nick was certain the upstairs chambers were usually used by whores as a place to take their johns, with a kickback coming to the tavern owner from their pimps.

"When did the 'gent' reserve the use of the rooms?" Nick realized that both rooms would have been paid for even if only one of them was used. This was to ensure that the conspirators had privacy. Once they came down the stairs, they could easily mingle with the crowd or slip out the back door. Nick had seen for himself the previous day how little notice was given to people's comings and goings there. This was also a mark of an establishment where illegal business was conducted, a kind of unspoken agreement to mind one's own business. If the authorities came calling—as he and John were now doing—it made lying to them so much easier.

"A month ago?" The man scratched his head. "It were raining, that's all I remember. Can't keep the floors clean with people tracking in mud all day."

As it had rained nonstop throughout the months of March and most of April, this was of no use at all. In fact, it was calculated to be utterly vague. And as the floor was filthy, Nick identified this answer as prevaricating, to say the least. He decided he was beating a dead horse.

Nick also knew it was useless to stake out the tavern to see if Annie, del Toro, or the "gent" returned. Nick's discovery of their hideout had rendered this place dangerous for them now, and they would not return. Even if they thought Nick was dead, they would assume the body would be found and the tavern would become known to the authorities.

"Let's go," he said to John.

★ ★ ★

Their next stop was the house Nick had seen Annie enter disguised as a whore and leave dressed as a youth. Unlike the tavern—a public house—this was a private residence, a single-story house joined on one side to its neighbor on the end of a row of similar dwellings. The house had been selected carefully, situated in Moorgate near the north side of the old city wall; the front door did not give out onto the street but looked down an alley, allowing the inhabitants to come and go unobtrusively. The open expanse of Moorgate on the other side of the alley, with sheep grazing placidly on the grass, only added to the privacy of this entrance. The row of houses looked to have been built at least in the last century for shepherds who kept their flocks on Moorfields for the London butchers. With a back door that led to a narrow strip of overgrown garden leading to a lane at the back of the property, it was an ideal bolt-hole for a traitor who could change her appearance like a chameleon. In addition, the house adjoining it on the other side seemed to be derelict, so there would be no nosy neighbors.

"Want me to go around the back," John asked, "in case she tries to flee?"

Nick shook his head. "No point. She'll be long gone."

The front door was locked. Looking up and down the alley to make sure they were not being observed, Nick kicked it in, instantly regretting it as a bolt of lightning shot through his head.

"I could have done the honors," John said, seeing Nick wince.

"Now you tell me."

They entered a dark hallway with two doors leading off each side and a door at the end, presumably leading to the garden at the back. The door to the left opened to a bedchamber; the door to the right revealed a room with a chair and table at the front near the window and a kitchen area with a fireplace at the back. Both rooms were narrow and ran the length of the house.

"I'll start with the bedroom," Nick said. "You take the other room."

The first thing that struck Nick was the vast amount of clothing hung on hooks and draped over chests—women's petticoats, stomachers, skirts of velvet and plain linen, stockings and garters, men's doublets and hose, even a codpiece. Hanging on the wall next to the window so that it received the most light was a lady's dressing table and chair; above it hung a large Venetian mirror of tin coated in mercury with a sheet of glass laid on top. Set into the front of the frame were tin candlestick holders to give light at night. Nick's mother, the Dowager Countess Agnes, owned such a mirror—a present from his father—and it had cost the old earl a king's ransom.

Scattered on the dressing table were cosmetics of every variety—kohl and charcoal sticks to darken eyebrows or, as Nick had seen, cunningly give the impression of stubble on a man's chin; a jar of ceruse, a white paste made of white lead and vinegar to give the fashionably pale look the Queen herself favored; a pot of vermillion to give the appearance of rosy cheeks and red lips. But there were also items that no lady would have on her dressing table—fake mustaches, eyebrows, and a pointed beard made from real hair, with a pot of glue and a brush so that they could be stuck onto the face. Nick had been in awe of the way Annie could transform herself not only into other characters—whore or lady—but into the opposite gender. This room was where the magic happened, much like the tiring room behind the stage that actors used to change their costumes. Nick's friend Will Shakespeare would die and go to heaven if ever he saw the contents of this room.

Draped over the headpost of the small bed was a flowing blond wig. Nick had seen it before on the head of the whore sitting on del Toro's lap in The Spotted Cow in Oxford. This was proof that Annie had been meeting with del Toro and had intervened when she saw Nick was watching him. Cleverly, she had removed him from Nick's surveillance. Now Nick recalled being passed on the road by a carriage when he was on the way to Oxford. He had not seen who was seated inside because the blinds had been drawn, but he would guess this was Annie, bringing a chest full of her tricks of the trade in case she had to disguise herself. As it turned out, her whore costume had come in handy.

As much as Nick was enraged by Annie's perfidy, he could not help but admire her skill as a spy. Seldom had he met anyone who possessed such consummate spy craft as she. If only she were working for Walsingham and not the Spanish. In some ways, he regretted the need to hunt her down and bring her to justice, which meant the headsman's ax. Such a waste of talent, he thought. But it would not stop him, however much Nick preferred not to have to do violence to women. A traitor was a traitor. And Annie had Simon Winchelsea's blood on her hands and had tried to kill Nick and Thomas. When it came to it, Nick would show no mercy.

Unfortunately, one of the signs of her professionalism was that he discovered nothing at her house that would tie her to del Toro, no letter buried in one of the chests under the wigs and other paraphernalia, no secret hoard of Spanish gold. John reported the same after his search of the other room.

"Seems like this was a place to store her disguises," John said, lewdly fitting the codpiece over his privates. "How do I look?" It was one of those absurdly inflated ones designed to make the wearer appear as generously hung as a prize bull.

"I've never understood the fashion for those," Nick said. "It suggests you have something to hide. Like a freakishly small . . ."

John threw the codpiece onto the bed as if it had burned him.

CHAPTER 18

The Palace of Whitehall

After they left the house in Moorfields, Nick had no choice but to continue on to Whitehall in order to inform the Spider of Annie's treason and her collaboration with a Spanish agent, as well as his conviction that she was responsible for the death of Simon Winchelsea and the attempted poisoning of Thomas. He was also convinced that Annie had arranged the assassination attempt on him, for he now knew for certain that the whore he had seen in The Spotted Cow had been none other than Annie.

Nick's snaillike progress through the London streets was due to the fact that each step he took sent a shock of pain through his head—it was like having the worst hangover of his life without the benefits of getting rip-roaringly drunk the night before. But he was also in the unenviable position of having to confess to Cecil that he had let del Toro slip through his fingers a second time. In short, Nick was in a foul mood, exacerbated by the fact that they had found no evidence at either the tavern or the house.

"I should have realized that the reason she was drinking so much was to make the flagon lighter so she could throw it at me," he said for the umpteenth time. "Stupid, stupid."

"I think that's pretty clever," John said.

Nick gave him an irritated look. "I mean, I'm the one who's stupid."

"No arguments there." But John slapped his friend on the shoulder to take the sting out of his words.

"Tell me again what happened when you followed Gavell and Stace," Nick said. "I'm afraid I wasn't too alert last night."

"You nodded off in the middle of my account."

After Rivkah had patched him up, Eli had walked with Nick back to The Black Sheep. The taproom had been full and the noise was agony on Nick's head, so Eli had helped him up the stairs to his bedchamber. John and Hector had followed them up.

"What the hell happened?" John exclaimed, seeing Nick's bandaged head.

"Softly, John," Nick moaned.

Hector had jumped onto the bed and rested his huge head on Nick's knee, his eyes looking mournfully into his as if to say, *Look what happens when I'm not around to protect you.*

"He was hit over the head with a poker by an irate woman in drag," Eli told John. "Lucky he's got a hard head." Then, grinning at the stupefied expression on John's face, Eli had taken his leave.

★ ★ ★

"I followed Gavell and Stace to a tavern and watched them drink all afternoon," John said as they made their way through Cheapside. "At some point, they were joined by Edmund."

"I thought they hated him?" Nick said, remembering how the hired thugs had attempted to beat Edmund up at Wood Wharf.

John shrugged. "They were pretty drunk, and Edmund was buying."

Nick could never remember Edmund being flush enough to stand drinks for everyone before. He hadn't appeared to have two groats to rub together. Perhaps Essex was a generous paymaster to his spies? Nick remembered Francis Bacon complaining about Walsingham's parsimoniousness; his presence at Leicester House must mean that he sensed profit to be made paying court to Essex.

They slogged on through the mud of the London streets. Early spring had been the wettest and coldest in memory. Nick remembered sleet falling on his journey to Oxford. But the gray clouds that had hung over the city for months had now miraculously cleared and blue sky could be seen above the buildings, although the sunshine did not penetrate where the upper stories of the buildings hung tipsily over the streets. It was only the more open spaces like St. Paul's Cross, Finsbury Fields, Convent Garden, Moorfields—where they had just come from—or the Royal Parks that received full sun, and there the trees would be beginning to show their buds. Here in the warren of streets in the heart of the city, it was perpetual dusk.

Still, the air was milder, and sensing the coming of spring, London's collective voice had miraculously grown less quarrelsome.

"Morning, gents," a grocer's lad called out cheerily. "Apples only five a penny."

"You can stick your apples . . ." Nick began. His head was throbbing, and the joyous sounds of London awakening to spring were more than he could bear. Even the birds cheeping raucously from the eaves was a torture. He longed for a cold, pelting rain that kept everyone huddled miserably indoors.

Quickly, John pulled Nick on.

"Misery guts," the lad yelled after them.

Nick was also sick of people staring at the bandage around his head as if he were Lazarus emerged from the tomb, so he took it off and stuffed it inside his jerkin. The last straw would be the palace guards making jests at his expense. He also did not want to advertise to the Spider how thoroughly Annie had bested him. If he was truthful, it was the fact that she had managed to outwit him a second time that was the real reason for his bad temper. His pride had been far more sorely injured than his head.

"Rivkah will have your guts for garters," John remarked.

"Only if you tell her," Nick said, smiling for the first time that day. The thought of Rivkah's professional pique filled him with gladness and brought back the feel of her fingers as she held his hand, the steadiness of her voice as she recounted an experience of such horror that it would have broken the spirit of someone with less courage. She had also told him that Thomas was out of danger and would live.

Suddenly, Nick felt churlish to be so out of sorts with the day. The advent of spring now appeared like a good omen: not only would his head mend, but he would track down Annie and bring her to justice. Even the knowledge that she was a traitor and a murderer could not destroy his everlasting thankfulness that now there were no more secrets between him and Rivkah, secrets that had kept him sleepless for many a night and had haunted his days.

★ ★ ★

Leaving John to drink a pint of ale with the off-duty lads at the Guard House, Nick made his way to Cecil's rooms. He walked straight in without knocking and, before Cecil could open his mouth to protest, told him that he had incontrovertible proof that Annie was a double agent working for Spain. As he spoke, Nick saw Cecil's irritation at being interrupted evaporate. By the end of his account, Cecil was positively beaming, a sight that Nick found a little unnerving, so seldom did the Spider show happiness.

"Why, that's absolutely splendid," Cecil said. "Well done." Then, as an afterthought, "How's your head?" Without waiting for an answer, he stood up and began pacing the floor, rubbing his hands together. With his small size and the hump on his back, which had caused the Queen to nickname him Pygmy, he looked to Nick more like a troll prowling in his cave. "We've got him now," Cecil said. "By God, we've got him."

"Sorry?"

"Essex. He's done for. The Queen won't tolerate this. A traitor and a murderess in his vaunted spy network. Oh, this is splendid." Cecil was virtually chuckling with glee. It was as bizarre a sight as Nick had ever seen. And as infuriating. Cecil seemed to have forgotten the death of Winchelsea and Thomas's near death. All he seemed to care about was showing up Essex for an incompetent fool and discrediting him with the Queen. It was as if he had been transformed into a malicious boy. He couldn't wait to run and tell tales on his hated adoptive brother.

"Remember that Walsingham did not want the Queen to know about del Toro," Nick cautioned. He still didn't understand why that was, but he was prepared to trust Walsingham's judgment, at lease for the present. Whether the Queen knew or not did not affect Nick's ability to search for del Toro and Annie.

"Are you mad?" Cecil said, stopping his pacing and staring at Nick. "She will have to know that Essex is employing a traitor. Walsingham is ill. He wasn't thinking straight."

It's you who isn't thinking straight, Nick thought.

"I sent a courier with a message informing him," he said.

"You did *what?*" Cecil almost shouted. "Damn. I shall have to act fast. Come on," he said to Nick.

"Where are we going?"

"Why, to inform the Queen about Essex, of course." Cecil looked at him as if Nick were a particularly stupid pupil.

Nick shook his head. "Not me."

"Might I remind you that you work for me," Cecil said.

"And you work for Walsingham. For whatever reason, he did not tell the Queen of del Toro's presence in London. I don't know why, but he must have his reasons. If you inform Her Majesty that Annie is a spy, then you will have to tell her that Annie is working with del Toro."

"Are you questioning my loyalty?" Cecil demanded.

"No. Just your judgment. I think you're letting your rivalry with Essex get the better of you. All you can think about is discrediting his spy network, a network that he set up in competition to yours. There may be more things at stake here than your personal hatred for Essex. At least wait until the courier returns with a reply from Walsingham."

"Get out," Cecil said.

Nick turned and left.

"I shan't forget your insubordination, Holt," Cecil shouted after him. "It will go ill with you and your family."

CHAPTER 19

Leicester House

Nick brooded on Cecil's none-too-subtle threat to his family all the way to Leicester House. Coupled with the fact that del Toro had confessed that he was talking to prominent recusant families, it meant that Robert and his entire family could be in grave danger. Nick had to own that one of the reasons he favored keeping the knowledge of del Toro's presence from the Queen—at least for the time being—was so that this aspect of the Spaniard's mission would not come out. He thanked God that Robert had not actually met with del Toro. In fact, Nick had Annie to thank for that, he realized, for she had whisked del Toro away before Robert had arrived at The Spotted Cow. And there were plenty of witnesses to attest to this, Alan the tavern owner for one.

Not for the first time, Nick found himself in a cleft stick: if he captured del Toro and Annie and brought them to justice, it would come out that the Spaniard was soliciting support from recusant families, Robert included, and that would place his own family in jeopardy. If he did not, then a murderer and traitor would go free.

"You did the right thing," John assured him after Nick had told him about his quarrel with Cecil. "Better to be on the outs with the Spider than with the Queen."

"I hope so," Nick said. "But if Walsingham dies, I'm fucked."

"Better pray that he doesn't."

★   ★   ★

Arriving at Leicester House, they went straight into the front entrance and up the stairs to the second floor. Nick wanted to search Annie's bedchamber before the Queen sent the palace guards over, as she surely would once Cecil told her that Annie was conspiring with the Spanish. He expected to find Essex in the building, frothing at the mouth at the accusations leveled at his beloved, but there was no sign of him. A servant informed Nick that Essex had left for Whitehall early that morning to take advantage of the beautiful spring weather by going hunting with the Queen. With any luck, Cecil was even now kicking his heels in the corridors outside the royal chambers and would be waiting all day for the Queen and Essex to return.

Annie's bedchamber was tidy, and only a few of her costumes hung from hooks on the wall—Meg the prostitute that frequented The Angel, and a man's doublet and hose. A scabbard with a knife in it was lying on the bedside table. Nick removed the knife from the sheath and examined it, but as with the knives of Gavell and Stace that he had confiscated after his fight with them at Wood Wharf, the dark, threadlike stains between the blade and the hilt could have come from any animal, and the blood itself was not proof it had been used to cut Simon Winchelsea's throat.

Once again, they found no evidence of collusion with del Toro, no papers or even letters in cipher. Aside from the two costumes, the bedchamber could have been the chamber of any young woman.

Nick and John turned the mattress, and Nick had just made a long slash in it with his dagger when there was a thundering on the stairs and Henry Gavell and Richard Stace burst into the room.

"What the hell do you think you're doing in Annie's room?" Gavell demanded.

"Annie is a traitor working for the Spanish," Nick said. "She also murdered Winchelsea and tried to murder Sir Thomas Brighton and me."

"You lie," Gavell said, his hand going to his sword. Stace squared up beside him, his dagger drawn.

"I'll pretend I didn't hear that," Nick said. The accusation of being a liar was an automatic signal for a duel of honor. Nick had no intention of engaging in one. For one thing, his head still hurt and he knew he would be slow in a sword fight; for another, he considered such duels to be childish, having less to do with chivalric honor and more to do with wounded pride.

Even so, he glanced at John, and they both moved away from the bed so they would have room to maneuver if Gavell and Stace attacked. John had his hand on his dagger but did not draw it.

"I saw Annie meeting with a Spanish agent with my own eyes," Nick said. "I'm afraid it's incontrovertible."

"You are a base liar," Gavell said, advancing on Nick with his sword drawn. "Ever since you came here, you have been causing trouble. It's not Annie who is a traitor but you."

"You're making a big mistake," Nick said, drawing his own sword.

"Not so brave without your dog, are you?" Gavell sneered. Then he lunged. Nick parried the blow and, at the same time, snatched up the coverlet from the bed and threw it at Gavell. It draped itself over one of Gavell's shoulders, and he shrugged it off.

"Nice try," he said, circling Nick, the point of his sword held rock-steady in the direction of Nick's heart.

Out of the corner of his eye, Nick saw John and Stace clash daggers, then break apart, circling each other warily. But he didn't have time to worry about him, as Gavell stamped forward and thrust the point of his sword at Nick's chest. Nick made as if he were going to parry the blow again, then at the last minute twisted sideways and watched as the point of the blade slid past him. He leapt behind Gavell and kicked him in the back, making him fall forward. Then he placed his sword point square in the middle of Gavell's back.

"Drop your sword," Nick said, "or I will run you through."

Gavell slid his sword across the room.

"Now tell your friend to do the same."

"Richard," Gavell said. "Do as he says."

Stace dropped his dagger and stepped back.

John kicked it under the bed.

"Now, gentlemen," Nick said, taking his sword from Gavell's back and motioning for him to stand. "I hope this is the end to this foolishness. The person you should be blaming is not me or John but Annie. She is the one who has betrayed you."

"Never," Gavell said. "She would never do that to His Lordship or to us."

Nick was surprised to see a kind of furious hurt in Gavell's eyes and realized that, for all his violence, he was a loyal man. He had defended his fellow agent in the only way he knew how—at sword point. For the first time, Nick felt a kind of respect for him.

"I'm sorry," Nick said.

He glanced at Stace, but if the huge man harbored a similar loyalty, Nick could not tell. More likely he just blindly followed Gavell's lead, much as Ralph dumbly followed Black Jack Sims's grandson Johnnie. Even now he was looking to his friend for instructions.

"Let's go, Richie," Gavell said. Then, to Nick, "You haven't seen the last of us, that I promise. We're going to make you pay for your damnable lies."

Once Gavell and Stace had left the room, Nick and John sat down on opposite sides of the bed.

"Phew," Nick said. "He almost had me. He's not a bad swordsman."

"That lout Stace knows how to use his knife, I'll give him that," John replied. "If you hadn't got Gavell to call him off, I'd have been in trouble."

Nick saw him wiping a smear of blood off his neck. "Are you hurt?"

"Nah," John said. "Just a scratch."

"Better not let Maggie see that."

"I'll tell her I cut myself shaving."

At that moment, Edmund ran into the room. "I just saw Gavell and Stace downstairs," he said. "What's this about Annie being a traitor?"

Nick explained what had happened the previous day.

Edmund joined them on the bed, sitting down heavily and putting his head in his hands. "I just can't believe it," he said.

Nick remembered that Edmund was a little in love with Annie. He put his hand on his shoulder.

"I'm sorry," he said for the second time. "But believe it."

"And she is conspiring with this Spaniard, del Toro?"

Nick nodded.

"Oh, my God. His Lordship will be devastated."

"He'll be more than that," Nick said. "I'm afraid his spy network is utterly discredited. My guess is the Queen will pack him back to the Netherlands in a hurry."

Edmund looked up. "That means I'll be out of a job."

Nick hadn't considered this, but he realized Edmund was correct. He only hoped Edmund did not ask him to recommend him to Walsingham, for in all truth, he could not. Edmund was too trusting, too easily taken in. He was lucky to be alive after approaching the assassin on the London Road.

Edmund was still leaning forward, and Nick saw a chain around his neck with a ring threaded through it.

"A love token?" he joked, touching it with one finger.

Edmund dropped the ring back inside his shirt and sat up. "My father's seal ring," he said. "It was all he left me."

"Surely the farm . . . ?" Nick began, but then could have bitten off his tongue.

Edmund smiled bitterly. "The farm was sold to pay off his debts," he said.

Nick and John exchanged glances behind Edmund's back. The debts had been the fine that Nick's father, the old earl, had imposed on Edmund's father for enclosing common land. But it was not the fine that had impoverished Edmund's family—with good husbandry, the family would have recovered their former wealth in time—but that Edmund's father had been a drunkard and gambled the rest of his fortune away. After bankrupting himself, he had then hanged himself. Shortly after that, Edmund had come up to Oxford. Nick had heard rumors that a distant cousin of the family had paid for Edmund's education so that he could make his own way in the world after losing his inheritance. Now Edmund was going to lose his job with Essex.

Nick clapped Edmund on the back and stood up. "Let's go and have something to eat at The Angel," he said. "I'm buying."

But their plan was forestalled by the sight of Essex riding into the forecourt of Leicester House, his horse in a lather as if he had ridden it at a gallop from St. James's Park down the Strand, which afterward Nick heard was exactly what he'd done. He drew the horse up by wrenching cruelly on its bit and almost sitting it down on its haunches, its eyes rolling white with alarm. Essex flung himself out of the saddle.

"What the hell is this I hear, Holt?" he raged. He grabbed Nick's shirt and pulled him toward him. "What lies have you been spreading about Annie?"

"Unhand me, my Lord," Nick said.

Essex looked at his hand grasping Nick's shirt as if it were not his own. Nick thought he was about to see a famous display of Essex's choleric nature and braced himself for a scuffle; then he saw something click in Essex's eyes as if he had woken up and realized where he was. Essex let go of Nick's collar and stepped back, visibly trying to get his temper under control, but the veins in his forehead were bulging and he was breathing hard, spots of color staining his cheeks and neck.

"That low-born cripple Cecil has just informed the Queen that Annie is a traitor working for the Spanish," he said. "He said that this is information you brought him this morning. Is this true?"

"I'm afraid it is," Nick replied.

John had moved to stand closely on Nick's right side. Edmund had taken a tentative step toward Essex, then stopped midway. Perhaps it was loyalty to Essex, or perhaps it was a desire to remove himself out of striking range should Essex assault Nick. But it put him in an oddly ambivalent place, a kind of moral no-man's-land. Nick couldn't help thinking that if Gavell had been present, he would have done as John had and arranged himself shoulder to shoulder with his master, his loyalties clear.

Essex turned away and ran his fingers through his hair distractedly. Then, seeing his horse still unattended, he bawled for a stable lad. When a youngster arrived, Essex turned his full fury on the poor lad, berating him for not appearing sooner, blaming him for the horse's lathered state. Nick thought it badly done for Essex to take his spleen out on an innocent boy.

"Come inside and explain it to me," Essex said.

"We were on our way to The Angel to have a bite to eat," Nick said. "Join us."

Essex looked at him. "Are you refusing an order?" he asked.

Nick looked calmly back. "I take orders from the Queen."

"I speak for Her Majesty."

"I think not," Nick said, remembering the quarrel between Essex and Elizabeth. "Come on, John." He and John walked away. Edmund did not follow. "Are you coming, Edmund?" Nick called back over his shoulder.

"I . . . er . . . I think I'll pass," Edmund said.

"Nobody walks away from me, you piece of shit," Essex yelled after them.

"I smell burning," John muttered.

"What's that?" Nick asked, puzzled.

"The bridge you just torched between yourself and His Lordship. Not to mention the one with Cecil."

"Fuck them," Nick said. "I'm hungry. And we have a traitor to catch."

CHAPTER 20

The Black Sheep Tavern, Bankside

Nick spent the next three days at The Black Sheep. Hector was ecstatic to have his master around, but Nick had an ulterior motive. He wanted to let the news of Annie's treachery spread through the gossip vines of London and eventually reach her ears. With the prospect of war with Spain looming, any talk of treason would spread like wildfire in the city. His motive for going to The Angel the day he met with Cecil and had the fight with Gavell and Stace was to spread the word about Annie and his role in uncovering her treason. Patrons in their cups talked, and there was no better way of baiting his hook than to talk freely in a tavern, making sure he was overheard.

Nick was convinced Annie was still in London. If nothing else, the gossip would tell her that he was not, in fact, dead as she had thought. He knew she had gone to ground, but he hoped he could lure her out in order to finish the job that she had failed to do twice: once on the London Road and once in the tavern. Should she ever be brought to trial, it was Nick's testimony that could send her to the block. If Nick was out of the way, there would be no proof. Therefore, she had a powerful motive to try to kill him a third time.

The Spider had sent him a message saying that, even though he had ordered the ports shut down after receiving Nick's report about del Toro and Annie, del Toro had managed to slip through and take a merchant ship to Calais. An agent in France had reported that he had been alone when he disembarked, so evidently he and Annie had split up. The Spider seemed to imply that del Toro's escape was Nick's fault for delaying reporting in until the next day, even though he knew Nick had been half unconscious from the blow to his head.

Nick had shrugged at this message. It was Annie who had murdered Winchelsea and it was Annie he wanted. He was heartened when the Spider's message said that all shipping to Ireland had been suspended until she was caught.

Now that spring had finally arrived, he took Hector for long walks in Paris Garden and wandered aimlessly around Southwark, trying to make himself as conspicuous as possible but keeping an eagle eye out for anyone who approached him on the streets or seemed to be watching him. The trouble was, he had no idea whom he was looking for, as Annie was bound to be disguised. So anyone who came within fifty yards of him was scrutinized, be it a soot-begrimed blacksmith's apprentice or a beefy washer woman on the steps of St. Mary's Queen Dock. Nick was also relying on Hector to alert him to Annie's presence, whatever protean shape she took. That was Annie's one small mistake—making friends with his dog.

On the fourth morning, he was slouched on a stool in the tap room of The Black Sheep, breaking his fast with bread and small beer, when John appeared from his family's quarters at the back of the tavern.

"Where are you off to?" Nick asked.

"Another meeting at the Brewers' Guild," John said. He was carrying a small cask of ale under one arm. "They want to sample Maggie's brew before they make up their minds." He pulled a face. "Cadge a free drink, more like. Bloody sods."

"Can you do me a favor," Nick said, "and drop in at Seeth-ing Lane to see if Walsingham has replied to my message?" He frowned. "It's strange that he hasn't replied. I only hope it's not because he's dead."

"You would have heard, surely?" John said.

"Not necessarily. The Queen might want to keep it quiet because of the situation with Spain. Losing her Secretary of State and head of her spy network would make us look vulnerable."

"I'll stop by," John promised.

After doing some chores for Maggie—hefting barrels of her newly made beer up the cellar steps and into the taproom behind the bar in readiness for the evening's trade—he decided to have a wander around Southwark with Hector and then go round to Kat's and see how Thomas was faring.

★ ★ ★

Thomas was recovering but still looked wan. At least he was freshly shaved and wearing clean linen. No doubt due to female ministrations, Nick thought. He eyed the door that led to Kat's own bed-chamber. It was suspiciously ajar.

"Just in case I take a funny turn in the middle of the night," Thomas said, noticing the direction of his gaze.

"Ha!" Nick said. He signaled for Hector to jump up on the bed and drape himself across Thomas's chest. "Say hello to Thomas, Hector. He missed you."

"Get the big brute off." Thomas's voice was muffled by Hector's shaggy chest and forepaws.

Despite savoring the sight of Thomas thrashing around under his enormous dog, Nick nodded for Hector to move.

"I'm surprised you're not up and about," Nick said, surveying his friend, who was irritably picking dog hair off his nightshirt.

"Oh, I'm up all right," Thomas said, leering. "All these lovely ladies see to that."

But Nick could see this was pure bluster on Thomas's part. He still looked weak, and his forehead was beaded with sweat.

Kat breezed in. "Talking about me again?" She sat down on the bed and threw her arms around Hector. "Who's a beautiful dog, then?" Joyously, Hector began slathering her face, his tail beating on the bed, making the whole structure shake.

Both Nick and Thomas watched enviously.

"Heard you had your own run-in with a lovely lady, Nick?" Kat said, sitting up and wiping the slobber off her face with a corner of the coverlet. "One in drag, no less."

"Oh, do tell," Thomas said, perking up.

Nick told them about Annie and del Toro. He was just explaining how he intended to lure Annie out in the open by making himself a target when there was a hammering on the front door of the brothel, shouting down below, then the sound of someone racing up the stairs.

Henry, Maggie's fifteen-year-old son and John's stepson, burst into the room. If his presence in the brothel was startling enough—he had been strictly enjoined never to set foot in the establishment on pain of death by his parents—the expression on his face was even more so. He looked stricken. He didn't even blush when he saw Kat reclining on the bed.

"Nick," he said. "Father's been hurt. Badly." Here his voice broke, but whether from his age or from tears stubbornly held back, Nick didn't know. Nick leapt to his feet and took Henry by the shoulders.

"How?" he said. "Where?"

Henry shook his head and scuffed at his eyes with his sleeve. "Don't know. Two men brought him to The Black Sheep. I told Eli and Rivkah on the way over. They'll be there now. You must come."

Nick briefly held the boy to him. "It'll be all right, Henry. John is as strong as an ox, you'll see." His voice was even, but inside, Nick felt as if a fist were squeezing his heart.

Without bidding farewell to either Thomas or Kat, Nick and Henry ran down the stairs with Hector loping behind them.

On the way back to the tavern, all Nick could think was that John had been mistaken for him, that it should have been he, Nick, who was attacked, not his friend.

Please God, let him be alive. Please God, Nick kept repeating to himself as he ran down the streets. Then, *It's all my fault.*

As they neared the tavern, Nick heard Hector howling.

★ ★ ★

Nick expected to find the taproom in an uproar, but after he had shushed Hector, it was strangely quiet. Two men were sitting quietly on a bench near the fire. Nick was astonished to see that it was

Henry Gavell and Richard Stace. Nick heard Matty in the back rooms consoling a crying baby Jane.

"What are you doing here?" Nick asked.

"We're the ones who brought him," Gavell said.

Nick didn't have time to question him further. "Where is he?"

"They carried him upstairs," Gavell said, pointing up to where Nick's room was located. "The doctors are with him now."

Nick and Henry ran up the stairs and into Nick's bedchamber.

John was stretched out on the bed, his face white, his nostrils strangely pinched at the edges and his eyes sunken. A bandage was wrapped around his head, obscuring most of his hair. Nick gave a shiver of premonition. John looked as if he had been prepared for burial with a bandage to keep his jaw from falling open. Maggie was on her knees beside the bed, holding one of John's hands and weeping.

Henry rushed to kneel beside his mother, putting his arms around her.

"Is he . . . ?" Nick began to say, but couldn't get the word out. He was paralyzed by the facsimile of a deathbed scene before his eyes.

Rivkah came to him quickly. "He lives," she said, putting a hand on his arm. "His pulse is weak, but he lives." Those were almost the exact words she had used for Thomas.

Nick suddenly felt as if his legs wouldn't hold him up. He sank down on a stool and put his head in his hands.

"He is in a coma," Eli said, his face grave. Then in a low voice so Maggie and Henry would not hear, "We fear he may not wake."

Nick lifted his head. "What can I do?"

"Nothing," Rivkah said. "All we can do is wait."

Nick stood and went over to the bed. He looked down at his friend lying so still, so deathlike that the covers over his chest barely moved.

"I'm sorry," he said, reaching down and touching John's hand.

"Sorry?" Maggie said, looking up at him. "You're sorry?" Then suddenly she was on her feet, beating at Nick's chest and face with her fists, screaming into his face. "What was he doing in Seething

Lane? He was only meant to go to the Brewers' Guild. You should have gone yourself rather than always getting John to run your errands. You call him a friend, but he is nothing but a servant to you. As are we all to your exalted kind, Your Lordship." She spat out this last, and Nick flinched.

He did nothing to defend himself but stood there, the blows thudding against him. In a strange way, he welcomed her anger, her fists striking his face. It was a kind of atonement for the guilt he felt. She was right. He had treated John like a lackey. Nick was no better than Essex. Not only had Nick used John to do his dirty work, but he had dragged all those he cared about most in the world into a cesspit of lies, treason, and death. Now his best friend lay mortally injured and might never recover. If Nick could have changed places with John, he would gladly have done so. Now, because of his abominable pride, it was too late.

Then Henry was pulling his mother off. "Don't," he said. "It isn't Nick's fault."

"It is my fault," Nick said. Then he turned and left the room.

★ ★ ★

In the taproom below, Nick sat heavily on a bench, his hands loose between his knees. Hector came over and leaned against his legs. Nick draped an arm over the dog's flanks and pressed his face into his neck.

"Sorry about your mate," Gavell said.

Nick sat up. "Forgive my manners," he said. "I must thank you for bringing John here." He got up, went behind the bar, and drew off three tankards of ale. He gave one each to the men and sat down with the third. Of course, it was possible that the two men had attacked John themselves and then, posing as Good Samaritans, brought him to The Black Sheep in order to get closer to Nick on his home turf. Nick knew he should not take anything they said at face value.

"Tell me what happened," Nick said, turning to Gavell.

Gavell was looking at him suspiciously. He took a drink, wiping his mouth on his sleeve, perhaps a delaying tactic in order to get his story straight. Nick waited, idly fondling Hector's ears but keeping a sharp eye on Gavell's expression for any sign that he was lying.

"Me and Richie figured that if we staked out Seething Lane, sooner or later we'd catch you going in to report to Walsingham." He gave a small smile. "We thought we'd rough you up a bit to teach you a lesson."

"Fair enough," Nick said. So far, Gavell's account had the ring of truth. Nick had gotten the best of them in two fights, and it must have rankled them deeply. He could imagine them brooding on their humiliation and plotting revenge.

"Then we saw your friend go in. We wondered if he were just meeting you and that you'd come out with him, so we waited. Then we saw this man come round the side of the building. He looked suspicious-like, as if he'd been hiding there. When your friend came out, this other man hit him with something from behind."

Gavell looked at Nick. "It wasn't sportsmanlike," he said, "to come at him from behind. A dirty trick, if you ask me."

So was waiting to ambush Nick in Seething Lane, Nick thought. This was where their story began to sound implausible.

The lines around Gavell's eyes crinkled in amusement.

"Think I'm just a thug, don't you?" he said. "But I have my standards."

Nick nodded. "I don't doubt it."

"Anyway, me and Richie shouted and ran over. The man was going to hit him again in the head, but he scarpered when he saw us coming."

"Did you get a look at him?"

Gavell shook his head. "He was wearing a cloak with the hood pulled up."

Conveniently anonymous, Nick thought. Only John could tell him what really happened, so there was no evidence to gainsay Gavell's story. Even if John woke up, there was a very real possibility he would remember nothing of his attack. Rivkah had warned Nick that memory loss was a common side effect of severe blows to the head.

"Could John's assailant have been a woman?" Nick asked.

Gavell opened his mouth to protest, then shut it again. He looked into his drink. "I hate to think it."

That, at least, was an honest answer, Nick thought.

They sat in silence for a few moments. Nick was picturing John facedown on the ground, his assailant poised to give him his death blow. Wary as he was of Gavell and Stace, he would always be grateful to them for intervening.

"Anyway, I checked to see if he were living," Gavell went on. "Then I got Richie to pick him up, and we brought him here."

"Why didn't you take him into the house on Seething Lane?" Nick asked.

"We thought his wife would prefer it if we brought him here," Gavell said.

When Nick looked startled, Gavell chuckled. "We've done our homework on you and your friend," he said. "We're not as dumb as we look. Well, I'm not," he added. "Now Richie there"—he nodded at his friend leaning against the bar happily consuming his fourth tankard of ale—"*is* as dumb as he looks. But there's no harm in him. Born like that."

Like Ralph, Nick thought.

"Why did you set on Edmund at Wood Wharf?" Nick asked.

Gavell shrugged. "Can't stand the little git. Always licking Essex's arse. Showing up when he's not wanted."

To a man like Gavell, who had probably been born into poverty and made his own way in the world since birth, a man like Edmund, who had been raised in comparative wealth as the son of a prosperous farmer, was incomprehensible. What Gavell took for weakness and sycophancy was probably Edmund's anxiety at the very real prospect of penury. The highways and byways of England were filled with landless men looking for work. Edmund must be terrified of becoming one of them—unshaved, ragged, starving, wandering the countryside like packs of feral dogs. It made Nick feel all the more guilty that he couldn't, in all conscience, recommend Edmund to Walsingham when Essex returned to the Netherlands.

He wondered whether Robert could take him on as a secretary or recommend him to someone in Oxford. Nick made a mental note to ask his brother when he next saw him. After all, he owed Edmund his life.

Before Nick could defend Edmund to Gavell, Eli and Rivkah came down the stairs. Both were somber.

Nick stood, expecting the worst. "How is he?"

"The same," Eli said. "I'm going home to study some of my books about head injuries. I may learn something there that will help, but I think the only thing we can do is keep him quiet and wait. Sometimes the brain has a way of healing itself. We don't know why. So far there is no sign of swelling. If that should happen, I will have to relieve the pressure on his brain."

"How will you do that?" Nick asked, fearing the answer.

"By removing a small piece of his skull and draining out the blood," Eli said. "The ancient Greeks did it, and I have seen it done in Spain."

Nick shuddered. "Was it successful?"

Eli shook his head. "The procedure is simple enough, but the shock of it can kill the patient even if the subsequent infection does not. I'm sorry I do not have better news."

"Pray for him," Rivkah said, putting her hand on Nick's arm and giving it a squeeze. "We will be back later. If there is any change, send for Eli at home and me at the infirmary."

Nick and Gavell sat down again. Maggie had stopped wailing, but somehow her silence was worse. Nick was afraid to go up in case he provoked her again. He felt utterly helpless. He couldn't even help with the baby, as he could hear Matty singing a soft lullaby to her in the back room.

"I'd better get Richie back or he'll drink himself blind," Gavell said after a while.

Nick nodded. "Will you inform me if you spot Annie?" That would be a test of Gavell's story, Nick thought. If they truly wanted to catch John's assailant and the murderer of a fellow agent, they would do as he asked, even if that meant betraying a friend.

Gavell nodded glumly. "I reckon. But I still can't believe that lass could be capable of such a cowardly act."

★ ★ ★

After Gavell and Stace left, Nick took a piece of parchment and wrote on it: *Closed until further notice: sickness in the family.* Then he nailed it to the front door of The Black Sheep.

CHAPTER 21

The Black Sheep Tavern, Bankside

Instead of walking around Southwark, Nick spent the next week wandering around London with Hector. He now realized he should have done this from the first, that Annie was not likely to cross London Bridge into his territory, that she would have more chance of stalking him in the city. He had given Hector a handkerchief of Annie's that he had taken from her room at Leicester House to smell, but in a city as large and populated as London, Nick knew even Hector's nose would not be able to track her.

Each night he returned to The Black Sheep to keep vigil beside John's bed while Maggie slept with her arms pillowed under her head on the coverlet. Maggie had forgiven him, or at least she did not rail at him anymore but went about the tavern quietly, almost without speaking, even to her own children. Nick would have preferred her to take out her anger at him, to scald him with words of reproach and vituperation, to bruise his face with her fists. It was what he deserved.

Nick, Maggie, and Henry spelled each other beside John's bedside, seeing to his needs, dribbling water and clear broth into his mouth in order to give him some nourishment. Rivkah and Eli came multiple times a day, each time checking for bleeding in John's brain. Each day they did not find it, they counted it a good sign. But still John did not awaken out of his deathlike slumber.

The tavern remained closed. Customers came to ask about John, then went away again, shaking their heads. If they were angry that they had lost their chief source of entertainment and gossip after a hard day's work, no one gave a sign of it. Instead, small gifts were left outside the door or placed shyly on the bar top—homemade pies, a bucket of fresh milk for the baby, cress and asparagus newly picked from Paris Garden, a bunch of wildflowers, an enormous carp. Even Black Jack Sims, the local crime lord, sent one of his heavies round to ask if there was anything he could do. Maggie turned him away—she would have no truck with criminals—so the man left a gold angel on the bar top and silently left.

Codpiece arrived by barge with a servant carrying a huge basket of luxury foods, like quails' eggs and white manchet loaves made only with the finest flour for the royal table, custard possets, honeycombs, plucked capons for making broth, and many other good and nourishing things. And a magnificent coverlet made from a dozen lambskins expertly stitched together by the Queen's ladies and backed with crimson velvet. This was especially welcome, as lambskins were used not only to keep the gravely ill warm but also to prevent bed sores from forming.

"A gift from the Queen for the invalid," Codpiece announced to an astonished Maggie, who could only bob a shy curtsy as if to the Queen herself and then run back up the stairs with tears in her eyes. Nick noted Codpiece's deliberate use of the word "invalid" to signify an assumption that John would recover and therefore give hope to Maggie. At that moment, Nick felt an enormous affection and gratitude for his friend's delicacy. And toward the Queen, whose emissary Codpiece was.

Just before he left, Codpiece handed Nick a piece of parchment. "I know it's not a good time," he said. "And the title is unfortunate, to say the least. But the Queen has invited you to a play put on by the Earl of Leicester's Men at Whitehall on May Day. Will has written it and would especially like you to come. The Queen will understand if you are absent."

When Codpiece had gone, Nick glanced at the title of the play. *The Ghost.* It was to be performed at the palace in five days' time on May first. Nick crumpled the paper in his hand and stuffed it in his pocket. Codpiece was right; given the circumstances, the title couldn't have been more ironic.

Kat came over every day and saw to the children, making sure their clothes were cleaned and darned, that they were fed. Her girls took it in turns to clean the tavern and the private family rooms and take away John's bedding to be laundered.

Three days after the attack, Edmund showed up. He seemed ill at ease and did not stay long, refusing the offer of ale.

"Will he die?" he asked.

Nick remembered him using those exact words about Thomas. "We don't know." He had made the same reply then. It was strange how history was repeating itself. Compared to the sensitivity Codpiece had shown, Edmund seemed curiously detached. Nick remembered how Edmund had not defended himself against Gavell and Stace's attack at Wood Wharf, merely curling himself up in a ball with his hands over his head waiting for the kicking to stop. Again, Nick wondered at Essex's lack of judgment in hiring Edmund, a man who seemed to have such an abhorrence of violence.

"I'm sorry," Edmund told Nick, as if sensing that something more sympathetic was required. "I know you and he are good friends. It must be terrible for you."

Nick didn't reply. His haggard and unshaven face spoke volumes.

Edmund put a hand on Nick's shoulder. "I know how it feels to lose someone you love."

Nick was left with a strange feeling of having received formal condolences after a funeral.

The one conspicuous absentee among the well-wishers was Essex. He had shown himself capable of compassion when Thomas was poisoned, but as he doubtless considered John Nick's servant, the wounded man was obviously beneath his concern.

No one except the immediate family, Nick, Eli, and Rivkah were allowed upstairs. Maggie stood watch over her husband like a she-wolf, making sure there was no noise to disturb him except the soft sound of her voice murmuring endearments, begging him to open his eyes for the love of God, sometimes berating him for leaving her a widow a second time. When Nick would hear this, he would put his arms about her and hold her while she wept inconsolably into his chest, even in her grief trying to smother the sound so John would not be disturbed in whatever place he had retreated to.

"John has the best wife in the world," Nick whispered. "And when he wakes up, I will tell him that."

Maggie gave him a watery smile, her lips trembling. "He knows," she said.

Even more forlorn than Maggie was Matty. Nick had not paid her much attention as she looked after Jane, the baby. From her days as a cinders in Whitehall Palace until he had brought her to live at The Black Sheep the previous autumn, Matty had developed the habit of keeping in the background. In the palace, she had been a night creature, tiptoeing into people's bedchambers to make up the fires for the morning. Her unobtrusiveness was deeply ingrained, although Nick had seen signs of more confidence in her of late, especially when she sat with Henry in a corner of the taproom in the evenings. He was teaching her to read and write, and sometimes Nick saw her laughing at something Henry said.

One night, as Nick sat with Hector beside the fire in the empty taproom, she approached him. The first he was aware of her presence was her small hand on his shoulder, which made him jump.

"Matty," he said. "Is all well?"

In the darkness of the room, the dying flames of the fire flickering on the walls, dressed in her nightdress, Matty looked as ghostly as when she had lived all her days indoors like a woodland creature that came out only at night.

"Is he going to die?" she whispered, tears leaking from her eyes.

Suddenly, Nick understood. It had been John who had first interviewed Matty when they were investigating the murders of the Queen's ladies-in-waiting; it had been John who had first shown her kindness and gained her trust. And it was John's baby that she looked after now. Not only was she mourning the loss of a friend, but she must be terrified she would be sent back to the palace if John should die.

Nick knew he could not reassure her as if she were a child, that he owed her the truth. "We don't know, Matty," he said. "But be assured that The Black Sheep is your home. We are your family now, whatever befalls. This I promise."

He tilted up her chin and looked into her eyes. "Do you understand?"

"Yes."

"Good," he said. "Now go back to bed and say your prayers for John."

She turned away, then quickly spun round and planted a kiss on Nick's cheek before disappearing into the family quarters at the back of the tavern.

Even Hector was subdued. He lay on the floor of the tavern with his great head on his paws, his eyes mournfully following Nick. When Nick wasn't sitting staring at nothing, he was pacing up and down, unable to keep still but not able to set his hand to anything. His mind was in turmoil. He simply could not forgive himself for putting John in harm's way. If only he had not asked him to go to Seething Lane. He should have known that was the first place Annie would look for him.

There was another thought at the back of his mind, but he couldn't come at it clearly. It had something to do with the fact that it had not been raining that day and John had not taken his cloak. Every time Nick thought he was on the point of understanding why this was significant, it slipped away. Eventually, he gave up, hoping that it would come back to him when he least expected it. Since receiving his own head wound, he hadn't been thinking clearly, but he knew that did not excuse him from culpability for John's grievous injury. He refused to think about what he would do if John died.

A week passed. As there was no change in John's condition other than that he seemed to shrink each day as his flesh wasted off his bones, and as there was no swelling Eli or Rivkah could detect over the site of the wound, Eli spent more time at the infirmary. It was Rivkah who came more often.

One evening, Nick watched as she picked up her cloak and, as was her habit when she went outdoors, wrapped it tightly about her and put up her hood.

"Any change?" Nick asked from the shadows of the room.

Rivkah jumped. "I didn't see you there." Then she shook her head. "No change."

"I'll walk you home," Nick said, lighting a lantern with a taper he'd lit from the fire.

"No need," she replied.

"Hector needs a walk."

Nick called the dog to him and took her basket. Then he opened the door so she could step out first.

They walked in silence, the lantern casting just enough light that the ground immediately in front of them was illuminated and they could avoid the potholes and deep ruts the heavy winter rains had made in the street. Hector coursed ahead, then doubled back, never leaving them for long, as if he were scouting ahead to make sure it was safe.

As if by mutual agreement, they passed Rivkah's door and carried on along the river. It was late, and the night was pitch-black. A mild spring breeze was blowing off the river, bringing the smell of river mud and seaweed, fish and the tang of smoke. When they came to a stone wall next to some steps, Nick stopped and set the lantern on the wall. Without speaking, they both sat down and gazed into the blackness ahead, the sound of the river murmuring at their feet, a giant slumbering presence in an otherwise empty world. Nick felt as if he and Rivkah had been cast up on a distant island, the mainland visible but unattainable because he had never learned to swim.

"What you said about loyalty to your people?" Nick began. He stopped and looked at Rivkah. She had thrown her hood back, and her hair was blowing in the wind off the water. He saw the white flash of her hand as she smoothed it back from her face. He looked back into the blackness ahead. "I feel the same way, except my people are not members of a race or even a religion, but those I love. My family, my friends, my neighbors."

You.

Now she turned to look at him, her face a white oval in the dark, her black hair indistinguishable from the night. "Love is the best kind of loyalty there is," she said. "Most people are loyal to ideas. They turn God into an idea in order to justify their acts of cruelty. But it is themselves and their desires whom they serve, not God."

"And what of vengeance on behalf of someone you love?" Nick asked. "Is that not also an act of loyalty?"

"You are thinking of the woman who attacked John?"

"And Thomas. And murdered Simon Winchelsea."

"You are not asking the right person. I have taken an oath to do no harm."

"You also have a saying, 'An eye for an eye.' What would you do if someone tried to harm Eli?"

"I would kill him."

CHAPTER 22

Somers Quay, Port of London

Nick had just returned to The Black Sheep after a fruitless day of wandering around London in the hopes that he could draw Annie out into the open when someone hammered on the front door. When Nick opened it, Henry Gavell was standing there.

"Come in," Nick said, opening the door wider. He assumed Gavell was paying a call to ask about John. Whether he was doing this out of the kindness of his heart or because he feared that John might awake and tell Nick it was Gavell who had attacked him, Nick did not know. He was surprised to see Gavell on his own and not accompanied by his silent shadow, Richard Stace.

Gavell remained standing in the street. There was a curious tension in his face, the skin stretched taut around the mouth, his expression flat. "I think I have a lead on Annie. I overheard Essex giving instructions to a sea captain. Apparently, Essex has stock in a ship moored at Somers Quay, bound for Antwerp. He told the captain to expect a passenger and that this passenger were to be hidden until after the ship sets sail tonight on the outgoing tide. Richie's keeping watch on the ship now."

Nick buckled on the sword belt he had just taken off and slipped a dagger in a sheath down his right boot.

"Let's go," he said. Then, as Hector got up, "Not you, pal. Sorry." Hector gave a mournful whine and flopped down on the floor again.

Although Hector was a strong swimmer, Nick was afraid that if he went into the water, he would be crushed between the ships moored at the quays, and the current near London Bridge could be fierce.

Twilight was falling as Nick and Gavell walked north over London Bridge, the sun sinking in red and pink ribbons behind Whitehall Palace and St. James's Park. Shopkeepers were putting up their shutters for the night. It was that time of day when the gender, character, and moral intent of those out and about in the streets underwent a sea change. Innocent shoppers—mostly women, household servants, or children sent on errands—had gone home. Empty carts driven by farmers that had come laden with produce to the city that morning were now trundling south again toward the countryside a few miles past the sprawl of Southwark.

Now Nick and Gavell were jostled by bands of loud, inebriated young men walking south along the bridge toward the brothels, taverns, and bear- and bull-baiting rings of Bankside. The only people going north into the city, aside from Nick and Gavell, were Black Jack Sims's lads—footpads and latch lifters, in the main— eager to prey on the careless and unsuspecting citizens of London. A few of them recognized Nick and grinned unashamedly. Their nightly commute from Bankside to London was as ordinary to them as if they were on their way to a night shift as stevedores at the docks. Like Johnnie, Black Jack Sims's grandson, most of them had been born into the criminal underworld of Bankside and knew no other life.

"Hello, Phil," Nick said to one of them. "Don't get nabbed by the bailiffs."

Phil grinned. "You know me better than that, Nick."

Then they lost sight of him in the crowd flowing in the other direction over the bridge.

Gavell was looking at Nick oddly. "You know that man?"

"Phil's one of the best latch lifters in London," Nick explained. "He can be in and out of a house in a trice, no one the wiser."

"He's a thief?" Gavell exclaimed.

Nick shrugged. "Phil's never been violent. Only steals from the wealthiest houses where there's rich pickings and plenty of money to buy more of what he nicks. He's got a wife and five children to feed. It's all the profession he knows."

"He'd still hang if he were caught. That's the law." Gavell looked astonished that Nick should know, and condone, such a man.

Nick was perhaps not as surprised at Gavell's moralistic attitude as he could have been. Though Gavell had doubtless committed many an illegal act in his life—with or without the sanction of his master, Essex—Nick had found that those who had managed to lift themselves out of poverty by finding a legitimate profession were often the most condemning of those who operated on the other side of the law.

Even his own brother Robert was scandalized by the company Nick kept, although he tried to hide it. It was not Gavell and Robert who were at odds with the times, but Nick himself. If he was honest with himself, he had been much like them before he had taken up residence in Bankside.

The younger son of an earl, he had kept to his exalted social class during his boyhood, he now realized, seldom mixing with boys from the village or surrounding crofts. And when he went up to Oxford, he mostly socialized with his own class, the sons of lords, earls, and gentlemen, or at least those boys fortunate enough to come from families who had money to pay for their education. Soldiering for a few years on the Continent had rubbed away some of the lines that divided the classes. In order to lead soldiers effectively, he had had to get to know them. They had mostly been poor men from failing farms, or even in one case an escaped prisoner about to hang for poaching, just like Simon Winchelsea. But on the battlefield, it was bravery and the bond that came from living at close quarters with one another in almost perpetual danger that counted, not the privilege of birth. Nick had been accepted as one of them, not because he was the son of an earl but because he was quick-witted, decisive, and courageous in a fight. The shared goal of staying alive each day created a strange kind of democracy, almost a brotherhood.

Once back in England, Nick had gone to live in Bankside, and this same sense of democracy existed among people who knew they were considered scum by decent society. His neighbors—whores, pimps, thieves, hired thugs, vagabonds, forgers, drunks, pickpockets, exiles, and actors—were all considered the dregs of society, but Nick had seen the human face of these social outcasts and called many of them friends. Somehow he doubted that in the wealthier neighborhoods of London, like the great houses on the Strand or the rich merchant houses in Cheapside, John and his family would have been gifted with such generosity and sympathy during their time of need.

They turned east off the bridge toward the Tower. This stretch between the Tower and the eastern side of London Bridge constituted the great Port of London, with its deep-water berths and long row of quays and wharves. Giant cranes set up along the wharves stood against the darkening sky like enormous gallows, their ropes and pulleys creaking in the wind that blew off the river; massive warehouses, their doors perpetually agape like giant maws insatiable for the goods that poured into London from Europe and the New World, lined the wharves. Nose to stern, the ships were moored from St. Katherine's Wharf east of the Tower all the way to London Bridge. There must have been a hundred of them. Even with night falling, the wharves were alive with stevedores stacking crates onto carts, which were then pulled by drays to the warehouses and stacked in geometrically aligned rows; customs officials with inky fingers checked off the crates as they were loaded and chalked coded symbols on them so they could be precisely stored and then instantly retrieved for delivery. It was a massive and complicated operation, but somehow everyone on the docks seemed to know their part and where each item should go. *The paperwork from the docks alone must be staggering,* Nick thought. No wonder his friend Thomas had uncovered widespread fraud at the Custom House last winter. To find a purloined crate of Venetian glass here, a bale of costly tapestries from Bruges there, would be like looking for a needle in a haystack. But discover them Thomas had.

Fortunately, Nick and Gavell did not have far to walk. Somers Quay was the wharf used exclusively by Flemish merchants, even though trade with Brabant had declined precipitously since the fall of Antwerp the previous year. The quay was the fourth from the bridge, and only one ship was moored there.

"There she is," Gavell said, pointing. "*The Dalliance.*" A sailor nonchalantly leaning against a rail on the ship straightened up and peered down at them.

"Are you sure she's on board?" Nick asked.

"Has to be. She'll be keeping herself out of sight until the ship sails."

"All right. Let's wait until full dark."

They left the wharf, and Gavell led Nick to the mouth of an alley opposite. The massive form of Richard Stace was leaning against the wall of a warehouse. He nodded to his partner.

"Most of the crew are on shore leave in the taverns and brothels until dark," Gavell explained. "Then they're supposed to report back to the ship to get ready to set sail. There's only a skeleton crew on board now, but they smuggled in doxies so they wouldn't miss out. We have to go now if we want to search the boat. The man on the gangway knows me from before. I slipped him some coin to let us on board."

After waiting for night to fall, they made their way over the road and up the gangplank. As Gavell had promised, the sailor guarding access to the ship let them pass without a challenge. Silently he handed them each a lantern containing a single tallow candle burning behind horn windows.

"Careful with them lights," he cautioned.

"You take the stern, and me and Richie will start at the bow," Gavell said. "We'll meet in the middle."

It was dark enough on the deck, but once Nick had climbed down the ladder into the first level of the ship, it was like night. His lantern gave a feeble glow, illuminating only a small circle around him. With the constant sound of creaking and the sense of the floor moving beneath his feet, it was like being inside a living thing, like Jonah inside the whale.

Nick moved cautiously forward, trying not to trip on coils of rope and, in some cases, the bare legs of a copulating seaman and a whore. A couple of the women watched Nick pass by with the same lack of interest they seemed to have for the sailor laboring on top of them.

"Anything?" Nick asked Gavell when he approached in the center of the boat. Stace was not with him.

"Nothing."

"She won't be on this level where the sailors' quarters are," Nick said. "She'll be hiding down below in storage, at least until the ship sails."

They descended another ladder to the next level and then down again beneath the water line, where the cargo was stored. Except for the dim light of their lanterns, it was pitch-black. As before, Nick turned toward the stern and Gavell to the bow.

Gingerly Nick made his way forward, listening intently. But all he heard was the rustle and squeak of rats as they scampered away from the light and the sound of his feet stepping around barrels and bales, crates and hogsheads of ale. There was only a narrow plank running down the center of the hull like a spine, the cargo packed above shoulder height on either side. Climbing onto a crate, he held the lantern aloft and looked along the small space between the tops of some bales and the deck above to see if Annie was hiding there, but the space was empty. Then he thought he saw a glimmer of light coming from the far end nearest the stern. From his many voyages to the Continent on ships just like this one, he knew this was where the gunpowder was stored for the muskets the sailors used if they were attacked by pirates, separated from the rest of the ship by a thick leather curtain and a wooden door lined with tin. The door was ajar and a faint light showed round the edges, flickering as if from a guttering candle. To take a naked flame into a gunpowder room was suicide. Perhaps Annie did not realize the danger she was in.

Stepping as quietly as he could, he walked toward the opening. Nick felt sweat running from his hairline into his eyes, not only from the fetid closeness of the ship under the water line but also because of the mortal danger of fire and gunpowder. He wiped his eyes on his sleeve, then carefully reached down and drew his dagger from his boot. The hull was too crowded with cargo for him to use his sword.

Just as he reached the door, he heard a sound behind him. He swung round and held up his lantern, but he could see nothing there. He turned back to the door and very gently pushed it open.

The tiny, triangular room was empty. A lit candle had been stuck down in its own wax on top of one of the gunpowder barrels. Cursing, Nick stepped into the room and pinched it out. That was when he heard the door slam behind him and the sound of a wooden bar being dropped onto iron hooks.

He heard footsteps moving away. Then he smelled smoke.

CHAPTER 23

Somers Quay, The Dalliance

Cursing, Nick set down the lantern and inserted his dagger into a crack in the door beneath the wooden bar. Then he struggled to lift it. Straining with the weight, he thought he had almost lifted it high enough when it dropped down again. Cursing, he tried again.

Now smoke was beginning to creep under the door in gray tendrils. Nick coughed and threw all his strength into his wrists and arms. Again, the bar seemed to be lifting clear, but then a sharp pain shot through his wrist and he had to lower the weight of the bar.

The smoke was thicker now, and he could hear an ominous crackling and feel the door beginning to grow hot. Desperately, he tried again, choking and almost blinded by the smoke. A lick of flame showed through the door near the hinges. Wincing from the pain in his wrists, he tried one more time and felt the bar lift and fall from the door. Pushing open the door, he was almost beaten back by the flames and smoke, but to remain in that confined space with those deadly little barrels of gunpowder was certain death. Placing his arm over his nose and mouth, he ran the gauntlet along the plank down the center of the cargo hold, the bales of cloth stacked on either side a mountain of fire, black smoke roiling from them, sparks singeing his hair and face, flames licking at his body as if he were falling into the very pit of hell.

Somehow Nick found the ladder leading upward. Once up at the next level, he began yelling, "*Fire! Fire!* Get up top. Get up top."

Suddenly the ladder was overwhelmed by a mob of terrified sailors and whores, some nude, all scrabbling and tearing at each other to be first up the ladder.

"One at a time," Nick bawled. He pulled one sailor off the lower rungs and threw him back. Then he hoisted a naked whore bodily up the ladder, boosting another woman, this one partially clothed, after her. After the women were safely up top, he stepped back to allow the men to climb to safety.

Luckily, most of the crew were on shore; otherwise the panic would have trapped them all below hatches, people being trampled to death in the frenzy to get out, blocking access to the ladders. The smoke was thickening, the hungry crackle of flames louder. Soon the gunpowder would explode. When that happened, they would all be shredded into bloody rags, the ship reduced to kindling.

Nick herded the sailors and their whores up the next ladder to the deck. "Get off the ship," he yelled, but they needed no heeding and were already swarming down the gangplank.

Nick looked around for Gavell and Stace and saw Gavell running behind the others down the gangplank to the quay. He assumed Stace was not far behind, although he could not see him in the crowd.

Knowing he was taking a foolish risk, Nick descended the ladder one more time to the second level. He knew going down deeper into the hold would be suicide. Holding on to the ladder, he yelled, "*Annie! Annie!*" but it came out as a croak, his lungs already clogged with smoke. He tried to listen for a voice calling for help, but all he could hear was a sound like the Apocalypse, a great roaring as if the world were falling in on itself and dissolving into ash; his eyes were stinging and tearing up and he could see nothing at all. Then the smoke and heat became too great and he knew he would die if he did not get out. Swiftly he made his way topside and ran down the gangplank, his face covered in soot, his clothes and hair singed, his lungs burning, the cool touch of the clear night air on his skin the most exquisite thing he had ever experienced.

A crowd had gathered on the dock to watch, as if it were some outlandish carnival attraction. "Get back," Nick yelled, waving both arms. "There's gunpowder aboard."

At the word *gunpowder*, the crowd scattered and ran, stumbling over each other, women screaming, men shouting and trying to drag the fallen by their arms along the street.

As Nick turned back to look at the ship, there was a tremendous flash, and the stern seemed to lift into the air and hang there, brilliantly illuminated from below by an almost celestial light. Then everything flew apart. Wood and iron rained down from the sky; Nick saw a running sailor pierced through the back of his shoulder by a sliver of wood with the ease of a rapier thrust; another was knocked senseless by a lump of metal; yet another was scored across the cheek by a flying nail.

The ship's back was broken, a smoking hole where the stern had been. Slowly, almost languidly, the bow rose in the air until the ship was almost vertically poised in the water; then the whole structure began to slide down into the river like a red-hot piece of iron quenched by a blacksmith. Nick watched as the flames of the burning hulk were progressively extinguished as the oily swell of the river rose higher up its sides, steam hissing at the water line. Suddenly the ship was gone, more quickly than Nick could have thought possible. Somers Quay, where the ship had been berthed, looked unnaturally empty, as if a tooth had been removed, leaving a blackened hole. Bubbles rose on the surface of the river, and all that remained of *The Dalliance* were charred spars and flotsam floating on the surface. The crowd gave a collective sigh, as if they had just watched the finale of a mystery play where devils had dragged a damned soul kicking and screaming through the open gates of hell.

Then the authorities arrived in force: customs officials, Beefeaters from the Tower, bailiffs who patrolled the warehouse district. As they tried to disperse the crowd and keep them back from the wharves, where sailors were putting out fires on other ships caused by falling debris and sparks, shouting and jostling started. The sailors from *The Dalliance* began to arrive, and seeing their beloved vessel destroyed, they began to drunkenly resist the bailiffs and Beefeaters, throwing wild punches and cursing as if they blamed the authorities for the loss of their livelihood. Soon a general melee of fighting had broken out from Somers Quay all the way to Billingsgate Fish Market.

Nick pushed his way through the crowd, dodging punches, sometimes returning them, looking for Annie. He could see no sign of her but did not really expect to. If by some miracle she had escaped the burning ship, she would probably have made off by now into the dark backstreets near the port.

Eventually he found Gavell on the edge of the crowd that had now gathered to watch the fighting and cheer on the sailors. He was standing on a hitching post so he could see over the crowd, his face pale, staring at the great gap where *The Dalliance* had been only an hour before as if he couldn't believe his eyes. He started when Nick took him by the arm as if he had seen a ghost.

"Did you see Annie?" Nick shouted over the noise. Then he realized that Stace was missing.

"I lost him after I talked to you," Gavell said, in response to Nick's querying look. "I thought maybe he had given up the search."

Or was hiding in the hold waiting to ambush me, Nick thought.

He studied Gavell carefully, but all he saw was a man in shock. This did not mean Gavell and Stace had not lured Nick to the ship in order to kill him; it simply meant something had gone wrong and Stace had failed to make it out in time. Either that, or Annie had seen her chance to remove Nick and had taken it. Now Annie was gone, and Stace was missing.

"Come on." Nick pulled Gavell down from his perch. "Richard may be in the crowd somewhere."

They searched the quays, then the nearby taverns, hoping against hope that Stace had decided to rinse the smoke out of his lungs with a tankard of ale. All to no avail. After what seemed like hours, they gave up.

"Maybe he's gone back to Leicester House?" Nick said, more to give Gavell some hope than because he believed it himself. Stace was not known for his independence of thought, following behind

Gavell like a faithful dog. If he hadn't shown up by now, Nick believed he never would. He had gone down with the ship.

Gavell obviously felt the same way. He was somber, and as the night wore on, he became more and more listless, as if he knew their search was hopeless. If not for the fact that Nick suspected the two men of luring him to his death, perhaps in league with Annie, he would have felt sorry for him. Despite the horror of their deaths, there was a kind of justice in both Stace and Annie going down with the ship, as this was the fate that had been planned for him.

Around midnight, Nick led Gavell down an alley running along the side of a warehouse to Thames Street. He planned to follow Thames Street west and then turn south to the bridge and so back to Bankside. He had no intention of admitting to the authorities that he'd been on board when the fire broke out. That would put him at risk of being sued by either Essex or the captain of the ship. In view of the bad relations between him and Essex, he had no doubt Essex would ruin him if he could. Besides, it wasn't he who had started the fire; it was Annie or Stace, Essex's own agents.

Nick couldn't help but feel that the sinking of *The Dalliance* was an ill omen for Essex, a sign that whatever Essex put his hand to, it would end in destruction. If it was Stace who had locked Nick in the gunpowder room, then it had been on the orders of Essex. Nick could not imagine Gavell and Stace acting on their own initiative. And if Essex had ordered Nick's death, then it was either because he was enraged at Nick for defying him or because he was somehow involved in the death of Winchelsea and the attempted murder of Thomas and John.

Guilty of treason or not, it was clear to Nick, Essex was cursed.

CHAPTER 24

The Black Sheep Tavern, Bankside

When Nick returned to The Black Sheep alone—Gavell had carried on to Leicester House, drawn by a glimmer of hope that Stace would be waiting for him there—he found Rivkah coming down the stairs after checking in with John.

"How is he?" Nick asked. But he knew from her expression that he was the same.

"What happened to you?" Rivkah exclaimed when she came closer and saw that Nick was covered in soot, his hair and clothing singed. She said this with a slightly hysterical edge to her voice.

For once, Nick knew not to joke. As far as he could tell, fire was the only thing Rivkah was truly afraid of.

Last winter, when drunken sailors had set fire to the roof of her house, Nick had gone through the door to get Eli and Rivkah out and had seen a look in her eyes that was more akin to a wild animal at bay than a human being. He had had to manhandle her bodily through the back door and lock her out. The sound of her frenzied curses and sobs still came to him in his dreams.

"One of the ships at the dock exploded and sank," he said. "I happened to be at the wharf and got a bit too close." He shrugged, hoping to appear casual.

Rivkah looked narrowly at him as she set down her basket and rummaged in it. But for once she did not question him further. Instead she said, "I have some ointment for burns." She handed him a small clay pot. "You can doctor yourself tonight. I'm going home."

Nick could tell that the reek of smoke in his clothes and hair deeply disturbed her.

After she left, Nick slathered some ointment on the worst burns, then climbed the stairs to see John. Maggie was asleep, her head resting on the bed beside John. Nick drew up a stool and sat down, taking his friend's hand in his. John's flesh was warm, but his hand felt lifeless and unresisting. Oddly, Nick noticed that John's finger-nails had grown and his chin was now covered with a beard. These signs of life seemed to mock the corpselike stillness of his body, the pale, sunken look of his face.

Nick bowed his head over his friend's hand. "John," he said. "If you can hear me wherever you are, we need you to come back to us." His voice caught in his throat, still croaky with the smoke he had inhaled. He felt a sudden desperation well up in his chest, as if he saw the long years ahead without his friend at his side. "Don't be a selfish arsehole. You've had a long enough rest. Now it's time to get up, damn you." He squeezed John's hand hard. "I need you. Do you hear me? I need you."

Then he felt a touch on his arm, and for a brief moment he thought maybe John had heard him and awoken. But when he raised his head, he saw Maggie looking at him.

Nick scrubbed at his eyes with his sleeve. "I was just seeing how he was," he said. "I need to get some clothes out of the chest, anyway."

He stood and turned his back on Maggie before she could say anything, the look of compassion on her face almost unmanning him. Randomly grabbing a handful of clothes from the chest, he ran down the stairs into the taproom. There he sat on a bench in the cold, empty room, his arm draped across Hector's back, staring at nothing.

★ ★ ★

The next day, Nick heard that the body of a woman and a man had been found floating in the river that same morning. They had been drawn downstream to Sabbes Quay, halfway between Billingsgate and the Tower, and snagged between two broken pilings. If they were Annie and Stace, then the poetic justice of their bodies being discovered like Simon Winchelsea's was not lost on Nick. Aside from the sex, the corpses were too charred to be recognizable, but the burned condition of the bodies made it virtually certain that they had come from *The Dalliance*. If Gavell had told him the truth about Annie being on board, then either the female corpse was one of the whores who had not made it out, or it was indeed Annie.

Remembering Annie's intelligence, her fearlessness, the quick wit with which she had bested the Puritan preacher at St. Paul's Cross, not to mention her extraordinary ability to transform herself into any character she chose, Nick felt unaccountably sorrowful. He had to keep reminding himself that not only was she a murderer who had tried to kill him twice, but she was a traitor to his Queen. It was better for everyone if it were Annie who had died on the ship.

As for Stace, Nick felt only a mild regret.

★ ★ ★

That same day, Nick walked over to the infirmary to find Eli. He had a favor to ask, and he could not, in all good conscience, ask Rivkah to do it. Even so, considering Eli's own experience with the burning of his home, Nick felt guilty about asking him.

"You want me to examine the bodies found in the river this morning?" Eli asked. "The ones believed to have come from the ship that exploded?"

"Yes." Nick needed to be as certain as possible of the identity of the dead woman.

Eli looked at Nick thoughtfully. "Rivkah told me you were pretty singed last night. She said you told her you had been on the dock when the ship blew up."

"That's right."

"Mmmm."

"What?"

"Only that the burns and smoke inhalation I can hear in your voice could not have been the result of standing a hundred yards away on the dock, if you'll excuse me for saying so."

Nick sighed. "I'll explain what really happened on the way."

Eli grinned. "I'll get my bag."

★　★　★

St. Mary-at-Hill, Ward of Billingsgate

The remains of the burned corpses had been taken to the crypt of St. Mary-at-Hill in the Ward of Billingsgate on Lovat Lane just off Eastcheap. They would lie there for a few days to see if someone claimed them, then be buried without ceremony in Potter's Field.

When Eli removed the sheets from the bodies, Nick stepped back and tried not to gag. The twisted, blackened things did not resemble human beings so much as overcooked lumps of pork. And the smell was disturbingly similar.

"Have you ever wondered why Jews do not eat pork?" Eli asked conversationally, as if he had read Nick's mind. "One of the reasons is because it is so similar to human flesh. It would be hard to know what one was eating."

Nick swallowed down bile. "Get on with it, will you?" He made a vow never to eat pork again.

Taking out a stylus from his bag, Eli began to poke at one of the bodies. "Definitely female," he murmured. "You can tell by the width of the pelvic bones." The breasts had been flattened by the trauma to the body.

"Can you tell if she was wearing men's attire?" Nick asked.

Eli looked at him oddly, then scrutinized the corpse. "There are scraps of material on her legs. Here"—he pointed—"and here."

Nick saw flakes of what looked like burned parchment.

"Thin hose would have burned away, so I would say she was dressed in a skirt and bodice made from some heavier material."

He began to examine her hands. "Ah, now this is interesting." Eli pointed to one of her fingers. At the base of a blackened

stump—what would have been the first finger on her right hand—
were the partially melted remains of a ring. Carefully, he eased it
off and gave it to Nick.

Nick held it close to the lantern the sexton had loaned them for
the examination of the bodies. He scraped the metal with his finger
and saw a faint sheen of gold beneath. The stone in the setting was
cracked and discolored, but Nick could make out the red of jasper.
He remembered admiring such a ring on Annie's finger when they
had first met at Leicester House and thinking the stone was the
same fiery color of her hair.

Sadly, he put it in his pocket. He would return it to Annie's
family if he could. The only thing he thought odd was that the
body was wearing only one ring; when Annie had been dressed as a
lady, as was her rank, she had worn multiple rings. Perhaps she had
donned the disguise of a whore to come aboard the ship. It would
certainly have prevented anyone from asking what she was doing
there. She could have gone below deck and hidden in the cargo
until the ship set sail.

"I've seen enough," Nick said. "Thank you."

Eli covered the body again with the sheet.

"If it's any consolation, she probably died from breathing in
smoke and did not burn to death." His mouth turned down, as if
he was remembering the gruesome fate of his family.

Nick put a hand on his shoulder. "Thank you for doing this,
Eli. I know it's not easy."

"What about the other body?"

"Is it a man?"

Eli nodded. "Judging from the size and girth. And then there's
this." He pointed to a thick blackened line around the waist. Clearly
a belt.

"I'll send someone round to see if he can identify him," Nick
said.

Even if Gavell could not recognize the face of his friend, the
enormous size of the corpse certainly fit. That, coupled with Stace's
continued absence when he had nowhere else to go, would make
the identification as certain as it could ever be.

On his way out of the church, Nick dropped a sovereign into the hand of the priest. "For the woman," he said. "A service and proper burial in your churchyard with a headstone."

"What shall I inscribe on the grave marker?" the priest asked.

"Protea."

In Greek mythology, Proteus was a sea-god, known as the shapeshifter. In view of Annie's skill at changing her appearance, and the way she had died, Nick thought it apt.

CHAPTER 25

St. Mary-at-Hill, Ward of Billingsgate

Two days later, Nick attended the service for Protea, aka Annie O'Neill, at St. Mary-at-Hill. He and Gavell were the only mourners. He had sent a message to Leicester House informing them of the time and place of the funeral, but neither Essex nor Edmund had chosen to show up. Nick remembered the way Essex had been unable to keep his hands off Annie in his study when Nick had been eavesdropping; he recalled how Edmund's eyes had followed her every movement with a besotted shine in them. Their lack of concern for her mortal remains bespoke a shallowness of spirit that did not surprise him in Essex but came as a shock to see in Edmund. In Nick's opinion, loyalty should not end with death, even if it had been misplaced in life.

The day of the funeral turned out to be one of those first sweet days of spring when the shoots that had lain sleeping in the ground all winter seemed to rise up at once and burst through the earth. In the cemetery, daffodils and hyacinths, snowdrops, early-blooming irises, clover, buttercups, and daisies rioted in the grass around the graves. The cherry trees showered white and pink snow on the shoulders of the pallbearers as they carried the coffin to the graveside. Although Nick had been taught that spring was Nature's allegory for Christ's resurrection, somehow this burgeoning of new life made the graveside obsequies all the more depressing, the thunk of the soil spaded onto the coffin all the more ominous. It was as if the brilliance of the flowers, the living smell of new grass, the joyous trilling of the birds, were props in a morality play to remind the onlookers that the beauty of life was a cruel illusion; that, in reality, all flesh was grass.

After they had watched the small box lowered into the ground, the grave filled in and covered over with sod, Nick and Gavell went to a nearby tavern. Nick would rather have gone straight home, but it was Gavell who had suggested the drink, and as it was traditional after a funeral, Nick had agreed.

In contrast to the loud jollity of the other patrons rejoicing in the balmy spring day, they were subdued. Still convinced that Gavell and Stace had somehow been involved in the attempt on his life on the ship, Nick was on his guard.

Gavell finally broke the silence. "I'm leaving the earl's employ."

"Why?" Perhaps Gavell had a guilty conscience and felt responsible for his friend's death.

Gavell looked down at the table and touched a wet spot there with his finger, a pretext for not looking at Nick. "Essex is returning to the Netherlands." Then he raised his eyes to Nick's. They were as blue as a pitiless winter sky. "His Lordship was more concerned with the loss of his precious ship. He couldn't have cared less about Richie and Annie." His voice had grown hoarse. "I was taken in. Thought he were a gentleman."

This, coming from a hard man such as Gavell, was a devastating critique. Infallibly, Nick had found, the opinion of servants about their masters was correct. They always saw the person beneath the facade, beneath the actor and sycophant at court. Before servants, one did not need to put on an act, for there was nothing to gain from their good opinion. Nick had witnessed such a moment with Essex and the stable lad the day he had broken with him.

The other explanation was, of course, that Essex had been furious when he learned that not only had he lost one of his own men, but Nick had survived. Perhaps Gavell was disaffected not only because of the loss of his friend but because Essex had refused to pay him for a bungled job.

Perhaps Gavell and Stace had never intended to help Nick catch Annie but had lured him to where she was hidden in order to do away with him and ensure her escape to the Continent, not dreaming that it would have turned out the way it did. In that case, Gavell would feel responsible for Annie's death as well as his friend's.

The one thing that niggled at Nick was the means of his death: why run the risk of placing a burning candle in a room full of gunpowder? Why not a knife in the back or a garrote around the neck? Either would have been a far more effective means and would have ensured that no one else would have died by accident, let alone the killer himself. Or herself? Had it been Annie who had persuaded her friends Gavell and Stace to bring Nick to her on the ship so she could get rid of him once and for all? She knew he would never stop looking for her, which effectively meant she could not show her face in England again. But then how was she to advance her family's fortune at court if she could not return to London unless the only witness to her link to del Toro was dead?

"Edmund is going to the Netherlands with Essex," Gavell said.

Nick was surprised. He could not imagine the squeamish, timid man he knew faring well on a battlefield. But perhaps Edmund had no choice, seeing as he had a living to make. Choice was a luxury only the very wealthy could afford, including him, Nick thought guiltily. If it hadn't been for the hold Cecil had over him because of his recusant status, Nick would have been free to do anything he pleased.

"They belong together, those two," Gavell said savagely. "As I said at Wood Wharf, Edmund's an arse-licker. Only says what he thinks Essex wants to hear. And Essex is only too pleased to listen. Pah!" He scratched at the stubble on his chin. "You knew him when he were a lad, didn't you? Edmund, I mean."

"Yes." Nick pictured Edmund standing in their college quad looking wistfully after them as he and John made off for a tavern. "You shouldn't judge him too harshly. He's had a hard life."

"Ain't we all?"

No, not all. Nick had had a happy childhood with plenty to eat and a family who loved him. He thought of Matty, and of the beggar girl, Allie, whom he had found starving on the steps of St. Paul's last winter. Both girls had been rescued from their miserable lives:

Matty had gone to live at The Black Sheep; Allie had been adopted by a kindhearted former cook called Mistress Plunkett, whom Nick had met during his investigation the previous winter. But there were thousands of others who were not so fortunate. And looking at Gavell's face, its hard planes of bone, the sinewy toughness in his arms, the wizened look that no doubt came from childhood privation, Nick could imagine him as a survivor growing up on the streets of London, fiercely defending his right to exist with his fists and a dagger.

"Someone tried to kill me on the ship," Nick said, watching Gavell closely.

Gavell looked surprised, then offended. "Weren't us, if that's what you're getting at," he said.

Nick held his gaze.

Gavell stared defiantly back. "Think what you like," he said eventually. "I admit, I didn't like you."

Nick noted the use of the past tense.

"Thought you was a turncoat," Gavell went on. "Someone who decides to change his allegiance when the wind starts blowing from the north."

When Nick looked none the wiser, Gavell sighed. "I knew you worked for Walsingham and that his agents were being targeted by a killer. We figured you joined Essex to save your skin. Kind sticks to kind."

"Because Essex is an earl and I'm an earl's son?"

"Something like that." Gavell shrugged, a characteristic gesture that told Nick that Gavell had long ago given up trying to understand his betters. "But then you saw to Annie's burial, proper like, even though she were your enemy."

Nick regarded him thoughtfully. He had assumed Gavell was nothing but a hard case, a bully-boy, with little on his mind except a primitive loyalty to the man who provided his pay. He was ashamed to admit he had thought this because, unlike Francis Bacon, with his blood ties to the greatest in the land, Gavell was from the poorer classes. Mistakenly, and unforgivably, Nick had assumed this meant he had no honor. That did not mean, of course, that Gavell and

Stace had not tried to kill him on *The Dalliance.* Following the orders of one's master was also proof of fealty.

Gavell held up his tankard. "To loyalty," he said.

"To loyalty," Nick replied.

But loyalty to what, and to whom?

Walking back to Bankside alone, Nick meditated on the irony of his toast after the funeral of a traitor. But Annie had been loyal to her family, her clan. She must have thought working for the Spanish was the best way to restore her family's fortunes. It didn't make her treason right, but it was something Nick understood. Blood was, after all, thicker than water. He wondered to what lengths he would go to protect his family, those he loved, and prayed he would never be put to the test.

CHAPTER 26

The Palace of Whitehall

Annie's death meant that Nick's letter to Walsingham over a week before was now moot, although he was still puzzled as to why he had not had a reply.

But he did receive another letter. It was from his brother, Robert, who said he was coming to London to see how John was—his own steward was John's brother—and also to purchase a house in the city; that he would be staying at The Mermaid Tavern so as not to put a burden on Maggie at this terrible time; that he would send Alan, his page, with a message when he arrived; that Elise, his sister-in-law, and their mother, Agnes, sent their love.

Nick was glad Robert was coming. For one thing, it would bring solace to Maggie and the entire Stockton family back at Binsey House. John's parents were both dead, and his brother could not get away from the estate, nor could his married sisters come to visit. So Robert would carry their love and take news back with him. As head of the family, this would be deemed not only appropriate but also a great kindness and a public sign of Robert's deep regard for the Stocktons, who had served the earls of Blackwell for generations, something to be talked about with approval in the villages and crofts on the Blackwell estate. It was a country custom but one that had been followed time out of mind.

Nick also had another reason for being happy to see Robert. He wanted to warn him of what del Toro had revealed, that he had intended to seek Robert out as the head of a prominent recusant family, perhaps to persuade him to join cause with Mary, Queen of Scots, and a treason plot to assassinate Elizabeth. Nick's blood ran cold when he thought that Robert and del Toro had so very nearly crossed paths in The Spotted Cow.

Del Toro was back in Paris, but that did not mean another approach might not be made. With Annie gone, there was now no witness besides Nick himself to testify that del Toro had had his sights on Robert at all. Nick wanted it to stay that way.

★ ★ ★

Nick was in a wherry being rowed across from Bankside to the Palace of Whitehall. It was May Day, and he could hear the bells of London proclaiming the holiday with joyous abandon. Even in Bankside, a maypole had been set up in Paris Garden, and people were flocking to the fields with picnic baskets. A May Queen had been chosen—ironically, one of Kat's girls—a sylphlike, fair-haired creature whose profession had not yet marked her face with cynicism and suspicion. In Bankside, it was not considered odd to have chosen a whore to be Queen of the May when, traditionally, it was a virgin who was chosen; in fact, the community would have been hard-pressed to find any female who was not beyond the pale of the law. There were a few such living in Bankside, of course, Mistress Baker for one; but as she weighed fifteen stone, was homely of countenance, and possessed biceps that any wrestler would envy thanks to a lifetime of lifting heavy batches of bread from the oven, she was automatically disqualified in favor of the willowy, and enthusiastically willing, Ursula.

The joke already circulating was that she was going to be the Virgin Queen for the day. The fact that this jest depended on an almost treasonous reference to the Queen's vaunted virginity made it all the more hilarious.

Nick would have much preferred to see in the May with his neighbors and friends, especially Eli and Rivkah, but he had decided to accept the Queen's invitation to the May Day festivities in the tilting yard. The play Essex was putting on in her honor—*The Ghost*, written by Will Shakespeare—would be in the evening. Even though Will was only on the outer margins of the acting troupe—being a lowly horse stabler and scene shifter—he longed to write plays and had secretly submitted his play to Essex for his approval.

Before deciding to attend on the Queen, Nick had volunteered to stay and watch over John so that Maggie could go to the May Day celebrations. But Maggie had refused.

"It wouldn't be the same without John," she said. "Matty, Jane, and Henry are going with Rivkah and Eli. You go and enjoy yourself."

Nick wasn't planning on enjoying himself. But once he was in the boat, such was the beauty of the day, the sound of the bells, the caress of the breeze on his face that the gloom that had descended on him since John's wounding and Annie's death began to lift just a little.

Compared to the last time Nick had been rowed across the river to Leicester House, this ride was a delight and not a misery of cold wind and rain, even though he and Edmund had sheltered beneath an awning on that previous voyage. Then, Essex had sent his own barge, hoping to entice Nick into his employ. Now Nick and Essex were on the outs, but Essex could not prevent Nick from attending—he was coming at the Queen's behest.

"Terrible thing that ship going up in flames," the boatman observed. He said it evenly, hardly out of breath despite the vigor with which he was plying the oars and the way he constantly scanned the water for other boats, maneuvering out of their way with consummate skill.

Nick should have been prepared to discuss the sinking of *The Dalliance* with a boatman. All those who plied their trade on water feared fire above all things, as they lived and worked in a world of frail wooden vessels with only a thin plank between themselves and eternity. Astonishingly, most of the sailors Nick had known had not been able to swim, although the boatmen who plied the Thames were usually good swimmers, having grown up on the river. But Nick did not want to relive the experience of the ship exploding, nor the sight of Annie's and Stace's burned corpses. He grunted a response and hoped the boatman would drop the subject. No such luck.

"I was talking to one of the sailors who escaped," the man said. He broke off to yell a curse at another boat that was crossing perilously close to his bow.

It contained a party of two ladies in summer dresses and parasols to keep the sun off their white skin and their beaux at the oars, their fine cambric shirts open at the necks to catch the breeze, their faces red and sweating in the warm sun. "Sorry," one of the ladies called, waving her parasol. The material of the parasol caught the breeze, and the boat rocked alarmingly, scraping the hull against the side of the wherry. The women shrieked and stood up; the men cursed and told them to damn well sit down and shut up. Both women complied, pouting, oblivious to how close they had come to overturning in the middle of the river.

"Fucking idiots," the boatman muttered with the contempt of a professional forced to watch amateurs give his livelihood a bad name. "They'll be in the drink soon enough, mark my words. Them ladies will sink like stones in them dresses." He said this with a little too much relish, Nick thought.

"Anyway," Nick's boatman continued, pulling smoothly away from the disaster waiting to happen in the other boat, "this sailor told me a mad man came running from the cargo hold shouting that the boat was on fire and to get out. If it weren't for him, the sailor said, they'd all be cinders. Said that he hoped the man escaped. Must have, seeing as the rumor was he saw a trollop asleep before the fire broke out. Said he tried to wake her but she was too drunk, most like."

Annie, Nick thought. But why was she asleep if she had just tried to kill him? Perhaps this was the proof he was looking for: that it had been Stace, not Annie, who had shoved him into the gunpowder room. Now that he was dead and Gavell was leaving Essex's employ, Nick would never be able to prove it. And perhaps there was no need; being blown up was punishment enough for Stace. After all, that was the death he had intended for Nick.

Gavell was another matter: he might try to exact revenge for the death of his friend, even though it was Nick who had been the intended victim. It would be just as well if Nick did not let down his guard, even if Gavell had appeared friendly at Annie's funeral.

But even if Annie was not responsible for the attempt on his life, Nick was certain she had killed Winchelsea and had attempted to kill Thomas and John. Justice had been done.

Let it go, he told himself.

The boatman lapsed into silence as he concentrated on steering through the crowded part of the river that ran alongside Whitehall Palace. Boats were three deep at Whitehall Palace Stairs, with revelers being dropped off for the May Day celebrations. As many of them were already drunk despite it being only morning, getting these passengers safely from the rocking boat to the dock took time. One severely inebriated man fell in, much to the amusement of not only his companions but himself. He was hauled out by his friends, his starched linen ruff sadly drooping, the dye in his vermilion hose running into his slippers like blood.

"Just call me Neptune," he hiccupped, "risen from the deep."

"A tosser, more like," the boatman remarked, rolling his eyes.

At last, it was his boat's turn to dock at the stairs. Nick paid the boatman and climbed out.

"Want me to come back for you later on?" the boatman said. "It'll be bedlam trying to get a boat then."

Nick was tempted, but he did not know when the play would be over. He told the boatman as much.

"Good luck to ye, then," the boatman said cheerfully, and shoved off to go seek out another fare. The first day of spring was one of the busiest days in a boatman's year; he would be up and down the river perhaps fifty times or more that day, but despite his exhaustion at the end of the day, he would be very much the richer.

Nick joined the stream of revelers flowing through the palace toward King Street and thence to the tiltyard west of the palace grounds, through the Great Court and main palace gates. On his way he passed by the chapel where the body of the Queen's youngest lady-in-waiting had been found last winter. She had been placed on the altar and had looked as if she were sleeping. This reminded Nick of what the boatman had told him about the sailor on *The Dalliance* who had seen a woman sleeping in the ship and been unable to wake her. He remembered how the sailors had tried to go up the ladders first until Nick had thrown them back so the whores could escape first. Most probably, the sailor the boatman told him about had been too concerned with saving his own skin to try to rescue a sleeping Annie.

This thought made Nick sad, a mood that was completely at odds with the merriment of the people around him, jostling each other in their eagerness to reach the tiltyard and the festivities there, shouting out greetings to those they recognized, the women arm in arm to steady themselves on their high cork-healed slippers, the men slapping each other on the back.

All were courtiers, all richly dressed in their brightest colors with flowers and greenery adorning their hair, as was the custom on May Day. Some paused to stare at Nick, for he had not bothered to trick himself out with flowers or greenery or even his best shirt and doublet. He had, however, bathed and shaved. That was the best he had been prepared to do when he was racked with worry over John and still deeply perplexed by the strange twists and turns of this recent case, a case he knew had been solved by Annie's and Stace's deaths but nevertheless still bothered him.

Why, then, this deep unease, a feeling that he had missed something? It must be the specter of John's death that was haunting him, Nick thought. He resolved to try his best to join in the fun of the day, but in all truth, he was dreading it and would have much preferred to be in Bankside just then. Or anywhere else except the court. As with Annie's sad little funeral, the celebration of Nature's renewal of life and the hope of a good harvest seemed deeply ironic in view of John's perilous condition. Nick said a quick Ave Maria that, like the seeds lying in the ground all winter, John would awaken from his deathlike sleep.

In Moorfields, Finsbury Fields, and Convent Garden, as well as outlying districts of London like Shoreditch where the city had not yet overtaken the countryside, and on village greens all over

England, maypoles would have been set up. These giant poles, fashioned out of birch trees, were chopped down by the young men of the village at dawn and trimmed of their branches so they were smooth, except at the top, where they were left leafy and green to symbolize new life. Decorated with flowers and ribbons by young maidens, the pole was then erected in the middle of a green sward by rope and tackle, shirtless young men eagerly showing off their brawn to the catcalling and giggling girls.

In poorer communities, a cart was used as a throne for the crowning of the Queen of the May, but at the palace, Nick saw that the royal enclosure on the viewing platform for the jousting had been festooned with flowers so thickly that they completely hid the wood beneath. In the center of the stage was the throne, no doubt borrowed from one of the lesser audience chambers, covered in a green velvet banner with the face of the mysterious Green Man worked in silver thread over it. On either side of this throne, and slightly raised on their own small platforms, were two other thrones—one for the Queen, traditionally dubbed Maid Marian for the day; and one for her chosen consort, Robin Hood. Nick would lay his last groat on Essex having been chosen to play Robin Hood for the day, perhaps as a sop to his pride before Elizabeth packed him back to the Netherlands.

The maypole itself was the tallest and most elaborate Nick had ever seen. He imagined that the Queen's chief forester had been tasked with finding one of superior stature months ago. Silk ribbons of every hue fluttered from its topmost branches, and like the stage, every inch of the pole had been festooned with flowers. St. James's Park and the countryside around must have been denuded of spring blooms in order to cover such a monstrosity, Nick thought, thus denying poor villagers one of the only really colorful and beautiful things in their otherwise drab lives.

Still, Nick thought, it did make a pretty show. He wandered in the direction of the tables spread out along where the barrier for jousting was usually erected and helped himself to the free wine being served in pewter goblets by an army of royal pages, for once all wearing clean livery. Nick noted that a fair number of them had obviously been sampling the wares; the boy who served him belched loudly.

"Pardon me, Your Eminence," he muttered. The boy was so far gone in his cups, he had mistaken Nick for an archbishop.

"You are forgiven, my son," Nick solemnly intoned, making the sign of the cross over him, then deftly grabbed the wine ewer from him when the lad gagged and turned a faint greenish hue.

As the pages ranged in age from eight to sixteen, the younger boys had obviously not yet learned that, with wine especially, a little went a long way. Nick suspected that more than a few of them would be discovered puking in the bushes and sleeping it off under the table by the end of the day.

Perhaps they had the right idea, Nick thought, emptying his goblet and refilling it. He sauntered off, still carrying the ewer, leaving the poor lad heaving behind the table. If he drank enough, there was a chance his bleak mood might improve.

The tiltyard was full of courtiers now, awaiting the arrival of the Queen as Maid Marian, and her consort, Robin Hood, who-ever that might be. After that the Queen of the May would process in and be crowned. Then the dancing around the maypole would begin.

Nick sat down on one of the top tiers of the viewing stands, blessedly empty, as everyone else had formed up on either side of the entrance to watch the approaching procession. Nick leaned back and closed his eyes. The sun was hot on his face and he felt himself growing drowsy, the buzz of the crowd getting fainter and fainter until it was a distant hum, like bees moving over a lavender bed in a summer garden. Then a trumpet sounded to herald the arrival of the Queen, and he opened his eyes and looked straight at a young man standing at the edge of the crowd. Nick was about to close his eyes again when the young man turned. Nick sat up.

The man looking back at him was Annie.

The man started moving away behind the crowd and managed to push his way through the onlookers around the gatepost of the tiltyard. Fearing that Annie was there to assassinate the Queen, Nick sprang to his feet and pursued, fighting against the crowd. Just as he reached the exit, Elizabeth swept through, dressed in green silk worked with silver thread and pearls. On her head was a jaunty hunting hat tilted down over one eye. She carried a silver bow and a quiver of arrows to signify her role as Maid Marian. She was arm in arm with Robin Hood—Essex, of course, trying to look jolly, but his mouth kept turning down when he forgot to smile—dressed in Lincoln green with a sharply peaked hunting cap on his head and also carrying a silver bow and quiver of arrows. Codpiece danced ahead of them, thwacking anyone within reach with an inflated pig's bladder on a stick and calling out obscene greetings. He was covered in bells and jingled like a purse full of change.

Cursing the delay, Nick made a hasty leg. Codpiece bonked him on the top of his head. When Nick looked up, irritated, Codpiece winked.

"Hello, Richard," Nick said. "Less of the pig's bladder in the face, if you don't mind."

The Queen's eye fell on him.

"Ah, Nick," she said, stopping. She bent to whisper in his ear, giving Nick the full treatment of her breath, eye-watering from a mouthful of rotting teeth. "Congratulations on resolving our little problem."

Possibly not so resolved, Nick thought, plastering a smile on his face for his monarch. Elizabeth was, of course, referring to the death of Annie, a rogue agent and traitor.

"Thank you, Your Majesty," was the only fitting response before so many witnesses. He couldn't very well tell her that a ghost had just appeared right under the royal nose.

"Don't be a stranger," Elizabeth said loudly, plucking a flower from her hat and tossing it to him. What others heard was a much-coveted open invitation into the royal presence; what Nick heard was a command to give the Queen a full report by day's end, or else.

The Queen sailed past, inclining her head graciously to her fawning courtiers, each of them eyeing Nick enviously because she had stopped to speak with him and not them. Not only that, but she had given him a favor; in chivalric terms, the flower she had tossed him was tantamount to choosing him to be her knight for the day. The scowl on Essex's face clinched it. Others in the crowd had understood the implication of Elizabeth's gesture as well. But before they could latch on to him like voracious lampreys in hopes of the Queen's favor rubbing off on them, Nick slipped through the gate.

To his right was the Old Staircase leading to St. James's Park. Briefly Nick considered that Annie might have run that way, but then he concluded she would know she'd be much more inconspicuous in the palace complex, with more chance to blend in with other people, so Nick turned left toward the palace. He emerged into the great open road outside Whitehall. No sign of the young man. Nick entered the vast inner courtyard of the palace and looked around. Servants were scurrying to and fro along the gravel paths outside the building that housed the wine cellar and the great kitchens. Nick walked toward them.

"Seen a young man come this way a few moments ago?" he asked a young kitchen girl carrying a bucket of bloody chicken and duck heads to throw on the midden behind Scotland Yard, the furthest yard to the north of the palace.

"I wish," she said with a coquettish grin. Then she spoiled the effect by wiping her runny nose on her sleeve.

Nick sighed and pressed on. He entered the palace by the door near the wine cellar.

Instinctively, Nick was making for the river on the east side of the palace. If it were he who was trying to escape, he'd jump into the nearest wherry and be lost in the myriad craft on the river in the blink of an eye. But when he came out at Whitehall Stairs, there were no boats pushing off, only two that were disembarking passengers. Nick asked the same question he had asked the kitchen skivvy. He got only shrugs from the boatmen and blank stares from their fares.

"Want a ride, mister?" one of the boatmen called.

Sorely tempted, Nick nevertheless shook his head. The Queen wanted a report on Annie, and now he would have to tell her that he had seen her alive and well. Either that, or he was losing his mind.

He couldn't face returning to the tiltyard to watch the crowning of the Queen of the May and the dancing around the maypole, not to mention put up with Codpiece larking about at his expense. What he really needed was somewhere quiet where he could think, so he reentered the palace and made for the room he had been loaned last winter when he was conducting inquiries in a murder investigation. He knew it was likely to be empty, as it was kept for visiting dignitaries and contained such amenities as a fireplace with chairs in front of it, a window looking out onto the Privy Garden, and a four-poster bed.

As he suspected, the room was unlocked and empty. Thanking God for small mercies, he entered and closed the door. Instantly, a great weight of weariness fell on him. Instead of sitting in a chair by the empty fireplace, he opened the window to let in the soft, spring air, then took off his sword and boots and stretched out on the bed.

For days, it seemed, he had been keeping vigil at John's bedside, or accepting the condolences of his neighbors, all the while trying to come to terms with the deep guilt he felt about John being mistaken for himself. If only he had not asked him to stop by Seething Lane; if only he had gone himself. The day John was attacked had been one of the first days of spring weather; the other had been the day they went to the tavern where Annie and del Toro had met, and thence to her secret house. He had taken off the bandage around his head because he'd felt that people were staring at him like Lazarus coming out of the tomb—Lazarus . . . Annie's funeral . . . spring . . . the maypole with leaves growing out the top . . . Protea . . .

Nick tried to follow his thoughts, but they kept twisting like the woolen skeins in his mother's tapestry basket, hopelessly tangled. As a boy, one of his jobs had been to separate each strand and wind it back on its corresponding ball of wool: jasper like blood; emerald like new grass, like the new growth of wood and copse. But when he reached out his hand to take hold of one thread, it changed into another color and he had to start again.

* * *

Nick was walking in a forest of maypoles, each tree towering into the sky above his head, the trunks smoothly silvered, the tops covered in round balls of wool of every color of the rainbow, loose windings trailing down like ribbons.

An old woman lying on the ground blinked once at him; Nick tried to wave, but his arm was too heavy to lift. Codpiece stuck his head around a tree, winked as if he and Nick were in on some private joke, and then vanished.

Edmund walked by, his fingers playing with something on a chain around his neck, but did not say anything, did not even look at Nick. Then he, too, vanished.

No leaves rustled; no birdsong riffled the air; no brook tumbled over stones. Nick's footsteps made no sound, and when he looked down, he was not walking on grass but on green silk figured with silver thread. A single daffodil lay beside his foot; he picked it up and put it to his nose. It smelled of sandalwood.

Then Nick glimpsed a lock of red hair against silver bark.

"Annie?"

A low laugh. "Catch me if you can."

Nick started running toward a great golden light that glowed brighter and brighter the deeper into the forest he ran. Suddenly, he was on the edge of the forest. He stopped, breathless, staring. Floating in the air, impossibly huge, was a great fiery ship with pennants flying, sails bellied, and tilted to one side as if beating into the teeth of a gale. The flames did not consume it but made it as radiant as the sun. Leaning on the rail, high above him, was Annie, red hair streaming in the wind.

"Goodbye, Nick," she called. "Goodbye."

"Wait!"

Suddenly Nick was sinking, water climbing up to his waist, his shoulders, his chin. Desperately he tried to stay afloat, but he felt hands grasp his ankles, pulling him down. The murky green closed over his head and he saw John's face floating white and bloated, his hair lifting and swaying like seaweed in the current, his eyes open, fixed on Nick as if he had an urgent message to impart. Then, like a monstrous leviathan, the dark hull of the ship passed over them, and everything went black.

* * *

Nick woke gasping, drenched in sweat. The room had grown warm, the covers tangled around his legs, the faded tapestries on the bed close and hot and airless. He crawled off the bed and staggered to the window. Opening it wider, he leaned out, drawing in great draughts of fresh air, feeling the sweat cool on his back, his mind beginning to clear.

The sun had passed its zenith and was beginning its downward descent into the west, its rays striking Nick full in the face, causing him to squint. Beyond the palace, the citizens of London were returning to their homes, tired and happy, thankful that the first day of summer had come at last, praying for a good harvest so they would not starve this winter.

Somewhere out there in the maze of streets and alleys and low-rent dives, a dead woman moved among the living like a ghost.

CHAPTER 27

The Palace of Whitehall, the Great Hall

Although Nick was tempted to leave the palace and go out into the streets of London to search for Annie, he knew he must show up for the play. The great clock tower in the palace struck six. He had slept through the entire afternoon.

Praying that the Queen had been too caught up in the festivities to notice his absence, he ran down the stairs and along the corridors to the Great Hall.

The feasting was over and the servants were clearing the platters of meat and bread when Nick sidled into the hall. He managed to snatch a piece of bread and a leg of duck before a snooty valet whisked the tray away. The kitchen staff were fiercely proprietary about the scraps left over from a feast; they would be shared out in the kitchens, the royal cook getting the choicest bits, then the under cooks and so on down to the lowliest skivvy, who would be lucky to be able to suck the marrow out of a chicken bone picked clean of meat.

The dais where the Queen and Essex had feasted had been cleared for the play. Elizabeth's throne had been set in the center of the room before the makeshift stage; smaller thrones for Essex as Robin Hood and the Queen of the May, the pretty fifteen-year-old daughter of the Duke of Somerset, stood to the right of the Queen, with Essex on the end.

Eating his food, Nick went to stand in the crowd behind the thrones, hoping to remain inconspicuous. He spotted Edmund on the edge of the crowd and nodded to him. Nick was just thinking of moving in that direction when Codpiece popped up in front of him waving his infernal pig's bladder in his face.

"Who's the naughty truant then?" Codpiece said.

"Shhh," Nick hissed.

But it was too late. The Queen had craned round and seen Nick. She beckoned with a beringed finger.

"Thanks a lot, Richard," Nick muttered.

Codpiece gave an elaborate bow and skipped off, grinning.

Approaching the royal presence, Nick bowed deeply, "Your Majesty."

"Where in God's name did you skive off to?" demanded Elizabeth.

"Er . . . I fell asleep."

"Nice for some."

Elizabeth did look tired; the thick white paste on her face was beginning to crack, making it look like a mask covering her bony, aging face. The flowers on her hat and in a garland around her neck had wilted. Nick had to remind himself that Elizabeth was approaching old age and was beginning to have more and more bouts of crotchetiness as her energy for long public events diminished.

Nick also happened to know that May Day was not one of Elizabeth's favorite celebrations. In 1536, when Elizabeth was only three, her mother, Anne Boleyn, and father, King Henry VIII, had been watching the jousts in honor of the day at Greenwich. What poor Anne did not know was that, at that very moment, her personal musician, Mark Smeaton, was being tortured by that odious little toad, Cromwell, to confess that he had been Anne's lover. Without warning, Henry suddenly got up and left the joust, riding off for parts unknown, no explanation given. It was to be the last time Anne would see him. Shortly thereafter, she was arrested, taken to the Tower, and beheaded. May Day 1536 was the last time Elizabeth had seen her mother. It was one reason that, although she traditionally celebrated the day with jousting, she always appeared restless and did not watch the bouts for long.

Essex seemed oblivious to this dark royal anniversary and sat slouched in his chair, idly shredding the petals of the flowers that had adorned his clothes and scattering them on the floor like a sulky child. He was chatting in a distracted, bored way with the poor Queen of the May, who kept glancing uneasily at the Queen. She had noticed Elizabeth's mood but was too young to be aware of the significance of the date and too inexperienced to know how to jolly her out of it. Altogether, it was a sad contrast to the earlier scene in the tiltyard, with the sun shining brightly on the gorgeous court and Elizabeth in their midst, the brightest sun of all. Now the sun had definitely set, and Nick could feel the gloom of night descending.

"Sit down, for pity's sake," the Queen commanded.

As if by magic, a servant placed a chair on the Queen's left. Nick sat.

"Tell me about this traitor, Annie O'Neill."

So Nick did, trying to keep his voice low.

"Pity," Elizabeth said. "I was going to issue a patent restoring her family's ancestral rights next year. Her father would have been an earl again."

At the word *earl*, Essex leaned forward and glowered at Nick. He must have thought Nick and the Queen were talking about him. Either that, or he was still sulking about the loss of his ship and the fact that Nick had not gone down with it.

"Ignore him," Elizabeth said. "He's miffed because I've ordered him back to the Netherlands." She shot Essex an irritated look. "If he can't keep his own agents in check, he's better off on the battlefield. Isn't that right, Robin?" she called in a loud voice.

He hadn't heard her conversation with Nick so did not know to what she referred, but like the good obsequious courtier that he was, he smiled and kissed the tips of his fingers to her.

"Pah!" the Queen snorted, turning her back on him. Perhaps she had gotten wind that Essex and Annie had been lovers.

Nick saw an angry color rise in Essex's cheeks at Elizabeth's contemptuous dismissal. For a moment, Nick thought he was going to storm off in a snit, but evidently he wasn't that rash. Instead, he snapped his fingers at a hovering page carrying a ewer of wine and held out his goblet to be refilled. He drank deeply and held it out again. It was obvious that he had decided to keep his temper and his seat, but he would steadily drink himself insensible.

So much for poor Will Shakespeare's hopes of impressing his patron with his first attempt at a play. Essex had abandoned any attempt at polite conversation with the girl next to him and sat hunched over his goblet, glowering at the stage. Caught between Essex's black mood and the Queen's, the poor girl must have felt that summer had quickly become deepest winter.

Nick had not yet told the Queen that he was sure he had spotted Annie, alive and well, in the tiltyard that morning. He was debating whether to do so when there was a beating of drums from the stage and an actor stepped forward.

"Your Majesty," he said, making a deep bow to Elizabeth with an elaborate flourish of the hand. He bowed to the Queen of the May and then to Essex, as protocol demanded. The girl blushed. Essex grunted and slurped his wine.

"Gentles," the actor said to the rest of the audience, again bowing.

"Get on with it, man," the Queen snapped.

Nick saw the anxious face of Will peek around the curtains. Nick gave him the thumbs-up, but he could see his friend was so overwrought that he looked on the verge of vomiting.

"*The Ghost!*" the actor proclaimed.

Another drumroll and the curtains opened to reveal the battlements of a castle at night and two men standing guard. A third man entered stage left.

"*How now, good men. Hast thou seen it again this night?*"

"*Not I, Prince Hamlet.*"

"*Not I.*"

"*Well, 'tis but your fantasy. Good morrow to you both.*"

"*Stay a while and watch with us. We swear it is not a dream of fevered minds, but fact.*"

The Queen yawned. Nick winced for his friend. So far the play was not exactly gripping. Nick wondered what Will had been thinking when he offered it to Essex for the grand finale of the May Day celebrations. It was set at night, in winter, and, instead of the theme of new life, the action of the play was about death and ghosts.

Nick envisioned all the sad, drunken soliloquies in The Black Sheep with Will opining the play's disastrous opening night, and it would be Nick's ear Will would be bending.

Nick watched with a fixed look of interest on his face as the play proceeded, but he was not really paying attention. He was thinking of what the boatman had said about the woman the sailor had seen sleeping on The Dalliance before it caught fire. At first Nick had assumed the woman was Annie, but now that he had seen Annie alive and well with his own eyes, he realized it must have been someone else, probably a whore lured there by Annie with the gift of her jasper ring, then murdered so that if her body were found, it would appear Annie had perished. That meant that either Stace's death had been an accident—he had always moved slowly— or Annie had called on her friends to lure Nick to the boat.

Nick thanked his stars that he had had the foresight to ask Eli to look at the corpse. He had the jasper ring in his possession, intending to return it to Annie's family. Nick smiled wolfishly to himself. Now he would return it in person, just before he arrested her for murder and treason. Once in the Tower with all its fearsome instruments of torture, Annie would give up Gavell.

Nick tried to pick up the thread of the play: apparently, the ghost was the murdered father of Hamlet who had demanded that his death be avenged. As far as Nick could tell, Hamlet was thrown into a tizzy by this revelation. Nick couldn't really follow it, but the plot somehow meant something to him, although he couldn't for the life of him think what it was.

"*Swear.*"

His eye fell on Edmund, who had moved to the front of the crowd and was standing next to Essex. He seemed absolutely enthralled by the action on stage, his face pale with concentration, his fingers playing with the chain at his neck. At least Nick would be able to report to Will that someone was enjoying his play.

"*Or such ambiguous giving out, to note you know ought of me.*"

Well, that was certainly true of Annie, Nick thought. He had had no idea of how treacherous she was.

A faint snoring came from his right. Nick glanced over and saw that the Queen had dropped off.

The play droned on, people leapt about, and then there was a fight scene at the end in which everyone, so far as Nick could tell, died. The bodies were carried off by two stagehands posing as servants—Will was one of them, looking thoroughly tragic, and Nick could tell he wasn't acting—noble attributes were ascribed to the hero, although Nick had a hard time remembering why he was so heroic, considering he had been utterly indecisive for most of the play and was definitely a mamma's boy. Then the actors appeared on the stage and took their bows.

The desultory clapping wakened the Queen.

"Oh, marvelous," she shouted, throwing wilted flowers onto the stage. "Bloody marvelous. Well done indeed." Then she grabbed Nick's arm. "Help me up," she said. "I'm dying for a pee."

CHAPTER 28

City of London

Nick slept the night again in the palace, using the same room, so that he would be closer to the city the next day.

He arose at sunrise, about five o'clock, stopped off in the palace kitchens on his way out to beg some bread and small beer from the yawning servants, then walked to King Street, the road running west of the palace, and followed it north toward Charing Cross. At the cross, he turned right and walked east up the Strand toward the center of London.

His plan was vague. All he knew for certain was that he intended to revisit the house near Moorfields, hoping against hope that Annie would return to it. If she was running around London in disguise, then she would need her costumes and makeup in order to change her appearance. He was still astonished that she would have been so rash as to appear at court the day before, albeit disguised. Was she tracking him in order to complete her mission and kill him? Is that what her Spanish masters required?

Nick did not know what she was up to, but he intended to make himself an easy target. His former qualms about killing a woman had completely vanished. If he could not take her alive, then he would run her through with his sword without hesitation. She was far too dangerous to be allowed to live.

His route to Moorgate took him past Thomas's lodgings. On a whim, Nick decided to go in. Thomas was not in residence. After recovering from the poisoning attempt, he had decided to visit his home in the country despite being on the outs with his wife. He had left a jokey message for Nick saying that, if he died, Nick was to consider his wife the prime suspect. Considering how close his brush with death had been, and how much his wife hated Thomas, Nick did not think this amusing in the least.

He knocked on the landlady's door. No answer.

"She's gone to market," a voice said.

A stunted, malodorous figure emerged from the gloom of the hallway.

"Harold?"

"At your service." Harold, the usually out-of-work rat-catcher, gave an incongruous bow, his rattraps swinging from one hand.

"I thought you were . . . well, unemployed," Nick said.

Harold shrugged. "I keeps me hand in," he said. "Besides, me rates are cheap, and Mistress here likes cheap."

Nick remembered the empty grate in the fireplace even though the room was cold, and there was a big basket of logs on the hearth. He had been right about her; she was one of those women who was penny wise, pound foolish. Employing a hopeless case like Harold who, if Bankside gossip was to be believed, hadn't caught a single rat in his entire sorry career, was a case in point.

Mistress Shrewsbury was the type of woman who would buy one mangy turnip at the market and one scrawny pullet and then live on the soup for days. Then she would have to pay a quack an exorbitant fee for an elixir that settled her stomach after having given herself food poisoning. Given the size of her house in such a prosperous neighborhood, and the fact that she had only herself to feed—and her cats, of course, and from what Nick had seen on his last visit, they were so well fed and indolent that they wouldn't turn a whisker if a rat ran right under their noses—Nick could not imagine that she needed to live this way. She was obviously a miser, and now she had employed the worst rat-catcher in London, foolishly thinking she was saving money.

"How long have you been coming here?" Nick asked.

"Oh, ages."

Typical, thought Nick. Harold had been coming for months, and Mistress Shrewsbury was still complaining about her rat infestation. But it gave Nick an idea.

"Were you here the day Sir Thomas Brighton was poisoned?"

"I come every morning to inspect the traps."

Which were empty, Nick noticed. Any rat worth his salt could outwit Harold's traps. In the rat community, they probably passed around blueprints and discussed ways of springing them without injury. This thought diverted Nick somewhat from his growing impatience. Harold was infuriatingly obtuse. Having a conversation with him was as frustrating and pointless as explaining the finer points of geometry to an ape.

"Harold, did you see anyone?"

"A young man on the stairs."

Finally.

"Was he a lad?" It could have been the boy from the tavern down the street delivering the wineskin to Sir John.

"I just told you. A man. Young."

"Could it have been a woman dressed up as a man?"

Harold just stared openmouthed.

Nick gave up on that one. Obviously, the notion of cross-dressing had never entered his innocent—or vacuous—mind. "What was he doing?"

"Dropping something off in that man's room."

"Which man? The fat one or the thin one?"

Harold grinned. "Nah. Stealing from Peter to give to Paul." When he saw Nick's incomprehension, he added, "Nicked a wineskin leaning against the fat git's door and put it in the other git's room opposite."

Even though Nick usually avoided touching any part of Harold's disgusting clothes—more rags than cloth—he gripped him by both shoulders. Harold looked alarmed and glanced down at Nick's hands, then up into his face.

"Are you arresting me?" he asked.

"No, Harold, me old chum," Nick said. "But there's a shilling in this if you think very, very carefully before you answer my next question."

Harold's red-rimmed eyes came alive for the first time. He was a notorious toper.

"Would you recognize this 'man' if you saw him again?"

"Expect so," Harold said, hawking a gob of phlegm into the back of his throat.

Nick let go hurriedly and tossed him a shilling.

Harold bit it, then put it somewhere in the pile of rags he called clothes. "Ta, Nick."

"Did he see you?"

"Nah," Harold said. "I was in the hallway looking up at him." He pointed up the stairs, and both doors were clearly visible. "Then I went out back. I was crouched down at the side of the house laying me traps when he came out. Got a good old look. He had no idea I was there."

Better and better. As much as Nick tried to avoid being in close proximity to Harold, owing to his stench, Nick did not want to see him floating facedown in the river.

"Make sure I can get hold of you in a hurry," Nick warned.

Harold slung his empty rattraps over his shoulder. "I'll let you know when I go on me holidays, then," he said, and went out the front door, turning left toward the tavern.

Nick stared after him. To his knowledge, Harold had never made a joke before.

★ ★ ★

When he arrived at the small house in Moorgate, Nick discovered that the door he had kicked in had been repaired. Aside from his glimpse of Annie in the tiltyard, this was the first hint he'd had that she was indeed alive and no ghost. He kicked the door in again and entered.

Her bedchamber and dressing room looked almost the same as when he had searched it with John. Except, he noticed, items on the dressing table were slightly rearranged—the pot of glue for

sticking on beards was in a different place; the candles on the mirror had burned lower. And there was a faint scent of sandalwood in
the room. Annie's perfume. She had definitely been here recently.
The bedcover was more rumpled than he remembered, and there
was an indentation in the pillow. So she had slept here.

He checked the other room, but it was empty, although there
were charred logs and ash in the fireplace whereas it had been
swept clean before. He put his fingers on the ash; still faintly warm.
Another indication that the rooms had been recently occupied.

He sat down in a chair and prepared to wait for Annie's return.
Then his eye caught something on the floor, halfway under the
bed. He bent to pick it up. It was a forget-me-not, broken at the
stem. Staining the planks of the floor were yellow pollen stains and
a single buttercup petal. Wildflowers.

Nick got up and left the house. Looking over the wall onto
Moorfields, he saw that the entire area was covered with buttercups, forget-me-nots, and flowering clover. He went back inside
the bedroom and stood looking at the floor for a long moment,
then made up his mind. Leaving the house, he quickly walked
through the Guildhall district to Fenchurch Street, then south into
Eastcheap and thence east into the Ward of Billingsgate and to the
church of St. Mary-at-Hill.

In the graveyard, he saw an ancient crone placing flowers in a
tin cup on Protea's grave.

At Nick's approach, the old woman turned. Her back was bent;
long gray hair straggled over her face, obscuring it; a filthy shawl
covered her head. But the eyes under matted gray eyebrows were
not wrinkled at the corners or clouded with cataracts. They were as
green as the Emerald Isle, as clear as its mountain streams.

Nick's hand went to his sword. "Hello, Annie."

CHAPTER 29

The Mermaid Tavern

Nick had been gone from Bankside almost two days—all May Day and most of the next. When he returned to The Black Sheep, he found a message waiting for him from his brother. Robert had arrived and was staying at The Mermaid Tavern near St. Paul's; could Nick come by as soon as may be, as Robert had some urgent news for him?

Nick could guess what Robert had to tell him, as Nick had asked him to make some inquiries for him weeks ago, just after he returned to London. Robert had obviously thought the information he was bringing too important to entrust to a messenger; besides, Robert was keen to purchase a house in London. It gave him a good reason to come to the city without anyone getting suspicious.

On the third of May, Nick returned to the city of London, first leaving a message at Leicester House and then walking to The Mermaid, where he and Robert talked until after dark. Then he made his way home across London Bridge to Bankside.

The following morning, Nick went upstairs to his old room—now John's sickroom—to check on his friend. There had been no change except that John was progressively wasting away, diminishing before Nick's very eyes.

His eyes filmed over as he looked at the still figure on the bed.

"I will avenge him, I swear," Nick said to Maggie. Her face was haggard as she looked up at him from her vigil beside the bed, her eyes dull.

Then, to John, "Just hold on. Almost there. Be patient, my friend." Nick was conscious of echoing Walsingham's words to him when they were in the carriage on the way to Whitehall.

Nick turned on his heel and left the room, his face grim.

Hector looked up hopefully from his place near the front door of the tavern.

"Come on, then," Nick said.

Hector sprang joyfully to his feet and nuzzled Nick's hand by way of thanks. Nick had been leaving him at The Black Sheep to guard the family in place of John. Now Nick could see he might have a use for his gigantic hound. Besides, he had missed him, and the poor dog needed to stretch his legs after being cooped up for so long.

Before taking a wherry across the river, Nick let Hector bound around Paris Garden for an hour, stretching his long legs and sniffing at every rabbit hole and clump of weeds in the vast area. The maypole was still standing, its ribbons blowing in the breeze from the river. Hector urinated copiously on it, marking it for his own.

When Nick climbed into a boat, Hector sat there panting noisily, his long tongue lolling, his face split into a tired but contented doggy grin. From time to time, he leaned over the edge of the boat and tried to lap at the river water, but because it was salty, he reared back, tipping the boat alarmingly and making the boatman catch a crab with his oars.

"Don't you realize the river is an estuary?" Nick said, ruffling the dog's head. "It's seawater, you dolt."

"There's a bucket of freshwater under the seat," the boatman said.

Nick held it for Hector to drink. He lapped up half of it, then, finally sated, rested his shaggy head on Nick's knees and promptly went to sleep.

"I could do with one of them," the boatman said, nodding at the slumbering dog, "for when I get awkward customers. One look from him and they'd sit down proper instead of arsing around and nearly tipping us out. Problem is, he takes up half the boat."

Nick caressed Hector's head. "I wouldn't part with him for a thousand gold angels," he said.

"Don't blame you. He's a right noble beast."

Nick had found Hector dying from a savage beating in the dock-land area of a Spanish port when he was spying on the shipyards some years ago. Hector had been a puppy, but still huge, and Nick had carried him back to his inn and nursed him back to health. Nick had named him Hector for his heroic refusal to give up and die despite multiple broken ribs and a fractured leg. Now they were inseparable, and as he was a sight hound, Nick had trained him to take not only verbal commands but visual ones as well. This silent communication between them had saved Nick's life on numerous occasions.

Nick had the boatman row him to Old Swan Stairs, hard by the western side of London Bridge. Before meeting Robert back at The Mermaid, he had to check something in a district east of St. Paul's and west of St. Mary-le-Bow. This stretch was known as Goldsmith's Row, and it had been the center of the manufacture and sale of gold and jewelry in London for hundreds of years. Nick chose a jeweler at random and entered the shop.

When he came out, the bells of St. Paul's and St. Mary-le-Bow were chiming ten o'clock in the morning. By five after ten, Nick was walking into The Mermaid. He nodded to the barman and a serving wench who was making the rounds with a tray balanced on her hip. In the back room was a man he recognized. He lifted his hand to him and ran up the back stairs to where Robert had taken two adjoining rooms in the rear of the tavern.

"Do you have all the documents?" Nick asked, hugging his brother.

Robert pointed to a table set against the window. On it were legal documents, drawn up, an ink stand, sand, and sealing wax. Because the window was open to the mild spring breeze, the documents were weighted down with Robert's knife.

"All ready," he said. "What time did you ask him to come?"

"Half past the hour. He should be here soon."

Nick signaled for Hector to go into the other room, and after placing a bowl of water and a large lamb bone that Robert had saved from his dinner the night before on the floor for him, he put his fingers to his lips and then shut the door. Hector, he knew, would remain silent unless Nick told him otherwise.

Both brothers sat down in chairs on either side of the fireplace. Between them were a flagon of ale and three goblets.

"Will he come, do you think?" Robert asked.

"He'll come," Nick said.

In their discussion the previous evening, they had decided to restore Edmund's farm and ancestral lands to him.

As the present earl, only Robert had the legal power to give those lands to Edmund, as they had reverted to the Binsey House estate. So Robert had summoned Francis Bacon to the inn late last night and asked him to draw up the relevant documents. Robert and Nick had chosen Bacon because they knew he would report back to Edmund after he returned to Leicester House. That way, Edmund would know Robert and Nick were in earnest.

Now all that was required was Robert's signature and seal, Edmund's signature and seal, and Nick's signature as a witness. In the message Nick had left at Leicester House the previous day, he had briefly explained to Edmund what he and Robert wanted to do. That was why he was certain Edmund would show up. Tomorrow he left for the Netherlands with Essex, so today was his last chance to restore his family's fortunes.

Nick had thought long and hard about this decision. In his way, Edmund had been loyal to his father, although Nick considered that loyalty misplaced, considering Edmund's father's venal character.

There was a knock on the door.

"Come in," Robert said.

Edmund entered. His face was flushed, as if he had been running. Both Robert and Nick stood up and shook his hand.

"Have a seat," Nick said. He poured ale into the goblets and handed one to Edmund first, then one to Robert, and kept one himself. Holding up his cup, he made a toast.

"To the reversal of wrongs," he said.

Edmund held up his cup but hesitated before drinking. Nick smiled at him and drank. So did Robert. Then Edmund took a small sip and put his goblet down on a side table next to his chair.

"I cannot thank you enough, my Lord," Edmund said to Robert. "This is a great day for me and my family. A great day indeed."

Ten years Nick's senior and sporting a bushy beard instead of a clean-shaven, scarred face like Nick's, Robert looked like a benign uncle. He beamed. "Nick and I thought it unfair that the son should have to pay for the father's crimes."

At the word *crimes*, Nick saw spots of color appear on Edmund's cheeks, but he smiled nonetheless.

"Not many would see it like that," Edmund said.

"My brother is a just man," Nick said. "As was our father."

Edmund looked at him quickly, his expression unreadable. His eyes kept straying to the table by the window and the documents waiting to be signed.

"Shall we?" Robert said, indicating the documents.

Edmund leapt up. Robert and Nick approached the table more slowly, Nick hanging back, as he was going to be the last to sign.

Robert bent over the table, inviting Edmund to do the same. He read out the legal language conferring the land to Edmund as the oldest son, to revert to him and his heirs in perpetuity.

"Is that to your liking?" Robert asked, when he had finished reading.

Edmund gave a great sigh. "Oh, yes, my Lord. I thank you with all my heart."

Robert picked up a pen and dipped it in the inkwell. "Then let us sign and affix our seals without more ado."

Edmund was fingering the chain around his neck.

Robert signed. Then he held the lump of red sealing wax to a candle flame until it softened, dripped a great drop onto the parchment, and without taking off his seal ring, pressed it firmly into the wax.

Courteously, he handed Edmund the pen.

Edmund signed. Then he put down the pen and unclasped the chain around his neck. He took off the ring threaded there and held it up. "This is my father's seal ring," he said. "But, as you can see, it has lost its seal through age and use." He showed them the blank metal where a family crest should have been. "I can draw my family motto on the seal from memory, if you are willing to accept that as a substitute?"

The brothers looked at each other.

"It's a bit irregular," Robert said.

"It's not Edmund's fault the ring wore out," Nick replied. "I say, let him draw it. That, along with his signature, will make it legal."

"Thank you," Edmund said. He was looking at Nick strangely, as if seeing him for the first time.

"All right," Robert said.

Edmund bent to the document again and carefully inked out an image. Then he sprinkled sand on it to dry the ink and blew off the excess.

"Now," Robert said, picking up the document and coming to stand beside Nick in the middle of the room. Both brothers were now facing Edmund. "If you would sign as a witness, Nick? It won't be legal otherwise."

"Before I do," Nick said. "I have something for you, Edmund."

While Robert had been speaking, Edmund had been smiling at Nick expectantly. But when Robert had picked up the document, his smile had faltered. He now looked uncertainly at Robert and then back at Nick. "I really could not accept anything more. You have been too kind as it is." His eyes had become watchful.

Nick dug his hand in his pocket. "Oh, I think you'll want this." He withdrew his hand and held it out palm up toward Edmund. In the middle of it was the small medallion Hector had found in the shed at Wood Wharf. "In fact," Nick went on, "you returned to the wharf to search for it the day Stace and Gavell beat you up. At the time, I thought you were just following me."

Edmund stood as if turned to stone.

"At first I thought this was some kind of medal worn on a chain about the neck," Nick said. "Except it had no hole in it to take a link, and I noticed that the chain you wore already had a ring on it. So that got me thinking. Today I visited a jeweler, and I asked him about this. Want to know what he told me?"

Edmund did not reply.

"I'll tell you anyway. He told me that solid seal rings are expensive to make. Like Robert's, who inherited it from our father and our grandfather before him and so on. It's made from a single chunk of gold. That gold is poured into a cast with a family crest engraved on the bottom. When it cools, the whole ring comes out in one piece, crest and all. That way, it doesn't wear out as quickly. But it costs a fortune."

Nick took a couple of steps toward Edmund, who backed up against the open window.

"But people who can't afford a seal ring made from solid metal, or who are too mean to pay for it, like your father, I might add, choose another method. They take a gold or silver coin—in your father's case, a shilling—and give it to a blacksmith. Illegal, of course, but when did that ever stop your father?"

"The blacksmith heats the coin," Nick went on, "then hammers the silver flat so all trace of it being legal tender is gone and only a round disc remains. Then a crest is engraved into the top. It's affixed to the top of an existing ring with heated metal. Problem with this method is that the seal can come loose. That's what happened to this"—Nick took a step closer—"when you were torturing Simon Winchelsea."

"What?" Edmund stammered. "Me? You can't think? Annie is the one who murdered him; she is the traitor."

"Give up the act, Edmund," Nick said. "I have proof. Not only for Winchelsea's murder but also for Thomas's poisoning and even the assassination attempt on me."

All at once, Edmund's eyes became flat and reptilian. Nick now knew he was looking at the real Edmund, the man who hid behind the hapless, lonely ingenue who used his formidable acting skills to get close to the people he hated.

Nick remembered Machiavelli's dictum: keep your friends close, but your enemies closer. Edmund had clearly taken this to heart.

"You fucking smug, self-satisfied, lordly little prick," Edmund snarled. "You always thought you were better than me, didn't you? You and that oaf you call a friend. Shame he didn't die. I hit him hard enough."

Nick's hand went to his sword. "You thought John was me."

Edmund laughed. "You still haven't figured it out yet, have you, Holt? I knew it wasn't you. It was John I wanted to kill. Your best friend. The friend you were always going off with at Oxford. A servant. That's all he was. But me?" His face twisted with hate and something else, perhaps puzzlement. "I was a gentleman's son, but you preferred to keep company with riffraff. I suppose you thought I was unworthy of you because we had lost everything?"

Now Nick realized what had been bothering him ever since Gavell and Stace had brought John back to The Black Sheep gravely injured. The day had been warm; John had not taken his cloak with him, nor a hat. Thus, his attacker had known precisely who he was when he had tried to kill him. Edmund's malice had always been aimed at Nick; Winchelsea's death was an anomaly. Poor Simon had simply been in the wrong place at the wrong time, but the killing itself had triggered something long dormant and festering in Edmund and had set him on his bloody path of revenge.

At least Nick now knew that his guilt about John being mistaken for him was completely unfounded.

"It was never about agents, was it?" Nick said. "Winchelsea saw you with del Toro, so you had to get rid of him. Why did you put out his eyes, Edmund?"

Edmund shrugged. "He saw me. It seemed fitting, somehow."

Nick swallowed. Edmund's nonchalant response revolted him. Here was a man who was completely detached from other men. Indeed, Nick wondered if Edmund even saw others as human beings at all, subject to cold and hunger and desire as he was himself. In all probability, Simon, Thomas, John, the nameless woman on *The Dalliance*, Stace, and even Nick himself—no matter how much Edmund hated him—were merely obstacles to be gotten rid of by whatever means possible.

But there was also a love of cruelty in Edmund, the kind that made small boys pull the wings and legs off flies and take delight in their helpless suffering. The correlation between Winchelsea recognizing Edmund and losing his eyes for it confirmed this. And the poisoning of Thomas. It took a particular kind of devilry to subject another human being to a slow and painful death through poison. No wonder Edmund had hesitated to drink; a poisoner would suspect others of the same evil. That was why the punishment for poisoning was being boiled alive in a vat of oil or lead. A hideous death befitting a hideous crime.

Nick glanced at Robert, who was standing gray-faced beside him. He regretted dragging his brother into this, but Nick needed him as a witness.

"You had to kill Winchelsea because he realized you were selling information to the Spanish."

"What's my country ever done for me?" Edmund said. "I needed the money if I was ever to buy back my family land."

"Killing Winchelsea gave you an idea, didn't it, Edmund?" Nick went on. "Target Walsingham's agents, and everyone would be looking at a political motive. But the motive was always personal, wasn't it? Like Hamlet."

"Exactly," Edmund said. "Hamlet was a hero."

"Hamlet wasn't a traitor."

Nick saw Edmund flinch at the word. He remembered how rapt Edmund had been during the performance of *The Ghost*, how enthusiastically he had clapped when the actors gave their bows, the only member of the audience who had seemed to enjoy the play. But then its theme had mirrored Edmund's life—a son avenging a wrong done to his dead father. Of course Edmund would regard Hamlet as a hero. He himself was a hero in his own mind. What was it his family seal said? *Ego permanere. I will remain steadfast.* And the symbol for it was the evergreen tree, unchanged whatever the season.

Ever since his father died shortly before Edmund came up to Oxford, he had kept his hatred of Nick and the Holt family alive, nursing it by putting himself close to Nick, trying to insinuate himself into Nick's life. When that had not worked, they had gone their separate ways. But Edmund had not forgotten Nick. In fact, Nick was certain Edmund had come to London and attached himself to Essex's spy network not only to be close to Nick but to rival him in his profession as Essex was trying to rival Sir Robert Cecil, his hated adoptive brother. Perhaps, as with Nick at Oxford, he had tried to become friends with Essex, but Essex had spurned him more unkindly and openly than Nick had done, contemptuously treating him as an inferior, a servant. In his own mind, Edmund must have thought history was repeating itself, that Essex was treating him like he believed Nick had treated him at Oxford. This must have fueled his hatred even more.

Edmund's decision to follow Essex to the Netherlands was not made out of loyalty but from expediency. He needed to get out of England and allow the memory of Winchelsea's murder to fade. Then he would return and try to kill Nick again.

He must have been astonished to receive the message from Nick the day before. Perhaps he had even thanked God that he had not succeeded in killing Nick on the London Road.

It was time to talk of Oxford.

"You went to Oxford to meet up again with del Toro," Nick said. "Why was that when you had already seen him?"

"He owed me money," Edmund said sulkily.

"But you couldn't find him. Then you heard I was in town, and you remembered where John and I used to drink."

"The Spotted Cow."

"Did you know that you missed bumping into del Toro by a few minutes?"

Edmund's gaze sharpened. "You lie."

"No. I was tasked to trail him. I didn't count on Annie whisking him away under my nose."

"Annie?" Edmund looked genuinely confused.

"In her whore getup. Very convincing. And as I had not had the pleasure yet of meeting her, I didn't recognize her. She spirited del Toro away. When I came back to the tavern after trying to find them, you were talking to Robert here."

"What was Annie doing there?" Edmund asked. For the first time, Nick saw panic in his eyes.

Nick was too weary and too revolted to answer him. As Francis Bacon had advised, he was laying out all the pieces so that Robert could witness them, but he had no stomach for rehearsing such evil. It sickened him to the depths of his spirit.

But Robert was doing more than just standing in as a witness. He had brought with him some interesting information concerning the stranger who had attempted to assassinate Nick on the London Road.

"You murdered a former servant of your family," Nick said.

Again, Edmund shrugged. "He botched the job. I realized I had to remove him as a witness."

When Nick had seen the name of the man who died—Walter Harcourt—he realized that Edmund must have murdered him when Nick had rolled into the ditch away from the horses' hooves. Then Edmund had wounded himself in the shoulder to make it look convincing. Nick had been completely taken in.

"I wondered at the time why you did not invite the man you claimed was a messenger into the inn to get warm. It's what I would have done. But then," Nick said, "you couldn't have me seeing him."

"He wasn't much of a servant at the best of times," Edmund said. "Typical of him to bungle it. I should have done it myself."

"Why didn't you?" Nick asked.

Edmund smiled. "I had already wounded myself. Stupid, really. Did it on the spur of the moment without thinking. I should have run you through when you were in the ditch, but I couldn't get the damn horse to calm down."

Nick remembered seeing Edmund struggling with his rearing horse, and by that time he was bleeding heavily from the shoulder.

"Besides," Edmund said, "on the way back to London, I got to thinking that it would have been too quick if you just died. You needed to suffer more, like I have suffered, like my father suffered. That's when I decided to go after your friends. Those Jews would have been next, by the way."

Nick looked at him. All pity for Edmund had fled. Whatever he had suffered could not excuse the evil that lay at the very center of his being, an evil that was almost palpable in the small room, like the stench of sulfur from the flames of hell.

"You can come out now!" Nick called.

The door to the adjoining room opened and Harold the rat-catcher, and Hector, came out. Nick signaled to Hector to stand beside him. To Harold, he said, "Is this the man you saw on the landing picking up Sir John's wineskin and entering Sir Thomas's room?"

"He's the one," Harold said with satisfaction.

"Congratulations, Harold," Nick said. "You just caught your first rat."

Nick waited long enough for Harold to savor his triumph, then nodded at the door. "Hop it," he said.

Harold left the room without a murmur. He had been thoroughly briefed by Robert before Nick or Edmund had arrived, and he knew it was for his own safety.

"You too, Robert," Nick said.

"I'm not going anywhere."

This was said in Robert's big-brother voice. Nick recognized it from his childhood scrapes and smiled. When he was five, he had climbed onto the roof of the barn and then slipped down the side until he was hanging from the edge by his fingertips, the ground fifteen feet beneath him. Robert had come running and had instructed Nick to let go, saying he would catch him. When Nick was too scared, Robert had said exactly the same thing: "I'm not going anywhere." So Nick had closed his eyes and dropped. Robert caught him, set him safely down, and soundly cuffed him for putting himself in such danger.

Robert's stolid presence at his side was like a small candle burning in the vast darkness that was Edmund and the legacy of hate he had inherited from his father. And on Nick's other side stood Hector, perhaps loyalty incarnate. The dog's very stillness told Nick that all Hector's senses were directed at Edmund and his desire to protect his master from threat. Another small light burning bravely in the great darkness.

"You slipped up when you came to Thomas's room with Essex," Nick went on. "You told me you were going to throw the wineskin on the midden out back."

Edmund frowned, trying to remember.

"But how would you have known there was definitely a rubbish heap if you had never been to the house before?"

"Every house has one," Edmund sneered. "That doesn't prove anything."

"True," Nick said. "But the way you stated it with such confidence told me you were absolutely sure there was one, which meant you had been there before. I didn't realize at the time, but I knew something was wrong and it niggled at me. Harold's identification just confirmed it."

Edmund glanced at the knife on the table. Robert had forgotten to remove it when he picked up the documents. Robert suddenly realized his mistake and took a step forward, but Nick put out his hand and stopped him. Now it was his turn to protect his brother.

Suddenly Edmund lunged for the knife. Hector sprang at him, and Nick threw himself forward at the same time, sword out. But Edmund had fooled them. As soon as Nick and Hector started to move right, Edmund moved left and leapt out the open window.

"Shit," Nick said.

Then he followed Edmund out the window.

CHAPTER 30

City of London

Luckily, the room was only one story above the ground floor, and there were barrels of ale stacked against the wall under the window. Even so, Nick landed hard, and a searing pain shot up his legs. He jumped from the barrels to the ground, praying he hadn't broken any bones. To his relief, his legs held him up. Glancing right and left, he saw Edmund limping down the alley east on Budge Street in the general direction of Billingsgate Fish Market and the docks. He was favoring one leg, and Nick thought he had probably twisted an ankle on landing. From the front of the tavern, he heard Hector baying and the voice of Robert shouting something. Nick had stationed Gavell downstairs in the taproom in case Edmund should try to escape. He should have put him outside but hadn't thought Edmund would be reckless enough to jump out the window.

Stupid, stupid, he chided himself.

"This way," he yelled, and set off at a run after Edmund. He knew Hector would pick up his scent and the others would be following close behind.

The warm weather had brought out all of London onto the streets. Edmund must have realized that he had a better chance of escape if he forsook the back alleys and kept to the main thoroughfares, no doubt hoping to get lost in the crowd. But Nick was able to keep him in sight, partly because he had the use of both legs while Edmund was limping. Still, Edmund was running for his life, and this gave him an edge in both speed and cunning. He dodged between shoppers and barged others aside; once Nick almost lost him as he entered a tavern and came out the other side, but Nick was prepared for this, as Annie had done the same thing, and he was determined not to be taken in again.

Only when Edmund veered left on Walbrook Street and made for the Royal Exchange at the junction of Cornhill and Thread-needle Street did he almost lose him. Nick skidded to a halt at Bank Junction where these two streets converged and surveyed the great open area in front of him. Thronged with people shopping for goods ranging from precious metals to expensive imported wine to bolts of silk and velvet, it was a sea of people in constant motion. Almost anything could be had at the Royal Exchange for a price, and trade was especially brisk this fine May morning. But most people were strolling through the area, and Nick spotted Edmund's head bobbing through the crowd, parting it like a rampaging bull trampling a wheat field. Then Edmund looked back and Nick saw his face, white and staring, his mouth open as he drew in great gasps of air.

Nick took off after him, ignoring the shouts and curses of people he was forced to elbow out of his way. When he got to where he had seen Edmund, he looked around and saw him doubling back toward the river. If Edmund caught a wherry, Nick would likely lose him. Somewhere above the hubbub, he heard Hector baying and knew he was tracking Nick through the city.

When Nick looked back on that day, he couldn't explain why Edmund did not make for Old Swan Stairs, directly in front of him, but suddenly turned and ran toward St. Mary-at-Hill and the graveyard where Protea was buried. Perhaps he knew that the chances of a boat being immediately available to him were slim to none and that waiting for one would give Nick the precious time he needed to catch up; perhaps he could not run any farther and had decided to seek sanctuary in the church if he could just get to the altar and lay his hands on it, claiming the protection of the church for forty days. After this, he would have to either surrender to the secular authorities or confess his crimes publicly and then abjure the realm. As this meant he would go unpunished, Nick was determined Edmund should not gain asylum. Perhaps Protea herself, the mystery woman Edmund had murdered on *The Dalliance*, was also of this mind, for when Nick arrived, he saw Edmund leaning on her gravestone trying to catch his breath.

Nick circled him, sword drawn, and placed himself in front of the gate that led to the church.

"It's over, Edmund," he said. "In a few moments, my brother and Gavell will be here. You cannot escape."

Edmund's mouth twisted at the corners. Nick couldn't tell if it was a grimace or a smile.

"I will never surrender to you," Edmund said. "You will have to kill me first, as your family killed my father."

"Your father took his own life," Nick reminded him.

"He had no choice. He was bankrupt."

"He did have a choice. As did you," Nick said, slowly walking toward him. "You are leaning on the gravestone of the woman you murdered on the ship. How will you explain your choice to her?"

Edmund looked down, surprised, and stepped away from the grave. "I know of no Protea," he said.

"That's the name I gave her, thinking she was Annie."

Now Nick and Edmund were facing each other perhaps ten yards apart, swords drawn.

"Tell me who she was, so I can have the name changed on her tombstone."

Edmund shrugged. "Just a whore I picked up on the docks. Told her there was good business to be had on the ship with the sailors, gave her one of Annie's rings. She thought it meant she had to fuck me." He laughed. "That suited me. Afterwards, I strangled her and left her in the cargo hold."

Again, Nick was stunned by the casual manner in which Edmund referred to his killings. He showed no more emotion than if he had put down a fox that had been raiding the chicken coop. Briefly, Nick wondered if Edmund was insane, but there was no manic gleam in his eyes such as Nick had seen in gaze of the lunatics at Bedlam. Edmund's eyes registered no grief or joy, nor anger, but a kind of deadly boredom, as if the world did not interest him except as a means of satisfying his desires.

Only his fingernails, bitten to the quick, a habit even in his Oxford days that Edmund had not succeeded in conquering, suggested something that ate at him without mercy, some torment inside him.

"And it was you, of course, who locked me in the gunpowder room and started the fire."

"Naturally. Shame you escaped. Again."

Edmund had been the man the sailor had seen escaping the burning ship. What had niggled at him when the boatman imparted this bit of gossip to Nick on his way to Whitehall was how improbable it was for a sailor not to have recognized someone from his own crew.

"Richard Stace did not escape," Nick said. "You have his death on your conscience too."

Edmund just shrugged.

It was fitting, Nick thought, that their final confrontation should end in a graveyard with the dead lying beneath their feet. Edmund's passage through the world had been marked by death: his father, Simon Winchelsea, the unnamed whore, and indirectly, Richard Stace. That he had failed to kill Thomas, John, and Nick did not signify. He had intended to kill them and must bear the guilt of it on the day of reckoning.

"Nick!" It was Robert's voice.

Nick glanced over his shoulder. "Stay back," he shouted.

The momentary distraction was all Edmund needed. He leapt forward and slashed at Nick's sword, striking it out of the way, then quickly thrust before Nick could bring up his guard, and Nick felt the edge of the blade slice through the shoulder of his sword arm. Immediately, he changed sword hands. He could fight almost as well with his left as his right.

He saw Edmund's face register rage for the first time. "Oh, well done," he mocked. "All that expensive training with a sword master."

Nick did not reply. He closed on Edmund, driving him back toward Protea's grave. Edmund was beginning to parry and slash wildly now, clearly tiring, his twisted ankle slowing him down.

A kind of fury was building in Nick as he drove Edmund inexorably back. Gone was the pity he had felt for him at Oxford when they were boys, gone the sympathy for the misfortune of Edmund's family and the guilt that his own family had wanted for nothing. Even if all this was true, it did not exonerate Edmund from his crimes, nor did it explain them. At the heart of Edmund was a great evil, and this evil must be purged from the world if the world were to survive in any form that Nick recognized, a world in which loyalty was based on love and not hate, on protecting life, not taking it.

Nick's blade pierced Edmund's side, and Edmund staggered but remained upright. His doublet began to darken with blood.

Nick was also bleeding from his shoulder, and droplets of blood flicked onto the gravestones as he moved. The next thrust of his sword took Edmund square in the chest. Edmund blinked and looked down at the shaft of steel protruding from his flesh, Nick's hand still holding the blade. He looked up at Nick and smiled. It was one of the most ghastly things Nick had ever seen.

"Finish it," Edmund said.

Even on the point of death, Edmund clung to the belief that his father had been a victim, that he himself was a victim. This was the heart of his delusion, Nick realized, the seed that had grown into a great black flower. And now Nick suddenly understood why Edmund was smiling. He would die a victim. In death, he would be vindicated. In his own mind, he saw himself as Hamlet, the tragic prince, done to death by an unjust world.

All this passed through Nick's mind as he held the sword. He could withdraw it, and perhaps Edmund would live long enough to be tried and executed. But looking into Edmund's eyes, he knew he was begging to be allowed to die with his illusions intact.

"Kill me."

Holding Edmund's gaze, Nick stepped forward and pushed his sword up to the hilt into Edmund's chest. Their faces were only inches apart, almost like lovers, and Nick felt a great sigh issue from Edmund's lips, and with it a bloody froth. Edmund's legs col-lapsed under him, and Nick caught him under the arms and sat him down, the sword still buried in his chest, grotesquely erupting out his back. Gently, Nick leaned him sideways so that his cheek rested against Protea's gravestone.

Edmund's eyes were beginning to dull, but he was still alive. He tried to speak and his right hand twitched, beckoning. Nick put his ear to Edmund's mouth.

"I wanted to be you," he said.

And died.

CHAPTER 31

The Black Sheep, Bankside

Sitting at John's bedside in The Black Sheep, Nick was haunted by Edmund's final words: "I wanted to be you."

He kept seeing Edmund as he had been at Oxford, his wheat-colored hair falling on his forehead, his hesitant smile, his bitten fingernails, the way his eyes looked down and a flush of color suffused his face when Nick and John spurned him. Nick kept asking himself if things would have been different if he and John had invited Edmund into their company. Would a simple act of kindness have been enough to turn away the evil that Edmund had been bequeathed?

Nick had to keep reminding himself that the taint of Edmund's father's sins and his self-murder had already laid their mark on Edmund's soul by the time he came up to Oxford, like the first spot of rot in an apple. What was it the Old Testament said? That the sins of the father were visited on the children unto the third and fourth generations?

"Could we have done differently?" Nick asked John.

He told John everything that had happened since he came across Annie in the graveyard of St. Mary-at-Hill.

★　★　★

"Annie," he had said.

"Nick," she replied, a youthful voice issuing strangely from the guise of an old woman. "Put your sword away and come with me."

"How can I trust you?" Nick said.

Annie laughed. "You can't. That's why I'm taking you to meet someone who will vouch for me."

That someone was Sir Francis Walsingham, His Nibs himself, and he was not in a good mood. He nodded curtly to the two chairs in front of his desk, favored Annie with a smile, and then glared at Nick.

"What the devil have you been up to?" he barked. "You expressly disobeyed my order to leave Annie alone."

"I did no such thing," Nick retorted. He was caught off guard. He had felt all along that Walsingham was keeping something from him, but even more strongly, he felt he had been used as a pawn in a devious game, and he didn't like it. Not one bit. He felt his anger mounting. "You asked me to track down the person who had been murdering your agents, despite saddling me with Essex. I did. I discovered Annie and del Toro conspiring together. She even tried to kill me."

"How's the head, Nick?" Annie inquired.

"Still hurts."

"It was only a love tap, don't you know," she said. "Wouldn't have killed a fly, let alone a big strapping fellow like you."

Nick recalled that it had been Annie who had bent down to his prone body and informed del Toro that he was dead. She had gone for a head wound because she knew they bled a lot and would make a more convincing injury. Suddenly Nick realized that, by knocking him unconscious and declaring him dead, Annie had actually saved his life.

As if reading his mind, she winked at him, the effect more grotesque than friendly, considering her getup.

He looked at the woman sitting across from him with a new respect. He had known she was highly intelligent and had admired how she could magically change her appearance and character, but he had not suspected how accomplished an agent she was, nor how ruthless. The best agent he had ever seen, if he was honest. Bar none, and that included himself. He had made too many mistaken assumptions in this case.

Walsingham cleared his throat. "I suppose he deserves some explanation," he said. "What do you say, Annie?"

She grinned. Not a pretty sight, seeing as she had blacked out most of her teeth. "I'd say he's earned it."

"On one condition," Walsingham said to Nick, raising a finger. "That you do not reveal any of what I am going to tell you to anyone. Especially the Queen and your friend Codpiece." He said this last with a small moue of disgust that told Nick that, great spymaster that he was, Walsingham had no idea that Richard, aka Codpiece, was Elizabeth's personal spy on her own court.

"Agreed." Nick sat back and folded his arms.

Walsingham sighed. "Annie is, and always has been, working for me. Initially, I put her in Essex's network to keep me apprised of what he was up to. Then, later, to keep him from sniffing out what *I* was up to. I sent you into his network for the same reason: to keep Essex occupied with finding a murderer so he would not be tempted to look . . ." Walsingham paused as he searched for the right word. "*Higher*, shall we say."

"Higher?" Nick repeated. Then the penny dropped. "As in Mary, Queen of Scots, higher?"

"I told you he was bright," Annie said.

Walsingham nodded. "That woman has been a thorn in the side of Her Majesty for almost twenty years. Not only that, but she is positively lethal. As long as she lives, she will be the figurehead of every assassination plot in the land, as well as a perpetual excuse for war with France and Spain. She cannot be allowed to live." He struck the table hard. "But we have never been able to obtain actual evidence—written evidence—that she condoned any of the numerous assassination plots on Her Majesty," he went on. "And the Queen demands proof of treason if she is to sign a death warrant for her cousin."

"And now you have the proof?" Nick asked.

Walsingham frowned. "Not yet," he said. "But we hope to have it by the end of the summer." He indicated Annie. "Annie is the go-between between the Spanish . . ."

"Del Toro," Nick said.

"Just so."

"She made initial contact with del Toro the night Winchelsea was murdered," Walsingham said.

"As a whore," Annie said. "I was hiding in a doorway and snagged him, set up our meeting in Oxford. Safer, we thought, than London. Saw Simon in the shadows watching. He was a good tracker was Simon." She crossed herself. Walsingham pretended not to notice, but Nick saw his mouth set in disapproval.

"Then after receiving the letters in Oxford, Annie brought them to me first," Walsingham said.

"Ran into you here," Annie said, grinning. "Literally."

Nick recalled the young man he had bumped into on the doorstep of Seething Lane. He had thought nothing of it. Just one of Walsingham's myriad runners, he had thought at the time.

To hide his embarrassment, he said to Walsingham, "Who is the English traitor?"

"Anthony Babington." Walsingham leaned back in his chair. He looked exhausted, and Nick reminded himself that he had just suffered a relapse and had returned to London only a few days ago. Annie had told him this on the walk over to Seething Lane.

"His Nibs being away," she had told him, "was a major pain in the arse. Normally, I could have hidden out at Seething Lane, but with His Nibs being gone, I had to shift for myself. The only way I could be safe was to constantly change my appearance."

"Why risk going to court on May Day?" Nick had asked her.

"I wanted to explain things and I knew you'd be there."

"Then why did you run away?"

"Because you drew attention to me and were asking all and sundry if they'd seen a young man. You blew my cover, you big loon."

Another mistake. But understandable, Nick thought, considering the torturous nature of the case. Nothing had been what it seemed: Annie the traitor was Annie the patriot; unassuming, shy, bungling Edmund was a devious and devilish murderer and traitor; except for the deaths of Winchelsea and Stace and the unnamed prostitute on *The Dalliance*, all attacks had been personal and not political. Even del Toro, a Spanish agent and sworn enemy of the state, was working, unbeknownst to himself, for Walsingham.

★   ★   ★

Nick turned his attention back to what Walsingham was saying.

"Babington and his coplotters have found a way to contact the Scottish queen. They are sending messages to her in the bung of an ale barrel that is delivered to her household. And her replies are sent out the same way."

"And you have intercepted them," Nick said.

Walsingham allowed himself a thin smile. "We've done better than that. The man who delivers the ale is in my pay. We read each letter, copy it, and then reseal it and send it on its way. She is a vain and impetuous woman. It is only a matter of time before Babington gets her written approval for his plot. When that happens, we will have her." He closed his fist.

"It was imperative that del Toro be allowed to make contact with Annie," Walsingham went on. "He had brought the Spanish ambassador's approval of the plot to be passed on to Babington."

"That's why you allowed him to land at Dover," Nick said. "And pass unmolested through the country."

"Correct."

"And that's why you were adamant that he had not murdered Winchelsea," Nick said. He sat forward in his chair so he could be sure that he had Walsingham's attention. "But you had no proof of this. He could very well have been Simon's killer. If I had not found Edmund's seal, del Toro would still be a suspect."

At this, Walsingham had the grace to look down. But when he looked up again, there was steel in his eyes. "I would not have arrested him even if I had seen him cut Winchelsea's throat myself," he said. "He had to be allowed to deliver his letters and then return to France to report to the Spanish ambassador that all was well."

"Even if you had seen him put out Winchelsea's eyes?"

"Even so."

Nick sat back in his chair. He no longer felt anger, but a kind of weary revulsion. No matter what Walsingham said to the contrary, his agents were expendable pawns in his great game of espionage. A religious fanatic, he would cheerfully watch the whole world burn for the sake of his Queen and the realm. In this respect, Walsingham was no different from his Catholic counterparts in the Inquisition. Perhaps, in his way, he was no different from Edmund himself, who had justified his actions by claiming loyalty to his father. For Walsingham, loyalty to his Queen justified all manner of betrayals.

The Bible that Walsingham was rumored to so assiduously study had not been written by God, as he thought, but by Niccolò Machiavelli. It was he who had given religious and political fanatics their first and only commandment: "The end justifies the means."

To Nick's ear, this was the most demonic statement he had ever had the misfortune to read.

"Robert Cecil does not know," Nick said. It was a statement, not a question. He thought of how the Spider had set him to tracking del Toro to Oxford, and how eagerly he had run to the Queen to inform her that Annie was a traitor, impelled by a burning desire to discredit his hated adoptive brother, Essex.

"He does now," Walsingham said.

Nick could imagine how that conversation had gone. The Spider would have been informed that he had very nearly destroyed the biggest and most important sting operation in his master's career. And he had done it out of a personal animus against Essex. *He must be devastated by his ineptitude*, Nick thought, wincing inwardly, knowing that he would bear the brunt of the Spider's deep professional embarrassment.

"Robert is young and has much to learn," Walsingham said, as if reading Nick's mind. "I thought I was protecting him by not telling him of the Babington plot, but I was mistaken. I underestimated his hatred of Essex."

"Protecting him?" Nick said.

Walsingham gave a weary smile. "Do you think the Queen will thank me when I force her to sign her cousin's death warrant? Robert's father, Baron Burghley, and I know that, if I am successful, and I pray God that I am, it will mean the end of our service to

Her Majesty. She will never trust us again. She will never forgive us for forcing her to spill royal blood. I had promised Robert's father I would keep him away from the taint of this. Young Robert is to succeed me, you see."

Suddenly, Walsingham looked very old and shrunken in his chair. His greatest espionage triumph was simultaneously his greatest failure. The irony of it was staggering.

"But to look on the bright side," he said with an attempt at jollity that was grotesque, given the bleak outlook for his future, "an early retirement from public service will allow me to spend what little time I have left with my family."

Nick thought that in all of Walsingham's grim life—his witnessing of the Bartholomew Day Massacre, the early onset of cancer, all the blood he had seen spilled and ordered to be spilled—he had never experienced a single day that could have been called bright. Even now, on this warm spring day, a fire was burning in the grate; the windows were closed against the cheerful sound of the birds; thick curtains were drawn against the brightness and warmth of the sun so that the room resembled more a place for the dead than a place for the living. No doubt it was his doctor who had instructed him to keep out the fresh spring air—unlike Eli and Rivkah, most doctors considered fresh air dangerous to the health—but it seemed fitting somehow. Walsingham was entombed alive by his obsession with Catholic plots and conspiracies, an obsession that was slowly killing not only his body but his soul.

And yet, blighted as Walsingham surely was, Nick still respected him. There was no question that he was a genius at what he did. If there was a man who could permanently remove the threat of Mary, Queen of Scots, after nineteen years of imprisonment and Elizabeth's refusal to send her to the block, he was sitting before Nick on the other side of the desk.

As a Catholic, albeit a recusant one, Nick could not condone this. But nor could he condone assassination plots against his own queen. He was caught as surely as a fly in amber. And, for his family's sake, his brother in particular, he would have to remain caught.

Nick glanced at Annie. She was in the same position as he, forced to cooperate with a government that was inimical to her faith if she were to help restore her family fortunes.

"It goes without saying that you must not breathe a word of the Babington plot to anyone," Walsingham said. "On pain of death."

Then, as if as an afterthought, he added, "Anthony Babington is a young recusant." He smiled. "Like you, Nick."

CHAPTER 32

The Black Sheep Tavern

"So you see, John," Nick said, "Walsingham's last words about Babington were intended to remind me that I am well and truly on his hook. I'll never escape."

Nick looked despairingly at the still form of his friend lying on the bed. They were alone in the room, Maggie having been persuaded to go downstairs to spend some time with her children.

How could he keep wading through the moral sewers of the espionage world without his best friend beside him? He and John had been companions since before they could talk. With Robert being ten years older than Nick, John was more of a brother to him than a friend. They had done everything together since they had been old enough to run outside and play: caught fish in the Windrush, poached rabbits off a neighbor's land, built castles out in the woods, and when they were older, stood guard outside the barn while the other learned about the birds and the bees with a willing local girl. Then later, they'd guarded each other's backs in vicious knife and sword fights in low taverns and back alleys in Spain and France. Nick could not imagine going through the rest of his life without him.

He put his head in his hands and pressed his fingers to his eyes. "Stuff Walsingham."

Slowly, Nick raised his head.

John's eyes were open.

Nick grabbed his hand. "John," he said. "You're awake. My God. You're awake."

"It was Edmund who attacked me," John said, the sound of his voice raspy, as if his vocal chords had dried up.

"I know." Nick squeezed his hand. Typical of John to think of the case first.

"He's the killer, Nick, not Annie."

"I know that too. I've been telling you all about it."

"I'm afraid you'll have to tell me again," John said. Then he frowned and squinted at the window. It was dusk. "How long have I been asleep?"

"More than a week."

"A week!"

Nick couldn't help but smile at the amazement on John's face; then his smile turned into a laugh, a little unsteady at first, but once he began, he found he could not stop. Tears coursed down his face. And every time he thought he had himself under control, he looked at John scowling at him for being the object of ridicule, or so he thought, and started again.

The sound brought Maggie, Henry, and Matty carrying the baby running up the stairs, followed closely by Hector. Hector leapt on the bed, careful not to land on John, and began slavering John's face, his tail pounding joyfully on the bed.

"He knows you need a wash," Nick said. "You stink."

Then Nick removed Hector so Maggie could take her husband in her arms. Up to now, she had not made a sound, just stared numbly at John smiling up at her, his wits and memory intact, the man she loved come back to her against all hope. As soon as she felt John put his arms around her, she began to sob, the sound tearing out of her like a barbed arrowhead being withdrawn slowly from a deep wound.

"Come, children," Nick said. "Let's leave them alone for a while." And he led them quietly downstairs.

★ ★ ★

The next day, Nick put a sign on the tavern door: OPEN FOR BUSINESS: JOHN WOKE UP.

Almost immediately the place was crowded with well-wishers, people who had spent a week in unaccustomed and unwelcome sobriety, and the frankly curious. Despite Maggie's strenuous and vociferous objections, and Rivkah and Eli's quieter and professional ones, John insisted on being carried downstairs and placed in a chair padded with the lambskin the Queen had given him as a gift. Here, on his throne, as Henry called it, John sat while the entire population of Bankside, it seemed, came to pay court to the man they regarded with as much awe as had the friends and relatives of Lazarus.

As John's doctors, Rivkah and Eli were much caressed and admired, and their standing in the community, already high, rose astronomically. John insisted they sit on either side of him, like lesser members of the royal family, in order to take the credit for his miraculous recovery.

Only Nick and Eli could see that this made Rivkah profoundly uncomfortable. Without her cloak and concealing hood to protect her, she felt exposed. She did not mind when neighbors and former patients came into the tavern, but by the second day, strangers from the city of London itself were making the trek over the bridge to see the man who had woken from the dead. Then she would look down, uncharacteristically tongue-tied, and Eli would have to answer for her. On the third day, she stayed home. Nick missed her but was glad that she was spared the torment of notoriety. Eli also stopped coming after the fourth day, but it was not shyness that kept him away but fear of persecution for heresy.

"There are many who would say that what we did with John was a blasphemy," he said, his face grave. "The unlettered call it a raising from the dead, and this is a dangerous rumor. They do not understand that it is a natural waking from a long sleep. Of what kind this sleep is, we do not yet know. But we do know the patient is not dead, for his heart beats and his lungs fill with air. The irony," he went on, "is that Rivkah and I did nothing but stitch the wound on his head and keep him warm and fed and clean. His body did the rest. Somehow, for reasons unknown to science, severe head wounds heal themselves by putting the body into a long and profound slumber. It is a miracle of nature, not of medicine."

John had lost much weight; now he had awoken, he could not stop eating. And so neighbors and friends brought gifts of food whenever they came round and sat and watched John eat with a satisfaction that revealed they considered themselves a small part in his recovery.

Will Shakespeare dropped by with Sir John Staffington in tow. While Sir John went to sit by John to congratulate him on his recovery and watch him eat with a look of profound admiration on his face, as if he had discovered a kindred spirit, Nick took Will aside. He could see the young would-be playwright was down in the dumps despite his happiness for John's recovery.

"*The Ghost* was a disaster," he said mournfully. "When the Queen told Edgar—he was the one who came out to introduce it, you remember?—to 'get on with it, man,' I knew it was all downhill from there."

"It helped me solve my case," Nick said, refilling Will's tankard. As usual, Will was more than a little tipsy. He and Sir John must have started early, as it was only midday.

"It did?" Will said, brightening.

"The theme of revenge and loyalty," Nick said. "That was the heart of the motive. Of course," he said, slyly, "I know what a classicist you are."

Will goggled at him. "Are you accusing me of nicking the plots of Greek tragedy?"

"The name of Orestes did spring to mind," Nick said.

Will buried his nose in his tankard. Then he looked at Nick, his eyes twinkling. "Don't tell anyone, especially that git Marlowe." Will and Christopher Marlowe had an intense, if mostly friendly, rivalry.

"*Swear.*" Will said this in the deep voice of Hamlet's father's ghost.

Nick laughed. "I would, but I can't make up my mind. Whether 'tis nobler . . ."

Will punched him in the shoulder, making Nick spill his drink. "You bastard."

"I swear."

*   ★   *

That evening, Nick stopped by Eli and Rivkah's and asked if they wanted to go for a walk in Paris Garden.

"You go, Mouse," Eli said. When she turned to get her shawl, he winked at Nick. Nick gave him two fingers.

As they strolled along the riverbank, Nick told Rivkah how Edmund had begged Nick to kill him.

"Did I do right?" he asked, stopping and looking out across the river. In the rosy dusk, there were still plenty of craft on the water, some lit by lanterns hanging from stanchions on the sterns. To the east, gulls circled and canted in the darkening sky over Billingsgate, swooping down behind the bridge to snatch up the offal thrown by the fishmongers into the river. Their plaintive cries came to him clearly. A lone raven beat the air upstream, cawing for its mate.

"You ended his torment," Rivkah said, putting a hand on his arm. "And you prevented a far more hideous death."

She was referring to the death of traitors. If he had lived to stand trial, Edmund would have been dragged on a hurdle to Tyburn amid jeering crowds lining the route, hanged, cut down while still alive, and then disemboweled, castrated, and cut into quarters. Only then would he have been beheaded. It was the most hideous and most agonizing death the state could mete out. A nightmare even to contemplate. Even being burned at the stake for heresy or boiled alive in a vat of lead for poisoning were not as hideous, as death came quicker.

"I suppose," Nick said.

"You are not convinced?"

Nick turned to look at her. Behind her the sky flamed violet and rose, the sun a gold sovereign slowly slipping into the velvet pocket of a gorgeous dress.

"His last words were, 'I wanted to be you.' I have thought and thought about that, and now I think it was the last lie he told."

"What do you mean?"

"I think that, by killing him, he made me him. Do you see? I think he really meant, 'I want you to be me.' He wanted me to kill him out of revenge for Simon, Thomas, John, Protea, Stace, his former servant, all those he murdered or tried to murder. When I thrust home my sword, I felt . . ."

Nick faltered and looked out at the river. He could now barely make out the shapes of the wherries plying to and fro on the water.

How quickly day fades to night, he thought.

Nick looked back at Rivkah, who was quietly waiting for him to go on. Backlit by the sinking sun, her face was in shadow, her expression unreadable.

Nick took a breath. "I felt like God."

Rivkah stepped close to Nick, so close he could feel the warmth of her body. She took both his hands in hers.

"Listen to me, Nick," she said. "I think you are right; I think his last act on earth was to finish what he had begun. To destroy you. To infect you somehow with the poison of his hate." She squeezed his hands hard.

"Do not allow that to happen. You can pity him. You can regret you were not kinder to him in your youth, but know that you will never, *ever*, be like him. He could never have been you, and you will never be him. Don't let him make you a traitor to yourself. Do you understand?"

Despite his melancholy, Nick smiled at the ferocity with which she had spoken. Perhaps it was this that he loved most about her, her indomitable strength that fought tooth and nail for the good and would never surrender to evil.

"I understand," he said.

Then he bent his head and kissed her on the lips.

AUTHOR'S NOTE

Marguerite Yourcenar, the author of *Memoirs of Hadrian*, one of the greatest historical novels ever written, once said, "Everything is too far away in the past, or mysteriously too close."

The historical novelist is like a camera trying to focus on the distant scene of the past. Sometimes the image can become blurred because it is too remote, the historical facts too alien to our own time; sometimes because it is too close, the characters too contemporary for them to be true to their own era. The trick is to find that sweet spot between fact and fiction that will bring the image into sharp relief. Consequently, I have mingled documented facts and real historical figures with fictional characters and events. Even the language my characters speak is a blend of period diction and a more contemporary rendering in order to make Elizabethan speech more familiar to the modern ear.

Wherever possible, I have maintained the Elizabethan spelling for place names (although spelling was not yet standardized in the sixteenth century). For example, the modern Covent Garden was originally *Convent* Garden, because the open fields in the sixteenth century were originally the grounds of an abbey and nunnery, seized by Henry VIII during the dissolution of the monasteries. Over time, the word *convent* became *covent*, most likely due to the way the original name was pronounced by Londoners.

One change I have made to the historical record concerns Robert Devereaux, second Earl of Essex. At the time of the events described in this novel, which takes place during the spring of 1586, he was in the Netherlands with his stepfather, Robert Dudley, Earl of Leicester. Essex participated in the Battle of Zutphen in September 1586 (where Sir Philip Sidney was killed) and was knighted on the field by Leicester, returning to England in late 1586 covered in glory.

I have invented a fictitious reason to get him back to England. It is entirely plausible that Leicester could have sent him to the Queen with personal dispatches, although there is no historical record of this. What is documented is that he and his entourage spent the months abroad feasting and quarreling and generally causing trouble; it is not a stretch to imagine that the ailing Leicester must have found this very wearing on his nerves and longed to get rid of his stepson for a few months.

Essex's turbulent and changeable temperament is well documented, so much so that historians have speculated that he had some kind of personality disorder. He was certainly capable of rash, not to say, suicidal, actions; for example, in 1598, he deliberately turned his back on Elizabeth after they had argued; when the Queen slapped him for his gross insult, he almost drew his sword on her in anger. The action that eventually brought him to the scaffold in 1601 was a bungled attempt at an uprising in the city of London. He was arrested before he could force his way into an audience with the Queen at Whitehall with an armed posse.

The historical record holds that Elizabeth shows particular favoritism to Essex only after his return from the Netherlands in 1586. For plot purposes, I have made him the Queen's favorite a bit earlier in the year.

Essex did not form his own spy network until 1592, but I have chosen to make this earlier, also for plot purposes.

The reason for these changes is the huge, looming shadow that is the Babington Plot—second only to the infamous Gunpowder Plot as the most sensational assassination attempt in all of British history.

Led by Anthony Babington, a recusant Catholic, this was a plan to assassinate Elizabeth and put Mary, Queen of Scots, on the English throne. Walsingham got wind of the plan thanks in part to a double agent working for him called Gilbert Gifford, a Catholic deacon who was one of Mary's agents. It was Gifford who passed on the letters written by Babington to Mary at Chartley Castle, where she was being held, and the single reply from Mary to the conspirators that sealed her fate. It is almost certain that Elizabeth knew Walsingham was intercepting Mary's letters, but, again, for plot purposes, I have chosen to keep her in the dark.

I have substituted a fictitious Spaniard, del Toro, for Gifford. After Mendoza, the Spanish ambassador to England, was expelled in 1584 for his complicity in the Throckmorton Plot, Spanish agents originated in Paris.

Annie O'Neill is also fictitious, although the history of the O'Neill clan is historically accurate.

A brief word about spy networks: Unlike the CIA, they were not financially or operationally supported by a government but by private individuals who had bought a network of informers who would channel information back to a central hub. Sir Francis Walsingham paid his informers out of his own pocket (which was why he was notoriously broke) and was only infrequently reimbursed by the Crown. All the information passed through his central office, in a house he owned at Thirty-Five Seething Lane. The location of the house within the city of London made it easier for informers to bring their information to him anonymously.

Informers, or spies, could be as diverse as chamber maids, diplomats at foreign embassies, merchants, valets, tradesmen—virtually anyone who had some connection to courtiers in a foreign or domestic court or government. The success of a spy network depended almost entirely on the central hub, where the thousands of scraps of information could be pieced together into a single narrative.

Unlike Essex, Walsingham was a genius at collating and interpreting disparate pieces of information, and he surrounded himself with similarly clever men. One such man was Thomas Phelippes, who was an expert code cracker and multilinguist. In July 1586, it was Phelippes who famously drew a gallows in the margin of his copy of a letter from Mary, Queen of Scots, to Babington. This drawing was made next to Mary's treasonous statement that she condoned the assassination of Queen Elizabeth I. It was this statement that led to her trial in the fall of 1586, and her death in February 1587 at Fotheringhay Castle.

Contemporary readers may feel that many of the courtiers who surround Elizabeth in the series seem excessively young (Essex is twenty-one; Sir Robert Cecil is twenty-two). However, in the sixteenth century, when disease was rampant and the average life expectancy was forty, people were considered mature at a much earlier age than in modern times. So it is no wonder that people not only married very young (some as young as fourteen) but also held court positions in their early twenties.

Finally, the fragment of the play-within-the-novel, *The Ghost*, is almost entirely fictitious, though it is, of course, based on Shakespeare's *Hamlet* (written between 1599 and 1602). The only line I steal verbatim is, "Or such ambiguous giving out, to note you know aught of me," and the word, "Swear."

ACKNOWLEDGMENTS

For their patience and support over the years, I'm grateful to a host of friends too numerous to mention. But a special shout-out to the following:

My agent, Carol Mann, for her steadfast support.

My editor, Faith Black Ross, whose invaluable advice helped shape this novel for the better.

My friends Leonie Caldecott and Georgina Dorkin, for their unfailing loyalty and encouragement.

My children, Magdalen, Helena, Charles and Benedict, for always having my back despite their busy lives.

And Greg. Always and forever.